RAVEN

ANNE GREGOR

OLIVERHEBERBOOKS

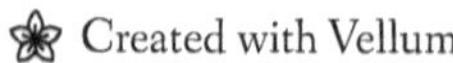 Created with Vellum

RAVEN

Sometimes in life there is a great divide between Before and After... no gradual gradient where a thing is one way and subtlety shifts, creating a new... thing... one intrinsically, at its heart, is the original but now has different shades, angles. No, some Before and Afters have all the finesse of a cannon shot on a still, foggy morning. Deafening. Jarring. Destroying.

Raven. River. Rowan. Always. Forever. Their parents had been gone four years, a lifetime— distant memories— smiles, warmth, love. Faded, like tarnished silver. Past and present divided... never the twain shall meet... Kipling had the right of it. Raven Byrne had her sisters, and that was enough.

PREFACE

Phytophthora infestans is a water mold— a fungus-like microorganism— and the cause of Ireland's potato blight. The Irish Potato Famine began in 1845 and hung on through 1852, killing a million men, women, and children— losing at least another million to emigration.

Many emigrants seeking cheap passage to America found themselves on overcrowded 'coffin' ships that had no regard for passenger safety. Little food and water during the six-week to three-month voyage. Squalid, close quarters below deck caused thousands to die during the journey, with more perishing from typhus once in port.

Countless Irish immigrants during the famine years landed in America poor, malnourished, lacking a trade, and speaking little English. They set up small ghetto communities on the eastern seaboard where the ships' passengers disembarked at the Boston and New York ports.

Their lack of skills and literacy forced the Irish into accepting the worst jobs. Working long hours and receiving little pay. America's expansion push called for cheap labor, and

Irish immigrants fit the bill. They built roads, canals, bridges, and laid track for railroads.

It was after the Civil War that the Irish began pushing westward alongside the railroad companies, helping the transcontinental crossing lay track across America. Many of these same Irish settled along the track, bringing their culture and religion with them. Atoka, Oklahoma, is one such place.

In 1852, Joseph Byrne, barely out of nappies, survived the eight-week voyage from his family's beloved Ireland to America's coast. Starting out in his young teens, Joseph survived working the transcontinental railroad line for eight years. By 1872, the Missouri—Kansas—Texas Railway, or Katy, reached Atoka, and Joseph found his home. In 1873, the twenty-three-year-old Irish railroader met the love of his life, Neakita, a Choctaw native. His wild Rose.

THE IRISH WOLVES TRILOGY FOLLOWS THE LEGACY AND DESCENDANTS OF JOSEPH BYRNE.

1

———

Triskelion Territory Designs was doing well for such a young company. Raven and her sisters kept to a strict business code of warm professionalism. Know the clients. Understand their vision and budget, and then add to that vision. After only three years, one of which was during their last year of college, they were making a name for themselves.

With their personal savings and the wise investment of their parent's estate, the girls had been able to purchase and renovate a brick-and-mortar three-story building in downtown historic Eufaula, Oklahoma.

The gorgeous, old red brick monument had existed since the 1920s, and with deft hands, and a decent budget, it was a stunner. The ground floor contained Triskelion's showroom and offices, a small kitchen, and powder room. The second floor was the sisters' shared kitchen and bathroom. The center island was dedicated to herbal tea, protein shakes, and smoothies. There was also a small gym, lounge, and entertainment space— if entertainment equaled a whiskey bar, flat screen TV, and sound system, which in Raven's humble opinion, it absolutely did—

Daddy raised his girls right. The bar's backsplash wasn't finished in traditional tile but a collage of old and new photos, family mementos, and special letters. One of many familial touches to keep their parents' memories, smiles, and especially their love close. The third floor was divided into three-bedroom suites. Perfection.

Raven and her sisters chose Eufaula because it nicely bridged the distance between existing clients and potential future clients in Oklahoma City, Norman, and Tulsa and hopefully reaching into other close states— Texas, Missouri, and Arkansas. They didn't mind commuting to see clients. They loved to travel.

Though the three sisters looked extremely similar, with long black hair, thanks to Native American heritage from both parents, obviously much stronger from their mother, mixed with pale Irish skin and hazel eyes— an admittedly striking combination. They definitely looked like family, clearly sisters, not triplet close by any means, but close enough to draw attention. They wore the same size clothes and shoes— that was hell growing up— and stood at 5'4". If Raven were being strictly honest. she topped out at a smidge over 5'3". The utter unfairness of being the oldest and yet the shortest! Ridiculous!

Since Raven and her sisters were separated by less than a year— Fertile Myrtle, they name is Lily Byrne— they were in college together. Her younger sisters didn't like the thought of separation, or their big sister leaving them behind, so both chose the online accredited high school route so they could take mostly concurrent college classes and finish early.

Rowan, the youngest, doubled down, always the overachiever, so that hand in hand in hand they'd loaded their dad's old, long bed Chevy with dorm life necessities, piled in the truck's cab, and followed their parents' Jeep for the hour and a half drive to Norman. Raven never missed her hometown of Bristow, Oklahoma, because she and her sisters returned as often as possible.

Raven, River, and Rowan had gravitated toward the arts— coloring to sketching to oil and watercolors on canvas; play-dough to modeling clay to hand-thrown pottery; felt animal puppets to monogramming school totes to intricate hand-embroidered countrysides... and decorating.

Give them a space... bathroom, bedroom, office, a treehouse for the love of God, and they would transform it into a sanctuary, a haven, a place to reflect, be at peace, a private nook of inspiration, or a cozy corner to quietly fade into the shadows.

Their talents had always brought them joy, as well as their family and friends. So, it wasn't a huge surprise to their parents that all three girls planned on majoring in Interior Design. Mom and Dad had forever encouraged their children to follow their passions. The girls only differed in their minors. Raven went for Art History, as any history appealed to her. River, more tech-savvy than her siblings, chose Digital Marketing, and Rowan, the youngest with the oldest soul, chose Information Studies, because, she had argued, personal libraries would need facelifts — the real truth— she just loved books.

By tacit agreement, the sisters chose academics over dating. Sure, they went to parties with each other and friends they'd met in class, had a date here and there, but, at the end of the day, they were passion-driven, led passionately by textiles and art, murals and museums, dreams of future clients— boys still coming into their own held very little appeal, except for a casual flirtation. There were those who felt deeply and those who just wanted felt up— they were of the former persuasion.

Raven had just settled at her desk to go through Triskelion's emails when, *un*surprisingly, a music complaint was thrown her way. "Is it absolutely, one hundred percent necessary, to play Dermot Kennedy radio every morning? Last time I checked, Spotify has a few other choices," River groused. "And no, Raven, I am not suggesting switching to Passenger radio, Lewis Capaldi, or gag, sea shanties."

"Oh, bless your heart River, you forgot yet again that I'm first, the oldest, second, awake and downstairs at least an hour before you— Every Single Day— and third, your taste in music sucks and would scare off potential clients in a millisecond."

River loved her sisters. Loved them. They were her best friends, her confidants, and her reason for living. They lost their parents. But together, each and every day, they chose to remember all the ways they had been cherished by their mom and dad. Their folks would never forgive the girls if they didn't grab happiness and success like trinkets at a Renaissance Festival.

Love, however, stretched thin when River promoted herself to Spotify Manager in the office— Screamer Rock or Red Dirt Country— did anything else need to be said? Rowan was chill but leaned toward Classical, like Pachelbel and Yo-Yo Ma classical, which Raven loved— but not... as much as her sister. So, yes, Raven did monopolize the radio. So far, a thankless undertaking.

"Suck my..." River began.

"River! Let it go, weirdo." Rowan finally chimed in. "Your music is questionable for, like, ninety-eight percent of the world."

Raven chose to move on. She knew from the hundreds upon thousands of ridiculous conversations had betwixt the three of them that throwing a timely non sequitur was effective upon occasion.

As Raven opened the main business email, she said, "How about we go over what we're each working on. I like everyone knowing the separate projects in case one of us has to step in for some reason."

Raven's scroll and delete of potential jobs versus spam emails stilled. Her cursor hovered over an email from O'Faolain Industries, LLC. What, in the absolute hell, she thought silently.

"What?"

"Why are you turning red?"

Both girls asked at the same time, noticing their sister's stillness, bulging eyes, and fly-catching mouth wide open for business.

No way, Raven thought. There was no way on God's green Earth this email was legit. O'Faolains were money. Like, clear your throat and cough up a diamond money. Oil of course. Oklahoma oil money plus a million other businesses— *that* is the O'Faolain clan. The Irish Wolves were practically a mandatory class in school. Again... no M F'ing way is this email real.

"Jesus, Raven! What in the hell is going on?" River demanded while Rowan watched her sister closely.

Raven cleared her throat, blinked her suddenly dry eyes, and admitted, "This may be junk, but oh my God, you guys, I am looking at an email from *THE* F'ING'O'FAOLAINS! They would like to interview our design firm to see if our..." Raven made air quotes, "vision... agrees with their newest venture. I..."

"No fucking way!" River, of course. "No motherfucking way is this legit." Exactly what Raven had thought sans the verbalization.

Rowan looked at both sisters as she swiveled her laptop in their direction. "Read it. Look at the address. It isn't spam. I think... maybe, it's real."

Raven's head felt fuzzy, like she'd had one too many shots of whiskey. Her eyes were tracking in slow motion. She watched as her sisters read through the same email that, no lie, had the potential of making their careers.

Rowan cleared her throat. There was a lot of nonexistent phlegm making its hacking glory this morning, obviously.

"Wolves Irish Pub. Wow."

"Possibly an Irish pub *chain*..." River whispered, also recognizing that this job, this single job, could set their future.

"If this is real you guys, it would make us." Raven carefully touched the screen as though any sudden movement had the potential to permanently delete. "He wants to set up a time to meet all three of us. Here."

Raven looked at River and Rowan and swallowed past the parched desert in her throat. "He..." Raven cleared her throat, "emailed last night at 11:30. We've got to respond." Cue three women breathing heavily— she'd laugh at the inappropriate noises if she weren't about to hyperventilate.

"Okay, okay... okay, no problem," Raven low-key screeched. "Let me draft a reply and we'll all pick it apart."

"The email is signed Bran." Rowan announced. "I suppose it could have been a secretary, but they probably wouldn't be working that late."

"Oh, God," River moaned. "The eldest son..."

No one said another word for the next thirty minutes while Raven wrote and discarded about ten drafts— good grief, it was one flipping paragraph. Reading over what she hoped sounded like a professional, but we're also super interested, few sentences, she placed the final period and looked up.

River and Rowan's unblinking eyes were trained on her. Waiting. Still, like prey becomes when a predator noses around. In this case, their instincts were on the money.

The O'Faolains were wolves. She'd only seen pictures, but it was always the three of them together. A pack of drop-dead gorgeous wolves. And one of them was coming here.

Shaking off her unease and clearing her suddenly dry throat — again— a potential habit that must cease, Raven told her sisters. "This is huge. We know it's huge. We also know what we're capable of, and if we land this job, and I realize it is a big IF, as they are probably interviewing several design firms, we'll blow their minds with our awesomeness!"

Using her sisters' final edits, Raven made the last few changes, read the response a final time, and pressed... Send.

Bran waited in his father's office at their Muskogee O'Faolain compound. The property was situated in a highly wooded area overlooking the Arkansas River. The over 1,500-acre spread boasted several ponds, with one large manmade pond close to the main house.

Dad had overseen *that* pond project personally. Admittedly, one of Bran's favorite parts of the property, though they gave him a hard time about the outdoor extravagance. He kitted it out with a fishing dock and decking secured with round, concrete pilings. The walkways and railings were built from ipé, a South American hardwood. One end had been left open to create a beach. The small, smooth rock didn't tear up a person's feet.

There were picnic areas, chairs and pads for laying out, fish cleaning stations, covered cabanas, and a badass bar that could be closed and winterized during the cold months, comfortable barstools, TVs, stereo, rows of liquor and mixed drink ingredients, a cooking flat top and grills, two refrigerators, and an ice machine. All of which was powered by electricity running from the main house. Basically, Dad built a luxury pool-pond/wilderness-pub.

Bran was not complaining.

The main house had plenty of room for his dad, him, and his brother Patrick, but knowing that in time his father might remarry, and the brothers would eventually have families of their own, they decided to build separate homes on the property.

Pat's house and Bran's own had been completed for a few years, but neither had taken the time to personalize them. They stayed at their dad's for the most part anyway, as travel for work cut into a large chunk of their weeks. The compound had become home base to all three of them more than any other place they'd lived.

Bran should be reviewing their company's latest financials, but an article popped up about some ancient, underground city in Midyat, Turkey. Bran loved history. If it pertained to a war, all the better. He could study weapons, maps, and tactical maneuvers for days. He and his brother had spent countless hours recreating ancient wars with army men.

His notifications dinged as he was flipping through pictures of part of the city that purportedly had been home to some 70,000 people. He wondered if he'd hear back from Triskelion Territory Designs today. Good, discussing the new pub venture was on this morning's agenda.

His dad asked Bran to find an interior design firm to head up Wolves Irish Pub's flagship location in Tulsa. His Gran's good friend had recommended Triskelion. One of the company's designers had updated the older woman's high-rise condo in downtown Tulsa, and she raved about the results. That recommendation, along with the company's name, appealed to Bran, and he emailed them last night.

A triskelion was an ancient Celtic symbol and Territory presumably referenced what was once considered Indian Territory, then later Oklahoma Territory, before becoming a state in

1907. Bran's own family hailed from some fishing village on the Irish coast. Gran had told him that much. He didn't think she'd ever researched much further . So, with their historically significant name as well as a rec from Gran O'Faolain's friend, he rolled with it.

His father, Hugh, and his younger brother, by only a year and a half, strolled in about the time he finished reading the reply email. He and Pat were both built almost identically to their father, Hugh, all tall, running from 6'3" to 6'4", Dad being the tallest. He and Patrick ran more toward lean muscular frames, while their dad was an all-around bigger, broader guy.

Bran and his brother had white-blonde hair, the only nice thing their birth mother, Helen, gave them. Dad sported close-cropped dark brown hair and a well-kept full beard with the beginnings of white streaking his temples and chin— Bran and Pat were still put out that they couldn't grow a decent beard to save their lives. All three men, though, had the same slightly tanned, golden skin. They were also very close. Bran's best friends.

"Nice to see you both could move on from scratching your sacs long enough this morning to show up," Bran deadpanned with a smirk, knowing full well they, like him, were hard at it well before sunrise.

His father leveled Bran his, don't fuck with me look, while Patrick unsurprisingly, quipped, "Suck my dick." Followed by, "Where's breakfast?"

Dad reminded him, "Sara's husband had a follow-up eye appointment after his cataract surgery. Feel free to cook us something after the meeting, son."

Bran always appreciated Dad's way of low-key bitch slapping someone. However, in this instance, Patrick *was* a fantastic cook, and Dad *did* love a full breakfast spread.

Getting down to business, Patrick asked Dad, "Learn

anything at the Petroleum Alliance's golf open? When was that, Monday?"

"Yes. In Oklahoma City," their father responded in his quiet, gravelly monotone. "I shared a cart with the Governor for several hours. It's clear the White House is turning a deaf ear to his plea, and that of the Oklahoma Energy Resources Board, to reduce the nation's need for imported Russian energy. It's concerning."

The three men sat silently for a moment, contemplating the ramifications of the government administration not recognizing the importance of utilizing the resources at hand. But thank God, the running, and the giant headache, of the family's oil business had been bought out a few of years ago by share-holders.

His father had recognized that the business, at least for him, was going in a direction that took way more politicking than he was willing to endure.

Oil had made their family billionaires, and since selling the majority of the stock, their interests could be focused on more pleasurable ventures. They had investments in various busi-nesses all over the world, which is why traveling was such a huge part of their lives.

He and Patrick had been groomed from a young age to take over in their father's stead, so when he came to them about five years ago with a proposal to sell, Bran admitted, the news was met with relief.

"Well, energy resources are a concern, but one that we won't be solving this morning," Bran said, hoping to ease the tension from his father's shoulders. Oil may not be their end-all everything now, but some responsibilities took time to shake.

"Right," Pat continued, "where are we on Wolves?"

"I found a design firm, in Eufaula of all places. Comes with

Diana Gaines' seal of approval, and we all know how she likes her shit to be just so."

That even got a smile from Dad, as he knew the elderly daughter of a natural gas mogul was a... stickler for all things fashionable and appropriate. Diana did truly love Gran, and they'd been friends since childhood, so the boys, which included his father, tolerated her show of treating them like inferior employees that would never cut it in the Gaines' household.

"That's only thirty to forty minutes from here. I assume traveling to Tulsa wouldn't be a problem," Pat said.

"Diana told Gran that they work all over Oklahoma, Texas, and even in Arkansas. Triskelion Territory Designs. The logo is a Celtic triskelion with Native American symbols. I liked it," Bran admitted. He would have to make a point to ask the owners the story behind their name and logo.

Busy looking up the company, Pat added, "It's run by three sisters. Hmmm," he paused. "The company is only three years old. There are no pics of the owners, only their credentials. They all graduated from OU in Interior Design. Weirder, they all graduated the same year."

"Maybe they decided to go to school later in life. A career pivot, like us," Bran added.

"And what in the hell does it matter what they look like, Pat? Jesus. Is their website good?" Dad asked, drumming his fingers on his ebony wood desk, an antique from some royal court in Europe that was bequeathed to Hugh upon his father's passing.

"I didn't say it mattered," Pat shot back, "only that it's odd. The website is legit. I couldn't have done better myself. Lots of before-and-afters. The color scheme is subtle, pleasing to the eye. Very easy to navigate."

"I emailed them last night and actually just received a reply before you guys came in." Calling up his emails again, Bran read the reply.

Good morning Mr. O'Faolain. We appreciate that you're considering our company for Wolves Irish Pub. You mentioned coming to Eufaula. We would be pleased to meet with you at your convenience. Let us know when, and we will block off several hours.

After you tell us about the project, your needs, wants, and what you expect from our team, we will, if you choose to go with us, create a portfolio of options and our personal recommendations. We would, of course, need to see the space and speak to your Hospitality management team.

We look forward to meeting with you,
Triskelion Territory Designs

"Professional," Dad admitted. "Well-spoken and to the point." High praise from the O'Faolain patriarch.

"I'll be packing for the Kentucky Derby in a few days. And, by the way, Bran, you've never said whether you're going or not," Pat lifted his eyebrows in good-natured irritation. "The three of us could make a run to Eufaula this afternoon or tomorrow."

"That's not a bad idea. That way, if we do decide to go with them, they can set up a meeting with James or his sister to look over the plans for the projected opening date and so on." James O'Connor was one of Bran's best friends from school. His family ran a hospitality business that opened bars and restaurants all over the world. Wolves was an important project for Bran's family. The Irish pub was meant to honor Bran's grandfather, Jonathan O'Faolain, who had passed away a couple of years ago. The O'Connors were the only team they would trust with something so personal.

"Today won't give them enough time to rearrange their schedule."

"You're right, Dad. I'll email them back and ask for tomorrow morning if that works for everyone." Bran looked at both men, who nodded in agreement. "While I do this, Pat, call James and see what his schedule looks like next week in case we do go with Triskelion. We'll want to get things going as soon as possible."

"I'll make the call in the kitchen where Sara hopefully left some hidden treats."

As Patrick sauntered off, Dad asked, "Have you spoken to James lately? I spoke with Dean O'Connor at the Summit Club the other day. He didn't come out and say he was concerned about James, but he certainly inferred it."

Dad paused, and Bran looked up from his email. His father's direct gaze leveled on him, awaiting Bran's response.

"It's been a couple weeks. I got some initial pricing for the pub. The usual shit." Bran ran over the brief encounter to see if he may have missed something. "If there was a problem, I was not aware of it."

"Keep it in mind then."

Conversation over. *Will do, Dad.*

3

———

Had anyone walked into the offices of Triskelion Territory Designs at that moment... they would have turned right back around and gotten the hell out of what looked like the *Twilight Zone*. Witnessing three women frozen, staring blankly at computer screens, no eye twitching, no tapping pens, no music, no nervous throat clearing. Just three mannequins awaiting their turn to be beamed up to the mother ship.

Rowan was the first to break the silence— one hour and twelve minutes to be exact— AER (After Email Reply).

"Guys, we have work that needs doing. The waiting sucks, but surely it would help if we did SOMETHING while we wait."

"You're right, sis, let's move on with our..." River began but was interrupted by several loud notification pings exploding from their laptops, phones, and watches— it was a battlefield of pings.

"Oh Jesus, Oh Jesus, Oh Jesus..." The extent of Raven's articulation.

"Jaysus, Mary 'n Joseph as Nan likes to say," River said absently.

Raven noticed that all three of their hands were hovering over their mice. No one had clicked to open. "If he's changed his mind or found another firm, we'll get over it. I'll reply that we appreciate his time and that if things change to keep us in mind for this or any other project."

Raven cringed at expressing rejection aloud before it had even happened. She had to get her shit together.

"Okay, sisters, forget my negative bullshit." River and Rowan looked up with wide hazel eyes, probably the same look she was giving them, a combination of terror and hope.

"Rowan," Raven said decisively, "open the email and River and I will sit by you, and you'll read it to us."

Chairs moved side by side by side, deep breaths in— and out — click.

Thank you for getting back to us so promptly. We have a tight deadline for when we want the pub up and running. Time will not be your friend. We will stop by your office tomorrow around mid-morning if that's acceptable. We don't expect to take up too much of your day.

Bran O'Faolain

Silence. Crickets. The calm before the storm.

And then— all hell broke loose.

The girls knocked over their chairs, they jumped up so fast. Then knocked into one another as their happy dances took up a considerable amount of space. As did chest bumping, high fives, jazz hands, and a millisecond of Ring Around the Rosie before collapsing in a boneless, wheezing pile of hair and limbs onto the soft, wool area rug.

Grinning at one another from their prone positions, Raven suggested. "Okay, how 'bout we make some smoothies, turn the music back on, get our work done for the day, go out to a celebratory dinner where we feast, imbibe, and come up with some excellent talking points for our new VIP possible clients." Raven took another breath and finished with, "Tomorrow morning, we'll get up, work out, beautify, and get our professional faces on."

"Hell to the yes, Rave!" River said while bopping her sister's nose.

"You know I love a good plan," Rowan agreed in her quieter way. "We'll have to get off the floor first, though."

"Oh," Raven reminded them, "I'll need to phone Mrs. Barclay and see if I can swing by her boutique Monday instead of tomorrow morning. I just hate to reschedule more than once if the O'Faolains are late, forcing us to change other appointments."

"Good thinking," River agreed. "I have a few calls that I can do today instead of tomorrow if the clients are available."

"I'll do that too," Rowan said. "Might as well free up the whole day... in case."

And just like that, serious determination painted each of their faces. They had been working their asses off for the past few years for just such a moment. Raven was going to fight for this job. They all would, she knew. Work now, then prepare. As if their minds were linked, three sets of hazel eyes looked toward the large portrait of their parents. Daniel and Lily Byrne. Never forgotten. Loved always.

Raven recalled when they'd finished their sophomore year in college. They could hardly wait to complete the next two and start *living*. Finals done, the girls had loaded their bags in the car, got on the road, and headed the short drive home to Bristow for the summer.

An online General Physics class the only hindrance to weeks of rewatching every episode, including the holiday specials, of *Great British Baking*, Gordon Ramsay anything—ironic since Raven hated to cook— and, most importantly, doing some preliminary outlining for establishing their own interior design company— a business plan, registration, licensing, insurance, marketing, financial projections, and location.

Their Mom and Dad had planned on being home the following day from Atoka. They'd been asked to speak and give a presentation at the Atoka Museum on Irish railroaders settling down in the area, the spread of Catholicism because of it, and the commingling between the Irish and Native Americans. In *SpongeBob* speak— their best day ever.

They'd called Raven the day before, and she'd put them on speaker so all the girls could hear. They wanted them to know that because of all the tornadoes around and torrential rain, a banner year apparently, their return may be delayed. The sisters' drive from Norman to Bristow had been continuous rain but not horrible, so Raven never gave it another thought. Oklahoma is known for its extreme weather.

It was the last time they would hear their voices. The last 'drive safe.' The last 'I love you.'

Daniel and Lily Byrne died the following evening. Poor visibility, heavy rain, straight winds, and a semi-truck pulling an empty 48-foot trailer making it more susceptible to the high winds. Eyewitnesses said the trailer had been swaying violently before it swung into oncoming vehicles, dragging the semi in its wake. Their car stood no chance against it. Surviving over seventeen tons of tornadic metal— nonexistent.

Past and present divided...

Raven knew her parents watched over them. She knew they would stand beside her and her sisters during this meeting with Mr. O'Faolain.

4

———

Bran, Patrick, and their father found Triskelion easily enough. The sisters had done a commendable job keeping the old-world feel to the three-story brick building while managing to make the entrance fresh and inviting. The heavy, wooden door painted emerald green, had a simple bronze placard attached:

Triskelion Territory Designs
Byrne Sisters

"Cool feel to the place." Patrick may not love history as much as Bran did, but he did appreciate it when an effort of preservation was made.

"Nice," Dad said. Hugh the Loquacious.

"We're earlier than I'd planned. Hopefully, we don't screw up their schedule." Bran had planned to have their sit down with the sisters around ten or eleven, but Dad and Pat decided the warm, sunny day would be wasted on the road and wanted to get business out of the way so they could enjoy the sunny weekend. Bran didn't try too hard to change their minds.

They were all home with no plans and decided they officially needed to start preparations for Open the Pond Day... or, more appropriately, Open Club Pond-Pub Day. So, with very little arm-twisting involved, they convinced Bran to get the boring shit with Triskelion over quick and early— 8:30 am arrival— stop by a grocery store that hopefully had a good meat market, grab some steaks and head back to the compound to get everything ready for a weekend of relaxation.

Thinking of what Dad had said about James yesterday, Bran had texted him on the way to Eufaula and asked him to join them for the weekend.

"Hey, James just texted me that he's down to hang out but not to buy any gas station garbage meat. His words, and he'll bring everything we need."

"Glad you thought to include him, Bran. It's been a long time since we've all hung out." Patrick added, "It will also give us a chance to talk to James about Wolves and, I guess, about our meeting this morning."

As the O'Faolain's walked through the front door, it wasn't the simplistically lovely creams and greens of the office space Bran noticed but rather the horrible music filtering through the office's stereo. Thankfully, it was on low— *Bangarang* by Skrillex (thank Pat for the awful music lesson), paired with the women's— presumably the owners'— colorful argument filtering down from above— and the smell... what the hell.

Dad looked as though he was bracing himself. Patrick said, "Great fucking song." Bran could only wonder what he'd done to piss Diana Gaines off.

~

RAVEN WAS ABOUT to cut a bitch— or two. The morning had started off so well, and the dinner celebration the night before had been fun and productive. Morning workouts and beautifica-tion— done and done. Baking cookies for their, hopefully, newest clients— burnt.

She shouldn't have made the attempt. River was the baker, but she was too busy fussing with her hair, and it should be noted here that they ALL have Straight. Black. Hair. They wash it, dry it, and brush it. It hangs to their waists. Gale force winds wouldn't change its trajectory. Straight, no fuss needed.

So, the fact that there were burnt cookies and a BURNT COOKIE SMELL in the office was simply NOT RAVEN'S FAULT.

"Suck it, Raven! It's fucking cookies, for the love of God. Cookies!" River screeched. "A five-year-old could have made them."

"I was nervous about this morning, you absolute *asshole*! And turn this horror movie music OFF!" Raven would love to have a redo. Hear her alarm go off, gently touch her phone screen to end the beep, dreamily stretch, and hop out of bed. But no... this hellscape was still in play and looking comfortable.

"I don't like to involve myself in your ridiculous bullshit, but I'm telling you both now, shut, the absolute fuck, up!" Raven and River froze, slowly swiveling like animatrons toward their youngest sister, and looked in awe at the youngest Byrne. The one that never raised her voice and so rarely cursed.

"Holy fuck, Row— you legit just used the F word." Cookies forgotten, River was all smirk.

Raven attempted to slow her roll. "Umm, sis, you all right?"

Rowan, even-keeled Rowan, didn't miss a beat. "Actually, girls, I'm not okay." Smoothing her hands over her behind, she asked, "Do you love my dress?" Before Raven could respond, Rowan continued - and here, she puts a hand beneath her flowy summer dress, all pale yellow and lovely, and made a giant production of pulling out a panty wedge.

"No-show panties, right? Lies," she cried. "Absolute, one hundred percent bullshit lies."

Rowan's clone then proceeded to pull the offending undergarment down her legs, wad them up, and throw them in the trash can.

"There. Those faux-no-show pieces of absolute shit can rest in peace in the trashcan." With a maniacal look in her eyes, she says all Laura Ingalls Wilder sweet, "Riv, would you mind switching the music to something a bit more peaceful, and Rave, would you help me open up the windows downstairs to air out the... ash in the air?"

Alrighty then. Put in their places, the three girls marched downstairs while River, thankfully, switched to Passenger Radio. Crisis averted? No.

As they hit the ground floor, it became apparent that hell on earth was no simple saying— they were prophetic words, a phrase saved for a priest's dramatic Christmas Mass meant to scare parishioners into making better choices the next year— words to describe the nightmare facing them, and currently staring in horror, at Raven and her sisters.

They froze like deer in headlights on the stairs. No sudden movement, folks... disaster will pass by.

Oh God, no. No, no, no, no, NO! Bran O'Faolain was standing by Raven's desk,

mouth ajar. Could it get worse? Yes.

Raven recognized the men who accompanied Bran. Oh, Jesus Lord, have mercy and angels surround them in this time of need... *great* need, Lord.

The eldest son brought no lower-level employees to witness this humiliation. It was none other than Bran's younger brother Patrick and their *father*, Hugh. The head of the whole damn O'Faolain dynasty. Dreams— crushed.

SHOCK KEPT all six people in the room immobile. Bran couldn't speak for his dad and brother, but it wasn't the mortifying conversation they'd just been privy to, nor was it the campfire aroma of the office space. It was the three women staring at them with varying degrees of horror.

Stunning. They were all stunning. The first wore a pale yellow dress, and Bran could only surmise... no panties. Yellow had dimples, only noticeable because her mouth was wide in shock and horror. The last woman to step off was lovely in a black pencil skirt and navy silk button-up. Blue was the only one of the trio with cat eyes, accentuated with dark liner. Bran imagined she might be the ferocious one.

However, his attention was riveted to the middle one. The smallest of the trio, or rather the shortest, as they all seemed to be of a size. That one. She wore a fitted black blazer paired with yellowish-green slacks. Stunning. Bran was having a hard time remembering why they were even there. He was thirty years old, for fuck's sake, and couldn't think of a single charming thing to say. Blazer had the type of pouty porn star lips women usually paid for— ones he would dream about.

Pat's whispered, "Holy shit," seemed to fracture the stasis the three men found themselves in. Time had stopped, and now, thankfully, it was ticking again.

Dad, the great orator of the 21st century, stated the obvious with, "Perhaps we need to reschedule."

With those five words, a bomb seemed to detonate around the women. Hands were flailing and gesticulating about. Bran heard a whispered 'No,' then an equally quiet 'Oh God,' followed by a 'We're fucked.' Attempting to shake off the shock of seeing Triskelion's designers, especially Blazer, he found his voice.

"My apologies, ladies, we had a change of plans for later today and decided to get an early start. I should have... called," he finished lamely.

~

RAVEN WOULD LIE DOWN and cry— later— but not right now. Damage Control. It would be like trying to stop the flow of arterial bleeding from a severed limb— using butterfly bandages. Impossible. Ridiculous. But damn it, it was her burnt cookies that had started this nightmare.

Forcing herself to look each man in the eye before addressing Bran, Raven began with, "The only apology necessary here, Mr. O'Faolain, will be issued from my sisters and me." One of her hands surreptitiously moved behind her back, and with relief, Raven felt her sisters' small hands grasp her own.

"Forgive us for our absolute lack of professionalism this morning. There is no excuse, so I will not make one." Raven attempted to keep eye contact with the eldest son, but his dark eyes were intense. He and his younger brother were similar in looks, much like Raven and her sisters, but where the youngest O'Faolain appeared carefree, chin length, shaggy white hair parted on the side, showing off his shaved sides, the oldest, Bran, took after his father. Reserved and serious. Though he had the same white hair as his brother, Bran styled his in a French crop with a high fade. A shiver shot straight up her spine. Gorgeous. Distracting.

"Well," River began, and Raven immediately stiffened beside her, "I will offer up an excuse. We cleared our calendars for your," and here she tipped her head in the three men's direction, "*mid-morning* appointment."

If Raven didn't feel her sister's hand shaking like a leaf, *she* might even have believed her bravado.

Raven held in a groan as River finished up with, "So, you see, gentlemen, we did have reason to believe we were quite *alone*, unlocked door notwithstanding."

Raven was about to attempt introductions when Rowan's quiet, steady voice stopped her.

"Would you consider a do-over?" Rowan let go of her sisters and took a step forward, right hand extended. Beginning with Patrick, then Bran, then finally shaking hands with Hugh. "I'm Rowan Byrne. Nice to meet you."

Raven stepped forward, with River right behind her and said, "Raven Byrne." Followed by the shaking of hands attached to slightly bewildered men. Echoed by "River Byrne."

"How about my sisters and I take you to the local café for breakfast while our office finishes airing out and then come back here for the meeting."

Before Bran or his family could respond, Raven added, "We won't take much of your time. Once we've heard your plans for the pub, we'll ask our questions. We have already compiled some of our own questions as well as a list of vendors in your area that we think will handle the quality you're after in the desired time frame." Raven finally forced herself to stop. Begging would commence if she kept rambling.

To Raven's shock, Bran simply replied, "Breakfast sounds good."

BREAKFAST *WAS* good but served with a heaping side of awkward. Patrick, usually the most vocal, had clammed up. Bran heard him mumble something to Blue, she snorted in amusement, then they both kept eating. No help there.

Dad said— absolutely fucking nothing. He didn't even say his order aloud, only pointing at the pink flyer with Today's

Special in bold print. Biscuits and gravy, bacon, hashbrowns, and toast.

Yellow looked at his dad once in silent question, for what he wasn't sure, before blinking once, twice, a lift of eyebrows, then back to her bowl of oatmeal. Bran could feel the uncomfortable beginnings of sweat forming under his light jacket and wanted nothing more than to strip the damn thing off, but it was as though normal behavior had deserted him— he would just sweat and suffer. Lifting his arms to take his jacket off seemed like it would draw way too much attention his way.

Finally, his eyes found Blazer. She was moving her fruit and side of sausage links around her plate. Her fork had yet to make a trip to those gorgeous lips. She looked painfully uncomfortable. He hated that they were so embarrassed. Honestly, he and his brother could come to blows over the television remote. So no, none of them were horrified by the bickering banter. It began and ended with the shockingly lovely appearance of the sisters. Definitely not middle-aged women looking to switch career gears.

Bran had unknowingly built a false narrative around the Byrnes. When a person expects middle-aged ladies, done with raising their families, who perhaps decided to create a business together, and instead sees three young, gorgeous, and obviously talented women standing before them... of course, the O'Faolains were stunned. His father, uncommunicative in public at the best of times, even appeared flustered behind his beard.

"Tell me, Ms. Byrne," Bran placed a ridiculously delicate cough against his palm when all three women looked at him.

"Please, call me Raven."

Thank God. "Raven, then," Christ, he sounded like part of the *Mister Rogers' Neighborhood* cast, "I wondered how the name of your business came about."

"Oh," she breathed. Like he'd handed her a life vest, saving her from drowning. Her eyes flipped to his immediately, hope in conversational salvation turning her pale cheeks pink.

RAVEN WAS DELIRIOUSLY relieved a talking point had been presented. The silence of breakfast was deflating. How did she answer a question that didn't need *the long version* but deserved one? Their parents had been successful academics, professors, published authors, and madly in love. As role models go, none came higher. The pressure to please was neither verbalized to the kids nor quietly hinted at. Even so, it manifested unintentionally within each of their children. Pleasing their parents became a love language for Raven and her sisters.

A thank you for all the love without strings— to parents who emboldened their children to reach for greatness.

Growing up, the girls spent the summers in Ireland with their grandma and grandpa while their parents headed the college's study abroad program. Their father and his family were extremely close.

Their mother grew up in foster care. Lily Byrne never knew who her father was, but she did know her mother was a Creek Native American that had lived on the Muscogee Nation reservation in Okmulgee, Oklahoma, until she was a teenager. Lily was told that her mother had left her with a neighbor and ran off with her boyfriend. It was later discovered they had both died a few months later of drug overdoses, and over the next several years, her mother's family had either passed away too or moved to parts unknown. When she married Dad, his family became hers, and she always taught her daughters to stay close. Family was everything.

The Byrne part of their family, and other Irish-born families that had lived in America for years, eventually moved back to

Ireland— the many wonders of America not enough to keep them from their native Emerald Isle. Many of those had served in the U.S. Army during WWI and decided to stay in Europe once the War ended, sending for their loved ones to join them later.

Descended from a long line of Irish Catholic immigrants, and the blood of both Oklahoma Choctaw and Creek had always been a great source of pride in their family.

The summers were magical and, without question, the shiniest of bright childhood memories. Not to say that with her and her siblings causing havoc, Nan Byrne could, would, and still did, scare them toward the straight and narrow. County Roscommon would forever be the sisters' favorite place on earth.

Family heritage should be honored. "Our father's family is from Ireland, but his ancestor worked the transcontinental railroad after the Great Famine. He eventually settled in Oklahoma and married a Choctaw woman. His descendants eventually moved back to Ireland. Our Nan still lives on the original Byrne land. Our mother was orphaned as a child, but her mother lived for several years on the Muscogee Nation reservation. Her mother was Creek.

"My sisters and I embrace both sides of our heritage with pride," she smiled, first at the O'Faolains and then toward her sisters, knowing any mention of their parents was special.

"With a last name like O'Faolain, I assume you have family in Ireland?"

❧

"I BELIEVE MY GRANDFATHER, Jonathan O'Faolain, had family from a small fishing village in southern Ireland. Unfortunately, people always think they have years to ask their loved ones questions, and when they pass, you realize how foolish it was to have wasted the time. Our Gran has said she plans on really working on the family's ancestry. Your story makes me want to dig a little deeper into our history as well." Smiling at his dad, he added, "I know we come from fishermen, which might explain my father's infatuation with ponds." He noticed the Byrne ladies hid smiles. They knew Bran must be teasing his dad about something.

Looking at Raven, or, more accurately, his newest obsession, he asked, "Pat mentioned that all three of you went to design school at OU, and," he paused as Patrick's head whipped toward him— he probably thought Bran was about to bring up that his brother had noticed their website's lack of pictures, "he said you all graduated at the same time. How did that come about?" River and Rowan smiled. Patrick and Dad looked up from their plates, curious as well.

"Oh, well..." Raven began, casting looks at her sisters. "I was born on February 16, the same year River was born on December 20, and Rowan the following year, November 1. So, you see, we are so close in age that River and Rowan chose to do online high school so they could finish much faster than my traditional route.

We all took concurrent college classes too. I didn't take as many in high school as they did, though. I was able to help them study and still work part-time. Eventually, we took several of the same college classes during their final year. It's sort of convoluted," Raven chuckled, "but we figured it out and then moved to college at the same time."

"I'm impressed," Bran admitted. And he was. They'd known what they wanted and made it happen. A close family. He liked that as he and his family were close. "Should we head back to your office?"

Raven was satisfied with the meeting. They had managed to, if not impress the O'Faolains with their knowledge and sensibility, at least proven they understood Wolves' vision. Being of Irish descent themselves hopefully swayed them a bit. When the girls had told them of their summers spent in Ireland, she could see their interest peak further.

Raven stood first. Everyone was seated in the corner lounge, with information on the pub's size and location spread before them on the coffee table. "Well, gentlemen, I know you have plans to get to, so we won't keep you longer. I hope we are still in the running to decorate Wolves after this morning's debacle," Raven smiled, internally dying, thinking of it again.

"Of course, you're in the running," Bran assured. "We'll need to discuss amongst ourselves and meet with a few other designers, but I'll get back to you hopefully within a week."

Bran and his brother were gorgeous, the shocking white of their hair and all that golden skin— ridiculously handsome. And one would never guess Hugh was their father. Older brother, maybe. She knew once she and her sisters cried themselves sick over this morning's horror, they'd enjoy comparing notes on the handsome O'Faolains. Raven was about to thank them all for their time when Patrick spoke up.

"Bran would love to see the rest of your building if you have the time. He loves historical sites."

Raven watched Patrick glance at his brother. Something must have passed between them because Bran agreed, saying, "I have been curious about what you've done with the other floors."

Hugh, Raven noticed, simply crossed his arms over his broad chest with the look of someone attempting to endure.

"Oh, of course! Like River told you earlier, we are free the rest of the day." Raven glanced at her sisters. "We created a space that is both a comfortable home and work environment."

Proud to show off the space, the girls started their assent up the wide, wooden stairs, the three men following closely on their heels.

Continuing as tour guide, Raven launched into the history of the town and the building's part in it.

"River focused her talents below in the offices. She's not only brilliant at design but building websites and handling social media." She nodded in her sister's direction as they walked into the open space on the second floor. "So, she naturally knew how she wanted our work area to flow and what made customers feel welcome."

"I was impressed with your site, River. I've built a few myself, and it isn't easy to make them look good but also be functional." Patrick's flattery had River blushing. How hilarious.

"I spearheaded this floor. It's completely open except for the bathroom. We wanted a space to read, watch movies, workout, and of course, enjoy a nightcap," she smiled as the men gravitated toward the bar.

"The tea, smoothie, and protein shake bar is in the middle," Raven pointed toward the juicer and blenders, fresh bowls of fruit and vegetables. "The fridge and sink are obviously on the left, while the rest, of course, is the good stuff," indicating the fully stocked bar. She laughed as she glanced at Bran, catching his smile.

"There seems to be a theme here," Bran replied. "Irish and American whiskey, with plenty of Scottish whisky to even things out."

"Damn," Patrick said. "Consider me impressed."

River's infectious smile bloomed, "You see, we got our mother's features and hair from her Creek ancestry. Her mother was Creek as Raven explained earlier, and even though our father's family carries Native American blood, they're as Irish as can be.

We got our vampire skin from him. And our love of whiskey, of course!"

Hugh, Raven noticed, couldn't stop a small smile from making an appearance.

Bran asked, "Do your folks live in Eufaula? Is that why you settled here?"

BRAN REALIZED he'd made a mistake as soon as the words left his mouth. All three women just... stopped. He, Pat, and Dad winced in the sudden silence. The sisters shifted closer to one another. Obviously, for comfort. Shit.

"I'm sorry," Bran started, "I shouldn't have asked such a personal question."

Raven shook her head slightly as though sloughing off a thought or memory.

"No, no. Of course, it's okay, and our parents were amazing people who should be remembered."

She would have gone on, but Rowan seemed to realize she didn't want to continue.

"They both were killed in a car accident right after finals our sophomore year at OU." Waving toward the bar area, Yellow/Rowan? explained, "Rave worked ages on the memory wall."

Bran, Dad, and Patrick moved closer to see the pictures, postcards, and mementos that created the backsplash. He saw pictures of the Byrnes when they were little girls bouncing around who he assumed were their parents. Grins as beautiful then as now. Some pictures at a cottage in, he presumed, an Irish countryside.

Rowan tried to save the men from feeling awkward and

chose to change the subject while imbuing her words with light-heartedness.

"I designed our living quarters on the third floor if anyone still feels like trekking up another set of stairs..." pointing half-heartedly toward them.

Surprising everyone in the group, including himself, Bran imagined, Hugh said, "We might as well see the rest."

5

Dad was not happy. "Patrick, what were you thinking to not only hire Triskelion before we'd even left their office without discussing it with your brother and me first? Then you invite them to our home with an invitation to stay the night Saturday!"

It took the thirty-five-minute drive for him to ask. They'd just turned down the driveway to their compound and were waiting for the electric gate to slide open when he turned in his seat to face his youngest son.

"I..." Patrick began before Dad cut him off.

"I'll tell you what you were thinking, or rather what you were thinking with, boy, and it wasn't your head," he fumed. "At least not the head atop your damn shoulders."

This last came out in a low growl that, once upon a time, would have had Bran and Pat quaking in their shoes.

Bran decided to throw his brother a life preserver. It was strange, though, that their dad was so fired up about it. He knew his father well enough to realize he would have chosen the Byrne sisters. There were simply too many advantages with their Irish heritage and their time living in Ireland to blow them off. Not to mention they were extraordinarily talented. Their Eufaula property was proof of that. Something else must be bothering the old man.

"Dad, leave off Pat, for fuck's sake. Patrick has never been foolish, and you know it. We were going to hire them. If they could come back from the fiasco we walked in on this morning, their talents probably have no equal." Dad didn't say anything else. A promising sign. Crisis averted.

But then Patrick chose to bring up the weekend. Jesus. Moron.

"Exactly." Justification riding his words. "Plus, I imagine you wouldn't mind staring at Raven with your mouth hanging open again, Bran," Patrick tacked on, smiling.

Unfortunately, he wasn't wrong. "Last time I try to help you out dickhead," Bran replied without heat.

"And," Patrick kept on his roll, "James is already going to be here. It'll save time all the way 'round."

Dad's mouth was starting to thin again. Perfect... annnnd... Pat wasn't done.

"I texted James to be prepared for an impromptu meeting with River... the Byrne's, rather, Saturday morning."

I should have let Dad kill him. Know when to shut the fuck up, brother. Seriously. "Great, Pat." Please let that be the end of Chatty Patty.

"By the way, Dad, thanks for the save back at Triskelion. I felt horrible that I asked about their parents." Remembering their sad faces squeezed his chest all over again.

"They're good girls," was all his dad said.

~

"I wish we could call Mom and Dad. They wouldn't believe us," River spoke from behind Raven. Her sisters were chilling in her bed while she packed things from her closet. They decided to do it tonight instead of tomorrow so they could concentrate on work.

She and her sisters had been switching positions in each other's rooms to multitask, discussing the day and packing for the O'Faolains. Just thinking about that sent swarms of butterflies through her stomach. Raven wouldn't relax until they were officially hired for the job. Barring another catastrophe, it seemed a sure thing.

Rowan pulled Raven from her thoughts. "I would like to believe they know," she said softly in answer to River.

Missing our parents every day was natural. Thinking of them every day was healing. Becoming sad every day was dangerous. They discussed this often. They had seen a therapist individually and together for a year and knew what problems to look for in themselves and each other.

Determined to lift the mood, Raven said, "Well, Row, if they know specifics like that in heaven, then they know that their youngest daughter, screeching like a banshee, tore her panties off and walked around three grown men au naturale."

River burst out laughing. "Oh my God, Rave, I'm literally dying. I may pee myself," she squealed.

"You are an absolutely horrible older sister!" Rowan started lobbing pillows into Raven's closet. She was laughing now too. "I've considered hypnotherapy to erase the whole morning from my memory," Rowan managed to sound traumatized, but her eyes were glowing with mirth.

At this point, it was laugh at it or cry.

River asked, "Hey, sis, are you packing any sexy nighties while you're in there? The way you were making eyes at Bran, I'm surprised the man didn't have ocular hickies."

Raven stuck her head out and stared at both sisters. "In all seriousness, was I obvious?" Putting her fingers to her eyes, she massaged gently. If only it would massage away the embarrass-ment— From. The. Whole. Morning.

"You know I have no experience with men. I mean, none of us do, but God, I'd die if I thought he noticed me noticing him..." As she trailed off, she uncovered her eyes and saw both sisters watching her.

"Come sit on the bed with us," River offered.

"It wasn't obvious. Truly," Rowan added. "But, sis, you realize *he* never stopped staring at *you*, right?"

Raven popped up and straddled her sister's lap, holding her shoulders down with her hands. "Don't play with me, Rowan. You'll regret it." Raven tried an unblinking stare.

River laughed, "She's not lying. He's way into you." Thoughtfully she added, "It will make this job slightly tricky if we're all not careful."

And damn, if River wasn't spot on. This was not a job to screw up by fraternizing with the client. Double damn.

"You mean because Playboy Patrick O'Faolain acted like a blushing nincompoop if you so much as glanced in his direction, River?" Rowan asked, still pinned to the bed.

"No way!" River knocked her older sister off her youngest, taking her place. Except she grabbed her shoulders and started bouncing Rowan up and down.

"It's true!" she screamed while laughing.

"Oh my, I'm exhausted," River said, hauling herself off Rowan before collapsing beside her.

They all lay in silence for a minute. It was true Irish luck that they'd landed this job. Raven was still shocked. They all were. Perhaps even the O'Faolains were, she mused.

"One last thing before we go to bed," River started. "Raven, you're right. None of us has any experience with men. I know we chose to wait. We put school first, and then we put work first," she paused, adding, "but don't you guys think it's about time we got some experience? Like, put ourselves out there? Not on a street corner or anything, but accepted a few dates here and there?"

Surprising her older sisters, Rowan was the first to respond. "Yes. I say hell yes, actually. We need to make our love lives a priority. Raven?"

"You guys are right. I mean, I'm not adding a stripper pole downstairs, but... I may add that black and nude nighty I bought last time we went shopping in OKC."

Her sisters lay on Raven's bed for a while longer in silence. Possibly doing what she was, considering what it would be like to let a man into their lives. What it would mean, and how it would change things.

6

———

"What's up, O'Connor?" Bran went in for a hug. James was one of his closest friends, and Patrick's as well. They'd gone to high school and then college together. James and his sister, Jo, took over the family business, O'Connor Hospitality, LLC. They opened and managed restaurants all over the world.

"Hey Bran, Pat was just filling me in on the Byrne sisters. He thought I might hit it off with Raven— after business is concluded, of course."

Bran's whole body went stiff. What in the absolute fuck was Pat thinking? No, Bran hadn't spoken to him about Raven, but still... what the hell? Both James and his brother burst out laughing.

"Holy shit, Bran, you should see your face! I owe you twenty bucks, Pat."

Bran realized his mistake immediately. It had been so long since he'd taken an interest in a woman, he'd obviously forgotten how to play it cool.

"Fine. You caught me out. I do, in fact, find Raven fascinating, but did Pat tell you about how he stammered and blushed when he tried to talk to River?"

"Okay fuckface, I didn't blush. I... couldn't think of what to say, and I... mumbled," Patrick finished weakly.

"So, is the third sister as pretty as your two?" James asked.

"They aren't ours by a long shot. We literally just laid eyes on them, but they make an impression. And you know Pat has no plans to stop being a playboy, but yes, Rowan is just as beautiful," Bran admitted. At this point, his father stood and headed toward the patio doors.

"I'm going to make sure Jerry stocked everything at the pond for tomorrow."

Since Patrick spontaneously invited guests for the weekend, they all decided to put off the big cookout until everyone arrived Saturday. Tonight, they'd play pool or cards and catch up. However, something was going on with Dad, Bran thought. After this weekend, he thought, they needed to spend some time together.

To take attention off his dad's odd behavior, Bran asked James, "Whatever happened to Jane, by the way? I thought she was going to be the one for you."

James' face shuttered. He was attempting, unsuccessfully, to hide his feelings. Dad was right then. Something happened to put that ill-disguised look of pain on his friend's face. He glanced at Patrick, and he gave a slight nod, acknowledging he'd noticed.

"It didn't work out," was James' answer.

Bran placed a hand on James' shoulder, "I'm sorry to hear it. If there is ever anything you need to talk out, Pat and I are always here for you."

Patrick agreed. "You should have told us, James. We aren't so busy we don't have time to listen."

James was fighting some deep hurt, apparent from his

rapidly blinking eyes. After a moment, he said, "I might need to, but not tonight. Okay?"

Patrick and Bran said, "Of course," and "I'll be here," at the same time. For now, the issue was dropped in favor of whiskey and pool.

"The girls are whiskey drinkers, by the way." That lightened the mood as hoped.

"Damn. You O'Faolains know how to pick them."

A PERSON WOULD THINK Raven and her sisters were on some exotic safari in Africa instead of a narrow road somewhere in Muskogee County, less than an hour from Eufaula.

Necks were craning this way and that, oohs and aahs for a patch, not a field, but a *small* patch of blooming daisies.

Look, the sky is so blue.

Roll the windows down. The air feels amazing.

Aren't the trees huge?

Much to her chagrin, Raven was no better. At least for River and her, this weekend was a double whammy. An exciting new job *and* the rush of seeing Bran and Patrick. This James might be a possible match for Rowan, though. Her youngest sister made a noncommittal noise when it was mentioned last night.

Raven wanted to rally the troops one more time before they entered the compound. "Remember, girls, first and foremost, we are here to work. The meeting with James O'Connor starts in an hour, at ten. For all the notice we were given, I still believe we came up with a few good starter ideas. Let's make the most of that time because it sounds like we've been invited to one hell of a cookout this afternoon."

"And" River couldn't help but add, "our second, but just as important goal, is to get out there and experience some shit!"

Three fists hit the air with resounding Yesses!

Security cameras must have picked them up because the ginormous, black gate they rolled to a stop in front of was already opening. These people live on another level— or, how Okies say it, 'a whole 'nother level.'

Raven kept reminding herself to breathe, and calm down, for the love of everything Holy. Do Not Sweat. Bran and Patrick were uber-wealthy and influential, yes, but they were also down-to-earth, funny, and kind. Hugh was... quiet.

"Oh God, guys, look at the house!" River said reverently.

It was literally a glass house— nestled in the trees with three levels of gorgeous glass, black metal roof, and wraparound, floating hardwood decks. Stunning. Raven couldn't wait to see how the place was decorated.

"Wow," Rowan started, "I mean, seriously, wow. Seeing this house might be the biggest perk of landing the Wolves job."

Agreed.

River had just put their Jeep in park when the front door swung open, and no, it wasn't a normal front door, but some intricately carved heavy, metal monster. Patrick and Bran waved and started walking toward them. Another man with golden blonde hair and of an age with Bran stayed by the door. It must be James. Further back, still inside, stood Hugh.

Raven smiled and waved back to the brothers. The back-drop was fantastic. Bran in worn jeans and a T-shirt was better. The faded slate blue of his shirt made his white-blonde hair really shine. Bran kept his hair in a very *Peaky Blinders*, Tommy Shelby style. What would this man look like in a Tweed cap? Shit, Raven! Focus on work. Work first, she reminded herself.

Bran came to stand right in front of her. He towered over her. She didn't care. Sore necks were a doable price to pay to be this close. He smelled of warm spices, not cologne. Intoxicating like whiskey.

"Hello."

One word, but paired with his sudden intensity, made her shiver. "Bran." Good Lord, could Raven sound any more porn star breathy? "Thank you so much for having us."

"I..."

He began to say something and then paused, cupping a hand around his neck in a strange show of discomfort. Oh no. Maybe he wished they hadn't come after all.

Raven quickly added, "My sisters and I only need to stay for the meeting with Mr. O'Connor, and then we can get out of your hair. I'm sure you have plenty going on without added houseguests."

COULD HE BE MORE AWKWARD? What was she, twenty-four or five, and she was more composed than he was. Bran almost said, 'I wanted you here,' but that sounded autocratic, more in line with how his father would handle the situation.

He settled for, "I'm really glad you're here. We all want you to stay and enjoy the weekend." She smiled tentatively. Hopefully, he salvaged the second meet and greet.

He desperately wanted to touch her. Maybe a pat on the shoulder. He was losing it. Pat had probably hired a videographer to tape his ineptness. They were probably filming behind that giant oak bordering part of the drive right now.

Shaking off the *Funniest Home Video* he was currently starring in, Bran told the sisters, "Let Pat and I grab your bags." He had to stop staring. Hopefully, his mouth hadn't been hanging open, or Patrick would never let him live it down.

Addressing all the sisters, Bran said, "We thought you ladies might want to get situated in your rooms, and then James is ready to sit down anytime you three are."

They nodded yes, and he heard a thank you, and that's perfect. Bran thought it was just as shocking to see the three of them together as it had been the first time. It was stunning to see them side by side.

As Patrick moved away with River and Rowan, bags in hand, Bran went to pull Raven's bag out. She was close to his side. Her loose white button-up, jeans, and sandals were casual but classy. She was classy. She wasn't a flirt— he almost wished she were. It'd make it so much easier to make a move, any move.

Before he lost the moment, Bran wrapped his fingers around her left forearm, lightly running his palm downward 'til it encircled her hand, squeezing gently before pulling away. "I'm really glad *you* are here." Bran grabbed the overnight bag and shut the rear door.

Bran barely caught the words, but as they turned to follow their family, he heard Raven whisper, "Me too."

RAVEN WAS TRYING to appreciate the décor of modern, clean lines mixed with antiques, but there was nothing in her head but Bran. When he'd leaned close to her body and lightly touched her arm, her hand— when he said he was glad *she* was there, not she and her sisters— *her*... a critical pivot happened in her mind. Raven thought... *knew* that meeting Bran was important. She would be careful because of business but still pursue the connection. She knew he felt it too.

Bran said his dad had two guest suites on the second floor and hoped she didn't mind that two of her sisters would have to bunk together. "One room has a King bed, and the other has two queens. Both have en suite bathrooms."

"Oh, that's more than fine, Bran. We could all room in one,

no problem." They'd caught up to her sisters by then, and having heard Bran and then her response, they agreed.

River looked at Patrick and said, "Raven's right. There's no reason to mess up two rooms. We'll take the one with two beds and be more than comfortable." Looking to Rowan, she asked, "Isn't that right?"

Ever the realist, Rowan agreed. "We'd probably end up in the same bed anyway." Eyeing Patrick, Bran, and James, who they picked up at the front door, she continued, "It's so much easier to gossip about the hosts that way." The three men laughed as intended.

"Here are the rooms. Choose both or one as you'd like." Bran indicated the two open doors. "We'll leave you ladies to get settled. Come back downstairs to the bar lounge when you're ready, and James can walk you through the preliminary specs for Wolves."

Before taking his leave, Bran couldn't help himself. He briefly placed his hand on Raven's lower back. It could have come across as casual, he supposed, but not when she looked up at him, and they both paused, staring at one another. So, casual was off the table.

Once he, Patrick, and James were seated at the bar, with Dad joining them a moment later, James set in on him.

"Holy fuck, Bran. Did you not just meet the girl?"

It was true, so Bran didn't take offense, but it *did* grate to have one of his best friends call him out in front of his dad. "I wasn't aware I needed your approval." The surprise and then hurt that passed across James' face instantly made Bran regret the cold words.

"I know you mean well, James," Bran began, "and I don't

mean to be short, but in this, with Raven... I won't tolerate interference. From anyone." Patrick and his dad lifted their heads to look Bran in the eyes. Both nodded and looked away without a word, for which Bran was thankful. He was feeling too off-kilter and sensitive to have a family dust-up.

"Understood." Bran knew he and James were good when his friend clapped him on the back and smiled.

"What did you think of Rowan, Jamie?" Patrick used his childhood nickname to rib him and lighten the mood.

James smirked, not rising to the bait. "I wasn't aware River wasn't up for grabs too. So, we're all *not* being business professionals right now?"

Patrick's jaw clenched, barely, but it did. Bran knew his brother well enough that James' comment hit a tender spot.

"I would prefer, that is..." Patrick cleared his throat and looked at their dad. He must have gotten some signal from the old man because he ended with, "I'd ask you to keep your distance from River, James."

"Jesus, fine! I never dreamed the O'Faolain boys were the Love at First Sight type, but hey, I thought Jane was the one too. Just be careful. That's all I ask." James went from jovial to pensive in a blink. He was going to have to tell them what was going on sooner rather than later.

Patrick quickly exclaimed that he was miles from in love but thought he and River would be friends.

Bran was about to reply when the Byrnes walked in.

"So, what do you think, James? Will you or Jo have time to meet us at the site next week?" Fifteen minutes into the meeting, Bran knew they'd hired the right design team. After an hour and a half, he knew they were brilliant. Each sister had their own strengths, but they flowed beautifully together. Where one excelled, the other two gave them the floor. It was quite something to witness. From the looks Pat and his dad threw Bran's way, they, too, were impressed.

"Sure, Bran. I'll text Jo and have her send me our schedule." James smiled at the sisters saying, "My sister will really love meeting you three. Jo will try to kick me out of the entire project and gang up with you guys."

RAVEN AND HER SISTERS LAUGHED. "I can't wait to meet her and see the space. If it's possible to let us know by Monday or Tuesday when everyone's free to meet, we'd appreciate it." She glanced at her sisters, who nodded their agreement. "We'll rearrange our schedules accordingly."

"Jo works seven days a week." James tried for amusement, but there was a grimness to his words that belied his smile. "Before you leave tomorrow, I'll have some options for you."

Raven felt Rowan's fingers touch her thigh under the table. Something or someone was putting her on edge. Tonight, she'd get it out of her. For now, Raven covered her hand with her own.

"Mr. O'Faolain." Rowan stuttered to a stop at Hugh's sharp look.

Raven squeezed her sister's fingers tighter and noticed River scooted a fraction closer to her other side.

"Yesterday, you mentioned Wolves wasn't only a new business venture but a tribute to your late father. I... I... I'm quite good at finding just the right pictures or mementos to serve as a remembrance wall."

Hugh stared at her sister for a touch past comfortable before answering. "I've things you can go through."

Good Lord, that man needed a serious attitude adjustment, Raven thought. To turn attention from Row, she brought up the last few items that would need to be addressed sooner rather than later.

"I think we've got everything we need for now. I *would* like to discuss poured concrete bar tops with your contractor and if they believe an epoxy coating will hold up under continual use and cleanings. It's durable and looks high-end without costing a premium.

"Perhaps when we meet later next week, it might be arranged." Raven looked over her notes one last time. "My sisters and I discussed earlier that a nontraditional, more sleek approach to the bar tops would be a lovely foil against warmer wooden beams and paneling.

"Now that we've seen this house, it is a very similar concept. Old and new. Sleek but approachable.

"One only has to look at how distilleries have modernized

their whiskey bottle labels. Keeping up with the times while still appreciating the past. Exactly what a good Irish pub should be, unless you're in Ireland, of course, and then it's all 'Ye get what ye get, and ye don't throw a fit, lass.'" The last thing Raven wanted to address, she hesitated over, but, for heaven's sake, this family had the means.

"The last thing on today's list— absolutely not a must-have: if any of you are traveling to Ireland in the next few months, there is a company that designs the most gorgeous wooden platters made from whiskey barrels. Perfect for tasting menus, charcuteries, desserts, even flights of whiskeys.

"The company is situated outside of Dublin and crafts all sorts of items perfect for Wolves. They don't ship to the US, but I imagine shipping could be arranged if someone were to buy directly." Before any of the owners present could yea or nay her idea Raven added, "We will, of course, begin sourcing craftsmen in the states as well."

THE OWNERS of Triskelion Territory Designs knew their business. No denying that. "We can all agree that in the coming few weeks, there will be a hundred more Q&A meetings. Between Triskelion and O'Connors. However, work time is over." Bran stood up and stretched. "Let's all change into pond wear and meet out back, I'm ready for a drink and some barbeque."

He noticed Raven glance at her sisters with wide eyes as they started moving toward the stairs. "So, pond wear?"

Bran heard the laughter in her voice and decided to dig at his father as payback for his atrocious behavior toward Rowan. "Pond is somewhat relative here. This property boasts several good fishing ponds, but the one we're enjoying today is manicured to within an inch of its life. My father spent more money on it than building this house." Dad's look darkened. Perfect. Bullseye.

The girls' laughter trailed behind them as they headed upstairs to their rooms or room rather.

Bran waited until he was sure the sisters were out of earshot before asking how everyone thought the meeting went. "They were pretty damned prepared for a few hours' notice."

Patrick appeared preoccupied but agreed with Bran's assessment. "Before Dad reiterates my negligence in not speaking to you guys first about hiring Triskelion, after that meeting, I have zero regrets. I think Wolves is going to look slick as shit."

Dad tipped his head in acknowledgment. "Very capable." He surprised Bran by adding, "I like the idea of a remembrance wall. My dad would have appreciated it, and I know your Gran will be pleased."

"You're awfully quiet, James. Did the sisters meet with your approval?" Bran knew they did, but he wondered if James had caught anything he'd missed. After all, O'Connor's business was opening clubs and restaurants. They usually hired their own interior designers, but James knew this was a special project for the O'Faolains and they would be taking a more hands-on approach.

"I wasn't crazy about working with such a new company. Pair that with women fresh out of college— however, my concerns were unfounded. You guys lucked out for sure, and if I know my sister, once she meets the Byrnes, she'll be hiring them for other projects."

Bran was relieved hearing that. He could tell Patrick was as well. "Dad. Any concerns, or are we good to move forward?"

"With you boys mooning over two of the girls, I don't imagine a nay at this point would fly. I had reservations, similar to James', but I believe Wolves is in good hands with the O'Connors and the Byrnes at the helm."

"I wasn't aware any mooning was taking place except with Bran." Pat looked at his brother with his trademark smirk while flipping him off. "What did you think of Rowan, James?"

"A man would be lucky to have any of them turn their eyes in his direction." A non-answer if Bran had ever heard one.

"It's a good thing you have so little interest because I believe she has no interest in you either." Count on his brother to knock a person down a peg.

His father stood. "We'd better go change. I'll head on out as soon as I'm ready. Everything is stocked. Bring the girls with you."

With that, Bran made his way upstairs. The whole third floor housed his dad's private rooms, office, and what would eventually be an impressive library.

As the three friends went to change, James' phone dinged. He opened things up, absently glancing at his screen as they moved toward the stairs. Patrick was in the lead, so it was only because Bran followed James that he noticed a hitch in his best friend's stride.

"Bad news?"

James kept climbing. "Nothing."

James had reached his door by this point. As he walked over the threshold, he glanced over his shoulder and said he'd meet him at the pond as soon as he returned some emails. Bran stood outside the door another minute. Answering emails was certainly valid. Before his father sold most of their company shares, three-quarters of every day consisted of calls and emails. All well and good, except Bran had witnessed James' face when he looked at his phone. It was despair.

What in the hell was going on with his friend? Bran toyed with the idea of reaching out to James' sister Jo. Maybe she would meet him and Pat for breakfast one morning next week. Something was going on, and it started with the end of James and Jane's relationship.

~

BRAN AND PATRICK led Raven and her sisters down a path of black rock pavers separated with gorgeous, multi-colored pea gravel. She could see the care Hugh had taken with this back acreage. The pond and plumage were impressive, and the fact that the pond overlooked the Arkansas River— seriously impressive.

"Holy shit, Patrick. I don't think we brought fancy enough swimsuits and coverups for your dad's pond."

River wasn't wrong. When a person had the money this family did, they should expect this type of... scene, but the O'Faolains never put themselves on a pedestal. They appeared... low-key.

Raven's feelings for Bran, however, were anything but low-key. She still felt the heat on her lower back where his hand had pressed. What did it all mean? She was naïve about dating, but she sure as hell wasn't an imbecile. He genuinely seemed interested in her.

Raven was willing to see where the attraction took them. Patrick was interested in River, but her sister believed it was an innocent flirtation. Both of her sisters thought Bran's attentions had the potential to be... something with potential.

"The envy of all other swimming holes across the world." Raven waved expansively, taking in the woody-chic scene.

Once her sisters and Pat pulled slightly ahead, Bran told Raven that everyone thought the meeting went well.

Warmth filled her chest. "I'm glad we're on the same page. We are so stoked to work on Wolves with the O'Connors. My sisters and I are determined to blow your minds," Raven laughed. "Seriously, though, the Irish theme is in our wheelhouse. We'll kill it."

Bran laughed at her cockiness, hip-bumping her off the path. "Hey! What was that for?"

Over his shoulder, Patrick yelled, "Immature boys like to hit the girls they like." To which he and her sisters chuckled.

Raven looked up at Bran as she made her way back to his side. His blush was hysterical, but she decided not to call him on it. They were almost to the bar when Bran asked if she might consider going out with him sometime. Her brain short-circuited for a moment. Holy shit! Well, she didn't have to wonder if he was interested.

"Sure. That would be great. I'll be traveling to Tulsa more often now."

"I know you're coming at the end of next week to see the space and meet Jo, James' sister. Maybe I could take you out to dinner Wednesday in Eufaula."

Internally freaking out, Raven smiled, in an un-manic way—she hoped. "I would love that."

Bran smiled back, "Good." He briefly touched her back as they joined everyone else.

8

"Some set up," River looked about her appreciatively. "You O'Faolain men know what's what in Pond Chic, or at least you do, Hugh." Dad's lips tilted up at the good-natured gibe.

"Consider me your bartender for the day." James flipped a glass up in the air, missed, and it landed on the bar. Thank God it was plastic.

"We're in good hands then." Bran met Raven's eyes as she raised her brows at the show.

"Dad, how about you start prepping the steaks and veg while I put on a playlist of everyone's favorite tunes. Bran can continue standing there staring at Raven, and James can keep embarrassing himself."

"Good plan, Patrick. Hugh, I'll help you with the food." In a stage whisper, River leaned toward the older gentleman and said, "I think we all know Raven isn't an option for your sous chef."

That got Raven's attention. "Hey! That was not my fault. A few of the cookies even looked edible."

"Bran, you should check the Eufaula obituaries and see if

any poor soul died recently from eating dumpster charcoal." Laughing, Patrick stepped behind his brother to dodge Raven's ice cube missile.

Ignoring the antics, Hugh told River he would appreciate the help. Pat finished cueing up the playlist he'd created earlier. Everyone contributed their favorite songs before the meeting with James had started.

As Patrick bluetoothed into the system, he informed them, "You can learn a lot about someone from the music they enjoy." River agreed with him, of course. Knowing Patrick's tastes... concerning.

Bran saw Raven look in River's direction before finding Rowan— a mix between a grimace and resignation played over her features. Rowan smiled slightly and shrugged her shoulders.

Bran enjoyed having the Byrnes here. It was relaxing. They were practically strangers, but there was an ease— not necessarily for his dad, but he was smiling here and there. *Under Pressure* pumped through the cabana's system. Bran watched James smile.

"That's one of mine. No one can top Queen." Lining up glasses on the bar, James asked for drink orders, and the three sisters rapid-fired their orders.

"Jameson Black Barrel. Double. Neat. Not chilled."

"Bushmills Black Bush. Double. Neat. Not chilled."

Noted, Bran thought. Tucking away the information of his newest obsession.

"Glenmorangie 18. Two fingers will do. Neat. Not chilled. Thank you, James," Rowan added.

"Surrounded by all things Irish, and the little lady goes for Scottish. Nice." James flashed the youngest sister a smile.

Bran hoped the two could be friends if nothing else. James was clearly not over his ex, but that didn't mean he didn't need to date, even if it was platonic.

"I would have liked Slane, but I don't think you have it," she laughed. At this, Hugh's head jerked up. Sure as shit, his dad was scanning the shelves of spirits. He must not have found that particular Irish whiskey either. His jaw tensed like he couldn't believe his oversight.

Bran laughed to himself. Dad didn't seem to care for Rowan overly much, but he obviously didn't like not having her drink of choice. Amused, he caught the tail end of what Pat was saying.

"...Byrnes have good taste."

Bran smiled at Raven. "Not super shocking, considering their heritage."

"Dad was a man who enjoyed his whiskey of an evening while he graded papers or worked on his own writing to publish," Raven said. "Mom liked her herbal tea... Hey! That's one of my songs." *Maybe.*

"Jesus." River rolled her eyes. "I call dibs on the hammock. This song could put a Red Bull taste tester to sleep."

"Don't you dare badmouth Matthew Nolan!"

The girls were all smiles as they ribbed one another. Their relationship was a lot like his and Patrick's. Bran led Raven to the bar where they could sit and watch James attempt to bartend. Raven asked James to tell her what his team had worked on so far for Wolves.

Bran let the conversation wash over him, happy to simply sit close to Raven at the bar. Occasionally, their thighs touched accidentally, and once, not so accidentally. Raven turned toward him then and smiled, acknowledging the contact. He loved that she was aware of him even while engaged.

"Hugh and I have everything ready for a late lunch. Until it's time to eat, how about we check out what's so special about this pond," River suggested.

Grinning at Raven and Rowan before moving her gaze to Patrick, River yanked her coverup off and tossed it to Rowan, who caught it easily. She stripped her own off, joining her sister as they danced to *Chasing Rainbows* by The High Kings and Badscandal.

Raven hopped off the bar stool and stripped her coverup off before running to join her sisters at the water's edge.

Reaching River and Rowan, she whispered, "Bran asked me out, and oh my God, you guys. I'm freaking the fuck out. I hope he didn't see how badly I wanted to jump up and down."

"When? Where?"

"I knew he was going to ask you," River said smugly. "Even though I was internally wishing to die over breakfast— After the Incident— no one could miss Bran staring nonstop at you."

"He wants to come to Eufaula this coming Wednesday for dinner, *and* I don't believe you noticed anything over breakfast, River. We barely remembered how to walk, let alone have cognitive thought— After the Incident."

"We can *all agree* this is exciting! I'm so happy for you, Rave."

"I wonder if you'll get a goodbye kiss tomorrow," River laughed over her shoulder as she moved a little closer to the water's edge.

Raven really, really, really wanted that kiss.

"I like all of them. They are good people. Mom and Dad would approve," Rowan added. High praise.

"Okay. I trust you both to tell me if you think I need to pull back." Looking at two sets of hazel eyes, she admitted, "I want this. Him. And I may be pissed, but if you tell me to slow down, I'll hear you." As she took the hands of her best friends, hand in hand in hand, she had a question for Rowan that she didn't want to let slip by.

"Row, why have you been so tense this afternoon?" Raven held up a hand to stop her protest. "Don't bother denying it. I could tell in the meeting something was bothering you. I don't expect to have your every thought, we all need privacy, but I'm asking you to tell me." Still linked together, the girls stilled. Waiting.

"I'm not sure I can verbalize, guys. Will you be satisfied if I tell you the moment *I* figure it out?"

"Yes," they answered immediately.

"Okay! Let's get our feet wet and see how cold this pond is!" As Raven led her sisters down the soft, graveled bank and into the gently lapping water, they found the temperature near arctic — producing squeals and laughter.

DAD, Patrick, and Bran resembled nothing short of slack-jawed gargoyles. The Byrne sisters clothed were something to write home about— in swimsuits... God save them! As his Gran often muttered. Truer words...

Each wore a tiny, black bikini differing in style and coverage. Raven's body... her body... Christ. Forcing his gaze away from her firm, pale skin— all lean strength and full curves— Bran glanced at Pat, whose eyes were lasered on the middle Byrne sister as though she might hold the answers to life, and then passed to his father, who was likewise in an awed stasis. James only looked amused by the women's laughter.

Trying to break the spell of the Byrnes, Bran attempted to speak, but before a word could emerge, the aching melody of *Nothing Compares 2 U* washed over him. Raven and River high-fived Rowan.

"Good tune, Row!"

"Sinéad O'Connor! Love!!!"

"Do you think Rowan played this for me or you, Hugh?"

James had obviously noticed Dad being an ass to her and was trying to rib him. Totally deserved.

"For herself, I imagine." Dad was back to surly but still entranced by the view.

Quickly realizing the water wouldn't get any warmer, the women stretched out on the loungers close to the water's edge. River twisted her body around and hollered at Patrick, who was still staring. "Keep the tunes coming, Pat!"

His brother, ridiculous smile in place, immediately grabbed his phone and started scrolling. *Western Feel* by Bartel Union started playing.

"Hey, Dad, let's put the steaks on. I'm starving."

"Yeah, Dad. Give me the veg, and I'll start that." With one last glance at the triple threat, Patrick admitted, "Anything that keeps me from embarrassing myself."

"I didn't think you were even close to wanting a serious relationship, Pat." James wasn't joking. Their schoolmate honestly looked surprised.

"I'm not," Patrick answered quickly, perhaps too fast. "I admit I like River. Hell, I think all the sisters are great, but I have no intention of dating a woman who would expect... commitment." He managed to make commitment sound like a dirty word.

Bran and their dad didn't say anything. Patrick might be telling the truth. As he believed it anyway. Pat wasn't wrong either. A man would have to be an idiot to think any of the Byrne sisters were casual dates. Bran knew this. He didn't care. There was no stopping now. He didn't want to stop it. Waiting until Wednesday would be a trial. Thankfully, Eufaula was close to Muskogee and Tulsa.

Dermot Kennedy's *What Have I Done* started playing. Bran didn't need to ask himself that question. He knew exactly what he was doing.

RAVEN and her sisters had already showered and put their pajamas on. Old, oversized t-shirts and boyshort panties, lingerie was staying tightly packed away for this trip. Raven was marginally embarrassed at herself for packing it in the first place. Did she think she might traipse around the O'Faolain property in silk and high heels? Not even on a dare.

They were busy going over the day, the amazing food, the drinks, the men... when a knock sounded.

All three sisters froze, staring at one another. River shoved her off the edge of the bed. "Geez, Rave. Answer it."

"Why me?!"

"Chances are high it's for you, dumbass." Rowan's smile got her moving.

Cracking the door open, the glow of the hallway lights highlighted the white hair of the eldest O'Faolain brother. "Bran." Did that sound as ridiculous to him as it did to her?

He took in her damp hair trailing down her front and said, "Sorry to bother you. I can see you're ready for bed and getting up early. I... would you mind stepping out here for a minute?"

Glancing back at the bed hidden by the half-opened door to see her sisters up on their knees, making shooing motions to get out, Raven answered, "Of course." Of course... worse and *worser*. She slipped into the hall, cringing at her getup, and faced Bran.

"I won't see you until Wednesday."

"Yes," Raven breathed out. Bran ran his hand through his hair. Was he nervous? Annoyed? When he suddenly moved toward her, Raven took a step back, her back now plastered to the wall next to the closed door. He stepped closer still, his hands very slowly, very gently, coming to rest on the sides of her arms. He looked... like he was on a mission. As long as it included... her.

"Today was one of the best days I can remember having."

"We thought so too. Thank you so much again for including us." Raven internally cringed at including her sisters. She *thought so too. Thank you for including* me. Is what she should have said.

"Will you call me tomorrow once you're home?"

"Yes." Internal wince. Think before speaking. Recall a smidge of IQ.

Books made flirting seem so damn easy!

"Would you let me kiss you goodnight?"

Unexpected. Thrilling. *Exactly* what she wanted. Anything to keep her from speaking out loud.

"Yes." 911.

He started to slowly bend to her level.

"You're short."

"Yes." Fucking kill me. "I meant to say... I am." She might need medication. Or a brain transplant. Instead of trying more conversational gambits, thank you, little, tiny baby Jesus, he solved the height differential by sweeping his arms around her back, palming her ass, and lifting her up. Her legs automatically wrapped around his waist, and between his arms and the wall's support, Raven was precisely where they both wanted her.

Bran groaned as his hands flexed for a moment on her panty-clad behind before pressing her more firmly against the wall. His broad palms swept her sides to her neck, cupping one side of her face and bringing his mouth just shy of touching her own.

Bran feathered kisses over her jaw, her surprisingly sensitive ears, her eyes. Finally, the side of her mouth.

They were both panting at this point, sharing each other's warm breath. His smelled of smoke and peat, whiskey. Hers smelled of toothpaste— cringe, but once his lips were finally pressed to hers, all thoughts of Crest were forgotten.

"Raven... you are driving me insane. I feel like we've known each other forever. Like I don't want to let you leave."

Do not say it, Raven. Do not. "Yes, exactly." Cyanide in her tea, perhaps?

With that, Bran braced one hand behind her head and... made her forget everything, *everything* but the feel of his body. His heat, his hands, his mouth. His tongue gently, almost lazily, against hers. Raven's body was slowly burning. She couldn't breathe. She didn't care.

A moment or a day might have passed when a throat clearing behind them finally registered. Bran stiffened but refused to release her when she gently pushed to get down. Resting his forehead against her own, he asked, "What in the fuck do you want, Pat?"

"Making sure the girls had everything they needed before I turned in." Pausing dramatically, he continued, "I can see I needn't have concerned myself."

"Correct. Leave."

Raven couldn't see Patrick because Bran's bulk blocked her view, but she heard his chuckle and the retreating footsteps.

"Sorry about him, Raven. Though," and here he paused to kiss her neck, "we probably needed interrupting."

"Yes." Oh. My. God. She was downloading a thesaurus immediately! As Bran slowly lowered Raven to the floor, she felt as though her whole body was boneless.

"Will you call me when you get home tomorrow?"

"Yes."

Raven slipped back into her room and almost knocked down her eavesdropping sisters. "You little shits!" she hissed at their smirking faces.

"Umm, Row and I are both bigger than you... soooooo... just shits."

Ravan, face flaming, more because of the kiss than her sisters, sighed, smiled, and admitted, "Best. Kiss. Ever! He wants me to call him tomorrow! Did you hear him ask me?" They both grinned like deranged Cheshire Cats.

"Yes."

"Yes."

9

———

Wednesday night in Eufaula, the sisters were reviewing their schedules, a lowball of whiskey in hand. "Okay, ladies. Current clients are complete or almost. I know we all made sure our schedules were free."

Raven heard herself speaking, but her mind was ridiculously focused on one thing and one thing only. Bran. They had been texting and calling one another since Sunday afternoon. They were like teenagers for the love of God, but what the hell, she felt like one. He was quickly becoming her epicenter. Bran had driven to Eufaula Monday *and* Tuesday night to take her to dinner.

"Rave," River began, "I love you, but we all know we have our shit figured out at Triskelion. As far as Row and I are concerned, the only thing left to discuss before we head to Tulsa is what we think Bran's intentions are toward you and if we are all okay with them."

Well, then. No beating around the bush. "We've known each other less than a week. He *has* no 'intentions,' I'm sure." Except that he appeared to want to see her as much as she wanted to see him. Things were going fast, but it was more like speed dating. Getting to know everything about one another as fast as possible.

Bran had not asked for anything more than to spend time with her. He kissed her goodnight after dinner once he'd walked her home. Thankfully, she knew her sisters were awake and waiting to hear about her dates. Otherwise, she would have been tempted to take things further. She was thrilled he was more interested in her thoughts than getting her into bed, but admittedly, she was ready, so ready.

Exasperated with her merry-go-round thoughts and her sisters, Raven stood and moved to look out the front window. Old-fashioned streetlights lined Main Street. They always looked like a *Beauty and the Beast* Lumiere army to her. She was aware she was trying to distract herself and put off answering her sisters. Sighing, Raven knew she couldn't get out of it. After all, she had promised to listen to them.

"Raven." Rowan's even tone warned her that time was up.

Gathering her courage, Raven turned around and faced the two people she loved most. "Honestly, Bran and I communicate every hour of every day, and he's taken me out twice already. I admit, easily to you two, that I am... falling."

Here she covered her eyes, "Jesus, who am I? A Victorian miss? I'm fucking obsessed with him and trying desperately to play it cool."

A single tear found its way down her cheek, bringing her sisters immediately to her sides. As they grasped her hands, she admitted her deepest fear. "This is probably a simple flirtation to Bran, and he hasn't a single clue that I'm falling for him." Raven freed her hands and held both up to stop her sisters from speaking. "How could he? But I don't believe he is the type of man to lead a woman on. Do you?"

Both sisters shook their heads no.

"Then, how about this... I promise to be careful. To tell you everything and listen to your advice. Let's enjoy seeing the Wolves' space tomorrow and meeting James' sister."

"And the swanky dinner that follows," River added. Both sisters hugged her, and they moved on. They trusted her as she trusted them.

Jo was amazing. A badass at business and one of the nicest people Raven had ever met. "You and James obviously have a clear vision of Wolves. I hope Triskelion's conceptualization of the pub blends with the O'Connors."

She and her sisters had spent the last two hours walking through the two-story space, measuring, taking notes, and tweaking their initial ideas. Jo told them where the bars would be, the stage, the kitchen, and the bathrooms already being roughed in.

"Oh, I think this place will be a dream between the four of us, and yes, I'm excluding James." Jo laughed and then laughed even louder as the four realized the men were assembled by the front door waiting for the women to take notice.

Giving a quick wave, River and the other ladies approached the men near the entrance. "This will be the most stunning Irish pub, Hugh. It's good you got this building before it went on the market."

"Our realtor knew we were looking, and when her friend mentioned the owner was looking to sell but wasn't in any hurry, I had her send him a very fair offer." Shrugging, he admitted, "I was more than fair. I knew of the man. He may have been in no hurry to get it off his hands, but easy money is easy money."

"This area," Rowan looked to Hugh and waved around them, "is going to be comfortable seating for guests waiting for a bar or table chair. Some of the artwork and perhaps a few mementos can go on this back wall, a teaser, if you will. Very few.

"We want patrons to *want* to see more— draw them deeper inside. That area to the right of the largest bar is already earmarked for couches and chairs. I thought that space would be perfect for special O'Faolain history pieces. Mostly your father's, of course."

She loved to see Rowan so excited about a project. Raven was already picturing the colors and fabrics for that area, wondering how Rowan would set it apart from the rest of the bar but still make it flow.

River left Patrick's side and walked back toward the lounge area. "Oh, Row, I do love that. Patrick told me the area you're considering will also have its own wait staff. A person could relax with a drink and feel like they're in the middle of an exhibit."

"That's right," Jo agreed. "The O'Faolain's want this pub to have everything. Fine dining, pub food served at the bars, family space, and live music. Something for everyone. I love the idea of that lounge being central to the family's memorabilia, Rowan."

Bran stood beside Raven, briefly letting his fingers touch her lower back. Raven let her body lean into his side momentarily before moving away. "James, the garage doors in the back are stunning. I hope the landscaper you hire plants plenty of flow-ers. Can you imagine how lovely it will be on nice evenings when the doors are open, and all the fragrant scents float in?"

Chuckling, James told Raven, "That's a Jo job. My sweet sister once told me I wouldn't know a rose from a radish."

"God's truth. Or your asshole from your elbow, but hey, we all have issues to overcome." Jo danced out of her brother's reach, moving behind Raven. "Have you girls seen enough for today? I'm starved, and I hear Gran O'Faolain has requested dinner be at her humble abode tonight."

At this unexpected news, Raven swiftly turned to meet Bran's eyes. "We're eating at your grandmother's?"

Her new mantra became— It's just dinner. It's just dinner. It's just dinner. It's just dinner... with the O'Faolain matriarch. Big deal. Oh God.

Bran went on, thankfully not reading her nerves. "We all live at the same hotel when we're in Tulsa. We bought out the top floors and renovated them several years ago. Similar to what you guys did with your building in Eufaula."

"Probably a touch bigger project than ours," River stage whispered.

Smiling at River, Patrick admitted, "Just a smidge."

"Dad told Gran Monday about you guys coming to town today and some of your ideas. She's dying to hear about them. Especially about the area that will commemorate Gramps. Dad thought you," he nodded toward Rowan, "could give Gran an idea of what you have in mind."

Rowan looked slightly taken aback but rallied quickly. "Oh, I'd like that. I want to display some family antiques in the lounge. I noted you have plenty at your Muskogee home and I assume you have several unique pieces scattered amongst your other homes as well. We might pick a few to include." Rowan paused to make a few more notes. "Yes. I would like to go over some things with Mrs. O'Faolain."

"According to my sister, my work here is no longer required." James managed to poke Jo's side. "Let's get out of here and change for dinner. Last I knew, Hugh, your mother doesn't tolerate tardiness. Even from you."

Dinner was lively and relaxing. It felt like they'd been getting together for years. In the past, he'd been on dates where he dreamed of nothing more than its ending. With Raven, he could listen to her all night— not that she monopolized the conversation— she wasn't reserved like Rowan or boisterous like River, but she was fully engaged.

She cared about what she said and what others said around her. She fascinated him. He knew she'd been nervous about meeting his grandmother, and she hadn't wanted him to know, but she'd shaken those nerves within moments of meeting Gran.

"You must have had your hands full, Mrs. O'Faolain, with your own son *and* Bran and Patrick." Raven smiled as his grandmother all but rolled her eyes.

"Call me Matilda or Tilly. That's what Jon called me. And as for the boys— I'm sure my hair would still be a lovely shade of brown instead of the silver it is now if they'd been better behaved."

"Oh, come on, Mother, I wasn't bad. The boys, though...."

"Hugh Darcy O'Faolain! Don't you dare tell lies at this table," she scolded.

Bran and Patrick laughed at their dad's expense until Rowan asked, "Darcy?" All amusement fled, and he felt his cheeks heat. After glancing at his dad and brother, they, too, had guessed the direction the conversation was about to turn.

Oblivious to their discomfort, his grandmother, all *pride* and no *prejudice*, enlightened the sisters about a fun family fact.

"Mother." A warning to stop. Unheeded.

"Oh, yes. Jane Austen has been my favorite author since I was a young girl, and my Jon let me name Hugh after Mr. Fitzwilliam Darcy."

"Oh, it is a beautiful name, and what a lovely coincidence that they're both the silent, broody type." Rowan sent a tiny smirk of a smile his father's way, causing the man to close his eyes and groan under his breath. River and Raven applauded the choice.

Patrick looked at Bran and smiled. It looked like they might dodge a bullet.

"Tell them about the boys, Mom." Dad's smile was all teeth. Dick.

"Jonathan was a sweet man, and I admit, despite his rough and ready ways, Hugh is very much like his father."

Gran paused to smile at Hugh, a loving mother, a side of her character she rarely let anyone see. But talk of grandpa tended to make her... softer, for lack of a better word. A benefit, though, was that his dad was full-out blushing now. He deserved it.

"Hugh chose the boys' first names but let me choose their middle names."

Bran was thankful no one asked why their mother hadn't been the one to name him and his brother. That would have been a conversation downer.

Raven glanced at Bran, merriment in her eyes. She had probably guessed where this was going.

"What did you choose for Bran?"

"Bran Knightley. *Emma*, of course. The last name went much better with Bran than George. Can you imagine, Raven? Bran George."

Raven was outright laughing now, her cheeks rosy with amusement— at his expense. He laughed too.

Smiling just for Bran, she said, "Mr. Knightley," she sighed, "helped Emma be her best self. He was kind, generous, caring, loyal, and gave excellent counsel." She looked at his grand-mother then. "You named him well, Mrs.... Matilda."

"And Patrick?" River asked, all sweet as she smiled at his brother.

"Patrick Brandon."

"Oh wow! My sisters and I have read the books and

watched the movies. *Sense and Sensibility's* Colonel Brandon was hands down my favorite of all her characters." She turned to Patrick and bumped him with her elbow. "You totally scored," she told him, grinning. Bran thought she was actually serious. Patrick looked bewildered at her compliment.

"River's right. We all love Jane Austen." Raven asked his grandmother if she was still a reader and what was the last book she'd read. The conversation around the table was easy, and he could tell his grandmother had enjoyed the evening.

Before taking their leave from Gran's penthouse, she pulled her grandson aside. If his grandmother had something to say, taking it on the chin was best.

Bran's always elegant grandmother placed her delicate hand on his forearm, looked him square in the eye, and said, "Finally."

Bran raised his brows at her, not understanding where she was headed. She finally had him alone? The dinner was finally over? Unwilling to guess, he waited.

"You've finally chosen well." And then, after a beat. "I approve. Don't screw it up."

Unexpected. Bran hadn't realized his feelings toward Raven were so obvious. "I... well..." Stuttering. Nice. "We have only known each other a few days."

"What the hell does that matter?"

"Language, Gran," Bran whispered, grinning at the only mother he'd ever known.

"I'm old and can say whatever I want when I want. But never mind that," brushing his interruption to the side with a hand, she doubled down, "Hours, days, months, years— Bran boy, it's all time. Your grandfather asked me to marry him after two weeks. So, save your nonsense.

"I realize young people today have to think every bloody emotion through, and that's fine. I just see what I see. You and Raven look at each other the way your grandfather and I looked at one another." Gran took his hand and pulled him down to her level, gave him a quick kiss on the cheek, and told him to go home.

This time Bran stopped her by placing a hand on her shoulder. When she looked back at him, he said, "I love you, Gran. Thanks for putting up with the three of us." Her eyes widened in surprise. Damn, he should tell her more often. She placed her hand over his and squeezed before turning to leave again, but not before he caught the sparkle of a tear.

He was still thoughtful and slightly bemused by his Gran as he held Raven's hand and they crowded into the elevator. He leaned down to speak in Raven's ear. "Jo has a car waiting out front to take you three to your hotel before she heads home. Would you give me a private minute before that?"

Raven looked up at him, as she was forced to because of their height difference, and smiled at him. "Of course."

THEY COULD HAVE EASILY DRIVEN home after dinner. It wasn't so late, but they decided to check out a few fabric stores and local artisans tomorrow morning. Tick a few items off their growing To-Do list.

Raven practically shoved River and Rowan through the hotel room's door. "Bran asked me to go to Ireland with him."

"No fucking way."

"Oh my God, Rave. No way!"

"For work, of course. I mean, I'm sure." Raven was sure of nothing. "He wants to look at the whiskey barrel artisans we admired outside Dublin. And," before she lost her nerve, she spewed out the rest, "he wants to meet Nan."

"I think shit just got real."

"Really real."

Really real about summed it up. Holy shit. She was flying to Ireland with Bran. On a private jet. In one week. Raven didn't know the itinerary. Honestly, she didn't know a whole hell of a lot, but she did know this— Bran asked her to go to Ireland. Just her. And she said yes.

10

Look at that— the good-old-boy gang's finally under one roof. It was exhausting surveilling three men and their families. When necessary, he also had to watch any women they dated if it seemed a potential relationship was blooming. Rare.

Such a lovely treat to have them all together. Minus that bastard O'Connor's ex, Jane. Good work that. It was almost too easy to break them up. At least he still had opportunities to twist the knife in James' back by sending pics of Jane with her 'other men.'

Chortling to himself, Sam had to admit, though he wasn't a braggart by any means, that his photoshop expertise was without peer. He'd fooled experts in the field before. Fooling the Three Amigos was child's play. Sam's strengths lay not only in digital graphic sleight of hand. He knew how to plant bugs and tracers— that he built himself.

He changed his appearance as easily as other people walked through open doorways. Hell, he had part-time jobs where the pieces of shit spent time— he couldn't work full time, obviously, if the majority of his days were filled with listening, watching, and following the three people he hated most. Actually, Sam's hate for Hugh O'Faolain was unmatched. Why go after Hugh directly, though? Hurting his family would hurt the most.

He lived for bussing their tables, topping off their water, bowing and scraping in a ridiculously obsequious manner. There was no room in his life for pride, nothing beneath him, because, in reality, his own opinion was the only one that mattered.

Everything he had once held dear had been taken by the O'Faolains.

His father, God rest his soul, had been a once devoted employee, a high-powered accountant for the family— and been discarded like trash. The perjurious heathens had slandered his father as an embezzler— no court hearing to uncover the fraudulency of the charges— just tossed out. Sam was sure Larry Delton never crossed their minds again. Well, the O'Faolains crossed Sam's mind.

His mother left them within months. Horrible woman, and good riddance. She never appreciated the level of intellect he and his father were burdened with. That, he could handle... his father being murdered less than a year later... he could not.

The coroners pronounced it suicide. Not true. His father was depressed, and from this oppressive abyss, he was forced to take a cocktail of prescription medications to cope with the injustice of losing his position. Taking too many was simply an accident. His dad would never have chosen to leave his only child.

Sam had been a classmate of the O'Faolain brothers and of James O'Connor. They'd gone to the same damn private Catholic school. The fact that they didn't recognize him, that he served them now, turned their sheets back, and plumped their pillows, might infuriate a lesser man. Not Samuel Delton.

No. He held on to the mere idea that one day his plans would come to fruition. That he would be there to bask in their despair. He would wait and watch. He would destroy every relationship they attempted to create.

It was glory. It was vengeance. It was justice.

GOOD THING SAM *didn't allow any detail to slide. He'd had the O'Faolain jet's numbers for months and periodically checked the family's traveling schedule. Usually, they were business trips, but when a trip appeared on the flight schedule right after that dinner, Sam knew there was a possibility that this was a pleasure trip. He was glad he'd followed his instincts and staked out the airport.*

Sam watched Bran O'Faolain and his 'possible' current amour board the family's private jet through night vision binoculars. He'd already entered the jet's tail number into his Flight-Aware app and knew it had a scheduled trip to Ireland.

He also discovered from the dinner the other night that the woman accompanying Bran was Raven Byrne, one of the owners of Triskelion Territory Designs, an interior design firm in Eufaula. Absently, Sam made a mental note to set up cameras in the offices there.

Typically, an overseas trip, usually business related, wouldn't have pinged Sam's radar. However, Bran had shown an exorbitant amount of attention to that particular Byrne. So, here he was, doing his due diligence.

Through the app, he would know when the jet made its return flight. He'd be waiting as they disembarked. Body language usually spoke much louder than words. If his intuition were to be believed, and it rarely failed him, Bran was getting serious with a woman. His first. Butterflies erupted in Sam's stomach, imagining the budding relationship's implosion.

11

Raven spent the day working from Jo's family home. The O'Connors' parents were in Florida overseeing the final touches on a restaurant opening. Jo assured her she was welcome whether the rest of the family was in residence.

Bran wanted to leave in the middle of the night or early morning, really— 3 o'clock. He said it was the best time. They would be exhausted by the time the jet lifted off, sleep for several hours, get some work done, and eat lunch. It sounded terrible, but he assured her it would help with the time difference once they landed in Dublin. She and her sisters had always just lounged around in pajamas for a day, so he might be on to something.

Jo had the family's personal driver take her to the airport in the wee hours of the morning to meet Bran.

Bran. A private jet. Ireland. Bran.

He was right. She fell fast asleep, covered with silk sheets and her head cushioned on a pillow cloud. She'd slept for hours in the down feather, silk, and leather cocoon. Now, a gorgeous salad with grilled chicken, nuts, and cranberries sat next to an even lovelier double shot of Bushmills Black Bush.

"Okay, Bran. You've won me over. I'm going to suggest at Triskelion's next meeting that my sisters and I purchase our own private jet. For business, obviously. I'm sure we can make little, tiny, monthly payments and own it outright in eighty years or so." Facing her, Bran was digging into his own salad, his with thin slices of steak and a fan of ripe avocado.

"I'm just glad you agreed to the early flight. Pat likes to leave late, but since we left Tulsa at three, we should arrive in Dublin by 6 o'clock tonight. Plenty of time to check into our hotel, change, and grab dinner somewhere." Smiling, Bran asked if she'd thought about some places she'd like to visit while they were in town.

Trying for a serious expression and tone, Raven listed her options. "Since you're quite a bit older than me," at this, she placed a hand gently to her chest, "I thought you might be too tired to leave the hotel. You booked us rooms at Fitzwilliam. We could always see if a table is available at Glovers Alley. However, if you feel up to it, we could grab some pub food at the Temple Bar." She batted her eyelashes at him, all innocence.

"Feeling yourself today, I see."

"Hey, no shame. I hear thirties can be a tough transition." Raven couldn't stop smiling as she sipped her whiskey.

"First, I'm thirty. *Just* thirty. Barely touching it. And you better fucking believe I'll be ready for the Temple Bar."

Bran threw her for a loop then, probably as payback for teasing him. "Did I mention that I booked the penthouse?" That got her attention.

"Oh? Where... will I be?"

"No worries. It's over 2,000 square feet. Plenty of beds." Devilishly, Bran paused, giving her time to think about sharing space with him.

"Glovers Alley is already scheduled to cook for us privately tomorrow night. The penthouse butler emailed me the arrangements this morning."

Raven let Bran's announcements settle. She knew very well he was trying to goad some response from her, though she was still unclear what her reaction *should* be.

Admittedly, this lifestyle was foreign to Raven, but the Byrnes were adaptable, resourceful, and certainly not shy... in business, at least. Taking another sip of Bushmills, Raven eyed Bran over the crystal glass.

"Consider me impressed, O'Faolain."

Changing the subject from sleeping arrangements. Even though she told her sisters she was prepared... so prepared... to sleep with Bran, it didn't mean she wasn't nervous. "I haven't visited Temple Bar since my family visited Nan a few summers ago. It was my mother's favorite pub in Dublin. Row was eighteen, and my dad ordered us all a shot at the bar to commemorate her legal-to-drink status." Raven took a moment to sift through her memories of that night. Bran noticed her pause.

"I'm sorry if this trip is painful for you, Raven." Putting his lunch to the side, he slid forward in his seat and grabbed her hand. "I would never have asked you to come if, for even a moment, I had considered it might make you sad." He added in a quiet, thoughtful voice, "Maybe I should have asked your sisters to come too. For moral support."

Oh Lord, Raven would not cry. Damn it. Swallowing the emotions she hadn't seen coming, she squeezed Bran's hand tighter. "Don't even think it, Bran. When memories are all one has, it's only right to take them out and relive them. I never want to forget. Anything. My parents deserve to be thought of even if it makes my sisters and I weepy sometimes."

Releasing a huff of air he'd obviously been holding, Bran scooted her lunch to the side of the table and moved over to sit close to her. "I know you and your sisters would stay with your grandmother when your parents were teaching abroad, but did you all visit often other than that?"

"Oh yeah. Dad and we girls have dual citizenship, which made travel easy, and he always missed Roscommon and his mother. His father, my grandad, died when I was little, so I don't remember him. He hated spacing visits with Nan too far apart since she lives alone."

She had to laugh at her dad, thinking Nan needed guidance. "I can't wait for you to meet her, Bran. Your grandmother reminded me an awful lot of my own."

"Jesus, save me. Did I remember to tell you what Gran thought of you when we had dinner at her place?"

"You certainly did not."

"Buy me a drink tonight, and I may be persuaded."

"Pat's right! You are a shithead."

"You have excellent taste in shitheads, then."

When their laughter settled, Raven leaned into Bran's shoulder and softly kissed his lips. "I really am so thrilled to be going to Ireland. With you." Bran kissed *her* this time. She ended up half sprawled sideways in her chair and half in his lap.

One of Bran's hands had just slid its way up her ribs. His fingertips a scant millimeter away from brushing the underside of her left breast when a woman's voice registered. Oh my God.

"My apologies for the interruption, Mr. O'Faolain," the flight attendant murmured, awkwardly frozen outside the galley while beginning a slow, backward retreat. "I can collect your lunch dishes and refresh drinks at a more convenient time, sir."

"No, Brenda, please come on back. My apologies for the PDA, and don't blame Raven," he laughed to cover any embarrassment for the women, "I can't seem to help myself."

Raven briefly touched her forehead to his before moving back to her seat. "My apologies as well, Brenda. I feel about sixteen right now." Laughing at themselves seemed to trigger Brenda's funny bone.

"I've witnessed worse," covering her eyes in horror, "so, so, so much worse."

"Was it my brother?" Bran asked jokingly. "Okay, Raven. We've work to get done before we land." Looking at Brenda as she cleared the dishes, he added, "Come in the cabin at any time. I promise to behave, and my girlfriend seems to drink copious amounts of whiskey and needs her refills."

"Jackass!" Raven laughed as she poked Bran's side. Silently dying over Bran's reference to her being his girlfriend. Telling herself to not make a mountain out of a moment. "Fine," Raven snapped with faux annoyance. "Let's work quick so you can get a nap in."

BRAN WAS the one who felt like he was sixteen. He was obsessed. Possessive. And aroused as all hell. He knew that this trip would either set the tone or write the ending of their budding relationship.

"Why don't we spend the rest of the flight making a list of places you and your sisters want us to look at for Wolves. I also want to add stops that are purely for fun."

"Agreed." Raven already had her laptop out.

"Tonight, we'll party, or as close an approximation as I can manage considering my age, get up early, start visiting some of your artisans, find some obscure pub for lunch, and visit some of the countryside. I'm sure the Fitzwilliam butler will have several suggestions." Ignoring Raven's snort of amusement, he went on. "I'll have Dom, that's the Butler's name, speak to you before we go out tonight."

"A man with a plan. I like it. Two nights at the Fitzwilliam, and then we'll be off to Roscommon. Nan's home is in a lovely town with the Curlieu Mountains as its backdrop. Oh, it also has phenomenal shopping and craftsmen. We can work *and* visit family. Have you ever been to Boyle?"

"No, honestly, we mostly travel for business. Obviously, my family has distant relations in Ireland. Our family is on the board of trustees for Trinity College in Dublin."

"You're joking?"

"I'm not," Bran smirked but admitted, "It basically means we had family that attended once upon a time. So, we show up to fundraising galas every few years, or if we can't make it, send a donation."

Your family is... wow... not intimidating, at least not to my sisters and me, but definitely... connected."

"Does it bother you?" Bran hadn't thought about how Raven would feel stepping into his world. She grew up in an amazing family too. Raven was intelligent, thoughtful, and put together, though he liked her hair wet and wearing a baggy T-shirt as she had at his dad's house. He hoped his family's wealth wasn't something that could come between them.

"Of course not, Bran. It just takes me aback at times. When you speak of butlers with the type of ease other people, like me, order some fries at McDonald's." She laughed as her hands were making directionless swirls in the air. "I mean... yes, it's different, but... but I'm with you, speaking to you. Not your wallet or your family's connections. You could be taking my order at a drive-thru, and I'd see a gorgeous towhead with a killer smile. Not your job. I'd want that smile directed at me every day."

Bran could only look at Raven. It was quite something to realize she held something in her that he hadn't even known he needed. He knew that with Raven, he wasn't just a means to an end like he'd been for his birth mother. He wasn't a convenience or a trophy to show friends.

He took her hand in his and laced their fingers together. She was tiny compared to Bran. Delicate. The thought of them parting ways when their trip ended didn't set well. Even though it was too soon, Bran wanted her to live with him. Damn it, he knew it was fast. It didn't matter. Gran didn't think it was weird. Great, he was taking love life advice from his grandmother now.

It felt odd to consider that he had feelings for a woman other than lust. He *did* want to rip all her clothes off the moment they hit the penthouse. He wouldn't, of course, but he wanted to... badly. Maturity was a real downer sometimes.

Instead of divulging his inner thoughts, the soft ones and the lustful ones, Bran leaned in to kiss her cheek. "I want to smile at you every day and have you smile back."

12

Raven and Bran spent about forty-five minutes in their penthouse, fifteen of that was speaking to Dom, the butler, about tomorrow's plans, and then they got a lift, from Dom, of course, to Temple Bar.

The bright, red facade always made her smile. The polished wood, chatter, music, and rows upon rows of amazing whiskies, were what this girl's dreams were made of. Sitting on a pair of barstools, munching on her favorite pub meal, fish and chips, Raven's knee kept brushing Bran's— she was extraordinarily happy.

"You keep smiling, Raven. Thinking about our accommodations or are these fries better than McDonald's?" Bran was teasing her about the sleeping situation. Little did he know what was packed in her suitcase. Spoiler— it wasn't a baggy shirt.

"The fries are amazing." Raven picked up two warm, crispy potato bits and shoved them in her mouth. After swallowing, she reached up to Bran's lips and gently swiped a bit of ketchup from their corner, quickly sticking her finger in her mouth and delicately licking the tip.

Bran's focus went from zero to triple-digit intense on her

mouth. "I just hope my snoring from the bedroom down the hall doesn't keep you up all night."

"You snore? Doubtful, or River would have texted me the moment she knew of our trip." Bran picked her hand up, the same one that had brushed his lips a moment before, and kissed her palm warmly. He was definitely better at sexy.

"She would have too, the bitch."

"You miss them?"

Raven thought about her sisters at home in Oklahoma. "It's not like, 'Oh no, I won't be able to sleep without them,' but more like... reminders to myself to tell them what I've seen and felt while we're apart. That probably seems silly, but... we are just so very close. We were before our parents'... accident. We're more so now."

"Not silly in the least, Raven. A testament to how strong your family's connection is. I imagine your parents would want just such a bond for the three of you."

Raven stopped herself from saying— Yes. Barely. She did have the ability to be articulate, but when Bran was like *this*, words did manage to escape her.

"Thank you. I told them earlier I would let them know how Temple Bar was when we get back to the room... rooms," she smiled at Bran, teasing him.

"My dad, brother, and I may be as bad," Bran admitted. "I don't think we've ever not spoken or texted one another every day."

"I haven't wanted to pry, but none of you mention your mother..." Raven open-ended the statement. She knew Helen Merrit O'Faolain was very much alive. She just didn't understand why she wasn't in their lives.

Bran tensed ever so slightly, and Raven thought she may have made a mistake bringing it up.

"Helen and Dad married young. I'm sure both families

believed it was a good match. Gran had to have, or she would have caused a scene."

"Bran, you don't have to explain if you don't want to." Raven placed her hands on his thighs and gently squeezed.

"No, it's fine. It probably seems weird. As I said, they were young and had me right away. Her family was old money with mountains of snobbery to go with it. You know Dad, he works hard. He doesn't expect others to do for him what he can do for himself— and Gran would have spanked his ass if he ever tried to act the wealthy playboy."

Brushing that thought aside with a swipe of his hand, Bran finished the story.

"Dad admitted to Pat and me years ago that he believed she'd never truly loved him. She considered marrying just another box to tick off. Marrying and having heirs was expected of her. So, she did. After the requisite heir and spare, she informed Dad that they would live separate lives from then on."

"Are you flipping kidding me? Jesus, what a horrible woman." Raven winced, "Sorry, Bran. I shouldn't have said that."

"Oh, you should. She was and still is. I don't think she ever held Patrick or me. She never spoke to us, only our nanny. We were strangers. We *are* strangers. We were all thankful when she moved back home with her parents. Last I heard, she's living her best life in Boston.

"I've wondered, you know, if she ever thought me... like, on my birthday or Christmas, or whatever. Honestly, I rarely think of things like that. It *has* always amazed me that Dad could have so misjudged the woman. I mean, I get it to a certain extent. She was extraordinarily beautiful, but he wouldn't have ever married for looks alone. He's deeper than that. No, Helen's acting skills had to have been top tier."

"There was something very, very broken in her," Raven said. "Do you think your dad misses her?"

"Oh God, no. He said he knew he'd made a mistake before the ink was dry on the marriage license. He was pleased to have an airtight prenup. Helen insisted as she believed her family would always be wealthier than her husband. She was wrong... really wrong, but the agreement stated that in case of divorce, both parties retained their individual wealth and properties.

"I believe she still considers foisting her sons' sole custody on her ex-husband a win. My father told us the day we were all his, only his, was the best day of his life."

Raven had to press her fingertips below her eyes to staunch the tears wanting to escape. It wasn't from sadness. Helen was sad, but not the lives she'd help create. No, the tears commemorated the wonderful man who'd raised his sons with love.

He was a worthy gentleman, no matter his taciturn moods. "You were fortunate. You and your brother." And then Raven couldn't help but add, "I never want to be within forty miles of that horrible woman."

"And you never will." Bran kissed her lips briefly, finished his Teeling, and said, "Let's go home, babe."

"Yes."

RAVEN STRETCHED while her eyes tried to sift through the various details of her surroundings, hoping to formulate some sort of recall. Light filtered through the heavy draperies that covered the floor-to-ceiling windows. King-sized bed. Luxurious sheets. Hmmm. Hotel. No, penthouse. Dublin. Bran.

Bursting out of the sheets like her bed was on fire, heart pounding, Raven really looked around. Flipping on the bedside lamp and quickly touching her phone screen to see the time, she grabbed a few extra pillows and bunched them up behind her back to lean on. It was just past six in the morning— and— she was alone.

Gathering more of her brain matter, Raven finally remembered the evening before. "Oh God," she said aloud, "he'll never let me live it down."

She scrubbed her face with her hands, hoping it would rub away the blush. They'd returned to the hotel, and Bran said he had some calls and emails he needed to return, suggesting she shower and change if she wanted. He wouldn't be more than thirty to forty minutes.

Raven showered. Dabbed a touch of rose oil behind her ears and at her wrists. Slipped on a silk nightgown with matching lace panties and a robe that hit right below her behind. It was slate blue and lovely. River had picked it out. She could hear Bran on the phone in the living room and decided to lie on her bed for a minute to check her emails and call her sisters.

She remembered telling the girls goodnight. And then, kill her now, she must have fallen asleep. Oh, Lord, and after Raven teased Bran about his age and needing naps.

Sighing, she drug herself from bed and padded over the thick wool rugs to the bank of windows. Drawing back the drapes, she sighed again over the view. Dublin was a sight. Better to get herself dressed and ready for the day. After all, she'd slept plenty, and Bran would want to rib her first thing.

BRAN LOOKED up from the dining room table to see Raven walk in. She looked amazing, as always. Loose, stylish denim jeans paired with a light blue button-up. Her hair was back in a thick, low ponytail, light makeup, and clear gloss brushed her lips. Sturdy tennis shoes— good for shopping and exploring.

"If it isn't sleeping beauty."

Bran noticed her cheeks flushed pink. "Oh, God. So, it begins. Before you say another word, Bran O'Faolain, I eat every word I dished out to you on the plane."

Bran barked out a laugh, loving every minute of her discomfiture. "If you're through eating humble pie, there is a full Irish breakfast, plus at least twenty other items under the lids of all these chafing dishes." He motioned to the long, ornate sideboard custom-built for this very room.

The entire floor was a mix of custom and antique. It was warm and comfortable, with enough clean lines for modernists to appreciate. He would definitely make this a reservation must the next time he was in Dublin.

"Oh, lovely. I prefer a smoothie and tea for breakfast, but," lifting up one of the domes, "these eggs look delicious."

Bran frowned. "Why didn't you tell Dom your preferences last night?"

Raven looked over her shoulder, giving Bran a slight frown of her own. "It was late, and I'm sure he had plenty of other tasks to complete before he could go to bed— including," she emphasized, "planning part of our day today." Raven continued with a shrug, "Aren't people supposed to 'when in Rome' while vacationing?"

"You're right. I just want you to be happy. I chose all this stuff and... momentarily became... irritated that you didn't have your choices too."

"Sounds like your inner Hugh was trying to join us." She laughed while putting a spoonful of eggs on her plate.

"Never say it's so!" Bran hung his head in mock shame.

"Seriously though, thank you for caring about me." Raven walked over, setting her plate down next to Bran's. "I wonder if we might ring the kitchen for some iced, unsweetened tea."

"Such a diva," he joked, pulling out his cell to text Dom. "Done."

Raven sat up straight in her chair, all business, looking Bran in the eyes. Her smile gone. Oh, shit. Bran attempted not to fiddle with his attire. He was greyed out today. Faded grey tee paired with equally faded grey jeans. Scuffed, but uber comfortable, grey Burberry sneakers. Slowly his body was tightening up. He'd not seen her look this serious.

"You will not. Under any circumstances, bribery or torture, tell my sisters that I fell asleep last night. Before we... that is, before you were off the phone."

Bran could not, under *any circumstances*, live without this woman. As he cleared the laugh from his throat and opened his mouth to answer, someone knocked on the front door. Hopping up, Bran placed a kiss on the top of Raven's head. "Hold that thought, babe."

"You aren't funny, you know."

Bran let Dom in with the tea, and the butler of all butlers took it upon himself to place the tea in front of Raven.

"My apologies that you had nothing to eat or drink this morning, Miss Byrne." Dom grimaced as if in physical pain. "I should have spoken to you about the menu as well." Bowing slightly, he vowed, "I shall endeavor to never, *ever* perform at such a lackadaisical level during your stay again."

Raven briefly scowled at Bran before turning all her attention to Dom. "I don't know what Mr. O'Faolain inferred in his message, but I can assure you, Dom, that breakfast this morning was a lovely surprise, and thank you for bringing up the tea."

Getting up from the table and ignoring Bran completely, Raven went into the living room. "Is it a convenient time for you to show me some of what you think Bran and I might like to see today?"

Perking up, Dom practically bounced over to the loveseat as

he pulled his tablet from a satchel that perfectly matched his suit. "I think you will be pleased, Miss Byrne."

"Raven, please, Dom."

"Of course, then. Raven." Dom laid out brochures on the coffee table, set his tablet next to everything, and began swiping through, what looked like a PowerPoint presentation.

Raven was oohing and aahing. Asking for distances between here and there, open hours, and even his personal recommendations that may not have made The Top 10 must-see list. Clever that, Bran thought. Who better to know than a local.

Raven sat back and stretched with a happy smile. Today's outing itinerary must meet her approval.

"Are we all set?"

"We are," she smiled in satisfaction. "Dom will be waiting for us downstairs as soon as we're ready to roll." Turning back to the butler, Raven thanked him again and said she'd see him in a few. Dom practically flew out the front door— lists of lists of more lists no doubt running through his brain.

"Where are we off to first?"

"A pottery shop. Not the one I had originally planned on visiting. Dom says this particular potter hand throws everything. *Everything.*" Raven clasped her hands at her waist in what could only be described as glee.

"She's located on Aaron Street," she continued excitedly. "After that, I thought we could just walk for a bit and see what catches our fancy. I told Dom we'd call him when we're ready to head to the whiskey barrel artisan outside of town. Does all that sound okay? Because, seriously, I can adjust the schedule in any which direction."

"It sounds like a great day ahead. I'm looking forward to it." And surprisingly, he was. Bran wasn't a shopper or a meanderer, but Raven's enthusiasm for finding unique pieces for Wolves excited him too.

Raven ran into her bedroom for a couple last-minute must-haves to throw in her tote, and they were off. Walking out the front door and into the personal elevator beyond, Bran took the opportunity to grab Raven's hand. She had to bend her arm at the elbow to accommodate his height, but if her smile were any indication, she wasn't mad about it.

RAVEN FOUND several pieces at the potter's shop. Flower vases, pitchers, and trays. She was most pleased with the whiskey barrel boards. They were everything she and her sisters hoped they would be.

Bran loved learning about the artisan's process. They had a great studio and spent a couple of hours in the back watching Michael Talbot, the head craftsman, cut, shape, sand, and finally work beeswax into the grain of the boards.

Bran asked Raven's opinion on what the pub could use and quantity. He was the one to sit down with Mike and place the order. This was the main reason she had wanted to come to Dublin. Mike's pieces were stunning and would be showstoppers at Wolves. Her sisters, Jo, and James would freak out when they saw some of her pictures.

Bran and Mike finally straightened from their bent positions over the rough table they'd been working over. Sawhorses holding up a mishmash of wooden panels were far removed from the sleek boardrooms Bran was probably used to making deals in, but the earthy honestness of Mike's workroom was perfect.

"Thank you, Mike." Bran shook hands with the owner and artist. "Remember to call me when you're ready to ship to the States, and I'll work all the details out." Bran's face was flushed with the excitement of success.

"It'll be no problem. I've your number, Bran. I thank you and your lady for the business."

Raven flashed Mike a smile. "You've made our whole trip. I can't wait to see what you create for Wolves." Holding her hand out to shake his hand, she added, "When next I'm in Dublin, I hope to have my sisters with me. They would love to meet you and check out your shop."

The older man looked at Raven and then at Bran. "You'll let me know when you marry." Not a question. "I've something in mind as a gift. Good day to you both, and safe travels."

As Mike walked away, leaving the two of them to find their way out, Bran looked quite pleased with himself. The marriage comment obviously not throwing him as it had her.

"You are one hundred percent off the hook for nodding off like Gran last night." Grinning down at Raven, he swung his arm around her body, dragging them close together.

"I'm ignoring the Gran comment because I'm too excited. Mike was great, right?"

"You and your sisters were spot on with this place. I can't wait to show some pictures to Dad and Pat." Giving her a squeeze, Bran quit walking and bent low enough to kiss her. She could kiss him the rest of the day.

Once the kiss ended and they stepped out of Mike's shop, Raven found breath enough to answer. "I'm pleased you felt the same way I did. As my dad would say, 'Mike's a proper talent, he is.'"

Bran's smile was broad. Both were feeling the success of their day. "How about we call Dom for a lift back to downtown Dublin and then set out for our afternoon of exploration? We need to work up an appetite before our special dinner tonight. Dom's assured me it'll be spectacular."

"Perfect."

"I just wanted to run the plans by you in case you think they're too much."

Raven gave Bran a questioning glance. "Why would they be too much?"

"I only hoped you would be able to stay awake for dessert."

"Pain and suffering will find you, O'Faolain. Pain and suffering."

13

Bran and Raven spent the rest of the afternoon exploring Dublin Castle, The Book of Kells, and the Old Library exhibition at Trinity— they got a special tour when they found out an O'Faolain was present. They stepped into colorful shops amongst the grand, historical buildings in the city, visited museums, and stopped at small cafés or pubs for appetizers and drinks. Dom would check on them occasionally, but he wasn't really needed since they walked everywhere.

Relaxing in a lovely bit of sun outside one of the café's outdoor seating areas, they both checked in with their families. River and Rowan asked a million questions and couldn't wait to hear how the fancy dinner went tonight. And what might happen after. They both threatened to disown her if she didn't call them the next day and give them a play-by-play. Raven smiled to herself. Hopefully there was something to report.

Rowan said she'd been communicating with an Irish artist that worked in both oil and watercolor. Rowan was very interested in some of his work for Wolves. He lived in Longford, which she and Bran would travel through on their way to Boyle.

Rowan said she sent an email with the artist's address and number.

Promising to talk to them tomorrow after she saw the artist, and with another promise to spill her guts about this evening, they hung up.

"All's well with your sisters?"

"Oh, yes. Row found an artist she wants us to check out in Longford tomorrow." Bran got his phone out and looked him up while she continued. "She sounded pretty stoked, and River agreed his work would look phenomenal in the pub."

"We'll be traveling on N4. That route leads us directly through Longford. Very easy."

"That's what they said. I'll call the artist in the morning before we head out. How are your dad and Patrick?"

"Dad's brooding about something. He'll tell me when he tells me. Patrick has been working all hours since we left on a website for Wolves."

"I didn't know he was going to build it himself. I assumed you would hire that out."

"Pat lives for that kind of thing. He'll spend three times longer building it than a design company because he's a perfectionist, but I do not doubt it will be what we want in the end. He mentioned that he is working with River on it. He said she is almost as good as he is."

That made Raven laugh. "Hopefully, he worded his praise differently to my sister."

"Coming from my brother, that was the highest of praise. I'm actually shocked he's sharing the project. He's usually quite territorial."

"River is as well. She wouldn't show Row and me a single part of the website until it was live. I'm glad they've become friends. I thought at first there might be some chemistry between the two, and maybe there is, but they seem very comfortable. Like they've been friends for years."

"I agree. Patrick doesn't need any more girlfriends, but a girl that's just a good friend..." Bran left the thought unfinished.

Raven knew only time would tell how Patrick and River's relationship evolved.

"Are you ready to walk back to the Fitzwilliam?"

"Sure, I want to shower and change, of course." Raven felt Bran's eyes heat as he stood up and held his hand out for her to take it.

"I want to have time to prepare for tonight as well."

Raven felt her whole body heat, and it wasn't from the shot of whiskey.

As they neared St. Stephen's Green, Bran could feel Raven's tension radiate through her cold fingers that were entwined in his— in her bunched shoulders and soft replies. Maybe he should let up on teasing her about possibly sleeping with him tonight.

He'd thought... well, they were both consenting adults. It should be an easy decision. They were both into each other. Maybe something else was bothering her. Not everything revolved around him.

Bran was about to come out and ask what was going on when Raven slowed further and tugged his hand to stop.

"Would you mind sitting with me for a minute? There's something I'd like to tell you." Raven indicated the black, wrought iron bench off the sidewalk.

"Sure." Now his tension was off the charts. What could have happened in the last ten minutes?

As they sat down, Raven clasped and unclasped her hands nervously. She smoothed her palms over her jeans and fiddled with two of her shirt's buttons.

"Okay, I'm just going to warn you. I'm about to word vomit on you, so... just let me get it all out."

Bran only nodded his head for her to continue. Now he was sweating.

"My sisters and I have always taken our studies and academics quite seriously. We knew in high school that we would own a business together someday. We even had a rough sketch of what that business would look like before we ever went to college. We never lost focus of our goals. We kept each other on the path. We dated some, very little. We preferred going out in friend groups to party. And then, after our parents..."

Oh wow. Holy motherfucking hell. He thought he knew where Raven might be going with this. He wanted badly to interrupt her 'word vomiting,' but he'd agreed to let her have her way in this.

"After our parents' passing, we doubled down on our focus. We spent every hour not in class learning about the ins and outs of starting a business. Permits, insurance, location, social media. By our senior year, we were working out of our small apartment, doing small design jobs on the weekends." Here she paused and finally looked at his face and not his chest.

"I, that is... we... we."

Her mouth was opening and closing. She was attempting to find the right words. Bran desperately wanted to help.

"So," with a few swirling, nonsensical hand motions, she finished with, "none of us has had sex. I mean, we're all big readers, especially romances. We've *read* all about sex. In great detail."

Stuttering slightly on the word *detail*, she persevered. "But... well, that was all I wanted to say. I didn't want to surprise you if something happens tonight between us, or... or perhaps not please you with my inexperience."

Before Bran could formulate a reply, she added, "I would really like to stop talking now."

Her attempt at levity worked. They both smiled at one another. "I appreciate your honesty, Raven. I do. As you've been honest, so will I. I've never slept with a virgin, and now I'm nervous I might not please *you. If* something happens tonight."

Here, he leaned forward and brushed his lips to hers. She sighed in relief at the contact. "Is it too soon to mention that I am now very, very consumed with thoughts of being your first? That I am caveman enough to want to be your last?"

"Not too soon." Raven hopped off the bench with renewed purpose and grabbed Bran's hands to pull him to his feet. "Let's get ready for dinner."

Strolling toward The Fitzwilliam, Bran was bemused to realize that he could relate to Raven's vulnerability. He was thirty years old, had had several lovers, and couldn't remember a single thing about the encounters. He suddenly found himself in similar territory with the woman walking next to him.

THE DINNER WAS INCREDIBLE. Unfortunately, neither Bran nor Raven was hungry. They were thankful Dom suggested the Glovers Alley tasting menu.

Her favorite had been the Carlingford Lobster. Bran loved the scallop dish. They both chose the same dessert, a mango, pineapple, and praline concoction. Heaven. The table was surrounded by balcony windows overlooking the city. It was a clear night, and the city's view looked like a painting straight out of a museum.

It was a fairytale evening.

The dishes were being cleared now, and Dom was setting up after-dinner drinks at the room's private bar. Bran had obviously remembered some of her favorite music from the pond party a few weeks ago because Dom queued up a perfect playlist.

Banners *Got It In You* started, and Raven couldn't help but sway toward Bran as they walked to the living room. He put his arm around her, running his hand down her side, his hand settling at her waist. His thumb brushed back and forth over her ribs, causing her to shiver. He looked down at her, a look of satisfaction at her reaction.

It was a special night. A night, if it went the way she hoped, that would remain one of the most special of her life.

"Thank you for all this, Bran. I would have been happy at a B&B. I never expected this business trip to be one of the happiest of experiences."

"I admit that this trip was a test."

"Oh?" Raven could see his hesitancy.

"Not for you. Or not just for you but for us. Would we get along? Would we run out of things to say to each other?"

"And?"

"We both passed."

Raven could only look at Bran for a moment. The candlelight showed off a few gold streaks in his white-blonde hair. "We have a couple more days together. You never know. Leave the toilet seat up once O'Faolain, and you'll wish for separate rooms."

Laughing, he turned to the butler, the only hotel staff remaining. "Thank you, Dom. Tonight was perfect."

"Oh yes, Dom. Thank you for everything. Today wouldn't have been as successful without your help and guidance."

"I have enjoyed serving both of you, though you didn't

require near what I'm used to procuring. I hope you'll both remember me on your next visit."

"I'll keep your number and let you know the moment we make plans," Bran thoughtfully added.

"And please thank Chef McFadden for us."

"Of course, Miss Byrne." Dom turned at the entrance and wished them a good evening.

Once the door closed, Bran pulled Raven into his arms. "Alone at last."

"Yes, we are. Do you want to grab our drinks and step out onto the balcony? It'll be cold, but I don't want to admit to my sisters that we were on the ninth floor of The Fitzwilliam, overlooking St. Stephen's Green, and didn't even have a peek."

Bran released Raven and bent to grab both glasses. Handing her the Bushmills. "Your usual, and Teeling Small Batch for me."

Taking a sip, they walked to the balcony, leaving the door wide open for a quick retreat if it proved too chilly.

She went to the railing and took a sip of her whiskey. "Dublin is beautiful." Raven leaned her back against him so he could circle her waist with his free arm.

"I didn't lie to Dom, you know. I imagine we will be back sooner than later, and I will let him know."

"The whole private butler thing seemed a bit silly, I admit, but he made today way easier. We had more time for fun because of it. Dom is a wonderful man and probably the most organized person I've ever known."

They remained quiet for a time. Both enjoying the view and the drinks.

Swiveling in Bran's arms until her chest was pressed to his front, she studied the strong lines of his eyes... mouth... jaw. He searched her face, perhaps hoping to ascertain her thoughts. He might be shocked. Raven's thoughts made her breathless. Bran's free hand flexed where it had settled against her side. Still watching him watch her, she quietly said, "I'm cold, Bran." Her full body shiver had nothing to do with the temperature.

She was committed now, Raven thought. Like coming out of a trance, Bran snatched her empty glass from her hand, making a clinking sound against his. All but tossing them on the dining room table, he reached back, grabbed her hand, and forcefully closed the balcony door behind them. Her nerves settled a bit, amusement bubbling in her chest over the eagerness that rode Bran's mad dash across the living room and into the master suite.

The bedroom also had balcony windows. The lights of Dublin twinkled over the bed like fairy lights.

Bran stopped in the middle of the room. Facing her, he took her hands. "Are you on birth control? I didn't think to ask until now. Sex with you is all I've thought about for weeks, and I never thought to ask, and now I'm rambling," he laughed at himself.

"No worries. River and I did a few months ago."

"That's good." That's all he said. He just continued to watch her. Like she might run if he made any sudden moves.

Hands linked, it was shocking to find hers steady and his shaking. As he'd yet to utter another word, Raven squeezed his hands and waited until his eyes stopped jumping all over the room and focused on her.

"I want this, Bran. With you. Tonight."

"I... you're sure, Raven? If you change your mind, I promise, I'll understand, and I *will* wait. You're worth that and more to me."

"I'm sure. I promise, if I do change my mind, I *will* tell you."

"Do you mind, then, if we move things along? I mean... shit... not in a rush way, well, kind of in a rush... for fuck's sake,"

Bran huffed in laughter, running a hand through his hair, making it stand on end. "I'm usually a lot more mature, I swear," Bran joked.

Raven laughed, as it sounded so much like something she'd say. Holding up her hand, she stopped Bran from continuing. "I completely understand. Remember me telling you my sisters and I read a *lot* of romances? Stop me if I'm wrong. You know I'm a virgin, and you want to take things slow. You're also incredibly horny, and you want to rip my clothes off, throw me on the bed, and have your wild way with me. You want my first time to be sonnets and roses, soft looks, and gentle kisses. Your body wants hard and rough and intense."

"Umm, well, yes. That about sums it up. Romances are... they are... intuitive."

Raven snorted at this. "Very intuitive." Raven decided to take the decision from Bran's hands and began unbuttoning his shirt. He stayed completely still as Raven parted the two halves. Using the flat of her palms against his bare chest, she ran them up and over his broad shoulders to slip the material from his body.

Their breaths shallowed at the contact. Raven silently wished the playlist in the living room was louder— much louder. Raven could barely make out Walking On Cars crooning *Colonize My Heart*. Dom must not read minds, or he would have already used an app to crank up the volume for her.

Bran was watching every move, like her undressing him was the most erotic moment of his life. With this in mind, she slid her hand back down his chest, slowly letting her fingers feel the grooves and valleys of his abs. When her fingers touched the waistband of his slacks, she paused for only a moment before placing two fingers lightly behind the fly, so her other hand was free to work the button.

Bran hissed air between his teeth. "Oh God, Rave. You're killing me."

Raven decided to hold off on the zipper and told Bran to take his shoes and socks off. In what could only be described as vampiric speed, he complied, pulling her back into his personal space as he stood up. Smiling at his exuberance, she rewarded him by sliding down the zipper.

With reverence, she braced her palms at his hips and, hooking her thumbs into both his boxers and pants, slid them down. Not very far, as the case may be. His very erect penis was... kind of hung up in the shorts.

Even romance novels had a few snags, she reminded herself. There was nothing for it but to carry on. Drumming up a nonchalance she didn't feel, she reached into the front of his trousers and gently wrapped her fingers around what, according to her books, was a *very impressive* erection.

"Raven, Jesus." Bran took over. He wrapped his hand around hers and stroked himself slowly. Once, twice, before removing her hand and ripping his pants and underwear the rest of the way off.

Raven went to move in close again. "Your body is... wow." Bran was golden. Everywhere. Sculpted, lean muscle, chiseled and grooved. Art. White hairs sprinkled his chest, trailing an icy path to his... Raven licked her suddenly dry lips. Nude Bran deserved poetry. She couldn't help but trail her fingers down the oblique channels currently framing Bran's imposing appendage.

"No. No, babe. If you touch me like that before I gain a modicum of control over myself, this will all end way before we want."

With that said, he reached for Raven and slowly spun her around. As one hand moved her long hair over her shoulder to rest down her front, his other found the zipper to her cocktail dress. Slowly, the black silk slip dress loosened and, with the slightest whisper, slid down her body.

Still facing away from Bran, Raven didn't move. She wore simple, black heels with matching nude lace panties and bra. She'd known, *oh, she'd known*, when she'd put them on tonight, that he would be able to see through the material.

"Fuck, Raven, you're stunning."

Raven shivered as his long, thick fingers traced down her back, flaring out and around her ass, squeezing her cheeks. His rough moan drew a soft moan of her own. He pulled her to him until her back was flush with his body, letting his hands glide around her waist and skim her flat stomach before cupping her breasts.

So good, so good, so good was Raven's silent mantra as she let her head fall back to see Bran's face. He kissed her then, fierce and wild, while partially turning her to unclasp her bra, devouring her mouth as he did. The bra landed on the floor. Bran lifted her in his arms. She was weightless for only a second before her overheated skin felt the bed's soft, cool sheets.

"I can't believe your mine." He took her heels off, placing each foot gently on the end of the bed. Bending close, he hooked his fingers in her panties and slid them down her thighs and over her knees before she lifted her feet enough to pull them free.

Overriding her first reaction to cover herself, Raven left her hands loose at her sides and watched Bran look at every part of her body. He put first one knee and then the other on the bed, straddling her ribs. His sex... mesmerizing. Before her hands could follow her wondering eyes, Bran's wrapped around her sides, lifting and shifting her just enough to place her at the head of the bed, throwing the mounds of pillows to the floor.

Raven's breath was sawing in and out of her throat in anticipation.

"I have to taste you," Bran said, his eyes roving down her body.

She'd always wondered, fantasized, about a man's mouth worshiping her body, and Bran was looking at her like a feast. Her core fluttered from his eyes alone, need making her slowly twist her hips in anticipation.

Bran kissed her then, his tongue an erotic simulation of what their bodies would do in truth soon. Leaving her mouth, he licked and sucked his way down her neck, her shoulders, and between her breasts. Leaning back, he watched himself squeeze both breasts, kneading them and rolling and pinching her nipples. While one hand continued to work a breast, his mouth worked the other, sucking the nipple in hard, licking little bites before blowing on the distended flesh. She was frantically writhing her body underneath his, frustrated at finding no purchase.

"I could spend hours on your tits, Raven, but not this time."

Bran's voice was hoarse as he took in the marks he'd left across her chest. He traced a reddened bite mark on the side of one breast.

After one last hot kiss to her nipples, he worked his way down her torso, ribs, belly button, and stomach. Learning her body as she longed to learn his. Raven's breath caught as his hands spread her legs apart. She felt warm breath at her center, lingering kisses on each side of her sensitive inner thighs. Her eyes squeezed tight. Waiting, waiting. Hot breaths against her lips. Waiting. Wanting.

"Raven. Look at me." Her eyes popped open. She looked down her body, flushed and beaded with perspiration. Her eyes found Bran's. His smile was dangerous. Slowly, making sure she didn't miss his intent, he licked up her entire seam.

She barely stopped herself from screaming. Her body jerked of its own volition with every swipe of Bran's tongue. Flicking her sensitive flesh forced mini shockwaves to course through her entire body while one of his long fingers shallowly pumped her channel.

"Hot. Jesus, so wet."

The slow in-and-out glide, paired with his tongue lashing her lips and the bundle nerves atop, had her exploding. Detonating.

She only realized Bran had moved because he was now kissing her mouth. She tasted her pleasure on his tongue. Books hadn't described the intensity of how erotic *that* was.

"I can't wait any longer, Raven," Bran warned. She felt his hard length grazing her wet folds. In answer, Raven wrapped her legs around his waist, anchoring her hands around the muscular tops of his shoulders.

"Now." That was the only word he needed. Reaching between them, Bran placed the head of his erection right where she needed it. The slow penetration— a glorious torture. Sweat beaded Bran's brow, his body tense. Raven knew he was doing his best not to hurt her.

Attempting to ease the fullness, she started to barely rock her hips. The friction of the small glide started to drive her body toward another orgasm. When Bran reached between them again to circle and pinch her hypersensitive skin, a second orgasm tore through her— Bran did as well. They both shouted when he was fully seated.

"So tight, baby. Jesus, your body is strangling me. So fucking good." He kissed her. Long, hot kisses. As her body started melting into his, Bran started pumping in and out. Slowly, carefully, until she began to match his thrusts, swinging her hips up to meet his. Bran became wild. He pulled out to the tip before hammering home, over and over, faster and faster.

"I'm going to come, Rave. Come for me one more time. Come on my dick, baby." Bracing his body further away from hers changed his position inside. He was hitting her just right. Oh God, her body was all raw nerves.

"Right there, Bran! Don't stop!"

"Now! Come for me now!" With one final thrust, he buried himself all the way. His shout of release and the spurting jerks deep inside her triggered the orgasm he'd demanded.

14

Having slept deeply, Bran was disoriented when he opened his eyes. Raven wasn't next to him. His head followed his hand across the deep expanse of the mattress, searching for the warmth of a woman. His woman. Ahh, there she was. He stopped the forward momentum of his fingers before they touched his quarry, not wanting to wake her. He let out a satisfied sigh. She probably moved away from his body because each time he woke through the night, he couldn't keep his hands and other body parts from touching her.

His. She was only his. Bran wasn't possessive over women— he and James had even dated some of the same girls in college. He never cared. He cared now. Rather deeply. Raven made him — he wasn't even sure— feel like he would no longer be him without her.

Raven's right arm was lying above her head on the pillow, the white sheet falling below her breast, her dark nipple and areola ruched from the cool air. The delicate, black triskelion tattoo on the side of her plump breast with a small Native American raven symbol beside it, the only spot of color marring all that creamy, pale skin.

The thought of sucking that tight bud into his warm mouth had his dick hard and aching. He wanted to wake her— badly— but knew she had to be tender. Tossing the tented sheet aside while studiously ignoring his one-track-cock, Bran quietly walked to the bathroom, deciding to shower and let Raven sleep a bit longer.

~

RAVEN WOKE to the sound of running water and an empty bed — Bran must be showering. Laying her head back against the pillow, she smiled, stretching her sore muscles. Last night had been better than her best fantasies. River and Rowan were going to flip.

As she continued to think of the evening past, a tingling started zinging from her core to her breasts. In truth, she shouldn't be considering sex again. She *was* sore. But— Raven sat up in bed— an idea percolating. She hadn't tried everything out she'd wanted to last night. Not nearly. Bran had been voracious *and* in charge.

She smiled as she got out of bed. She needed a shower, too, after all.

~

BRAN STOOD under the hot spray when he heard the bathroom door open. Damn. With sleep-tousled hair and puffy lips, Raven stood staring at him through the glass. Naked. He still couldn't believe this stunning woman was his. She'd *better* be his.

Her mouth was moving. It took a moment for his brain to catch up— for the words to register.

"I thought I'd join you. If you don't mind."

Her smile was tentative, but her eyes were fastened on his body. Determined.

"Good idea."

She grabbed a scrunchie off the bathroom counter as she walked by. Pausing just outside the shower door, she gathered all that thick, black, silky hair and did some wad and twist thing with the band that ended up looking sexy as hell.

He opened the door. "I missed waking up next to you," Raven admitted as she stepped close, her breasts smashing against his ribs. Her focus didn't stay on him, but strangely, she looked around like she'd never seen the inside of the huge walk-in shower before. Nerves, maybe, Bran thought. His erection was back to full attention, making his decision to let her recover — difficult.

Raven stepped away from him and went to one of the built-in seats, where the water gently misted, and steam climbed the walls. Bran watched, transfixed. She turned and sat, legs slightly parted, giving him a glimpse of her glistening, pink folds. Fuuuck...

"Come over here, Bran." Mind already blank from looking at her— he walked, somewhat dazed, to the other end of the shower. "Closer, babe."

No way.

No fucking way was his recently devirginized girlfriend considering...

He stepped close. Very close. In her seated position, his straining sex was at the perfect height.

He wanted— so badly— for her to be thinking— what he was thinking.

"I want to taste you, Bran. I want to know what you feel like on my tongue."

A bead of cum instantly pearled.

He groaned and grasped himself with one hand, slowly

stroking the head toward her parted lips. Her words alone made his balls tighten.

"You'll let me know what you like." Not a question.

"I will... you're sure...?" In answer, she leaned forward to swipe the precum off his head. Bran had to brace his suddenly weak legs. The muscles in his thighs swelled and twitched. His palms slapped the wall above her.

Raven wrapped her delicate hands around his swollen, throbbing length, leaned forward, and closed her mouth around him. Her tongue swirled back and forth across the sensitive underside.

"Jesus. Fuck." It was all he could do not to pump his hips as Raven bobbed her head farther down and farther still. Her hands stroking in tandem.

His will to remain still lasted seconds. He *had* to move. Bran couldn't *not* move. "Take more of me. Oh, God, baby, swallow me down. There— yes— shit!" Shallow pumps, her wet lips, tight throat, the sight of her mouth stretched around his shaft...

"Going to come, Raven!" Gritting his teeth, Bran tried to hold back. "Let me go, or I'll come down your throat!" he demanded. Her response was to move one hand to his ass and dig her fingers in, keeping him where he was.

"NOW! Raven, God!" Every muscle in his body locked up. "Swallow all of it," he growled. Spurt after spurt of his climax washed the back of her throat. Bran didn't think he would ever stop. The intensity left him weak.

Finished, she slowly let him slide from her swollen lips. His legs could no longer bear his weight, and he sat heavily on the shower floor at her feet.

Raven was silent for a moment, and then she smiled. "A person can learn a lot from books, right?"

"I'm building you a library."

THE TRIP to Longford was overcast and misty. It didn't matter to Raven. Nothing could dampen her mood, even clouds. She and Bran kept looking at each other and grinning. It was all so new to be in a relationship. She prayed it was a relationship. He'd called her his girlfriend more than once... but.

She'd talk it through with her sisters, though they would probably be disappointed she'd slept with Bran— well, a whole lot more than sleeping— without asking for some clarity of their status. Most important... were they exclusive.

Bran slowed their mid-sized SUV rental. A winding road led off Ireland's main highway or national primary road. "What are we doing?"

"There is a castle ruin just a mile up ahead. We have the time before meeting Peter Tamin in Longford. Are you up for a walk in the light rain, Miss Byrne."

Snorting, she laughingly replied, "I probably won't melt." Pleased with the stop, she tried to put her worries about their status on a back burner.

As they pulled up to a bit of beaten-down grass that must serve as an Irish countryside parking lot, the sun started to peek through the clouds.

Raven eyed the sky. "Oh, perfect, Bran. I think the sprinkling is about to stop too."

The rain-slicked stone from the long-ago tower sparkled in the stray beams of sun. "I have to snap a pic for my sisters. Will you take one with me? Your arms are a lot longer than mine." Smiling, she handed Bran her phone.

"Good to know I can be of service." They could never get the angle right where they were in the picture with the ruins behind them. She was too damn short. Bran suggested she hop on his back.

The picture ended up being perfect. They were both laughing, the sun was fully shining, and an Irish treasure was at their backs.

"I'm so glad we stopped."

They walked hand in hand around the old stone fortress, with its empty turreted windows and low crumbling fences surrounding the outer walls. Raven always loved castle ruins. Not that they were in ruins, which was a shame, but that it allowed her mind to conjure all sorts of stories about who once lived and worked in them. To appreciate the people that stood on the same bit of land she was standing on now.

Bran ducked under a low doorway to enter a stairwell that ended in crumbling stones about twenty feet up. The steps that were still intact were smooth, wide, and well-worn. Bran sat on one, taking her hand and pulling her to stand in front of him, his head just slightly taller than her own for once.

"Why don't you tell me what was bothering you in the car earlier?" He held up his hand to stop her denial. "You don't have to. It's just after the night we shared, and the morning, I thought you might feel more comfortable sharing your thoughts with me."

Bran grinned at the shower reference— she felt her face warm. But she knew she'd pleased him if collapsing on the floor was any indication. She was pleased with herself.

And he was correct.

"You're right. You know this is new for me," Raven shrugged, "but—"

Bran interrupted. "It's new for me as well, Raven. Surely, you realize that having sex with someone you aren't emotionally invested in is way different than what happened between us."

Raven looked at Bran for a moment. She understood what he meant. And yes, their level of closeness deserved openness and vulnerability. From both of them.

"I've fallen for you, Bran. Hard. You want me to open up? I will. I love you, and I became nervous that you might not feel the same. That it's too soon. That this might be a fling, and once our trip was over, we would be too."

Bran braced his hands on her hips and moved her to stand between his bent legs. "I feel the same. I love you too. I know it's fast, but Gran assured me that when you know, you know and not to be a... dithering idiot about it."

Raven could picture Matilda saying that and smiled.

"I want to make plans for our future once we're back in the States. We don't have to rush, but you're it for me."

Raven leaned forward to kiss his lips, bracing her hands on his chest. "My, aren't we so grown up. Speaking of our feelings. Making commitments." She kissed him again. Slow, easy. "You make me very happy, Bran."

Bran deepened the kiss and began undoing her pants in the process. Laughing, she tried to move out of his embrace. "Bran! You are *not* taking my clothes off!"

Easily holding her still, he got her pants unbuttoned and the zipper down. "Not all your clothes, babe, just the bottom half."

Grinning, he asked her to kick off her tennis shoes. She did — she was sooo weak when it came to Bran. She couldn't help the squeak of surprise when he stripped her jeans and panties in one go.

Bran stood, asked her to grab her shoes and clothes, then lifted her bare ass up, wrapping her legs snugly around his waist. He left the stairwell and headed out a crumbled back wall, where only miles and miles of green fields met them.

"Where exactly are you taking me? Outside? Naked! And why did I have to take my pants off first?"

"Simple, I wanted to feel your bare ass in my hands."

He gave her a look like she should have known that.

"I'm not an exhibitionist, Raven, but surely you're adventurous enough to let your boyfriend fuck you in a deserted Irish field."

Bran's deliberate, bold sex talk had her remembering all the dirty, nasty things he'd whispered in her ear as he took her over and over last night. He *knew* what it did to her.

As he walked them to a shallow indention surrounded by more fallen stones and boulders, he'd been squeezing the cheeks of her ass, his fingers coming so close to her core she was squirming before he set her on her feet.

"I lied. I want all your clothes off." He was already tugging off his light sweater, jeans, boots, socks, and briefs. Raven could only watch as he stepped into the shallow, rounded recess— She prayed it wasn't a medieval grave.

Fitting his back against the low, moss-covered embankment, uncaring of the damp, he asked, "Why aren't you naked yet?"

"Shameless, O'Faolain." Shaking her head, she pulled her own soft sweater off, placing it with her jeans. "I must be as well." As she straightened to unclasp the front closure of her bra, Bran's eyes were fastened on her every move. His right hand stroked his shaft. Raven was mesmerized as his thumb swiped a drop of cum from the crown. Her bra fell from her fingers before she climbed down as well.

Who was mesmerizing whom?

"I don't want to make you sore, but fuck, I can't think of anything else but being inside you again." Gently pulling her down, he split her legs across his thighs.

Her very center was spread open for him. Raven slid further up his thighs, working her core on his hard length, back and forth, back and forth, and back and forth again. Their breathing, already heavy, grew ragged. Raven slid further up on the last glide until his length found her entrance before she slowly impaled herself.

~

RAVEN'S BREASTS swayed and bounced with every up and down motion of her body. Bran grasped her hips, helping increase the friction between them, before sucking first one nipple and then the other into his mouth. He could already feel himself edging toward climax and knew Raven was close. Her tempo increased, and her moans became almost frantic, chasing her release.

"That's it, baby, come for me. I love to watch you— feel you tighten around me." As he knew it would, his words made her burn even hotter. She exploded, flinging her head back, as her hips continued to jerk and ride him until he followed.

She lay on his chest, her head resting on his shoulder. He gently rubbed circles on her bare back, soothing her.

He was so far gone. Insanely in love. Patrick would never let him live it down.

Raven lifted her head to glare at him. "You, O'Faolain, are a bad influence. Yesterday, not even twenty-four hours ago, I was as pure as the driven snow."

Her disgruntled tone might have worked if her eyes weren't sparkling.

"Now, look at me, naked in a pasture." She did smile now. "I'm so telling my sisters. You know that, right?"

Swatting her ass before he lifted her up, separating himself, he said, "I expected nothing less. I'm surprised you didn't wake them up already."

"Ha! I told them I wouldn't call until after we met with the artist, and I won't. You, however, will have to find something to occupy your time for at least thirty minutes while I give them all the details."

"You guys are ridiculous, but since I now feel like they're my sisters, I know when I'm beat. Let's get dressed. It's only another forty minutes to the address Rowan sent." They pulled on their clothes, then headed out of the ruin.

As they rounded the corner, an older gentleman in a worn brown jacket and cap came walking down through the field adjacent to the path they'd driven, a Cocker Spaniel trotting at his feet. Bran and Raven waved as they walked on to their car.

Raven hissed under her breath as they reached the door. "If that poor man witnessed us making... having sss... *screwing* in public, so help me God, I will make you pay. Somehow, I will."

Her face bright red, she got in the car and not so much slammed as shut the door with firm intent. Bran refrained from reminding her that the chance of meeting the man again were next to nil. Once he was settled in the driver's seat, he looked over, attempting a serious demeanor. "Shall I confess to your sisters what we possibly did in front of that poor man, or do you want to?"

He watched Raven suck in air so quick to reply she nearly choked. "You are horrible. Horrible!" Then she bent over, laughing. They both laughed until tears leaked from their eyes. After a few starts and stops, she finally got out, "We shall never speak of this, Mr. O'Faolain. I was going to tell them about it but I've changed my mind."

15

A s Sam began most of his mornings, he thanked his father's talent for turning a profit. Before the O'Faolains had shit all over his family and ruined his father's name and Sam's as well, come to that, his dad had invested— wisely.

Even after he lost his job, Thomas Delton had plenty of money to live the rest of his life comfortably.

The O'Faolain attorneys had only found two of his dad's accounts. There were three more that the stupid twats never uncovered.

Sam could have stayed on at his private high school even though he hated most of his classmates. However, the teachers caught wind of his father's supposed disgrace and made Sam's life hell. His dad had been convinced that Hugh O'Faolain had spread the rumors. Hoping to run them out of town.

The students were indifferent, but he could feel the sneering looks from James, Bran, and Patrick burning into his back. Every Single Day. Fuck that. He had his father pull him from school, and he finished online.

His dad's CPA license hadn't been revoked because the

O'Faolains magnanimously *didn't press charges. Dad admitted privately to fraud, skimming money off the accounts he managed. It wasn't true. His father told him he was forced into admitting guilt to keep his family from the embarrassment of court. He could still practice, but anyone who was anyone knew about Dad's supposed theft. He wouldn't work in Oklahoma again.*

The spiderweb of accounts was his dad's legacy. Thomas Delton was a numbers genius. Luckily for Sam, like father, like son ran true.

So, the ritual of thankfulness continued all these years later, honoring his father and mentor. "Thanks, Dad, for all the fucking money you left me. Turns out I'm damn good at investing too." It always tickled his funny bone that the O'Faolains had killed his father, granted, in a roundabout way, and ruined the Delton name, but Samuel was a multi-millionaire regardless of their intent.

Thanks to his inherited wealth, Sam was able to devote his days to 'working' jobs that allowed him access to the preening assholes. And damn, if he hadn't used the last few days of Bran's absence to his advantage.

This evening, Sam was waiting on Josephine O'Connor's table at a favorite Irish pub located in downtown Tulsa. She'd met up with two of the Byrne sisters for dinner and drinks, and more conveniently, a waiter at the pub experienced a bicycle accident earlier in the day and couldn't make his shift.

As luck would have it, Sam was a trusted member on almost every freelance shift work app— and knowing the waiter might have an issue— he refreshed the open shifts every minute for hours until the injured waiter's shift showed up. Sam accepted the job within seconds and was accepted.

So easy. Not as easy as loading remote access software to some of the laptops owned by a few of the exclusive members of

Those He Hated the Most, however. And hey, was it really his fault that the idiots left their electronics lying around?

Monitoring emails and messaging apps took an excruciating amount of his valuable time— but look at the payoff— three women of Sam's interest had their heads together laughing, and he was their waiter. Bingo, motherfuckers.

"More water?"

"No, I'm fine. Thank you."

I'll take some, please."

"I'm good right now."

"All right, ladies. I'm Charlie, and I'll be your waiter this evening. If you're ready to order, I'll take them now, or if you might prefer getting drinks from the bar first, I can grab those while you look over the appetizers."

The women smiled at Sam. So lovely. He would fuck any of them. Reminding himself not to flirt since tonight's disguise was that of a nondescript, prematurely balding man. His stringy, brown wig was tied at his nape in an unimpressive ponytail. He had expertly applied acne scars across his cheekbones, bright blue eyes covered with brown contacts, and cheap, stretchy-waisted black slacks, a black button-up, and black orthopedic tennis shoes completed his look. Not a wet dream walking.

It was necessary to cover his appearance completely. He was extremely good-looking, and he kept his body appealingly fit. He could easily get any of the women seated before him. He knew this because when he wasn't monitoring his enemies, he enjoyed picking up women with his boy-next-door charm.

He enjoyed getting them drunk, so their inhibitions were loosened. Sometimes he dropped a little something special into their drinks when they went to the restroom. It was one of Sam's favorite games. Most of the women made it easy, though. His looks helped too much at times, taking the challenge out of it.

When they first saw his media room, they did tend to freak out, but that just made his homemade pornos worth more on the dark web. He'd made a pretty penny on his video rental site. Renting was a genius idea. Keep them coming back. He still laughed at his name. @SammySoGood— King of Twisted Love Stories.

Shaking off the hard-on-inducing thoughts, he snapped back to his current job. The ladies rattled off their drinks. "I'll run get these and take your appetizer order then if you're ready."

Stroking the bartender's ego— 'Damn, bro, you're one of the fastest bartenders I've ever seen'— Sam got his drink order in record time.

"Okay, here we are," Sam said as he gently set the drinks in front of each of the ladies. Guinness with a full head, Jameson Black Barrel neat, and Slane, neat as well.

Grinning to show off his fake orthodontics, he told them that they could probably out drink every guy friend he had. That got them all laughing. That's right, Sam thought, I'm just your average Mr. Friendly.

"We aren't in a hurry, Charlie, so we are going to order a few apps before we order dinner." This was the middle sister, River, he believed. They all looked gorgeously similar.

"Perfect," he gushed, pen poised, "Let me have it."

"Irish nachos, Kells shrimp, and the St. Mullins mussels."

"Good choices, all. I'll turn this order into the kitchen and bring back tableware and napkins. Just ignore my coming and going. I like to swing by my tables more than some of the other wait staff." Let me do my job by ignoring me.

Not five minutes later, as he prepped the table for the apps and refilled water glasses, the ladies did as he asked and let him do his thing. They smiled at him but kept talking to each other.

"They're visiting Nan today and getting some more Wolves shopping in."

"When Raven called us this morning, she said they would be flying out on a late flight from Dublin tomorrow."

"I don't care about the timeline! Get to the good stuff already!" Josephine demanded.

The sisters laughed. "She confirmed that she is absolutely in love with Bran."

"And," the other sister finished, "Bran is absolutely in love with her."

Sam could hear them all squealing in delight as he went to check on the apps. His mind was whirring. He was happy to have confirmation of what he already believed, but now, he had so much to accomplish before the lovebirds touched back down in Oklahoma.

He knew from O'Connor's emails and messaging app that the Byrne sisters would be staying the night in Tulsa and working at Wolves tomorrow. This meant he would need to make a run to Eufaula tonight to see about setting up surveillance equipment at Triskelion. He would need plenty of pictures of Raven at her home and at the pub.

Preferably at Wolves. That would hurt Bran the most.

Hopefully, in a matter of weeks, he would ruin another one of the musketeers' relationships.

Dropping the appetizers off at O'Connor's table, Sam checked his watch. One more hour and a half, tops, and he'd be finished 'working' and walk out the back door. Always cognizant of not burning bridges, Sam would let the manager know he was extremely ill and couldn't finish his shift. He would be so upset that he couldn't finish his shift, he wouldn't accept payment. The manager would probably appreciate his work ethic, and Charlie would receive a great review on the shift app. Winning. Always winning.

Sam cared for the few tables he was responsible for until finally, the ladies called an Uber. They were all smiles and thank yous, generous tips and good nights. As soon as they departed the pub, Sam was working his way to the manager.

Glancing over his shoulder at the three beauties stepping outside, his whole body tingled. He loved his life. He loved that the very people who spit on his family would never see who was coming for them. He knew.

16

"I can't believe you're about to meet my grandma." Raven nervously put her right hand on Bran's thigh as he maneuvered their car across the private, wooden bridge that spanned the Boyle River, leading them into Nan's timbered enclave.

"Are you nervous she won't like me, babe?"

"No." And then again, "No. She'll love you because I do." Raven knew this. Her nerves were bubbling up regardless. "I think... it's just, besides my sisters, Nan is the last of my immediate family. I guess I still carry an old dream that I'd bring my first boyfriend home to meet Mom and Dad."

Raven smiled at Bran in reassurance that she wasn't going to break down, but she felt her smile wobble, and of course, he didn't miss it.

"Rave." Bran stopped the car once they'd crossed the bridge.

Raven waved her hand in front of her, brushing away the feelings. "It's fine. *I'm* fine. Honestly. Little girl fantasies... I... didn't realize." Once again, she fluttered her hand in a moving-on gesture. Bran caught her hand.

"Don't try to brush off your feelings like they aren't important." He brought her hand to his mouth and kissed her fingers gently before leaning across the center console and pressing the gentlest of kisses to her mouth.

Sitting back in his seat, he said, "Only boyfriend."

Umm. "What?"

"You're bringing home your only— ever— boyfriend. Not your first." He clarified.

"Lord have mercy. And men think women are difficult." Both were laughing as Bran started to drive again. Raven appreciated the distraction from her parents.

Looking around at the tree-lined road, Bran was impressed. "Wow. Very nice."

"The property has been in the family since the 1700s. It's a couple miles from town. Remote, but not *too* remote."

"How much land does your grandma own in this enclave?"

"I think almost eight acres. There are two outbuildings, and oh," she exclaimed, "I can't wait for you to walk the path leading to the river. Nan placed benches near the water, and there's a firepit. The wooded grove is mostly ash, hazel, and willow trees. It's perfect. River, Rowan, and I played hide and seek for hours in that grove."

The house came into view then. The 1800 square foot, two-story, whitewashed cottage with its light grey tiled roof was a vision. The red double door gave it a pop of color. Lovely and very Irish. The house sat on a neatly packed pebble drive that circled the house, green grass surrounded the narrow path.

The flowers, though, were the showstopper. Nan had planted every type and color in a brilliant, fragrant, wild display. There was no order to it, but the neat little dirt footpath that wound through it twisted into a perfect secret garden oasis.

Having come to a stop, she and Bran climbed out. She walked over and grabbed Bran's hand. "I want a flower garden just as wild and untamed as Nan's someday. I want my children to run through it giggling like my sisters and I used to." She smiled at him. Joy completely washed away the sad thoughts from earlier.

BRAN WAS MOMENTARILY STUNNED. Raven's smile was electrifying. He wanted nothing more in that moment than to give her all the flowers and children she desired. Thankfully, before he could fall to one knee and propose, an older woman, lovely white hair braided about her crown, stepped outside.

"Raven! My girl." Laughing, the older woman, who was still quite beautiful, started running out to her granddaughter. Raven yelled 'Nan' and took off. They met in the drive, wrapping each other up in warm hugs, kisses, and smiles. Each asking and answering a dozen questions.

"Are you well, my love?"

"Yes! How are your knees?"

"Fine, fine. Your drive? I spoke to your sisters."

"Good. Lovely, actually." Raven looked over her shoulder and smiled at the same time the intense stare of Bébhinn Byrne met his.

Raven was leading her grandmother toward Bran. "Nan, I can't wait for you to meet Bran." Having reached him, Raven stepped to his side once again. "This is Bran O'Faolain. Bran, this is my grandmother, Bébhinn."

"I am very pleased to meet you, Mrs. Byrne. Raven has told me so much about you and about your home. It is really beautiful here. Thank you for allowing me to stay the night."

He was rambling. Jesus, he could feel his face getting hot. He stuck his right hand out to shake her hand in greeting. He'd never been nervous about meeting new people, but meeting Mrs. Byrne was, in essence, meeting Raven's parents.

Thankfully, she didn't leave him hanging and stepped

forward immediately, cupping his large hand in both of her small ones, squeezing and patting simultaneously. Her hands were calloused and heavily veined but strong.

"You are welcome in my home, Bran O'Faolain. Call me Bébhinn, please. You've some Irish with that last name."

"Yes. My father's father's father's family was from County Kerry. Fishermen, I believe. Since Raven told me the history of the Byrnes working the railroad across the United States, I've wondered if any O'Faolains did the same, as we ended up in Oklahoma too."

"I enjoy genealogy. Someday, I'll have to get some information on your family and do some research."

"That would be great. My Gran would be very pleased to give you our history and help in any way she could."

"Okay then, let's get the bags inside. I've got rooms made up for you both with fresh linens and towels. And Raven, I made your favorite scones with orange glaze, and I also made some plain sugar biscuits in case Bran doesn't like scones."

As Bran grabbed bags out and the three bottles of whiskey they brought for Bébhinn, Bran stared at Raven until she caught his eye. "Rooms?" He whispered.

The shrug and smile as she turned to trail behind her grandma were *not* reassuring.

AFTER SHE AND Bran had left their bags upstairs, they headed down to have tea with Nan. "Before we go to the living room, I want to show you something in the sunroom." She threaded her fingers through his and led him to the side of the house where the lovely glassed-in room was. It had always been one of Raven's favorite rooms in the house.

It had a tiny reading nook and a table and chairs for morning tea. One side was dedicated to potting plants, and the whole room was filled with the earthy smell of soil and green. Nan had flowers spread out on worktables and herbs hanging from the rafters. The nook held an old sofa that she and her sisters still loved to curl up on to gossip— and to feel closer to their parents. Her grandma had an armoire off to one side that held her parents' urns.

"This is quite a room. I bet you loved it growing up."

"I did. I still do. So do my sisters." She let go of Bran's hand to walk over to the cabinet, all dark wood and scrolling motifs. It was old but lovely in the way antiques are supposed to look. Its age spots giving it character that newer pieces had yet to achieve.

She carefully opened the doors to reveal not just her mom and dad's resting place but the magical utopia she and her sisters had created inside.

Bran came up behind her and asked, "Holy shit, did you do all this?"

"My sisters and I worked on it whenever we visited Nan."

It was painted in pale yellows and greens with a profusion of brightly colored flowers that could be seen peeking around the edges of all the pictures and framed letters. The urns were set on one of the side shelves with their wedding rings and marriage license between them.

There were old photos of her dad and his family, young pictures of Nan holding her father and grandpa Sean smiling at them both, ones of her parents in college, and of her and her sisters when they were born. There were homemade Christmas ornaments and noodle necklaces they'd made their mom for Mother's Day.

"It's our memory cabinet. Not for feeling sad, but to never forget all the wonderful parts. We essentially wanted colorful displays and tiny vignettes that would draw your eye to different areas each time you look.

"You can't meet my parents, so I wanted you to see this. They would have loved you, Bran."

He studied the cabinet for several more minutes, asking questions about some of the pictures and laughing at a few of the childhood 'art' pieces. When he finished, he turned toward her and hugged her tightly.

"It's one of the most amazing monuments of love and family I've ever seen. Thank you for sharing it with me. Would you mind if I took a picture to show Dad and Pat? I would love to someday do this for Gran."

"Oh, what an amazing thought. You could have the inside painted all French blue with watercolor trees for all sorts of lovely family pictures and memories."

"Maybe you and your sisters could help us do that someday."

"They would be thrilled. I would be honored," she admitted, going up on tiptoe to give him a gentle kiss. "We'd better make our way to Nan."

THE CONVERSATION HAD BEEN LIVELY during tea. Grandma regaled Bran with tales of mischief Raven and her sisters had got up to in the summers. Nan needed a medal for not tying them to chairs.

Raven got misty-eyed when her grandma told Bran about her dad, and then once he and her mom had gotten married, she told him stories about them both. Some of the things Raven hadn't heard before. What a precious gift. She would share them with her sisters when she got home and ask for repeats when next the three were here together.

After tea, Bran had asked Raven if she would take him on a guided tour of the property and to the river through the grove. The intense way he stared at her made it clear what else he hoped to see on the walk. Her body knew too. She became hot with the same need reflected in his eyes.

She was about to answer with an enthusiastic yes, but her grandmother, who Raven believed, had known exactly what she was blocking, said she would love to tag along. Bran attempted to rally, but the brief look of frustration mirrored her own.

After exploring the property and outbuildings, they walked to the river. Nan enjoyed answering Bran's questions about her land, what surrounded it, who owned it, and for how long. Once they walked back, dinner prep began.

Bran cooked steaks for them and fish for her. Grandma had already prepped cauliflower, broccoli, and roasting potatoes before they arrived this afternoon. They had put the veg in the oven before heading to the river, so they were ready to serve. Raven tossed a salad before they all sat down to eat. It seemed easy and familiar even though it was their first time preparing a meal together.

The sun was low in the sky, shadows lengthening. There was a peace that Ireland always brought her. Perhaps because it had been her father's childhood home. If she and her sisters hadn't decided to make a go of their business in Oklahoma, they would have been very happy moving to Ireland.

Nan's outdoor table and chairs had a partial wind block from the attached gardening room at the side of the house, keeping a lot of the cool breeze off them. She should have gone to get a lap blanket, but it was such a lovely evening she didn't want to move, and Nan just brought out a bottle of Teeling whiskey and sliced fruit for dessert.

Finishing off her last bite of cauliflower, Raven told her

grandma that she wished this visit could have been longer. "I forget how much I need this place... and you."

Bran seemed right at home and clearly agreed. "I've really enjoyed today, Bébhinn. Thank you for the meal and hospitality."

"You did most of the cooking, young man," she chided. "I am very glad I got to meet you." Turning to her granddaughter, she smiled and took a sip of whiskey. "I would love a longer visit, and I expect one sooner than later, but I understand you need to finish work on Wolves. Of which you'd better send me plenty of pictures, Bran. I want to see what you and my granddaughters accomplish together. Do one of those video walkthroughs for me."

"I will," Bran promised. "I'll even include my dad and brother in the video so you can meet them. My dad will hate being filmed, which will make it even better." They all laughed at that.

EVERYONE WAS SETTLED for the night— in separate rooms. Bran was struggling to 'settle,' though. He needed sleep, tomorrow was going to be a long day of travel, but damn it, he was used to Raven sleeping next to him. It wasn't about sex, okay, Bran admitted to himself, not *all* about sex. He just wanted her close, and two doors down wasn't fucking close enough.

Decision made, he tossed the bedsheets aside, slipped a t-shirt on with his plaid pajama bottoms, and stealthily pulled his door open. The bedrooms were all on the second floor or what the Irish considered, the first floor, as apparently, the first level was the ground floor. Stepping into the hall and about to pull his door shut behind him, he heard a delicate cough at his back.

To say he almost felt his heart burst was no exaggeration. He literally almost died. Whipping around, he saw Bébhinn Byrne stepping out of her door. Her head was covered in some sort of... wrapper, and she was wearing a quilted robe cinched about her waist, covering her from chin to toes.

Bran was unable to move. He stared at her while she stared back at him.

"Oh, you couldn't sleep either?" Moving toward the stairs, she gestured for him to follow. "Let's not wake Raven, the poor girl. I was going to make some hot tea. I'll make some for us both."

Please, God and all his angels, let her not have been waiting to hear him trying to sneak into her granddaughter's room. Helpless to do anything but follow in her wake, he wound up sitting at the kitchen table while she put water in the kettle. Studying the tabletop, anything but eye contact, thank you very much, Bran ran his fingers across the worn wood. Smooth with age and the scars that came from its family.

Bébhinn noticed his interest and told him the table had been her husband's mother's. "Over the years, I tried to imagine a more modern setup, padded chairs, and whatnot— and then I pictured my Sean, sitting right where you are now, and our son Daniel, banging his silver baby spoon along its surface, smiling and laughing at the racket he was making.

"As my two greatest loves are gone from this world now, I don't reckon I'll ever part with the damn thing." Shrugging, she admitted, "As one ages, Bran, one becomes more attached to things that others may deem bin-worthy."

"I don't think loving this old table is any different than my dad framing the painted noodle necklaces my brother and I made him for Christmas years ago— that still hang on his office wall. If looking at something or touching something triggers happy memories, why not hang on to them? It's your history.

This table still takes care of your needs and will continue to do the same in the future. I imagine your granddaughters have sat here many times and that their children will one day bang their own toddler spoons against its weathered finish. This table should be cherished." Damn, when Bran saw Raven's Nan swipe at a tear as she turned back toward the whistling kettle, he felt his own eyes burn.

Bébhinn didn't speak further as she prepared their tea until she sat with him at the table. "I know you love each other, Bran. That isn't in question." Bran nodded his head in assent. "And, well, I wish there was a male left alive that could speak for Raven, but alas, wishes can be fickle. And so..." She raised her hands up in a helpless gesture.

Bran let her gather her thoughts. She felt she needed to speak to him about his and Raven's relationship. He could not fault her for that.

"As the Irish are fond of saying, 'You'll never plough a field by turning it over in your mind,' so I'll get to the point so we can both get to bed. The love is there, yes. I only want to ensure the commitment is as strong."

Cupping his hands around the delicate, floral-patterned teacup, he sat straight before answering, knowing this was important to her. "I love Raven. I didn't even know what loving someone besides my father and brother felt like. She is everything I never dreamed of because I didn't know to dream that big. I'm not sure exactly when or how I'm going to do it, but I'd like your permission to ask Raven to be my wife."

Bébhinn was mopping up tears with her special embroidered napkins before he was finished. He hoped they were happy tears.

"Oh, you sweet boy. Of course. Of course, you have my blessing. And I would tell you, that if my Sean and Daniel were still here, they would extend to you a hearty blessing as well."

She stood and walked over. Bran quickly stood as well. She gave him a brief hug, looking up, she placed her palm on his cheek. "Oh, boy... you have this old woman's blessing tenfold."

"You'll never regret it."

"Enough of the heavy stuff. Pour a wee bit of your whiskey in our cups, and let's off to bed."

Bran smiled and grabbed the Teeling from dinner. Pouring a hearty amount in each cup, he recorked the bottle.

"May I assume you'll manage to stay in your room the rest of the evening?"

"Yes. No problem." Clearing his throat in embarrassment, he followed the Byrne matriarch back up the stairs.

Before shutting her bedroom door, she quietly asked, "You'll bring her back to me when your work is complete?"

"A very easy promise to keep, and I'll do one better. I'll bring all three of your granddaughters."

17

Saying goodbye to Nan was sad but not as difficult as it usually was. The older woman had gotten up before dawn to bake some muffins for the road— Bran had two before they got in the car.

When her grandma hugged her tight a final time, she whispered in Raven's ear. "I'm so proud of you. Bran is everything I would dream for you."

Letting her go, she wished them safe travels and made Bran promise to let her know that Raven was home safely.

Buckling up, Raven grinned over at Bran. "Apparently, I now need someone to ensure I get home safe."

"Your grandma is old school, babe. I'm sure she realized years ago how capable you are of holding the fort, so to speak, but if there happens to be a big, strong man nearby, willing to take care of her little, tiny, baby girl... well, let him shoulder the responsibility."

"I foresee you and Nan ganging up on me in the future."

"You'll at least see reason about me tucking you into bed?"

"Mmhmm, now that I will agree to. Speaking of which, I thought I heard your voice in the hallway last night."

Suspiciously, the tops of Bran's ears and cheeks pinkened. "You did. I stepped out to use the restroom and met Bébhinn in the hall. That's all."

"Really? You seem flustered. Could it be you were caught trying to sneak into my room?" Raven couldn't help laughing at his blank expression.

"No. Just the restroom."

Changing the subject, he suggested they make some of their stops in Boyle for the pub but wait to eat lunch until they were back in Dublin.

"We'll need to be at the airport no later than three this afternoon. The jet is scheduled to taxi out at four. I have us leaving a few hours earlier than I'd originally planned, Miss Byrne." Bran wrapped his fingers around her hand, bringing her palm to his mouth for a soft kiss. "Perhaps you'll recall agreeing to spend the night with me while we hid in your closet this morning. I wanted all the hours I could get alone with you at the compound before your sisters steal you away for a tell-all reunion."

Raven blushed, remembering the desperate kiss. Patrick had slipped into her room while she was changing and pulled her into the darkened closet. She would have agreed to anything once his lips touched hers. Playing it cool, she smiled, saying, "Oh, I won't deny they'll want details, but umm... did you, by chance, tell your brother we'd be staying at the compound?"

Bran looked over, trying to gauge why she'd asked. "I did. Why?"

"He invited my sisters to meet us there. They said that Patrick told them we were getting in earlier than expected. So, we'd have time for drinks and a few stories before bed."

Bran cursed his sibling.

"That dickhead. I can't wait until he's got someone in his

life that he's dying to be alone with. He will rue the day." We both laughed at his attempt at sounding medieval.

"We should be in Tulsa by 7 o'clock. How long is the drive from the airport to your dad's?"

"Just under an hour, but I hadn't planned on us staying at the main house. I wanted to show you my home there. I can't wait for you to see the space. It's all but a blank canvas, a designer's dream."

"God, I'm happy my sisters and I didn't scare you and your family off the first day we met," she laughed as they crossed Nan's bridge. "I can't wait to see your place."

"I want you and I to decorate it together. There are plenty of places for the flowers you'll want, like how your grandma has them."

"Wild, you mean?" Where moments before Raven thought she could stay in Ireland with Bran forever, now she was giddy with excitement to be home. "I could ask Nan to give me the names of some of her favorites." Grabbing Bran's hand, she said "I'd love that."

"I guess we can stay at Dad's and then head over to my house in the morning if we can talk your sisters into waiting until after lunch to drag you off to Eufaula."

Raven contemplated the time difference. "Since we are gaining six hours on the trip home, we can sleep a few hours on the plane, still have enough energy to visit the family for a bit, and politely take our leave to sleep at your house. Sleep in, tour the house in the morning, and then let my sisters take me away. It'll be Sunday, so I can fill them in on everything we purchased for the pub, and they can catch me up on what's been done at Wolves while we were gone."

"I knew there was a reason I loved you. You, Raven, are an excellent planner. Let's get this day moving." Grinning at Raven, Bran added, "Remind me to ask Brenda where the 'Do

Not Disturb' button is located. I think we'll really need it for the return flight."

"You do that O'Faolain, and you might not make it to Oklahoma."

~

BRAN ALREADY HAD his phone out to call Raven as he left the Oklahoma History Center in Oklahoma City. The Board of Directors usually met in April, but a few members had COVID, so they agreed to put it off. Rescheduling had been a bitch, and it was now well into June.

He was pleased that the other members liked his proposal of a black-tie event for the Fall. Invitations would immediately go out to professors from Oklahoma universities who had devoted their careers to Oklahoma history, historical sites, and preservation. They would be asked to speak at a dinner. The influential guests would be asked to donate to the OHS and the projects and causes dear to the professors so that they could have the funds to continue working. Many of the professors to be asked had either just published books or journal articles. These would be provided to the guests in gift bags with donations from local businesses and artisans.

This was the first event he had taken a more active role in for the OHS Directors. Raven's parents' story had inspired him. The last professional engagement they spoke at was in Atoka, about the rich history surrounding the town and its people. Daniel and Lily would have easily made the list of professors chosen for this event.

It saddened him for Raven's sake that they couldn't be included, but he hoped she was pleased that her parents had inspired this year's fundraising.

He would be informed of the exact date for the event, but it should be sometime in mid to late December. The Dominion House in Guthrie, Oklahoma, was the chosen venue. Guthrie was full of history and historical ambiance. The Byrnes would definitely approve.

Raven answered on the second ring.

"Bran."

She sounded breathless, his favorite octave.

"What are you doing? I miss you desperately."

"I miss you too, Bran. I'm glad this feeling isn't reserved solely for me. I love you if I haven't told you yet today. How was the Oklahoma Historical Society meeting?"

"I love you too. The meeting went really well, actually. I was the one to come up with this year's fundraising effort. Your parents actually gave me the idea." He told her of his plans and hopes for the event.

Raven's silence was unnerving. Fuck.

"Oh, Bran. Oh, my. I... don't know... I can't begin to tell you... Damn it! You asshole, I'm trying to work at Wolves, and you're making me cry in front of the contractors." He heard her sigh before saying, "You are... so thoughtful. My sisters..."

Bran could hear her trying to stifle her tears. He wished he were able to hug her close.

"My sisters," Raven continued, "will be so very pleased." She changed the subject, probably to give her emotions a break. "When will you be home? I've found I don't like sleeping alone."

Bran groaned. "Rave, you're killing me. I'm heading to the airport now. I'm meeting Dad at the Congressional Country Club in Maryland for a few days of politicking and oil talk with a side of golf. Boring as fuck, and I still don't know how Dad suckered me into it. I must wish for Pat to be the oldest son a hundred times a day."

"How about this? I work my ass off at Wolves. Drive my

sisters to exhaustion, and then, in three days, I'll escape to your house—"

"Our house," Bran corrected.

"Our house... and we can have a romantic evening. Just the two of us. Because, if you remember, we're having an O'Faolain-O'Connor fun night of drinking and games this weekend."

"That sounds perfect, babe. I will think of nothing else while I'm gone. I admit that an evening planned by River and Patrick sounds slightly... scary."

"No shit, right? Those two spend way too much time together. As 'good' friends. I'm using air quotes you can't see but would totally appreciate if you could."

Bran was dying. Patrick would kill him and Raven if he knew they were speculating about his love life— which made it even more fun. "I'll call you tonight when I get to the Club. I love you, Raven."

"You're everything to me, Bran. Talk to you tonight."

Bran was swamped with happiness. He wanted desperately to call James and tell him what he was getting ready to do, but he was reluctant. James was good but not great. He and Jane breaking up was still a mystery. He hoped, for the sake of his friend, the relationship would someday be mended. James was at his best with Jane.

Patrick and Dad knew he was going to a jewelry designer in OKC before going to the airport. He was like a child at Christmas. He'd planned precisely what he wanted for Raven and had already sent his initial designs to the designer. All that was left was to see the completed ring and ensure it matched his vision.

He knew enough about his girlfriend to know that flashy was not her thing. She was Irish and Native American. Both cultures appreciated the land upon which they walked. When they'd been in Ireland, Bran had witnessed Raven being moved by the rugged beauty of an untarnished landscape, smiling when a fierce thunderstorm rolled in, and taking the time to smell the bloom of an early flower. She wouldn't appreciate a spectacle on her finger. He grinned at the thought.

Bran was confident that Raven wanted him. Not his wealth and social pull. Just him. This, over anything else, helped him design, what he hoped, was the perfect ring. Well, that and the opinionated Bébhinn Byrne.

Bran chose a 4-carat round-cut emerald. Set in a delicate platinum band. No diamonds. No frills. The band should have a subtle braid design to it. He thought to go smaller with the emerald, but in the end, he wanted the green to stand out brilliantly on her finger, forever reminding them of their first trip to Ireland. He could save diamonds for her ears, lovely throat, and wrists. The emerald would be the only thing to grace her ring finger.

Bran had intended to plan an elaborate scene to ask Raven to marry him. In the end, he decided she would love being surrounded only by her family and closest friends.

RING BOX SECURED in his carry-on luggage, Bran was set to leave Oklahoma. The ring was everything he'd envisioned. Raven would surely love it too. Before boarding his flight to Maryland, he called Raven again. She told him she and her sisters planned to put in extra hours until he and his dad were home. They all wanted to unwind and enjoy the quiet time of the O'Faolain compound.

"I love you, babe. I'll see you in a few days. I'll call you tonight."

"Have a safe flight, Bran. I can't wait to show you some of the flower garden designs Nan has helped me with for your... our home. I love you. See you soon."

Finally, Bran was home. Raven was slightly freaked out about how much she'd missed him. She'd been spending more time at the O'Connor's residence than in Eufaula the last few weeks, and Jo had fast become the fourth Byrne sister. Raven had spoken with her sisters, and they were all agreed that the O'Faolains and O'Connors were like long-lost family.

She, River, Rowan, and Jo had stopped at an authentic Mexican grocery store in Tulsa before coming to Muskogee after work. They had the most amazing, marinated fajita meat, guacamole, queso, and Pico de Gallo. Plus, they had huge sacks of homemade tortilla chips and soft tortillas. The guys were going to bow down to their culinary awesomeness... They *had* shopped for it...

Raven was at Bran's house, having kissed her sisters goodnight. *They* were both content waiting for The One, but she wanted them to find their happily ever after— yesterday. River was best friends now with Patrick. They spoke every day, all day. She said they were just close friends. They could tell each other things. Raven knew it was more than that, at least on her sister's end.

Rowan... she had always been a bit of a mystery. She still was. Something was going on with her youngest sister, but Raven knew she would only hear of it when Rowan was good and ready to share.

Raven knew Bran would be home any minute. She was antsy, pacing, hot then cold. Frustrated with herself, Raven took a couple of water bottles, a bottle of whiskey, and glasses to the patio.

When one of the sliding bifold doors finally opened, Raven turned from pouring drinks. Bran stood highlighted in the dim interior lights. She stood, admiring all that white hair slipping into his eyes. He'd shaved more of his sides, similar to Patrick's. He looked like a modern rendition of a Norse Viking, and when the light hit Bran's dark eyes just right, there were tiny glints of gold around the edges. His tall, lean muscles were covered with charcoal joggers and a light grey t-shirt. Delicious.

"You're home," was all Raven's brain could construct.

"I am."

"I have Teeling for you."

Bran reached for the glass nearest him. "Thank you."

Was she imagining things, or was Bran's voice husky AF? "Good flight?"

Taking a drink, he savored it for a moment before swallowing. "It was."

The intensity of Bran's stare was doing numbers on Raven's body. "Are you hungry?" Her voice had become as low and husky as Bran's.

"Yes."

Compelled to move closer, Raven walked forward, stopping a breath from touching his body. With her free hand, she, oh so slowly, placed it flat against his chest. Looking up until she could meet his eyes.

"I'm glad you're home."

He watched intently as she took a long drink of whiskey, pulling all the smoky heat past her lips. Bran placed his crystal glass on the table carefully before taking her glass and placing it next to his. His hands were free to trace the sides of her face, thumb across her mouth, her neck... he dragged his fingers lightly along her collarbone, down her shoulders, stopping to grasp her upper arms.

She was panting now, craving more, and needing to touch him back.

"I don't like being parted from you, Raven. Days felt like years."

"I didn't like it either."

Raven's breath caught as Bran leaned down to firmly place his mouth against hers. The pressure gave way to nips and licks, twists and turns, tongues and heat.

"Do not stop, Bran," Raven moaned as his tongue swept her mouth deeply before retreating.

"I don't plan on stopping until our presence is required elsewhere."

There was no more teasing. Bran pulled the chocolate-colored silk blouse over her head, stopping to flick his fingers over her hard nipples through the nude bra she wore beneath.

Raven's hands were at his waist, working her fingers into the waistband. They both went at each other then. She yanked his pants down, and he kicked them off with his shoes. He may have ripped her slacks as he pulled them off her. Her bra was next, his shirt, socks, panties, underwear... naked, finally. Then... skin, heat, fingers, hands, pressure, friction...

"Oh God, Bran... need... want."

Grasping Raven around the waist, Bran started dragging her up his body.

"Wrap your legs around my waist, baby... yes, Fuck! Already wet for me...."

Raven felt his hard sex at her entrance, breaching her slick folds. She could only moan his name and was about to beg, but then Bran thrust hard, not stopping until he was fully seated. He moved slowly, then faster. Her core felt like a livewire.

She was delirious with sensation, hands clenched on his shoulders. Her fingers dug into his skin as she started to pulse around his shaft— exploded.

"Fuck... baby, hold on."

Bran swung them around so that her back was to the closed door. Pressing her hard against the cold glass, he moved his hands to cup the base of her ass and thighs. In this position, he went harder, faster. Slamming into her sex over and over and over. She felt herself start to clench again with another orgasm.

"Raven, oh God, baby... gonna make me come..."

One last hard thrust had Raven screaming as the clench and release intensified. Bran yelled as his own release jetted deep.

Only the door at her back and Bran's hands kept her from sliding to the ground. Bran laid his sweaty brow against her equally sweaty neck.

"I was hard all the way home thinking of what I wanted to do to you when I got here. I need a better imagination, obviously. Holy shit."

"Did I mention I was glad you were home?" Raven laughed against his shoulder.

"I don't remember, but then, I think you fried my brain."

Bran slowly slid free of her body, setting her back on her feet. He was still semi-hard. His dick had yet to give up the ghost.

The glistening head drew her attention, mesmerizing, in fact. Raven placed her hand on his stomach, starting a path down his abs.

Bran placed his hand on top of hers to stop its current trajectory. "I have plans, babe, and they don't include another round on the patio."

Laughing, Raven left off. For now.

"Leave the clothes. I'll grab the whiskey. You want to know a secret?" Bran asked, picking up the lowball glasses. "I had very specific daydreams about my shower— you starred in all of them."

"I'd like to know about these daydreams, Mr. O'Faolain, and if I'm impressed, I might tell you about some of mine." Smiling, she turned and walked inside, giving Bran one hell of a lovely show.

18

Raven made Bran breakfast that they shared inside the screened-in porch. She didn't exactly make it, so much as toast it. Bagel and cream cheese. She said she wanted to make sure he was well and truly hooked on her before she attempted cooking for him. That love could only go so far.

Her burnt cookies were never far from their minds.

The house was set high enough that the porch had a great view of the Arkansas River. The screens were a bonus because they didn't have to share the morning with a hundred flying bugs. The little winged bastards managed to hit him directly in the face, over and over, until finally landing in whatever he was drinking. *Not* a perk of living in Oklahoma and why this room was a must.

Raven's phone dinged. She smiled while she was reading.

"One of your sisters?"

"Yes," she laughed. "River said to quit having sex and meet everyone at the pondominium. Eleven. She and Pat found new appetizers they want to try out on us. James and Jo are coming, too, and they'll be in charge of cocktails. It's a pre-dinner party, I guess."

"That sounds like fun. I hope you brought a swimsuit. But before we head over to Dad's, I want you to show me your landscaping ideas."

"Of course." Raven smiled absently as she contemplated the view.

Bran could tell her mind had wandered but knew she'd eventually tell him what was bothering her.

"I know I'm only months older than my sisters, but... I don't know... I'm still the oldest, and I worry. Unnecessarily, I'm sure."

"Hey, I'm only a year and a half older than Patrick, and there are times when I feel like he's my twin and we're equal in all things, and then there are moments when he goes on benders, partying too much or whatever, and all of a sudden, I feel this need to step in as the older, wiser brother.

"Sibling dynamics continually shift," he continued. "Hell, I've seen Rowan eye River with motherly affection when she's being extra... Rivery. Dad can make me feel like a naughty five-year-old, but most of the time, he's just my best friend. Which sister is concerning you? Or is it both?"

"It's River and... Patrick. I've never seen River so happy. Did you know they text all day long when they aren't next to one another? When just the girls are eating, I feel like Pat's there too." Laughing, she leaned toward the empty chair beside her and asked a pretend Pat how his bagel was. "That's what it's like!" she laughed.

"Jesus, I wish that shithead could have seen you do that. I've noticed he talks about River, but it seems like a genuine friendship. I don't think he would ever hurt her, babe."

"Oh, no, I agree they truly are friends. But there have been a few times late at night, and I know they're talking. Again, they're adults. There is no curfew or lights out. It's just... I can't quite put my finger on it, but I think River's feelings run much deeper than maybe Patrick realizes."

"I will talk to him about it. Make sure he understands to be very careful." Raven's look of alarm stopped his reassurances.

"Good Lord, Bran, no! She would never forgive me if it changed their relationship. I only worry, but I love them both, and I'm willing to let them figure their own lives out. I refuse to interfere unless... I must."

"I won't say anything then. I know Dad isn't complaining. Since becoming close to River, Patrick seems to have found a focus and purposeful intention in business. He has been a great asset to both of us in meetings and charitable events that he would typically hide from until the coast was clear. Okay, so we're good where River is concerned. Any sisterly concerns with Rowan?"

"No. Not really. Rowan has always kept her cards close. She's seemed, I don't know, unsettled lately."

"You're aware. That's probably all that's needed at this point. And have you considered that a lot of things have changed for you three in a short period? Not the least of which is her big sister in a relationship."

"That's probably it." She leaned over and kissed him. "I love you. I'm going to chill out. I'm not their mother, and I don't want to be. Thanks for letting me talk things through."

Raven pulled out her tablet to pull up some of the preliminary flower bed designs.

While Raven was distracted, Bran asked, "What do you think of hiring a full-time housekeeper who also... umm... cooks." Raven's instant inhale of outrage was priceless. If only he'd videoed it for blackmail with the family.

"You... you... asshole," she sputtered. "I can certainly learn how to do... something in... there."

"The kitchen?"

"That's what I said."

Realizing he needed to tone down his smile, he asked, "But baby, do you dream of cooking? If it isn't a passion, I can assure you I don't give a flying fuck if you never cook. I can't cook. Do you still love me?"

"I do. I... God, you're right. I despise cooking. Hate. It." Raven fist-pumped the air enthusiastically. "I'm being ridiculous. Start taking applications today!"

Bran took Raven's hand in his own once the laughter died down. "When will you be ready to move in with me? Full time. Not just weekends."

Raven let the silence fall between them. Bran's heart went from a normal thump to pounding.

"How about next week?"

Bran smiled at Raven's impish grin. "Now, who's the shithead? I'll expect you to hold to that."

"Byrnes keep their word... but... that housekeeper/cook position isn't going to fill itself. Perhaps while I put on my teeny, tiny, red bikini, you start penning that Help Wanted Ad."

As Raven pushed up from the table to leave, Bran slapped her ass and laughed at her squeal. "Consider it done." Grinning over her shoulder, she winked before disappearing inside.

Bran smiled as Raven walked away. God, he was a lucky man.

THANKS TO RIVER AND PATRICK, the afternoon had been full of sun, laughter, drinks, and food tasting. Bran hoped at dinner tonight he'd be able to corner River or Rowan and tell one or both of them that he had a ring. The ring.

He'd planned on putting it in the safe when he got home last night, but Raven had derailed those plans... in the best of ways. This morning while Raven was changing, though, and only after he'd called his father's longtime office manager about getting a housekeeper/cook asap, he placed the ring in the safe.

Her sisters would be the only two people who would know, without a doubt, what Raven would consider an epic proposal.

Raven was upstairs at his dad's with her sisters, showering and getting dressed. He and the other men were on the deck having a drink. Dad had hired a chef for dinner, so no one had to lift a finger tonight. Pat was probably put out.

"I saw Jo on her phone before she went to her room earlier. The call seemed intense. Is she still working seven days a week?" Bran only asked because he cared about James' sister and wanted to make sure everything was good.

Bran understood what a successful business deal felt like. It was a rush. A high that, before Raven, he didn't believe could be achieved outside a boardroom. He knew now that a business deal didn't come close to the satisfaction of his relationship with Raven.

"Yes, damn her. We have a client who will not allow us to do our job without checking and rechecking every decision we make five times at least. I told her to stop responding." Taking a drink of his Absolut, soda, and lime, James shook his head in aggravation. "No one should be expected to work all fucking weekend. Jesus."

Dad agreed. "She'll burn out if she isn't careful. I learned that working seven days a week while trying to raise two boys. It doesn't work."

"Jo's smart. She'll figure a balance that works for her."

"I'm sure you're right, Pat, but I feel like my sister is driven by something dark. I've tried to... you know... get her to talk to me about it. She didn't speak to me for two weeks after I asked her to open up." James shrugged. His disquiet was unsettling.

He loved his sister, and it must hurt him when he felt he couldn't help her.

"Damn, James. Sisters are a lot different than brothers. We just punch the shit out of each other. At least I punched Pat," Bran laughed, trying to lighten James' mood.

"Fuck you, Bran. You don't punch anything anymore unless it's your dick punching your zipper whenever Raven walks by."

Bran felt his ears get hot. Patrick was such a dick— but James, and even his dad, were laughing— and... it was fucking true.

Laughing, Bran took a long drink of Raven's favorite, Bushmills Black Bush, and flipped his brother off over the crystal rim.

"Every year, boys. Every damn year, I hope for a modicum of maturity from you both, but this is the shit I get."

"Speak only of Patrick's immaturity, Dad." Bran dodged a shove from his brother and laughing, changed the subject. "I haven't had a chance to tell you guys yet, but I met with the jewelry designer in OKC. He nailed my vision. The ring is perfect. I put it in the safe."

He felt joy and satisfaction at his family's well wishes, handshakes, and back slaps. Bran was nervous about bringing up the news in front of James, but he needn't have worried. His oldest friend was genuinely happy for him.

"When will you propose, brother?"

"I'm not sure. Soon. I hope to get a word with Raven's sisters at some point. Their Nan knows I'm going to propose, and she approves."

"No matter when you propose, here is *my* proposal." Patrick cleared his throat as if he was giving a wedding reception speech. "River and I will be in charge of all the food. *All* of it. Rowan and Dad will be in charge of the venue. Jo, the honeymoon."

Bran noticed his father's slight flinch at his brother's words.

What was up with him? He needed to talk to him privately before too much more time passed and see if there was a possibility that he didn't approve of the union.

It wouldn't change Bran's mind, but he wanted his father's approval. His dad was one of the best men he knew. His opinion mattered. A lot.

"You are so extra, Pat. You realize she has to say yes first, and then, if she does, all of the things you just listed would be up to her, not you, dumbass."

Patrick shrugged, not concerned at all. He was sure Patrick believed he would ultimately have his way. Knowing Raven, he would.

He heard multiple voices laughing and talking moments before Raven, River, Rowan, and Jo made their way to the deck to sit at the long table with the men.

"Hey, babe."

Raven bent down before sitting. Whispering, I love you, kissing his lips before finding her seat.

Bran reached over and pulled several thick strands of her hair through his fingers. It was beautiful. It always seemed to be shifting and moving around her lithe body. She smiled softly at him. Probably knowing that he was thinking sappy thoughts about her. He loved her smile of approval when she saw the open bottle of Bushmills. There was no hesitation as she grabbed it and poured her own drink.

Bran felt like poking her. Knowing she would blush.

"Raven committed to moving in next week. Permanently."

The blush stained her pale skin on cue. She gasped and looked at her sisters. Whoops, he assumed she'd already told them. Shit.

Side eyeing Bran, and not in a good way, Raven explained to her sisters. River and Rowan currently looked like crappies out of water, gills working overtime.

"I was going to speak to both of you tonight, but... someone," Raven raised her eyebrows in Bran's direction, "couldn't wait. I'll start packing as soon as we get back to Eufaula tomorrow. I will commute daily unless I'm meeting a client out of town, I promise."

"Tweedle Dickhead already told me to expect it," River laughed, poking her thumb in Patrick's direction.

"Hey now, Riv!" Patrick spluttered. "Knowledge is power." Pat sniffed with mock offense.

"You might consider saving your insight for the bimbos you date," James laughed as he air quoted 'date.'

Bran saw River stiffen. Barely, and if he hadn't been watching her, he'd have missed it completely. She laughed with everyone else. Raven didn't miss her sister's reaction. Her left hand that lay on his thigh tightened.

Damn. Maybe he should talk to Patrick after all.

Dad's housekeeper, Sara, poked her head out, smiling at everyone. "Mr. O'Faolain, the chef asked me to let you know dinner would be served at your convenience." The older woman winked at his dad. "Which means, young man, get your ass up and to the dining room. I'm off to home. Behave." With that, she sauntered away, enjoying her status as a woman too old and beloved to care if her words insulted someone. Sara was awesome.

Dad pushed his chair out and announced it was time to eat. Everyone began filing through the patio doors.

Bran scooted his chair back and slid out, waiting for Raven. She looked stunning this evening in a sky-blue wrap dress with butterflies at the hem. She was smiling up at him as she stood. He couldn't wait to untie that perfect bow at her waist.

Leaning into him, Raven placed her hands on his chest, stretching just a bit to place a kiss on his lips. She should wear heels more often— much easier to get to her mouth. Her lips started to leave his, so he placed his hands on her hips to keep her still— pull her closer. He deepened the kiss, dragging one of his hands up her body to cup the side of her head, giving him purchase.

He knew he was a man obsessed. He just didn't care.

Breaking the kiss briefly, they stood panting on the deck alone. "Shit, babe. Can we skip dinner?" Raven's tongue flicked her swollen bottom lip. Groaning, he took her mouth again, rougher, deeper. Bran wedged his hard length against her stomach, her hand coming between them to stroke him through his slacks.

This time Raven broke the kiss. "Let's sneak around the side of the house to your car."

Bran knew their escape plans were ruined when his brother's irritating voice bellowed outside at them.

"For fuck's sake, bro. Stop humping Raven. I'm fucking starved, and Dad won't let them bring in the food until we're all seated."

"I will kill him one of these days," he mumbled against her lips.

Laughing, Raven whispered, "No, you won't."

Her shoulders shaking with mirth, she kissed his mouth briefly— way too brief.

"Tonight, Bran."

Following Raven inside, Bran adjusted his hard-on into a less painful position and untucked his button-up, draping the bottom half of the shirt over his dick.

When he entered the dining room, everyone was seated. His brother got to Raven first and pushed her chair in. Her smile was wide as she met his eyes.

"Jesus, Bran. I thought we were supposed to dress for dinner. I must say, I'm not loving the untucked, wrinkled look."

He saw his dad duck his head to hide a smile. James laughed

straight at him. The girls all blushed.

"Dad, honestly, you should have stopped having children after me." As he walked behind Raven's chair to kiss her cheek before taking his own seat, he childishly flicked the back of his brother's head. His howl of pain was satisfying. As was their father telling Patrick to sit back in his chair when he was about to jump up to go after Bran.

"Patrick. Sit. You deserved that and more, I'm sure."

His father sat at the head of the table. Patrick to his left, River across from him. Bran was next to River and across from Raven. Jo was on Raven's left, Rowan on his right, with James taking the end opposite Dad. Any more people, they'd have to add in the extra table leaves.

THE FOOD WAS DELICIOUS. The chef had prepared several starters. Salad, crab cakes, chilled oysters and shrimp, and whole loaves of sourdough bread were placed up and down the table. The chef brought those out personally to tell them he used his four-year-old starter to make them.

The Byrnes all oohed and aahed— they said that they wondered at the bread's exceptional flavor and that it rivaled their own Nan's, who'd always kept a starter as her mother had. The chef's cheeks turned pink before he went back to the kitchen.

Bran could understand how overwhelming it was to have the Byrne's undivided attention. He could barely handle one.

Jo leaned over to ask Rowan what 'his own starter' was about. Bran listened to the explanation. Supposedly, it was an honor that the chef used his private starter for their bread tonight. That one had to cultivate the starter, caring for it like a child. For years. If a person ever gifted another baker with some of that well-tended starter, especially the older batches, it was considered a gift without measure.

Bran noticed the men practically ate a whole loaf to themselves while the women nibbled slowly on a small slice. If Bran were a woman, he'd still eat a whole damn loaf and buy a bigger dress if he had to.

Bran heard his phone vibrate a few times. Probably a text or email notification. He flicked the side toggle to silence it until dinner was over. The main courses were coming out, and work could wait.

RAVEN WAS ENJOYING THE EVENING. The food was amazing—the company was better. There always seemed to be laughter with this crew. She loved them all, truly. She was glad Patrick had interrupted her and Bran earlier, or she would have missed out. Smiling into her crystal tumbler of Bushmills, she admitted, she probably would have enjoyed that version of the evening too.

Bran noticed her smile and mouthed, "Tonight."

Raven noticed Patrick starting to open his mouth, but Hugh placed a hand on his younger son's arm. She also saw Hugh and Patrick share a smile and a laugh. They all enjoyed the game of picking on one another. Bran enjoyed it, too, even though he grumbled. She and her siblings were the same.

Raven watched as Patrick's attention was snagged on her youngest sister. Sitting back to see what was behind Bran's brother's wicked smile. Rowan noticed she held Pat's attention and looked at him curiously. Patrick smiled at Rowan, and she smiled back.

"Rowan, that's a beautiful yellow dress you're wearing tonight."

Patrick's eyes were sparkling way too much to *not* be up to something.

Rowan smoothed her hand lightly down the front. "Oh, thanks Pat. It's one of my favorites."

"Aah, that's right." Acting as though a thought just came to him. "You were wearing it when we first met."

Dawning horror started to turn her sister's cheeks pink. River was already hiding her laugh behind her linen napkin.

"I only wondered what you are wearing under—"

Patrick's hijinks were cut short by Hugh tipping his son's chair back. Patrick had to stop speaking to save himself from falling to the floor.

"Patrick!" Jo yelled. "Why in the hell are you asking Row something like that? You are such a shit!"

Most of the table couldn't cover up their laughter. Patrick's comment may have been the tinder, but Jo's scolding was the lighter. Everyone burst out laughing. Even Hugh glanced at Rowan and chuckled. She smiled back at the older O'Faolain.

Finding her gumption, Rowan shook her finger at Patrick across the table. "You tell *that* story, at *this* dinner table, and I can promise Patrick O'Faolain, you will wake up missing some of your favorite body parts."

They all roared then, even Pat, who, Raven was sure, never intended on it in the first place. She leaned over to Jo and told her that they would tell her about it after dinner.

James leaned into his sister's side and said, "And then Jo, once you get the details, you can come tell me."

"Fat chance, James. Chicks before dicks."

Across the table from Raven, Bran was laughing so hard he was wiping tears from his eyes.

"I am stuffed. What does everyone think of heading to Hugh's study for drinks, more drinks, and whatever dessert that amazing chef has prepared?"

A chorus of agreements answered.

∾

THIS WOULD BE a hard dinner to top, Bran thought as he made his way around the table to help Raven from her seat so he could walk with her to the study. Patrick was already helping River, James was helping his sister, the two bickering and laughing. He was about to walk back to Rowan, whom he should have helped before leaving her side, but she was already getting to her feet.

Oh, and there was Dad, pulling her chair the rest of the way out. Of course, when she smiled at him, and Bran could tell she was about to thank the old man, he abruptly walked off— his manners needed more than polish, Bran thought with a mental shake of his head.

He could tell his dad had hurt Rowan's feelings with his indifference. He had to speak with him before he did permanent damage to a relationship with a woman that would hopefully be part of his family once Bran and Raven were married.

Dismissing the family drama, Bran leaned down to Raven, kissing her cheek. "I enjoyed tonight. Our families are great together."

"Agreed. To both." She started giggling as they walked. "I swear I almost peed my pants when Pat brought up the dress. Oh God! I thought Row was going to jump across the table and stab your brother with a table knife."

Chuckling, Bran agreed. In the study, everybody was pouring drinks and finding spots to lounge. James and Patrick were getting a couple decks of playing cards out.

"Do you play any card games, babe? Looks like they're setting up tables," he nodded in their direction.

"My sisters and I are masters of Old Maid and Slapjack." River and Rowan heard what she said and laughed.

"Slap what, now?"

"Don't tell me you've never played? We Byrnes have slap-jack skills." This from River.

Rowan even boasted, "It's true. We are masters."

"Dad, have you ever played the game? I know Pat and I haven't."

"No, I'm looking it up now to see if they're pulling our legs."

"We would never," River gasped, fluttering her eyes.

"It's a real game. But... the American version doesn't seem to be much of a game."

"Oh no, Hugh," Rowan laughed. "Concentration and speed are key. The deck, or multiple decks of cards, are placed face down in the middle of the table. One person flips over one card at a time, face up— preferably a non-player, but we always had to play with one of us girls flipping, and Raven always cheated." Rowan raised her brows in a 'what can you do' look.

"I never cheated! That's bullshit, Row! You and River always ganged up on me."

Raven looked at Bran. "Don't you dare believe her, babe."

Laughing, he pulled her close to his side. "I'm not saying I believe her, but I will keep my eyes on you."

"Okay, let me finish the rules. The dealer flips the card over, ensuring no one sees it before it's flat on the table. If a Jack is laid down, the first person's hand to make contact, or slap the Jack, takes it and whatever cards are beneath. The winner is the person with the biggest stack of cards when the deck is gone. Easy, but requiring skill. Like I said." She huffed in Dad's direction.

"Oh," Raven added. "Be warned that injuries can happen. Sometimes someone doesn't slow their slap in time, and the winner's hand takes a beating." She pointedly looked at River.

"It was an accident, Rave. Jesus. Let it go, it's been ten years!"

"This sounds like just the game for Bran and me. I've always had better hand-eye coordination," Pat said, grinning.

"You only are setting yourself up for embarrassment." Turning to Raven, he asked if she would mind getting their drinks. "I got a few texts and emails during dinner. It might be something I need to deal with."

"Sure, babe. Look at your messages." Looking over her shoulder at James and Patrick, she said, "They'll be a few minutes more setting up the table and cards."

"I hope it's a sturdy table."

RAVEN GRINNED as she moved toward the bar where Hugh was getting more glasses and bottles of water.

"Ready to get your ass kicked, Mr. O'Faolain?"

"No, which is why I will most likely be the Dealer for this evening's entertainment."

Hugh glanced over Raven's shoulder and frowned. Raven twisted at the waist to see what had caught his attention.

Bran stood by one of the couches, staring at his phone screen. He was white as a ghost. She and Hugh moved toward him at the same time.

The banter ceased. No one moved. It couldn't be good news.

"Bran." No response. "Bran, what is it? Has something happened?

He raised his head— and looked at Raven with such anguish, such anger... disgust— her steps faltered. What in the world was going on?

"Has something happened?"

Bran choked on a harsh laugh. "You could say that. I've been played."

"What are you talking about? You're scaring Raven and making everyone else here uncomfortable," Hugh chided.

"I would ask Raven to explain, but she's way too good of a liar. I doubt she'd even know how to tell the truth."

Raven's face was flaming hot. She was scared, not for her safety, but the absolute dizzying disorientation swamping her body. She was shaking.

"Raven's been fucking another man, or more than one. Who knows."

Gasping, "That is a lie, Bran. A fucking lie. I have never cheated. Who... who has... has told you such things?"

"Oh, they didn't tell me. They did one better. They sent photos." Looking at his screen again, his countenance stiffened further.

Raven felt her sisters move on either side of her, someone at her back. Jo, maybe.

"You can't possibly believe that of me, Bran." Raven took deep gulping breaths. "I love you. You *know* I do. Please, show me the pictures, let me... I don't know. But Bran... I've only been... damn it, Bran... you know very well I didn't sleep around before us... I—"

She and her sisters were all shaking now. Bran advanced two more steps toward her.

"I know nothing but what these pictures tell me. Everything before— that was the lie. And you know what, maybe you've been planning this since before Ireland. Maybe you were a virgin, or maybe you faked that like you faked loving me."

Raven's head fell back as if he'd slapped her. She could barely see through the tears. Nothing could be worse than this— this horrible moment.

But... it could, actually, get worse. He wasn't finished destroying her.

"Or maybe you decided you liked sex so much you couldn't

get enough of it. And in Wolves? Jesus, Raven! My family's own fucking place? And here I've always thought my mother was the worst example of a woman."

Clearly, he thought Raven was worse than a cold-hearted bitch with no love for her own children.

Raven watched the other men finally start to move. It was as though the vitriol Bran had been coating her with had briefly frozen the other inhabitants in the room.

Hugh walked between his son and Raven. "I'm sorry for this. For whatever the fuck *this* is." He motioned behind her. "Won't you sit and have some water?"

Raven could only stare over Hugh's shoulder at the man she had believed, mere minutes ago, was her forever. This night... she could not have conjured the atrocity of this night... no... this was a level of hurt like she'd experienced only once before in her life, and still, her parents hadn't wanted to destroy her with grief. No... they hadn't meant to hurt her... they hadn't meant to leave her.

Bran's words were intentional. Whatever those pictures were, they were not her, but Bran's words were as final as her parents' deaths had been.

His words were meant to drive her from this room, this house, his side, his life— a different brand of death.

Still grasping her hand tightly, River took one partial step toward Bran. "I will never forgive you."

"River." Patrick's pained voice. He went to reach out a hand, but her sister shook her head. No.

"Please, River." Raven wasn't sure what she was asking. Perhaps she didn't want Bran to speak to either of her sisters as he had her. It was time to leave.

BRAN WATCHED as horror stretched Raven's splotchy, red face. Was she acting? Was it guilt? Could she *be* innocent? He was sick and sickened that he'd confronted her in front of her family and his.

River and Rowan were at Raven's side, having moved there in support soon after he began speaking, but Raven never so much as glanced their way. She never stopped staring at Bran, anguish washing her features. Is she just upset that she was caught?

"You can't possibly believe that of me, Bran." Her voice was so soft, so pain-filled, that Bran almost folded. He flicked his eyes to his phone screen, still brightly lit, a picture of Raven clearly enjoying the attentions of another man— in Bran's own fucking pub— he clenched his jaw tight and forced himself to look back at the woman who had betrayed him.

Patrick and his father looked at him as if he'd lost his mind. He had. From the moment he'd opened the anonymous text and flipped through several pictures of his supposed girlfriend. Undressing in a few. Leaning her back against Wolves bar, her arms stretched toward a man walking into them. His life shattered.

Nothing made sense.

He looked to where James was standing near the door. He was frozen. His face was white. He looked almost worse than Bran felt. He briefly met Bran's eyes, some emotion curling through his best friend that he couldn't understand. That he, frankly, didn't have the emotional stamina to attempt to understand.

The sisters had wrapped their arms around Raven, Jo at her back clutching her shoulders. Female solidarity. He didn't blame them for lending their support, though he desperately wished some for himself. They couldn't fathom Raven behaving that way. He couldn't fucking imagine it either.

"Please." He heard Raven whisper. "Take me home."

"Yes," River agreed.

"Of course," Rowan whispered.

Jo kindly added, "I will pack everyone's things myself and follow you in my car as soon as possible."

When the sisters started to lead their sister from the room, River and Rowan looked at one another. Rowan briefly touched her fingers to Raven's cheek. River nodded and continued with Raven, who looked about to faint— tears making silent, salty tracks down her cheeks. Rowan waited for them to walk by James and out the door before turning her attention to him and his family.

"You will regret what you said this night. The horrible, horrible things." Rowan was furious and shaking from it. "What you've done is unforgivable. My sister could never conceive of such a betrayal, let alone perform the act." At this, his father started to move toward Raven's youngest sister. Rowan whipped her head in his direction and put her hand up to halt his progress. "No. No, Hugh. It is over between our families."

Her mask of fury cracked as her breath caught, and she hiccupped on a cry. "I wish we'd never met any of you. You have destroyed my beloved sister. What our parent's deaths cracked in our hearts... you may very well be the final blow." Finished, she whirled back toward the door, James moving well to the side, and fled. A moment later, they heard the front door slam. Its reverberations ran through the room like aftershocks from an earthquake.

No one spoke, let alone moved for a full minute.

"You can fuck off, Bran. I don't care if you're one of my brother's best friends." Jo swallowed before forcing out her final parting shot. "The things you said to the woman you supposedly love... I don't know who you are right now. Maybe, I never did."

James tried to speak to his sister before she left. She wasn't having it. Bran's legs finally gave out, and he fell back onto one of his dad's couches. He placed his hand over his face and felt the hot burn of tears trying to escape.

"Why would you say those things, son?" Bran felt his dad sit down next to him. When he placed a hand on Bran's back in sympathy, he was done. He couldn't speak, so he handed his phone over. There was silence as the other three men passed it around.

"Fuck that. No way, Bran. No. *Way*." Patrick collapsed on his other side, letting his head fall against one of the couch's oversized pillows.

The hand at his back, his father's, fisted and became rigid.

"I'm sorry, Bran. I would like to think this is a misunderstanding, but..." he waved to Bran's phone, "how can that be?"

Pulling himself together, he sat up and looked at the men in the room. James was sitting silently in one of the chairs by the bar, having finally moved from the doorway.

"I agree, Dad. There was no choice but to break things off."

Bran let his head fall back, staring at the black beams supporting the vaulted ceiling. Sitting back up, he finished. "But I should have never said the things I did to Raven, and certainly not in front of everyone. Some of the things I said..." Groaning, he rubbed his hands briskly over his face. "I didn't mean them, damn it. She hurt me, and I wanted to hurt her back. When things cool..."

Why bother to finish that sentence. Things would never cool. Not for him.

His dad walked over to the bar and started getting out glasses and pulling a bottle of Elijah Craig Barrel Proof from the shelf. Bran could feel himself break into smaller and smaller pieces. He doubted the strong American whiskey his dad was pouring could fix what had happened tonight, though hopefully, it would knock him out.

"I'm getting drinks. We are all going to bed. James, you will not leave."

James raised his eyebrows at the command. "Okay."

Not done giving orders, he looked at his two sons sitting side by side and commanded, "Pat, you'll sleep in your brother's room tonight."

"What the fuck, Dad? I'm not fucking five." If Bran could have smiled, he would have at Patrick's outrage.

"No way... you can't make me."

"Mature." Dad took a deep breath. "We need to sleep. Cooler heads may prevail in the light of a new day. Patrick, your brother is upset. He may wish to talk, or... I don't know, find comfort in not being fucking alone." Probably like he'd felt alone after his wife had destroyed his life.

"I have something I need to do, though," Patrick finished lamely.

"You are not calling or texting River. Give the girls a moment. Now," he stopped to take a drink of his EC, "Jesus, that's strong. I've told you three what I expect, and I expect to be obeyed. Last time I checked, this is still my house, and you are still my children. And as you are a guest, James, you'll mind me in this too."

He left without another word. Bran tilted his phone up and swiped. The screen unlocked. Once more, the photo of Raven embracing another man tore him apart. He couldn't look at it one more time.

Standing, he pocketed his phone and went to the bar where drinks were poured and waiting. If the jet fuel fumes wafting around the glasses weren't clue enough, he read the label. 132.6 proof. Perfect. James and Patrick met him at the bar. Each man took their glasses and threw back the shot in one eye-watering go. In silent accord, they walked up the stairs and found their beds.

19

The car ride home to Eufaula was silent except for the occasional sniffle and hiccup. She'd felt this type of deep-tissue pain once before. Emotional gauntlets hurt.

And damn it, she needed to pull herself together, but Dermot Kennedy's *An Evening I Will Not Forget* started playing. Jesus, the absolute irony, and her hot, swollen eyes began to burn again. Tonight was a blow. A grenade. But it wasn't just her she needed to consider.

She had sisters. Where one went, the others would follow. Even if she asked them to let her go for a while— just a moment to shatter and scream— they would follow.

There was no dissuading them. Raven should know, if the situation were reversed, she would never let them go. So... she needed to plan. *They* needed to plan. To prepare for the inevitable fallout.

Drying her eyes on what looked like a dirty pair of gym shorts— whatever— she was past any level of eww. One thing did need to be cleared up first.

"River. Rowan. You do... believe me?" Good Lord, she choked on the last words. Tears were endless.

"Don't be an idiot."

"Of course, Raven. We'll forgive you for asking. This once."

Rowan looked at her briefly, the dash lights illuminating her own tear-streaked face. Raven wasn't the only Byrne hurting.

"Thank you, guys. I could never get through this without you both. I've... I'm trying to put aside what Bran... what he believes, what he said, I guess, and think of tomorrow and the day after. We need a plan. Triskelion is something we have control over. My relationship is not. I want to set what happened aside. For now. Until I can make sense of it."

"Agreed." River's voice was also thick with tears. "I'm one step ahead— as usual." Her attempt at levity warmed Raven.

"We'll be home in fifteen minutes, so I'm going to state all the obvious shit we three are aware of— there is a lot, so just sit back and take it in. Once we're home, however, we shower, separately, as we aren't filming a weird ass video for *Extreme Sisters* — gross— then we pick a room, grab a bottle of Row's Glen 25, and watch a movie until we sleep. Jo shouldn't be but an hour behind us. Tomorrow, I have a whole other list of things to do with the direction I think we should take going forward."

"You're an elite strategist." Row backward knuckle bumped River.

Raven was silently crying again. Damn it. Their support was so very, very needed.

"Sounds like just the thing, River." Raven's voice was shaky, and she knew she hadn't done well at hiding her continued distress. River cleared her throat. She hated making either of them sad.

"Here's where Triskelion currently stands— We finished clients pre-O'Faolains two weeks ago. We chose not to take on new clients until the first Wolves was all but complete, which is about two to two and half months away, I believe. We all agreed that the potential windfall of clients that would want us once

Wolves is regaled in the papers had the potential to skyrocket TTD. We are that good, so the gamble wasn't really a gamble, not even a calculated risk, in my opinion. A sure thing. Moving on," River continued.

Raven had turned to watch River swipe through her phone a few times before she paused, almost hesitant.

"What is it?" Raven asked.

River took a deep breath. "Okay, fuck waiting until the morning. I know what tomorrow looks like, and the day after, and the day after that fucking day. We've got this nasty situation by the balls. It will not destroy us. Any of us."

River looked straight at Raven. She swallowed back more tears. "Agreed."

Once River broke down what their life was going to look like, not twenty-five years in the future, but day by day, week by week, and month by month. It gave her a semblance of peace.

Rowan, ever stoic Rowan, surprised Raven the most.

"A mistake was made tonight. A big one, and I believe it will eventually come to light. But know this sister mine, our parents are proud of us, Nan is proud of us, and I'm sure as fuck proud of us. Whatever we put our minds to will not only work but flourish. I'm ready for a new adventure."

River whooped it up, and Raven even managed to laugh through her tears.

This hadn't been the plan a few hours ago, but Rowan and River were right. No one, and nothing would break them.

20

"You're sure this is what you want to do?"

Jo had spent the night with them, and all agreed that nothing of a serious nature would be discussed until this morning. River did make sure Jo understood that she and Rowan weren't simply backing up Raven because they were sisters. Raven had done none of the things Bran had accused her of.

"I haven't known you three for long, but I sure as fuck know that the load of bullshit someone fed Bran is just that. I had zero doubts last night and none today."

Raven needed to hear Jo say that. Having someone besides a family member believe her was relieving.

"We aren't rash when it comes to business, Jo. You'll have to trust that we wouldn't make this drastic change if we weren't *mostly* sure of success," Rowan explained.

"It's a big change, I agree," Raven admitted. "River's already made a gazillion spreadsheets. Our chance of success is high."

"So, would you mind breaking it down for me in a bit more detail. I support you guys, but I also don't want to walk out of here worrying."

"River, this is your brainchild." Raven nodded to her sister to take the floor.

"I wish I'd had time to put a PowerPoint together, but I'll muddle through. Oh, before I get into the good stuff, Raven, did you know you've been using my toiletry bag? You know I hate you using my makeup brushes."

"They must have gotten swapped when Jo packed. I've had that same one for weeks. I checked the initials." Mom had made the girls matching bags in her favorite French toile pattern. They had several pockets and special inside bags. The only difference is the initials. *RSB. RAB. RCB.* Raven Sorrel Byrne. River Aster Byrne. Rowan Clary Byrne. Mom and Dad wanted their children's names to be unique and meaningful. The first names honor the family's Native American heritage, and the middle names were all flowers native to Ireland. Mom's name was Lily. Always connected.

"The stitching is worn. No matter, I just noticed a couple things I don't usually use. Maybe we accidentally swapped them when we used the same bathroom to change. I put it in your bathroom before I came down and grabbed mine."

"Thanks. We really should get different colored bags, but I can't bear not to use the ones Mom made. Did you take my birth control out of your bag before you made the switch?" That's all Raven needed, to screw her periods up and deal with hormone imbalance for days.

River gave her a weird look, a slight thinking frown. "I'll make sure after the meeting."

Raven smiled. Her face was still swollen from crying and the extreme stress of the night before. She felt as though she were wearing her body, but not... *her* anymore. Time. She just needed time. And distance.

"Okay, so I'm getting ready to puke a plan all over your lap. Try to hold comments, questions, or suggestions until the end."

Jo nodded, very used to Riverisms.

"First, because we're damn good designers, we already have detailed notes of the bulk of what we committed to for the Wolves project. What has been ordered and what needs to be ordered. The vendors we have already vetted and approved included.

If we work from the moment we're done with this meeting, possibly into tomorrow morning, as some of us are psycho about detail..." She glanced at Rowan. Her peaceful expression remained unfazed. "We'll have our part of the promised design work complete.

"We realize you may have to hire another firm to finish the project, and though we hate the headache this may cause you and James, we are more than confident with what we're providing, which will include renderings, etc., making hiring anyone else, hopefully, redundant.

We are also signing a document that makes it clear, very clear, that we will accept no payment for this job. Not for hours of research, shopping vendors, work completed, or the files and notes we will turn over to you by tomorrow."

Jo tried to interrupt at this point. They knew she would balk.

River held her hand up to stop any interruptions. "No payment is an absolute, nonnegotiable, ironclad footnote to this plan, Jo. We will not accept one— single— cent from the O'Faolains. I don't know how Hugh or Pat feel, but we know how Bran feels."

River jerked her head to Raven when she heard a small gasp. "I'm sorry. I should have worded that more kindly." She bit her lip in remorse.

"Truth is never wrong between us. Please continue."

"So. No money. I will hire a local real estate agent to take photos and help sell this building. There's always been a ton of interest in it. It won't be hard, and I imagine we will more than double what we paid. Hire a packing company, shut our phones down, new numbers and emails— you will, of course, get all of this from us."

River continued the Noah's Ark of To-Do Lists until everyone seemed to melt under the avalanche of minutiae.

"Have you even spoken to your grandmother yet?"

Rowan volunteered to tap in for River. "We are today. She has always wanted to visit Morcote. It is supposed to be one of the most picturesque villages in Switzerland, and the weather this time of year is gorgeous. Raven is supposed to find a house to rent for two months. It will be the vacation of a lifetime for Nan, and she deserves it. And... we'll love it too, and... I'm sorry, Rave, but you need to be surrounded by as much love as we can get for you."

Oh, God. How long before the pain would ease? Tears squeezed from the raw corners of her eyes. She could only nod in agreement. The other women were dabbing eyes and attempting to pull the meeting back to order.

River managed first. "It seems like an unclimbable mountain of moving parts, but we only have to tick one item off at a time and eventually we'll come to the end."

"After Switzerland?"

"Once the movers pack our house up, we'll have it freighted to Dublin and stored in a facility until we're ready for it— a facility that is on the list of things to do." Even River sighed at the tasks ahead.

"I love you guys, and I know you all feel the same, so you won't be offended when I ask you this. Can you afford this move to another country *and* a two-month stay in Switzerland?"

"Valid concerns," Rowan assured her. "Financially, we are frugal. The money we received from our... parents, we invested and make a very nice yearly allowance from that alone. We did use some of it initially to pay off college and to buy this building, but I guess what I'm trying to say is that we *know* we cannot be excessive, so we won't be.

"Our Vrbo, or however that works out in Morcote, will be modest. We will cook and clean ourselves. We will not purchase or lease a new space for Triskelion until this place is sold. If we must, we'll live with Nan and work in Boyle until we have enough money."

"I would be honored to give you guys money or... a loan," she quickly tacked on at seeing their horrified faces.

Raven spoke, though her voice was scratchy. "We love you for offering, but Jo, we *will* succeed even if it takes longer than River's projections." They all smiled at that.

"Okay, so I have a nonmonetary gift for you three. I'm sure you'll appreciate that my gift is nonnegotiable."

"Oh, yes, please, we love prezzies!" River laughed, making grabby hands at Jo.

"Your To-Do List is... scary. So, and again, this is nonnegotiable. We will divide and conquer that bitch. I know an excellent moving service— they do it ALL— I will find a reputable storage facility in Dublin and a moving company to pick up your belongings and take them there.

"Also, one of my best friends from college lives in Dublin, and, drumroll, she's a badass real estate agent. If there is a space perfect for Triskelion that doesn't break the bank, she'll know already or find it. Lastly, I live to plan vacations that I never take. I will find you and your Nan the perfect, *affordable* rental. You will let me do this for you. Please let me." Jo's voice cracked at the end, and tears coursed down her cheeks.

The Byrnes were immediately on the floor surrounding their friend. Oh God, Raven hated leaving her in Oklahoma. One of many things hurting her heart.

"Ignore me, damn it. I told myself to stay strong."

"We're all breaking down around her, Jo. You never need to hide anything from us. We wish you wouldn't." Rowan tucked a piece of Jo's golden, blonde hair behind her ear.

"I really hate you guys are moving. I'll miss you horribly."

"First and most importantly, we accept your gift. Mom and Dad didn't raise fools." River smiled, squeezing Jo's hand. "Second, you *used* to plan vacations you never took. That ends here. We know you must see Wolves through 'til its opening, but after that, you will visit us in Ireland. In fact, you might want to consider spending half your time there and half here. And don't act like your family doesn't travel the world for jobs, and you just admitted one of your best friends lives in Dublin."

Jo sat up at this. The idea apparently held some appeal. Raven held her breath.

"You know what. You're right. I can do whatever the hell I want, and I want to live where my best friends live. At least part of the time. You guys just made my future seem not only bearable but brighter. I suddenly feel hopeful about all this. I hope you guys feel peace about it all too."

First, River squealed, then Rowan laughed, clapping her hands, Jo was beaming, and Raven... smiled and put her arms around Jo and her sisters in a group hug... too bad her body was so numb she couldn't feel it.

CALLING Nan was as hard and cathartic as Raven knew it would be. After Jo left with hugs and kisses and her own big To-Do List, the three girls sat around Rowan's desk and called their grandma.

"Well, this is a nice surprise. I get all three of my girls at once." They could hear the smile in her voice. Raven looked at River. She was to go first.

"We're all calling together because we have a surprise for you. And we really hope you like it because we can't take it back." River grinned at her sisters. The news about Raven's personal life wouldn't overshadow how excited they were for their grandma.

"A surprise? Oh, my, girls. You didn't have to do that."

She meant every word, but they all smiled wider because they could hear her interest.

"You better ask Mr. Dunn if he can take care of your house this summer."

"Whyever would I do that? What is going on?"

They decided to tell Nan that they'd already rented a place in Morcote, so she wouldn't back out. Jo said she'd have it figured out today. And as a going away present, nonnegotiable as well, she was having the O'Connor jet fly them. Nan would fly commercial since the flight was only a couple hours from Dublin. All three of them had literally cried at the gift. It would save them a lot of money— and be damned comfortable too.

"We decided to take a vacation since we just finished up a huge project, and we rented a place in Morcote, Switzerland, for Two Fucking Months! It'll be the most epic vacation, and we'll get to do it together. Nan, are you dying or what? Can you believe it?!"

"Language, River, but oh God, oh God, Oh God! You girls are teasing me, surely! Tell me you're teasing."

"We aren't joking, Nan." Rowan told her it was nonrefundable, so not to even think of saying no.

"I'm... speechless. Girls... this is... oh my," she repeated. "I have dreamed of going for years. And now, for two months. Oh my, oh my."

"So, is that a yes, Nan?"

"Of course! I'm so very blessed to have you three love me so much, but... girls, I don't understand about Triskelion. How will you be able to stay closed so long?"

Rowan took this part. "Well, Nan, that's the second part of the surprise. We made a big decision for ourselves, and before starting on the new venture, we decided it was the perfect time to vacay with our Nan."

Rowan grabbed Raven's hand and squeezed. Her sister smiled, encouraging Raven to embrace the plan just like they were trying to convince their grandma to do. It wasn't what she'd ever wanted for her or her sisters. However, there was nothing to do but move forward.

"We're moving to Ireland!" Rowan exclaimed. "We are selling our place here and packing up shop. While we're all enjoying the sights in Switzerland, movers will pack our home and business and ship it to Dublin.

"We should make a profit on our Eufaula property, which will give us a nice down payment for a place in Dublin. We have a very good friend helping us out with that. With a lot of it, actually. We are so excited, Nan. We'll give you all the details when we meet."

"Oh my," Nan uttered. "I never dared dream you girls would move so close. Never dreamed," she repeated.

Hearing Nan admit she'd been wanting them closer made Raven feel less terrible— less desperately terrible at least.

"We plan on arriving in Morcote two days before you arrive. Then we can get everything set up. River will send your flight details later today."

Rowan finally ran out of steam. Dreaded silence followed. It was a lot to take in, Raven admitted. She thought they did a good job at abbreviating.

River's eyes widened at the continued silence. "Nan? Are you there? Are you changing your mind about the trip?" Rowan shrugged. Raven was sweating.

"No, I'm more excited than I can say." Her words were cautious. "You aren't telling me something. Important. And why haven't you said a word, Raven? And how does Bran feel about you moving from Oklahoma? What's going on?"

Oh, God. They knew their chance of skipping over Raven and Bran was slim to none.

Clearing her throat in nervousness— back to the old habit— great. "I'm sorry, Nan. I should have started with that. We broke up last night." Raven cringed at the 'we.' It certainly was not mutual.

"I can't believe it, my sweet girl. What happened? This makes no sense. I just knew you two were meant for one another. Are you okay, sweetheart?"

She grabbed her sisters' hands for support and attempted to explain without many details. Bran's behavior would hurt Nan too.

"I thought so, as well. We just have too many things we disagree on. Too many differences in how we see the direction we want our lives to go."

"Is there a chance you might reconcile?" Raven could tell Nan was hopeful. She and Bran had been fast friends instantly.

Refusing to give her beloved grandma false hope, she answered honestly. Crushing them both. "No. No, there is no chance."

Rallying, Nan coughed delicately. "Okay then, Raven. I won't say I'm not sad about it, and I won't press you for what you are hiding. If and when you want to tell me what really happened, I will listen, and I will love you the same as I always have, and life will continue to move on. I will say, young lady, I can feel how much you're hurting now, but you are a Byrne, and you will come out a brighter star than you began."

All three girls were sniffling. Nan had a way about her, that was for sure.

"On to happier news," Nan chuckled, "I am already thinking of how much stuff I can get in my old suitcases and not be dinged for weight."

Aah, maybe there would eventually be light at the end of this dreary tunnel, Raven thought.

"The best surprise isn't the trip, you know."

They all gasped in surprise.

"My girls will be living in Ireland! Holy shite, your father would be over the moon."

All three girls laughed and, in unison, said, "Nan, language!"

21

Sam decided to enjoy the sunny morning and have coffee outside on the covered patio. What a gorgeous morning to look over surveillance footage. His work on the Byrne girl must have topped even Sam's high standards.

The night he sent the doctored photos to Bran O'Faolain from his burner phone, Sam's camera caught images of the girls entering their three-story walk-up not two hours later.

When Sam had gone to Eufaula, he'd been disappointed that they had such a reputable security system and that it was armed. Oh well, he couldn't always be so lucky. However, the small wireless camera he'd placed on the parking sign in front of Triskelion Territory Designs perfectly captured anyone walking by or entering the building.

That night, there were several photos of one of the Byrnes unlocking the front door— really, there was no telling those three women apart in black and white images at night— while another sister had her arms wrapped around, presumably, Raven.

Who needed TV drama? Fake bullshit. This, he thought, clicking through stills of James and Patrick, was real-life drama.

Sam sat up, staring more intently at his screen. These were photos from the hallway outside Bran's Tulsa hotel.

My, my, my. The spurned lover finally shows. Oh, yes. There he was again, leaving his rooms with a bag of sorts. Hard to tell in the dim light. Time-lapse showed he was inside for only twenty minutes. Probably headed to Muskogee.

How irritating. His cameras probably wouldn't pick Bran up again in town. Now he was doubly annoyed he couldn't get near that property. Sam had been trying to devise a plan to cut power to their Muskogee property so that he could infiltrate the compound to set up surveillance. One of the main issues was the generators they had, what they powered, and how long before they would kick on. Not enough time to do what he needed, he was sure. There had to be some way to see inside the private O'Faolain domain.

Sam took a sip of coffee, the steam caressing his upper lip. He would just have to enjoy settling for the knowledge that Bran's ex-girlfriend no longer resided in Oklahoma. Bran O'Faolain was too arrogant to assume she wouldn't be right where he dumped her.

He was done with Raven Byrne, but finding out where she was would be fun. Sam wanted to stay one step ahead of that cocksucking Bran. Not for the first time, Sam believed he was missing opportunities to hurt his enemies. Granted, destroying their relationships chipped away at their self-esteem and self-worth. That type of mind-fuck stayed with a man. It was satisfying... but...

Maybe he was thinking too small.

22

Bran had only just arrived at the Muskogee compound. After he left the airport, he'd had to stop at his hotel condo to grab some extra clothes. He wasn't sure where any of his shit was, honestly. His temper, his whole damn body, was raw. He was volatile, furious at himself, and knew, given the slightest provocation, he could slip into violence.

Almost two months had passed since that— night.

He missed her. God, how much he missed her. He had always believed that women as coldhearted as his mother had to be a one-off, but as soon as those photos had downloaded, he realized his naivety. He loved her still.

Entering his own house, he was relieved it was dark. The silence. He loved his family, but he'd eschewed the main house to avoid their well-meaning banter.

Bran parked in the garage, grabbed his clothes from the back seat, and walked to the main door to enter the code. Just inside the entry, a tall, wooden table carved with vines and leaves held some fancy architectural glass piece. It was clear with slate blue veins. He'd picked it up on one of his trips to Santa Fe at Holsten Galleries. The glass sculpture had spoken to him.

He tossed his key fob and wallet into the hollow middle. It probably wasn't meant to hold shit from his pockets. What did it matter? If he looked at the art any longer, he'd likely throw it across the entryway, so he kept moving.

Steadily making his way toward the study because he fucking needed a drink or three. He suddenly froze— mid-step. His study door was open and weakly illuminated by what would have to be the gas fireplace. The flickering shadows were snaking up the opposite wall from the entry.

He had personally turned off the house alarm but didn't remember if it had only been set on the perimeter. The entire property was monitored— which meant— he had to know the intruder.

Sure enough, as he stepped over the threshold, his father leaned one of his shoulders against the fireplace mantle. The big sonofabitch held one of his new Waterford Lismore Connoisseur Diamond Straight tumblers in his bear-sized paw. A gift from his grandmother— the whiskey glasses, not his father— he certainly was *not* a gift this night.

"Dad. This is unexpected." Not surprised, his father just stared at him with a grimness that meant Bran wouldn't enjoy the visit any more than he'd assumed. Only the flames moved over Hugh O'Faolain's still features. Bran turned to get himself a drink. He wouldn't get rid of his unwanted guest until the reason was given.

Whiskey in hand, Bran made his way to one of the chairs in front of the fireplace and eased his sore body onto the mahogany leather chair. He felt like he'd been in a fight, then a wrestling match, followed by a four-hour gym grind, and a car wreck to round things off. Never let anyone tell you stress and tension aren't bad for the body.

Not interested in continuing the stare-down, Bran broke the silence. Again. "I had planned on coming to the main house in the morning. Can whatever this is," Bran waved in his dad's direction, "wait until then. I'm exhausted and want to go to bed."

"Forgive me, Bran, if I don't believe you."

His dad straightened at this and set his glass on the mantle. Giving his son his full attention.

"You've avoided Pat and me for weeks now. Gran as well. Pardon my refusal in not giving any credence to your placations."

Guilt flooded his body. Damn it. Once he'd run out of excuses to meet them, he'd stopped answering their calls and texts. How had he gotten here? Ahh, yes, he knew the answer to that.

Regardless of the clusterfuck his life had become— after Raven— every colorless, loveless moment of his current existence could be defined as— after Raven, there was no excuse for treating his family badly.

Taking a healthy swallow of Tullamore Dew, he stood out of respect and looked directly at his dad.

"You're right, Dad. I've been a shit. My life is shit. Forgive me for how churlish and childish I've been." Bran's whole body seemed to deflate along with the words.

"I'll call Pat and Gran tomorrow and apologize to them too."

Still silent, his dad walked to him and took Bran's glass right out of his hand, placing it on the table by his chair. He then pulled his son into his large frame. Hugging him tight, one broad hand palmed the back of his head, forcing him to lean his head on his father's shoulder. Shocked at the display, Bran remained stiff for all of a minute. His dad didn't budge.

Bran felt the heat burning through his father's t-shirt, warming his tight muscles. Slowly, Bran put his own arms around his dad. He heard his father clear his throat. Bran's own eyes were welling with tears.

"It has killed me, son," he growled, "to see you hurting. I only ask that you don't cut me out. I... that is something I cannot bear."

Bran seemed to be hurting everyone he loved. To have upset his father to this degree... was past enough. He had to figure his shit out. "I won't do it again, Dad." His father had always been Bran's safest place after his mother left them. He'd forgotten how safe.

They stayed like that for another minute before gradually separating.

Picking up his drink from the mantle, Bran downed the contents, walked over to the bar, and placed the crystal in the sink.

Before his father walked out of the study door, he spoke one last time without turning around. "I'll let you rest tonight. I expect you at the main house by nine. James has been trying to see you as well. He said he has something important he needs to speak to you about. I'll let him know to drive down first thing."

"I understand. I'll be there." As he passed through the door, Bran stopped him. "Thank you, Dad. For... loving me."

His father's hand tightened on the doorframe before he moved on, but Bran heard, "Always," before he disappeared into the dark.

BRAN CALLED Patrick to see if he was home, in Tulsa, or out of town. He had never *not* known where his brother was. It was just another difficult pill to swallow. Pat was at their dad's. Good.

"Meet me in Dad's kitchen in thirty?"

"Fine."

Not super positive, but with Pat, Bran believed he could fix things. He made it there in twenty. Patrick was already flipping pancakes on the griddle.

Bran decided not to be a pussy and immediately owned up to his bullshit.

"Patrick." His brother briefly glanced over his shoulder before returning his attention to the food. "Pat," he started again. "I've been unbearable. I've been a shit brother when you've only ever loved me. Please, Pat, forgive me."

Patrick removed the last three pancakes and placed them in a stack on the plate warming next to the griddle.

Leaning against the counter with his arms crossed over his chest, all casually posed, Patrick finally responded— not casually.

"What the fuck, Bran? We're brothers. We're best friends. You wouldn't even see me." Patrick's cheeks burned scarlet with emotion, and his eyes were bright.

When someone says a person has to hit rock bottom... Reaping what one sews... devastating.

"I have no excuse, Pat. Raven... Jesus, brother, she's destroyed me."

"I would have understood. I *do* understand, for fuck's sake! You still should have let me be by your side."

"I should have. And I'll say the same thing I told Dad last night. It won't happen again." He and his brother didn't move from their counter leans. The steam from the pancakes curling between the stalemate.

"I've missed you, Pat. Please."

Finally, his brother relented. They hugged and banged each other on the back. He vowed to himself to never again shut his family out.

"Thank fuck that's done. You're such an asshole, Bran. Maybe now we can get this problem figured out. I miss River... all the sisters, of course."

"I don't know how anything can be figured out. Don't you think I've tried to find ways to forgive Raven? I can't breathe, sleep, eat... fucking think... without her."

"Since you've been hiding, did you know that none of the girls have spoken to any of us? Including Jo? Did you know that they quit— refused payment for the work they already did?

"They even sent files to the O'Connors, enough designs and drawings, and whatever else to finish the damn bar? But we've heard from none of them. No one. Dad told me last night that he was going to Eufaula today after we met with James."

Bran was stunned. He hadn't known. He hadn't wanted to know. "But... it's been well over a month... almost two! Surely Dad had to speak with Rowan about the wall for Grandpa."

"She emailed detailed instructions to Jo before they went radio silent. They were extremely detailed. In fact, they included design renderings. Raven and River's notes, files, and contacts for goods they'd already sourced were sent to Jo as well. The whole project has continued running smoothly. They did all the work."

"But they... there was no remuneration at all?"

Bran could understand wanting to leave the job because of how things had ended with him and Raven. The time they had to have spent after the breakup, the meticulous detail Patrick said they offered... His thoughts were spinning.

They quit but didn't quit. It sounded like they completed the damn job and refused a fucking penny for the work. Why do that?

Patrick placed stacks of pancakes on three plates. Dad must be on his way.

"I want you to know that whether you can fix things with Raven or not, I will talk to River again."

Dad walked in then and grabbed his plate, not bothering to

go into the dining room but sat down at one of the kitchen island barstools.

"Dad said that even if Rowan keeps hiding from him, he plans on forcing her to speak to him. We've texted all three sisters intermittently for weeks with no response. After James leaves, I'm calling River. If she doesn't pick up, I'll make her listen to voicemails every hour."

Jesus, this morning was full of revelation. "Why have you been trying to get ahold of Rowan, Dad? Patrick said she sent detailed notes to Jo about how she wanted Grandpa's memorial."

Frowning, he looked up from his pancakes. "I don't like the font for the placards."

Okay... Dad giving a shit about fonts. What in the ever-loving hell was happening this morning? Dad ate his breakfast like it was his last meal. He wouldn't answer any more of Bran's questions, guaranteed.

"So," Patrick continued to hammer, "just so we're clear, Dad and I are going to talk to the girls. Today."

"Perfectly clear." If clear looked like a fucking mud-bottom pond.

James arrived thirty minutes later. It was a sunny morning, so they sat on the patio overlooking Dad's pond and the river beyond it.

"I've already apologized to Dad and Pat for my behavior, James. Before we talk about whatever you need to talk to me about, I would also apologize to you. I'm sorry for the past few weeks. I haven't been myself since... that night."

James took a sip of his unsweetened iced tea, carefully setting down the Solo cup like he was handling fine china. Everyone was off these days— probably not as off as Bran— but off. He felt like his life was some alternate universe.

"Forgiven."

It didn't appear James was lying, but his focus wasn't on the apology. However, James' preoccupation with his phone was getting awkward. Bran glanced at his family. They both raised their eyebrows and shrugged their shoulders.

Finally, James seemed to come to a decision. He clenched his hands into fists on either side of his phone a few times before picking the device up— a deep breath, then a simple swipe to open things up. After clearing his throat, phone gripped in one hand, James finally looked at Bran.

"I can forgive you easily, Bran, because I've been going through the exact same thing you have, only far longer."

"Jane?" Bran could hardly believe it. He always assumed James might have cheated and was too ashamed to admit it or that she had wanted more of a commitment than James was willing to give. He'd always hoped they would get back together.

"I was going to ask her to marry me."

"Jesus," Patrick said.

"Fuck, James. I'm sorry you didn't tell us. We would have been there for you."

That got a 'this coming from you' smirk.

"Fine. Point taken." Bran didn't have a leg to stand on.

"I didn't tell you guys because I needed... or wanted to still be able to hang out with my best friends without them feeling like they needed to talk about it. I *couldn't* talk about it. I don't want to be talking about it now, but... if what I've been considering has even a sand's grain of truth... well, I ruined my own life, and waiting this long, I may have destroyed yours as well, Bran."

Dad, Patrick, and Bran all sat up and leaned toward James. Not liking the turn in conversation.

"Explain." Dad's low voice suggested without delay.

"You'll maybe remember that I took Jane on a trip to New York City right before Christmas this past year?" Seeing the nods of confirmation, he continued. "We'd only been seeing each other for a few months, but it was on that trip that I decided I wanted to marry her."

Jane was amazing, and she'd clearly been in love with James. He just couldn't picture her doing anything to jeopardize that. But then, he hadn't thought...

"By January, I'd found the ring and booked a week in the Maldives for mid-February. I thought it would please Jane if I asked her to marry me on Valentine's Day. Jo knew. She loves Jane like a sister. She even helped me plan a fancy dinner a week before we were to leave to surprise her with the trip."

James stopped to drink some tea, giving himself a moment. He picked his phone back up and started flipping through screens. What he was looking at, which none of us could see, made his jaw tighten. He closed his eyes, grimacing. Looking at them once again, he finished.

"The night before that fucking dinner, I received pictures from some anonymous asshole. Pictures of Jane on some hotel balcony with another man. Jane kissing the same man on the park trail where she runs."

As James explained, he was flipping through the pictures for them to see, but he pulled his phone back abruptly before he slid his finger over the screen to the next photo.

"I... I can't show the other two. God, this is hard. She was naked from the waist up, only wearing panties. Her fingers were on the waistband, about to pull them down. I can't allow anyone to see her like that. She was smiling at a man in front of her."

Bran was shaken. He understood the betrayal.

Dad stayed silent. Patrick was unusually reserved. "I'm sorry that happened. I wouldn't have thought her capable. I don't blame you for ending things."

James' eyes flashed with anger, and he slammed his fist on

the table, making everyone's tea slosh over the rims of the plastic cups.

"I've told myself that very thing for months. I have tried everything to purge that woman, those photos, from my mind. Nothing worked. I've thought a million times of begging her to take me back. Forgiving the infidelity. I love her that much— still."

James focused on Bran then. A strange combination of anger, fear, hope, and guilt.

"And then you got pictures of Raven. After a trip. Where I believe you became serious. Truly serious."

His father was the first to catch on. Bran was still reeling.

"Do you think they were faked?" Hugh O'Faolain unfolded his body from the table and stood, leaning into James' space. "Because if you've had this information and didn't come forward, I will fucking beat the ever-loving shit out of you. Start. Fucking. Explaining. Now."

James must have realized his health was in jeopardy. "I didn't know or even suspect until a few days ago. I was lying in bed feeling sorry for myself. Jo's been short with me. We only speak about jobs.

"I was thinking of Jane and her betrayal and then thinking of Raven's. I don't know... I don't fucking know why it didn't click when Bran first told us. I guess I was so shocked and sickened for my friend. Knowing how he felt, my older pain spiraled and became unbearable again. I just tried to shut it all out, and with Bran staying away, it was easier to *not* think.

"But that night. I can't explain it. Perhaps my brain had secretly been mulling our situations over. Their similarities. Too many similarities. We've been friends for years, you, me, and Pat. We've always dated. Sometimes the same women. None of us has been in a serious relationship. Until me."

"And then Bran," Patrick finished.

"Are you suggesting someone is watching you boys, our families? What do you think this is, James? And what of the pictures?"

"I don't *know* a goddamn thing, Hugh. I dreaded coming here today because I know how farfetched it sounds. I also didn't want to give Bran and me any hope where there is none in case I'm completely wrong."

"The pictures, though? I still can't see..." Patrick gently asked.

"I know this is a huge ask, Bran, but I spoke to a detective friend of mine at Tulsa's CID, and he gave me the name of a freelance forensic audio and video image analyst retired from the FBI. My buddy said if I got him the pictures, he'd pass them along to see if he could see any tampering.

"I'm sending him these today. All of them," James swallowed hard and blinked rapidly a few times. "I must know. This may be a reach, but... I have to make sure."

Bran was shocked. Every emotion was raging through his body. His chest was tight, and his ears were ringing. The elation that it was all some horrible setup from someone out there meaning to hurt them... devastation that he'd thrown Raven away without considering her character.

Bran grabbed his own phone. "I'm sending them in a file to you now."

"Tell your friend that we will pay quadruple what the analyst usually receives if he can prioritize this case."

"I was also thinking, Dad, that if the photos are proven fake, we have a possible psycho trailing us. We might need to consider extra security here and in Tulsa. At Gran's as well. You too, James. For you *and* Jo."

Patrick was right but fuck if this whole scenario didn't seem impossible.

James finished on his phone, setting it aside. "I sent the files and put in your request that it be a rush job."

"I'm calling River. I should have called all along. What if something's been wrong this whole time?"

No one spoke as Patrick found River's name in his contacts, not hard to do, as Bran could see her in his favorites. He put the phone on speaker.

A recording. "The person you are trying to reach is not available..."

Dad was already calling Rowan. "The person you are..."

Bran immediately tried Raven. "The person..."

Bran could feel panic streaking through his limbs. The adrenaline spike made his hands shake. "James, call your sister. Fuck..." Calm down, he told himself. They were safe. Oh, God. He had done this, driven her away where she was unprotected.

Deep breath in. Out. "Sorry. Call Jo, please. I don't like this."

"No problem." He was already calling. "I'll put it on speaker so we can all hear what she has to say."

"Hey, James."

"Jo, I'm here with Hugh, Bran, and Patrick." Silence. "There is a lot of shit going on with the Byrnes, and—"

"Listen, bro, I don't appreciate being on speaker, but since I am, you all might as well know that I will not discuss anything to do with them with you four. And James, I love you, but I know you would tell your friends what I tell you, so you're included on the no-tell list."

Bran started to speak, he wanted to yank Jo through the fucking phone, but James mouthed No with a hand swipe to cut him off.

"Listen to me, Josephine O'Connor. If you told me something in confidence, I assure you, I would never break it unless you gave me permission. That was uncalled for."

She was silent for a moment. Then, "You're right. Damn it, I'm sorry."

"Forgiven always, sis. I know you and the sisters are good friends, and I'm glad, but I need to know—" Again, she cut him off.

"I still won't discuss them, James. At least not right at this moment."

"Damn it! Stop cutting me off and just listen to what I have to say. It has to do with Jane too." That finally got her quiet, at least.

They all sat silently while James explained his suspicions about the photos and a potential stalker. About the detective, the analyst, and the sisters' phones being shut off. Their worry that something could be very wrong.

"I know Jane is fine, or she was last night." Looking sheepish, he admitted, "I know because I'm basically a stalker myself."

Jo was silent for a beat, digesting the news. It was a lot to take in, so Bran forced himself to stay quiet.

"I'm floored, James. I never knew why you and Jane broke up. I knew you were hurting, but... I hope the analyst exonerates both her and Raven to your satisfaction. I don't need the analyst to tell me they were set up. I'm also glad you've been watching over Jane. I make sure to call or text her at least once a week."

James' eyes closed briefly. Bran could tell his sister's love was a balm.

"But... and this is for you, Bran, and your family by default, I will not tell you anything about Raven, River, or Rowan. They asked me not to, and I will not break my promise. I *can* tell you that I speak with all of them daily. They are fine."

Dad stood up so fast his chair was thrown back, knocking into one of the potted plants, shattering the terra cotta. He and Patrick stood as well, watching their father warily.

"How do you know Raven isn't being stalked as we speak?

That her life isn't in danger? If there is a stalker, we've certainly never been aware of it." Bran's hands fisted the back of his chair, knuckles white.

Jo sighed. She was concerned. There was no flippancy in her answer. "I only believe she isn't currently in danger because you broke up with her, Bran. The same with James and Jane. He broke up with her and the pictures stopped."

"I still get a picture every once in a while," James admitted.

"James!" Jo shouted, clearly upset for *and* with her brother.

Bran's stomach dropped. "Jesus! So, whoever is doing this still watches the women. Jo! Raven could very well still be in danger. Surely, you see that."

"I understand, and I will pass all this information on to her. *She* will decide what she wants to do, and remember, Bran, five fucking minutes ago you thought she did everything in those pictures! So, don't tell *me* how worried *I* need to be now!"

Jo was right. What right did he have to anger— unless it was directed at himself?

"There must be someone with a grievance attached to both our families in some way. That being said, James, if you treated Jane in any way like Bran treated Raven when you broke things off..." she audibly swallowed down her emotion. "If it were me, I would never take you back. Even if you begged."

Bran felt the blow. His whole body bent forward, his hands landing on the cold metal of the table's top. He heard James admonishing his sister.

"No, James. Stop. She's right. I doubt you spoke to Jane the way I spoke to Raven. I've never done anything more devastating, so purposefully cruel, in all my life." Bran looked at his dad and brother. "I will spend the rest of my life, even if Raven is not in it, attempting to make things right. There will be no one else for me. But I agree with you, Jo. I don't deserve her forgiveness."

"You don't even know if she is innocent, yet you want her back?"

"I don't give one motherfucking damn if the photos are real or not. Raven's guilt could be no greater than my own. The photos only matter if we have someone after our families."

"Okay then, Bran. I believe you mean it. I still won't tell anyone anything about them, but, *when* you guys do find out the photos were altered, I will make sure the Byrnes are made aware of the situation. They can choose what to do about their safety."

"Agreed."

Bran looked at Dad and Patrick, who both nodded. They would track down the sisters whether they wanted to be found or not.

ALL THREE MEN were outside Triskelion Territory Designs in Eufaula an hour later. The blinds were drawn shut. The placard on the door they'd all admired upon their first visit had been removed. The tiny screw holes the only evidence it had ever existed.

"Oh God, Bran. Look."

Patrick was pointing to the window to the left of the door. A Real Estate sign was placed against the glass on the inside of the blinds. A For Sale sign— that had a separate Sold sign placed diagonally across the middle.

Gone. She was gone. She'd left him.

After he'd left her.

"We'll find them, son. We know they're safe. Josephine wouldn't lie."

Bran wasn't sure how long he stared at the Sold sign.

"They meant to never see us again." Patrick was leaning his

back against the door. "Sorry Bran, but I understand Raven wanting to stop contact, but why River and Rowan?"

Bran had to lean against the side of the building. His legs were weak. He felt so very cold. Empty.

"How is it hard to understand? What you do to one, you do to all of them. We hurt Raven, and they wouldn't allow us anywhere near her, which means we go nowhere near any of them."

"I guess you're right, Dad. It's just... River knew she was moving to who knows where and didn't say goodbye to me." Patrick sounded as lost as Bran.

"I don't mean this as a slight against you, Pat, but as your father, I've seen you with a lot of women. You treated River like a good friend, true, and I can't fault that. You made each other happy, but you made sure to keep her well away from... you. She probably didn't know you'd care if she wasn't there."

While Pat stewed over Dad's truth bomb, a glint kept catching Bran's attention on the parking sign across from them. With each slight wind gust, the metal would fractionally twist side to side. What was he seeing?

Bran walked across the sidewalk to the sign, bending so he could see the groove in the galvanized steel post. He finally saw what was catching the sun's light. Reaching out, he dug at the small disk, popping it off and letting it fall into his palm. There was a small magnet on one side.

"What are you doing, Bran?"

Bran turned around and held it up to his dad. "What in the hell is this?"

He thought he might know.

Let this not be what he was imagining.

Patrick and his dad both scrutinized the... device.

"Holy fuck. Is that a camera?"

Dad didn't bother answering Patrick. He was already calling the police.

"Pat, call James and tell him what we found. Have him call his detective friend and see what steps we need to take. Tell him Dad is calling the local police." Count on his brother. Pat was already talking to James before he finished.

Bran was calling Nan.

23

———

Morcote had to be the most glorious slice of land on this side of Heaven. When travel blogs insisted this was the place to go if a person wanted to leave behind the modern world, they weren't lying. They'd just arrived, and Raven felt some of the tension in her body relax. Not even two weeks had passed since Bran broke things off, and here she was, stepping off a private jet and walking into a whole new life— without Bran.

The drive to their villa in Morcote was surreal. Nothing this beautiful could surely exist. Raven and her sisters had pictured a quaint, affordable, heavy on the rustic, cottage with tight quarters, one bathroom— a nightmare with four women, but not impossible— bed-sharing, but the atmosphere would overcome it all.

They hadn't considered Travel Agent O'Connor.

Or the going away present that kept getting additional clauses, footnotes, and addendums— all nonnegotiable. River probably regretted her past word choices— it made it hard to put her foot down.

The first look inside the luxury villa that was now part of

Jo's parting gift had been nothing short of shocking for all of them: The property was for sale, but Jo talked the owners into renting it to her for two months. Raven shuddered to consider the expense of it all.

The main villa— as in there were other accommodations on the property— had seven bedrooms and multiple bathrooms. She and her sisters wouldn't even remember how to share after this vacation.

The indoor/outdoor pool was second in beauty only to the veranda, covered in flowers that flowed in a profusion of color, swirling around the entire property. The veranda overlooked Lake Lugano.

A separate three-bedroom villa dotted the lush scenery to the right of the veranda. Separate accommodation toward the back of the villa was set up for the home's service staff.

And surprise, Jo hired three housekeepers to live there while they were in residence. Arguing about the unnecessary expense got them nowhere. She only argued back. Raven asked if she didn't think three housekeepers was a bit excessive. She admitted that one of them was actually a private chef.

"I'm telling you guys, Jo has lost her mind. This..." Raven flapped her hands all around them, "... is insane!"

"Yes, it is," Rowan agreed. "But," she paused and looked around her once again, just as awed as her sisters, "Jo isn't changing her mind. It's a done deal, as she put it. So, I suggest we go jump on all the beds, unpack, and explore."

They were all grinning like loons now.

"Nan is literally going to shit!"

Before they could run off, Raven grabbed her sisters' hands.

"Thank you." Raven willed the tears stinging her eyes not to fall. "We loved Eufaula, and we loved the space we'd created... and you left it all, and... I'm sorry I wasn't strong enough to stay."

Rowan and River clasped their hands together, finishing the circle.

"We're together in this, as we've been together in everything else."

"We are each other's home, Rave. What we started planning as kids in Bristow, worked toward in college, and finished in Eufaula was amazing, but that really was just the first version of what we're capable of. Like a... trial run." Rowan smiled.

"Row's right. Byrne's Triskelion Territory Designs 2.0 will rock Ireland's world!"

"And, if you're concerned we'll miss Oklahoma, don't be. We will go back whenever we feel like it once we're established in Dublin."

"And Mom and Dad are forever in Ireland. There is nothing to hold us back from starting a new life. And," River grinned, squeezing her hand, "I'm kind of liking the beginning of this adventure."

Done with sadness, Raven smiled back. Before her sisters could anticipate her move, Raven dropped their hands and started running toward the bedrooms, laughing as she went.

"I'm the oldest, and I get the best room!" Sliding around a corner, she heard her sisters in hot pursuit.

"You tricksy sneak, Rave!"

"The shortest gets the smallest!" Rowan yelled at her back.

God, laughing, really laughing, felt amazing.

RAVEN WISHED she'd videoed Nan's reaction when she arrived at their villa two days later. She kept spinning in circles, trying to see everything at once. It was late afternoon, so they called Jo. Nan insisted on thanking her personally.

It was a warm, wonderful, tearful thank you, and Raven

could tell Jo was even more pleased with herself than before. The gift giver that keeps on giving.

"You'll come to Ireland to visit and let me spoil you."

Jo quickly realized that Nan wasn't suggesting. "Thank you, Mrs. Byrne."

"Nan."

"Right, sorry, Nan. I believe it will be around October. Hopefully, your girls will have a shop front by then. I was considering staying through the holidays."

"No way, Jo!"

"Are you serious?"

"That is the best news ever, Miss O'Connor." Raven was tickled. Jo was sticking to her word about visiting.

"I've got to go into a meeting with my folks, but my friend said she would start looking at property in Dublin immediately. So, hopefully, I'll have a list for you guys to virtually look at soon."

"That's perfect. Really perfect. I hope our Eufaula property sells fast."

Everyone said their goodbyes and promised to talk tomorrow.

They decided to spend the rest of the day getting Nan settled and making plans. Anything Nan had ever dreamed of doing or seeing while she was here.

THE SISTERS AGREED that the trip had been an extraordinary success. One that they were so blessed to have taken with their Nan. The memories they were squirreling away would stay with them forever. This moment was one of the most precious and catastrophic of Raven's life.

Creating bonds with the women in her family, stronger now

than they were even weeks before, was a blessing, especially in this quiet, humbling piece of the world where outside influences faded and the most basic of human bonds bloomed.

The impetus for the trip, however, still weighed heavily. Bran had shattered each well-constructed future plan. Raven thought he had destroyed her. This trip, her ability to find peace, taught her he hadn't. Still, she missed him.

Raven got teary-eyed when they took their rental car to Lugano to tour St. Mary of the Angels Catholic Church— Santa Maria degli Angioli— constructed around 1499. The beauty and absolute peace found inside its vaulted ceilings were awe-inspiring. Breathtaking frescos, stained glass, wooden pews worn smooth as glass, incense— it had been a glorious assault on her senses.

If Raven heard someone say they'd experienced a religious experience, she could honestly reply that she understood.

They didn't spend every day as tourists. Many of them were spent reading, gossiping, or being lazy as their 'personal' chef fed them.

Decadence, thy name is Raven Byrne.

They were celebrating the sale of the Eufaula property today. The real estate agent had closed and would send all the paperwork to Jo. Thankfully, they'd decided to make her their power of attorney for the summer until all their assets in the United States were safely shipped to Dublin or sold. She had the right to sign paperwork in their absence.

As predicted, they'd made a killing on the remodeled three-story. Raven hoped whoever bought it would love it as much as they had.

Row and Nan were floating in the pool while she and River were reading in lounge chairs under umbrellas, drinking whiskey and water— never mixed, of course— with their laptops in lieu of Kindles on their laps.

Rowan floated close and asked if they had narrowed down the Dublin properties. The first properties Jo's friend sent a few weeks ago had been great, just too pricey. River called the real estate agent herself to explain that they weren't afraid of getting dirty and overhauling a fixer-upper.

Saoirse Kennedy took requests with a Challenge Accepted type of attitude. Totally their kind of woman. So, the next batch of properties were more in line with their needs and finances.

She told them that there were basically ten main streets they should be aware of before opening a storefront in Dublin.

First was O'Connell Street. It was Dublin's main thorough-fare, laden with historic buildings and shops.

Grafton Street was about as upscale as it got and topped destination shopping list experiences every year.

Moore Street was a mixed bag, but its main claim to fame was hosting the city's fresh market.

Dame Street was Dublin's financial district. Kildare housed government buildings. Henrietta Street was home to King's Inn School of Law and palatial red brick Georgian-styled buildings.

Talbot had one potential property for Triskelion. The street had lots of shopping, chain stores, and the Talbot Mall, but she didn't feel the vibe was right for the sisters' design studio.

Then there was Crown Alley. This street was the life of the party, with pubs, cafes, and street art. Ailesbury Road... well, the Byrnes pocketbooks were not nearly deep enough.

So, Saoirse said, that left Cow's Lane. It was quirky, with a lovely mix of boutiques, cafes, tattoo parlors, bookstores, and tea shops— some of the sisters' favorite things— plus it was in the Temple Bar district, which meant an excellent choice of estab-lishments selling all that lovely whiskey.

"I think they both have a lot of potential." River continued to flip through the photos. "It's really the living quarters that throw the curveballs."

Raven agreed completely. "Both have generous storefronts that, with some work, would be nice. Truly lovely." She stopped at the one she was favoring. "There is one that, damn it, Row, there is something magical about the front. The windows and doors are a mix... old lines, charm, and sturdiness.

"The interior is heavy wood and vaulted ceilings, but rustic, certainly nothing modern or pretentious. It feels... like... the three of us somehow. The space we have left for ourselves will require a lot of sharing, though. Perhaps too much."

Damn it. There were just so many unknowns in their lives right now. Finances are at the top of the list. Raven knew they would make it. They had proven themselves in Oklahoma several times over. They *would* do it in Dublin too.

"We could make it lovely, and it would be— if it were housing a single or a couple in a relationship. It would not be a forever home, of course. Perhaps a lovely lounge and kitchen eventually. Living in it would be a test," Raven concluded.

A 'test' was being generous. Raven and her sisters would basically be sleeping, eating, and showering in three hundred square feet. It was doubly tough to imagine while currently lounging in a luxe villa.

"The second choice is very nice, as well. There's nothing wrong with it. The space we'd convert to our living quarters is much more generous. Perhaps even enough room for two full baths instead of one. Closet space that doesn't require rolling clothing racks in the living room." With all the cons of the first property's living quarters, Raven couldn't believe she was still entertaining it.

Sighing, she admitted, "River, you and Row make the final choice. I swear to you both, I will be thrilled with either."

Rowan floated to the stone steps leading out of the pool. She dried off and sat at the end of River's chair facing Raven. "Let me see them." She held her hand out for Raven's laptop. "I'll bite the bullet and decide. How's that?"

"Thank God."

"Please."

Raven's stomach was churning again today. She hadn't had much of an appetite since they got here, which was a real irritation because the food was exceptional. Rowan got onto her for losing so much weight. They agreed it was probably lingering depression.

She'd also barely spotted, and only once in Morcote since the whole birth control swap. She knew screwing up pills with River would mess with her system, but that was a few months ago when they'd done that, so it had to be simply stress— and trying to pick Triskelion 2.0 was definitely a next-level stressor.

"Looks like the three of us will have to go to Nan's if we want to stretch our legs," Rowan said. "I just emailed Saoirse and told her to make an offer."

Raven and River sat forward in their loungers.

"You did it?"

"Oh, God. I hope they accept."

"I think they will. Call it my Irish intuition, but I completely agree with you, Raven. There *is* something about that particular property. It's meant to be ours, so I think it will be. I can't wait to get started."

Nan gracefully walked out of the pool to sit at the end of Raven's chair. A plush cotton towel wrapped around her trim middle. Raven was about to take her laptop back from Rowan, thinking she wanted to see the property they'd chosen.

"I'm happy that's decided. Now, you can truly start planning the next step in your 'adventure,' as you call it." She wrapped her cool hand around Raven's ankle and stared grimly toward the horizon.

What was this about? Raven's already churning stomach rolled violently.

Nan finally faced Raven. "I won't beat about the bush, Raven. I've waited almost six weeks for you to come clean about you and Bran. I'm done waiting."

Her sisters both had wide, panicked eyes. A mirror of her own.

"Nan, please don't think I'm keeping secrets from you. It's only... I hate thinking about it, let alone speaking about it. My sisters know everything because they were there."

"What?" She turned to look at the other two.

Grimly, River explained that they'd been enjoying a family dinner at the O'Faolains. "Raven, if you want me to explain, I will. You can go on inside and get ready for dinner."

Raven saw her grandma's look of bewilderment. She needed to just say what happened and be done with it. Nan would never doubt she was innocent, and Raven would like Nan's advice.

She explained how the evening had been one of the best they'd ever shared. Bran had asked her to move in with him, and she'd accepted. How she'd planned on moving a lot of her things that next week.

"It all went so... wrong, Nan." Raven winced at the memories flashing before her eyes. Him whispering I love you. A gentle hand tucking hair behind her ear. His hand settled possessively at the base of her spine. Sharing a private look. Teasing.

"We finished dinner. I suggested playing games in Hugh's study."

"They'd never heard of Slapjack, so we explained the rules," Rowan added solemnly.

"Pat and James were setting up a table. Hugh was going to

be the dealer. We were all excited." River looked at her and asked again. "Can you finish?"

Raven nodded. "I was speaking with Hugh, about to get Bran and me drinks at the bar. Bran had told me he got some texts and emails at dinner he wanted to look at in case it was something he needed to deal with immediately.

"Hugh noticed first. Bran was visibly upset. Staring at his phone. I asked him if something was wrong. He... he didn't answer... right away." Tears started to roll down her cheeks. "Damn it, you'd think I'd be over this by now."

Nan took her by the shoulders and pulled her into a gentle hug, rocking slightly back and forth, the lounger creaking.

"Stop now. Stop, Raven. Don't say another word. I... shouldn't have asked. I don't need to bloody know a damn thing except that you were hurt."

Raven cried harder. It took several minutes to gulp down the tears and emotions clogging her nose and throat. "I shouldn't still be this upset." She looked to her sisters, begging them to give her some reason she was still this gutted over Bran's accusations. It's not like they were true, for Heaven's sake.

"Rave, he was your first boyfriend, your first sexual experience, and the love of your life. You *believed* it was forever. It was fucking forever for *you*."

"River Aster Byrne! This is no time for your... blasted language!" Nan exclaimed.

Raven finally breathed, a small smile tugging her lips. She would finish this story if it killed her. "The short of it, Nan, is this. Someone Bran didn't even know sent him pictures of me with another man. He wouldn't show them to me. I know they weren't me."

"Of course, they weren't you! Bran was acting a fool to believe any such bullshite about you."

No one mentioned the curse word.

"Did you tell him it wasn't you?"

"I did," Raven said quietly.

Rowan pushed. "Tell Nan the rest, sister. She needs to know it all."

So, she did. Every horrible, hurtful, scarring word that the man she loved, still loved, accused her of. As Nan became more agitated, throwing questions at her sisters as well, Raven's stomach became more and more nauseated.

"Sorry... I'm... oh, God... sick." Raven got up and started to rush indoors to her room. She barely rounded the door into the bathroom before she was dry heaving over the toilet. She felt cool hands scraping her hair back and putting it in a bun to keep it from dipping into the vomity toilet water.

Finally, Raven just laid her head on the arm resting across the toilet seat. Breathing slowly, testing to see if she dared move.

Rowan tilted a glass of water by her mouth. "If you think you're done vomiting, open your mouth a bit, and I'll pour some water in. Just swish it around and spit."

Doing as she was told, Raven was pleased to find her stomach much improved. It had to be a short-lived bug. She'd felt even more off the last couple of days. Hopefully, this was the end of it.

"Let River help you up, my love. We'll get you tucked in bed. I've got a cool, wet cloth for your face."

"I feel much better now. I've been off for a couple of days. I hope it's over now."

"Well, baby girl, it might be longer than a couple of days."

Nan's cryptic reply made all sorts of Oh Shit! alarms start ringing.

River helped her to bed. "Way to be positive, Nan. Geesh."

Raven tried to laugh off her unease as the three women sat on the edges of her bed. "No worries. Seriously. Whatever was wrong has passed— into the toilet." Her sisters laughed. Her grandma did not.

"Did you use... that is..." Nan shook her head like she was shaking off her hesitation. "When was your last cycle, Raven?"

Silence. Only the waves breaking against the lake's shoreline accompanied the silent stillness of her bedroom. She found her hands enfolded by River and Rowan. Neither spoke, though.

"Nan, I'm... on birth control." Face blazing at discussing this with the older woman. Still, it had to be said.

"Okay, okay, then. And, have you ever missed one of the pills?"

"No. Never. I only caught a bug. That's all this is."

And then Rowan dropped a truth bomb.

"Before we left Oklahoma to come here, didn't you and River discover that you'd switched toiletry bags— *and* birth control packs?"

"Yes. But that was forever ago." Oh shit. As soon as the words left her mouth, she felt her whole body go numb.

"We decided to keep going with the packs we were on since we'd been taking each other's for who knows how long. We get three months at a time, so if you started taking mine then... I was always three weeks different than you, Rave, right? So, we all wouldn't be on our period at the same time. It probably happened in May, right before you went to Ireland with Bran..."

River paused, obviously trying to do some mental math. "You would have taken your placebo pills and then immediately started taking my placebo pills. They're all white, I don't have sex, so I never even look at what week I'm on." She looked as sick as Raven was moments ago over the toilet.

"And our periods are light or spotty most months," Raven spoke softly, almost to herself. Looking up at River, she added, "I did this. I took your bag by accident. Your pills."

"We don't know for sure. I'll ask the housekeeper where we can get a test." Rowan got up without another word. Obviously, in search of a pregnancy test.

"This can't be. No way."

"We don't know yet, Raven, but if you are, that child will be so loved and so welcome into our family." Nan was crying as she hugged Raven.

Raven looked at River over Nan's head. River only shook her head and shrugged. That about summed it up.

Two LINES. Two lines. Two lines. Raven could still see those two lines behind her lids after she squeezed her eyes tight. Bran would never believe she hadn't gotten pregnant on purpose. It was a mistake. A foolish mistake and all hers. River was probably right. She had to have started her sister's placebo pills soon after she'd finished her own.

A mistake. How did she feel about it? It didn't feel like a mistake. Nan was right.

Not a mistake, then. A blessing. She would never utter the word mistake in reference to her child again.

She couldn't stay in the bathroom forever. So, she took a deep breath and splashed some water on her face. Staring into the mirror, she covered her flat stomach with one of her hands. She smiled then. Really smiled.

"You were never a mistake," she whispered.

Time to face the music. Raven opened the door and walked to the living room, where everyone had agreed to wait. They'd tried to hover outside the bathroom door, but she couldn't pee with all the whispering and shuffling about.

They all noticed her at the same time and stayed silent as she joined River on one of the sofas. She adjusted a pillow before finally settling. No one broke the silence, kindly waiting for her to decide how she wanted to tell them.

Clearing her throat, she cringed. What an annoying habit. "You've probably guessed. I'm definitely pregnant."

Nan dabbed at her eyes with a napkin. Her sisters waited for some cue to tell them how Raven was leaning emotionally so they'd know how to react. She helped them out.

She smiled and laughed, bringing her hands to her face. "And I'm thrilled."

Raven heard Nan laughing as her sisters' dog-piled her on the couch. They were all laughing and hugging and touching her stomach in wonder.

"We're going to be aunts, Riv. Can you believe it?" Rowan asked in wonder.

"Oh, Raven..." River's eyes were blinking back tears. "I'm so glad you're pleased. We're all going to rock this pregnancy."

River jumped off the couch and started running to the bedrooms. Rowan yelled after her. "Where are you going, weirdo?"

As River skidded across the wood floors, she answered without turning around. "Laptop. We have some serious adjustments to make to our future projection charts."

Raven chuckled but was swallowing past a suddenly dry throat. Her first nugget of fear wormed its way into her head. They'd just made an offer on the property in Dublin, and they had to move forward in *some* capacity to start making money again. But the building's living quarters... she barely held in her groan.

Adjustments indeed.

～

Four hours later, they'd eaten an amazing dinner of grilled fish and roasted vegetables, thanks to their fancy chef, stopped Nan from looking up baby names four times, and hammered out a new and improved life plan for themselves personally and professionally.

The housekeeper even sourced some ginger and honey drops to suck on. She swore it would head off the worst of the nausea and hopefully stop it altogether. She was sucking on one now. Since she wasn't a fan of laying her face where her ass usually held court, she'd suck on these drops 'til the cows came home if necessary.

"Nan, the three of us aren't knocked up," River smirked at Raven. "How about I pour us a nice glass of Jameson, and we go over the plans once more all the way through."

Rowan accepted her glass. "Sounds good. We may have missed something."

They probably did miss a few things, but not from a lack of trying. It was impossible to think of all the variables with so many moving parts.

Saoirse Kennedy called them before dinner to say the offer had been accepted. She'd send the initial paperwork tomorrow morning. It was a bank foreclosure, so the process would go more quickly.

To spare the expense of long-term vehicle parking at the airport, Nan's good friend had driven her. The same friend was scheduled to pick her up. They only had two more weeks in paradise.

"Okay," Raven began. "I'll start with short-term personal goals that should cover the last big Switzerland To-Do's. We have less than two weeks before we fly to Dublin." She looked at her grandma and smiled. "A private O'Connor jet for you this time, Nan."

She shook her head in wonder. "That Jo. I can't wait to hug her."

"We've got tickets purchased for the Funicular, seriously guys, I hope it's more awesome than its name. Funicular sounds like a weird surgery... on private parts. We do that in two days. We may all want to Dramamine up before that one. It's a mountain tram ride, and I don't want to scare anyone, but it was built in 1908."

"Older equals better built," Nan sniffed with attitude.

"When you're snuggled in a leather recliner with someone offering your favorite foods, drinks, and a facial on the 'not old' private jet— remind me about ancient things, Nan," River teased.

Ignoring the banter, Raven looked over her list. "We will choose between the two summit restaurants for a late lunch before tramming back.

"Next Tuesday, we've booked a crossing to The Swiss Customs and Smuggler Museum in Gandria. It's located at the base of Monte Brè. We'll be crossing Lake Lugano by a lakeboat they call them. Dramamine again?"

River and Rowan touched each other's stomachs. "Nope. Not pregnant. No nausea meds needed here, sis."

"Assholes." Secretly, Raven was pleased beyond measure that her 'Baby on Board' news was being digested into normal Byrne chitchat. The normalcy had a way of making Raven feel like this was the course she was always meant to be on.

River ignored Raven flipping her off outside of Nan's field of vision, as she ticked off the third biggest thing they wanted to do before going to Ireland.

"Next week, one of the last things, and most important things, we have left to do is drive into Lugano to their historic shopping district, Via Nassa. It has super posh boutiques, bookstores, jewelers, and, if the hype is to be believed, which I do of course, the best restaurants. This is the day we find the *perfect* thank-you gift for Jo."

So far, they'd been unsuccessful at finding— *it*. Jo was too special to grab the first thing they laid eyes on. Raven knew that when they saw it, they would *know*.

"Those are the highlights. Nan, if there is anything else you want to do, you'd better speak up. We are free agents and here to please you."

Laughing, Nan patted each of her granddaughters on the knee. "You three have given me a gift I will never forget. Truly. I thought I was just an old widow. Adventures only for the young. Now, I realize that... Though the two men I loved most in this world are gone— I'm still here, and damn it, not a word River, I'm going to stop dreaming and start doing. You girls have taught me to go after what I want."

Was Raven a giant blubbering boob as a rule, or, please God, just the pregnant version? Tears again.

"Brava, Nan."

"Is your widowed neighbor one of those things?"

River looked smug at Nan's gasp and touched her throat to grasp her nonexistent pearls.

"I have never heard of anything so ridiculous in my life, young lady."

Raven decided to save her grandma from further embarrassment. "Hey, I'm really exhausted. Would you all mind if we finish this meeting in the morning?"

"I'm tired too." Rowan's jaw cracked as she yawned. "It's been a huge day, especially for you, Rave. There is one thing we never touched on, and I was hoping you'd bring it up, but," she shrugged, "you didn't. We figured you could be anywhere from two to three months along. Let's assume you've knocked out the first trimester—"

River interrupted. "I just added finding a good OB/GYN in

Dublin. No worries, I'll do some doctor trolling tonight. Rowan bringing up how far along you might be made me realize you need to see someone ASAP."

"Oh. Yes, of course." Fighting the internal freak-out session was— difficult. Raven reminded herself she wasn't alone. She had a place to live when they got to Dublin. With the money Jo threw at this trip and the good price they got for the Eufaula building, they had enough to rent a small, affordable apartment not far from where they would be working double time on the remodel.

Within an hour of them telling Saoirse they would need a place to live while they worked, her assistant had several options. The hope was it would take only two months, as the downstairs business space had good bones. They agreed that it was worth a year or two of cramped quarters to see Triskelion flourish.

And it would.

"So, back to what I was saying." Rowan sighed at River. "We've given ourselves two months to open TTD, hopefully less. That would put you at four to five months along. About the time Jo expects to visit."

Where in the absolute hell was Rowan going with this? Besides giving her a headache?

"You never once mentioned telling Bran, but I know you, sister. You would never keep something this important from him. He's a total piece of shhh..." Rowan quickly swapped adjectives when Nan raised her brows. "He's totally not on my list of people I most want to be related to... but he is the father, and... you do love him still. Right?"

Rowan's last words were quiet, but they exploded inside Raven. Oh yes, she loved him still.

"Yes." Such a simple word of affirmation. Yes, had power. Yes. Yes. Yes.

"I will tell him in my own time. It was one of my first and fiftieth thoughts. For now, this child is in *me*, and... he doesn't want me. I will tell him, but not yet. Closer to the end." She had to breathe deeply several times to wrangle her emotions. "Please tell me you understand."

Nan spoke first. "Of course, we understand. I believe he has a right to know, but he gave up his right to the experience of seeing you bloom with his child when he... when he behaved foolishly."

"I agree, Rave," River said. "As long as he knows before you give birth, I'm good. Rowan and I will take good care of you and the wee bean."

Rowan got up and pulled Raven into a hug. "Go to bed. I will support your wishes. Always."

Later that night, Raven put her hand on her stomach, barely believing a tiny baby grew there. She and Bran were having a child, and she wished... desperately, that things were different, not just for herself, but for their child.

There were so many decisions to be made, a doctor for baby, managing their finances, remodels, telling Jo, telling Bran. Raven started to drift, closing her eyes. In the stillness between consciousness and sleep, she heard Bran whisper her name. She whispered his back.

THEY WERE DRIVING BACK to the villa from Gandria where they'd spent an amazing day exploring the museum, with only the tiniest bit of nausea from the boat crossing. Thank you very much, ginger drops. When they were almost back to Morcote, River got a text from Jo asking her to call when they were home. She had some news and wanted Nan there, as well.

They gathered in the kitchen to make the call. Jo didn't

waste time telling them everything. James' confession and initial suspicions when the men realized she and Jane's pictures were probably altered and meant to sabotage their relationships, the detective, the former FBI analyst, the boys' discovery that the girls had changed their numbers, their trip to Eufaula, Bran finding a camera attached to a signpost outside Triskelion's front door, and Hugh calling the police.

It made Raven's skin crawl to realize some psycho had been watching her. Taking pictures. To what end? To break up her and Bran? It seemed ridiculous.

"I can tell you, I was never more thankful that my conversations with those three were over a phone. I swear the O'Faolain testosterone packs a punch even long distance. They were angry I wouldn't tell them where you were or give up your numbers. I assured them that we spoke every day.

"Bran is concerned for your safety, Raven, and I suppose there is the smallest chance he's right, but he doesn't know you are out of the country. He just learned you were out of Eufaula. He's panicked. I get it. I promised to relate all this to you and allow you to decide if you felt you needed protection, which they would pay for, of course.

Rowan asked, "Do you still talk to Jane? See her, like, in public? Has she ever had anything weird happen to her since she and James broke up?"

"We do still speak. She's amazing. She never knew about the pictures. James broke up with her through text. No reason given. And I have had lunch with her a few times here and there. In public. I tried to reason with Bran that if the stalker's goal was to ruin their relationships, once he accomplished that goal, the women were no longer an interest.

"However, my closed-mouth brother admitted that he has received a few more pictures over the last several months. So, I don't really know. It could be that the stalker kept watch on

Jane because I still spoke with her. No one knows anything yet.

"I don't speak psycho. I could be wrong, and if you were coming back to Oklahoma, I would advise caution, but you aren't, so..."

"I agree. It is really creepy to think someone was following me. Taking pictures of me."

"Unsettling," Nan agreed. "I'm thankful the authorities are involved. Jo, are you okay there? Are your parents home, and have you told them?"

"Yeah, Jo. This is crazy news. You should never be alone until the person is caught."

"No worries. James called Dad and filled him in. Dad was furious that he hadn't told him about the issues with Jane. Mom guilted James for not letting her love on him when he needed it most. Which is all true, but I had to chuckle at them treating my big brother like a spotty teenager.

"What isn't amusing is that I now have a security guard assigned to me. Like, I almost got whiplash I had one so fast. How did Dad manage that? And, apparently, I'll have one until further fucking notice. Whoops, forgive the language, Bébhinn, but my a-hole brother didn't have to have one. We're driving together now. I'm in the backseat. The guard refuses to speak to me. So, I've decided to ignore Honey Bunny too and see how he likes it."

Raven could hear the laughter in her friend's voice. All three sisters burst out laughing despite the seriousness of the situation. It felt very good to speak of Bran and not cry. Progress.

River whispered in her ear that Jo had us on speaker. "Is that like his nickname? Honey Bunny?"

Catching on, Nan asked in her lovely Irish accent, "Is he precious, then?"

"Does he hop into the driver's seat?" Rowan allowed a slight

Irish accent to flavor her words. They all had a slight accent, very slight, but with months spent in Ireland as children, and their father, they naturally adopted the lilting brogue and musical intonations of the country on words and phrases here and there.

"Does he have a fluffy tail?" River... Jesus.

Struggling to speak through the telltale tremor of humor they could hear in her voice, she told them, "His hair is honey-colored like mine. James and I went to a petting zoo once, and I fell in love with a pet rabbit with long floppy ears. James said when I hugged it, you couldn't tell where I ended, and the rabbit began." She laughed at the memory. "I named him Honey Bunny and begged to take him home."

"I take it the rabbit stayed at the zoo."

"Yes, but *this* Honey Bunny is apparently all mine," Jo said.

"Child, I'm an old woman! You make me laugh any harder, I'm like to wet myself."

Once the laughter subsided, Jo went on. "Thanks, girls. I needed to laugh. It's been a stressful few days, I won't lie. I know you're safe, Rave, but I warn you, Bran is not going to give up."

Raven could tell they were taken off speaker so 'Honey Bunny' couldn't hear their side of the conversation.

"It's been almost two months since... that night. And I won't lie to my family, myself, or you. I love him just as much now as I did... before. And I'm happy that he *now* knows I'm innocent. Even though the results from the analyst haven't been done yet. Right?"

"Even with the rush, it'll be a few days."

"Since I know that I never was with any man besides Bran, ever, I'm unconcerned with the results. And perhaps I could eventually forgive him, but you all were there. You heard the things he said to me. He didn't just want to break things off. He wanted to break *me*.

"He cheapened every moment that had come before. He... well, it doesn't need to be rehashed. It won't change what he did. That he threw me away without ever, not once, thinking of giving me a chance to explain. My sisters have made huge sacrifices because of it. We will not divert from the plans we made. We will rebuild, recover, and stand on our own again. Stronger and wiser, I hope, than before.

"Not just because of Nan, but I think Ireland was where we were always meant to end up. I hate to ask you for more, but until we're on our feet in Dublin and settled, I would ask that you keep the O'Faolains in the dark. Just for a few more months."

River, Rowan, and Nan smiled softly and nodded at Raven. Harmony. She'd decided not to tell Jo about the baby until she visited in the fall. It was so new, and Raven wanted to see a doctor and make sure everything was as it should be before she told anyone else.

"Not a problem, but I know he'll keep trying to get ahold of you, Bébhinn, since the girls' phone numbers changed. I didn't explain that Nan wasn't answering because she'd broken her phone. I decided to let him believe, and probably partially out of spite, okay maybe all out of spite, that she just didn't want to talk to him. I still haven't forgiven how he spoke to you, Rave."

"And I appreciate you having my back. Truly. But I think it's time we move on. The past weeks in Morcote have given me distance... from the breakup, from Bran. My inexperience not only clouded my judgment and made me think our relationship was stronger than it was, but it allowed me to think I *need* Bran. I will forgive him eventually, but letting the hurt go is another matter. Just a few more months to make sure my feet are solidly under me. Then, it's business as usual."

"Team Raven all the way, baby." All the women cheered.

River asked to be put on speaker one last time before they hung up.

"Okay, Jo. See you in a few months. If the stalker isn't caught by then, I guess we'll all get to meet your Honey Bunny."

"I vote carrot cake to celebrate," Rowan snickered.

"I'll start building a nest in your bedroom," Raven threw in.

"With a warren to your burrow." My God, River was horrible.

"Okay, ladies, I'm hanging up now. Honey looks to be mangling the steering wheel."

It was the small things. Raven smiled as Jo hung up. She patted her stomach. Definitely, the small things.

24

———

Their final full day in Morcote saw the Byrne ladies sunning and reading on the veranda, munching on raw veg. No peanut butter, though. Mmm, crunchy, yummy, and oh so satisfying. Europeans just didn't appreciate the BEST spread *ever* invented. God, Raven wanted some.

If Dublin lacked her brand of choice, Skippy Super Chunk, there was always Amazon.

Yesterday, they'd driven into Lugano to shop at the fancy Via Nassa center. They wanted to get Jo's thank you gift squared away. After hours of popping in and out of stores, tea and biscuits at the outdoor cafes, and using their phone translators, with and without success, they finally happened into a small jeweler. This had to be it. None of the jewelry looked traditional. Everything in here looked one of a kind.

Translator app at the ready, she told the saleswoman that they were looking for earrings for one of their good friends. They'd at least narrowed it down to earrings three hours ago.

The robotic app voice asked them about color, stones, and something else she couldn't understand. River grabbed my phone and, thank God, took over.

"She has wavy blonde hair and gray eyes." River made a motion around her breasts, presumably the length of Jo's hair.

The saleswoman nodded and motioned for them to follow her. Nan smiled and shrugged, game to see what the lady might have, but clearly flagging from the long day.

And there they were. Like sunlight and angels were lighting up the display case. All three sisters smiled and pointed. That pair. No translation needed for the clerk.

Gray spinel gemstones surrounded with tiny oval cut black onyx. The gems were set in a lower prong platinum mount. They should set flush to Jo's lobe. The gray spinel gems looked like smoke. They would match her eyes perfectly, and the onyx would sparkle and reflect in her blonde hair. Oh, God, yes, these were it.

The jewelry store shipped the gift directly to Jo's home in Tulsa with a handwritten thank you note from all of them.

To our sister, Josephine.
Love, Thanks, and many Blessings Upon You,
Raven, River, Rowan
And your adopted gran, Nan

They knew it would be days before she got the package. Nan said to call her the moment they knew she'd received the gift. Her grandma was as excited as they were.

The gift had been the last thing on their Switzerland checklist. They were all packed now and ready to leave in the morning. The flight was scheduled for 9 o'clock. Raven would miss the easy days in Morcote. Especially after the shocking news they'd gotten last week. She admitted to being relieved that they weren't going back to Oklahoma, especially being pregnant.

Jo called last night to update them on the stalker situation. The analyst proved the pictures were faked, and whoever had done them was highly skilled. James' detective contact was helping with the investigation. So far, they had found several more cameras. Outside the O'Faolain's rooms at the hotel in the hallways, the most disturbing was the one they found at Jane's gym in the women's dressing area.

The pictures of Raven were taken from the camera outside Triskelion, but the ones in Tulsa, at Wolves, and the one in the back of an Uber where it appeared she was kissing a man, were taken from a regular camera. One with a powerful lens used from a distance. Distant or not, the fact that someone had indeed been following her was frightening.

The detectives were finding out who had access to the places the cameras were found. The list was excruciatingly long. The pictures had been sent from a burner phone to both James and Bran. They were getting closer to tracking where the hidden camera stills were being sent, but again, whoever set this up was very good at covering their tracks.

Raven didn't even know Jane, but she had been violated worse than anyone. Jo said she refused to see James, so Jo had to meet with Jane and the police while they explained what had happened. The police allowed her to leave town for a while as long as she always let them know where she was.

Jo said it was the very best thing Jane could do. Though she'd tried to convince her brother not to, James was going to follow her whether his ex-girlfriend approved or not— which she absolutely did not. Raven could sympathize.

Nan's phone rang during her peanut butter fantasies, unusual but not crazy. Her grandma obviously had a life outside her granddaughters. "I wonder if it's the widower, River." They both grinned at each other.

Nan sat up, stiff as a board. She and her sisters were instantly on high alert. None of them liked calls that got that type of reaction. It brought back instant memories of Mom and Dad and... that last night with Bran.

Raven almost hyperventilated when Nan responded to the person speaking on the other end.

"Bran O'Faolain. I'm surprised to hear from you."

Her grandma was all calm, cool, and collected. River whispered to put it on speaker. The first word he uttered was destroying. Raven bent over and covered her mouth. Not sure if she could stay quiet. Her sisters came over and sat next to her in the lounger.

"Don't give yourself away, Rave. You can bear this. Let's find out what he wants," Rowan whispered. She could only nod.

"...tried to reach River and Rowan for weeks."

Breath whooshing out of her, she couldn't believe what she was hearing— Not Raven— damn it, why was she surprised?

"Repeat what you said, please. The service skipped out." A lie, she only wanted him to repeat what he'd already said for their benefit.

"Listen, I know your granddaughters know everything that's been going on here in Oklahoma. James O'Connor's sister, Josephine, promised to tell them everything. And I assume they would tell you." He hesitated, probably not sure how much Raven would have told her grandma.

"Did Raven tell you about... the pictures... and... all of that?"

"She did."

"I know now that they were faked."

Nan didn't speak.

"Bébhinn, did you hear me?"

"I did, Mr. O'Faolain. Miss O'Connor let Raven know that the reports were confirmed. We, of course, didn't need the reports to know. Is there anything else? I'm quite busy." Cool. As. A. Cucumber.

River whispered. "Nan is a badass."

She could tell by his pause that Bran was thrown by her grandma's attitude. She was giving him none of her usual warmth.

"Please, Bébhinn, hear what I'm saying. There is someone, still walking free, that followed first James' girlfriend and then mine and took pictures of them. The pictures were altered, yes, but they were real pictures of Jane and Raven. I've been trying to call you for two weeks!"

"I broke my phone screen and had to get it repaired."

She wasn't lying. Before they boarded the Funicular last week, she'd dropped it face down, and it shattered the screen. Thankfully, Lugano had a repair shop that carried iPhone screens. She had just gotten it back yesterday.

"Jo said you were fine but wouldn't tell me anything else. I thought... I assumed you didn't want to speak to me. And I wouldn't blame you after what I did," he rushed to add.

"Had I had my phone, I would have taken your call. I am not known for being purposefully cruel."

Raven and both her sisters flinched. Nan had been holding back on her anger, it seemed.

"I deserve that... Mrs. Byrne. I hurt Raven. On purpose. I thought she had lied about her feelings. I have done nothing in my life as wrong, as brutal, and grievously spiteful as what I did that night. I will never be that man again. I threw the best thing in my life away, and I have suffered every moment of every day for the past two months."

Nan finally spoke. "I appreciate your remorse, Bran, I do, but I don't think you have even an inkling of the pain and suffering my granddaughter endured because of your words."

They could all hear that Bran was crying. Oh, God. She pictured him scrubbing his hands through his hair, making it stand up at weird angles.

"Steady," Rowan whispered.

"No rash decisions. It isn't just about you anymore."

The baby.

Voice hoarse and croaking, Bran tried to respond.

"I would give anything to change that night," he whispered.

Even Nan's stoic face showed some cracks of sympathy.

"Can you please, Mrs. Byrne, I'm begging, ask Raven if I might be able to see her? Or talk on the phone? Or text even? Or... even tell me where she is. I give you my word. I won't follow her. I... need to know... Not knowing even where she is sleeping at night is killing me."

Nan sighed. "She's been out of your country these past two months, and no, not Ireland. Her sisters are with her. She is loved."

"Would you ask her to let me speak to her? Please."

"And I am asking you to give her a couple of months. She has a lot of healing left to do. She is also aware that it took James coming forward only two weeks ago to make you consider she might not have been capable of what you accused her of.

"She's glad, we're all glad, that her name was exonerated, but the truth is, if James hadn't sent the photos off, would you be asking to see her now? These are the thoughts that Raven needs to consider and how they make her feel. How she feels about you.

"Give her two more months. She has told me that she'll let you know one way or another. I am asking you to respect her wishes, Bran. And don't think I don't understand that there is a person out there wanting to hurt your family and the O'Connors, that he was the catalyst of this mess, but *you* are the one who didn't allow her any defense."

"You're right, and I'll do what you ask though it will kill me. Two months seems like a lifetime."

It was a good thing Bran was in another country because Raven knew if he were in front of her, she would go to him, wrap her arms around his waist, and never let go. Her family was right. Had been right from the beginning. Time apart was necessary. Separation allows healing and personal growth.

She needed to be standing strong and in charge of her life once more before she let him in. She needed to know that if he didn't prove himself to be the man she needed, she could make it on her own. This child would always have two parents. They just might not ever be together again.

Oh, but she hoped— desperately— that one day, they could be a family.

"I've taken enough of your time Béb— Mrs. Byrne, but I need to ask, otherwise Dad and Patrick will throw me down a flight of stairs, if Rowan and River might consent to giving their numbers to them. They won't ask questions pertaining to Raven."

Everybody looked at each other with raised brows. What was this about?

"Why do they want their numbers?"

"Patrick has been sulking for weeks about River leaving and not saying goodbye. He'd like an explanation. His words, not mine."

She felt River shiver next to her. She had believed there were feelings between those two, but when Raven had tried to talk to her about it, her sister always blew it off and changed the subject.

"And who needs Rowan's?"

"I won't pretend to understand my father. He's been bent out of shape about something Rowan designed for my grandfather's memorial in the pub."

"What the hell? No way," Rowan whisper-shrieked. "The space was perfectly designed!"

Nan gave her a sharp look to be quiet. "What problem?"

Bran was hesitating now. They all leaned toward Nan's phone. Waiting. Waiting. Waiting.

"The font she chose for a plaque."

"Ahh. A font problem, is it? Okay. I'll pass the news on. If the girls decide to give out their numbers, they'll let Miss O'Connor know."

"I know you have the information from Jo, but she isn't taking the possible threat this stalker is seriously enough. They have knowledge of our routines, where we live, and who we see. This has been going on for a while. I can't stress enough that Raven needs to think about security. I will provide professional guards for all three sisters wherever they are now and wherever they may be moving to. It isn't just me asking. My family wants them all protected, as well."

"I promise to pass on all of these things to the girls. You have my word, but they will do as they want."

"Okay. Right." Bran took a deep breath. "It was really, really good to talk to you. I wanted, *needed*, some connection to Raven. Two months. Two more months," he whispered. Louder, he finished. Telling Nan, "I'd wait the rest of my life for her, so I can manage two months. As long as I have hope she'll contact me at the end of them."

"She will."

"Tell her I love her with everything I am. Tell her I don't deserve even a moment of her time, but I'm begging she'll give it to me."

Raven needed the time, she did, but two months would seem an eternity to her as well. She and Bran were of one mind in that she would wait a lifetime for him too.

25

———

Two weeks earlier.

S am had changed things up this morning. Instead of his plain, toasted bagel with butter, he'd added blueberry bagels to his last food order. He sat his breakfast next to his steaming cup of hazelnut coffee and adjusted the napkin in his lap.

Chuckling at his routine, Sam knew exactly what he was doing as he powered up his laptop. Allowing anticipation to build. He could feel his skin start to tingle. Checking his surveillance photos made him slightly giddy. It had been weeks of nothing. Something... his intuition hinted... knew change was coming.

Before he pulled up the first of his camera images, he clicked his 50s and 60s oldies playlist. His dad had loved listening to this playlist. Bobby Day's Rockin' Robin started playing. What a happy song for snooping, he chuckled.

He'd save the women's locker room gym pics for last in case he decided to exercise something besides his brain this morning.

He took his first bite of toasted blueberry. As the berry flavor burst on his tongue— paired with warm butter— damn, he'd have to switch his routine more often. He began to flip through the hotel stills, nothing, but he knew this would be the case. The O'Faolains didn't spend a lot of time in town these days. Bran was still crying over the breakup. Perfect.

James did nothing but work, whether alone, with his sister, or flying all over to meet his parents. He remained alone, though, so Sam wasn't concerned he was missing a new relationship. It would happen. Just not yet.

He instantly started thinking of different ways to fuck with their lives when they did move on. Perhaps a new girlfriend would enjoy a special evening with Sam. He would video all the amazing things she would do to him and for him. The thought of sending homemade porn to those pieces of shit might become his newest obsession. Along with these bagels, damn.

Okay, enough daydreaming. He moved quickly through the cleaning staff coming and going outside the family rooms. Nothing. No surprise. He flipped to Eufaula, though the sisters had been out of town for some time. Run off by the heartless Bran. He almost felt a twinge of regret where the youngest sister was concerned. He admitted to being drawn to her. He would definitely have to see where they went if they didn't show up soon.

He knew from the real estate sign that they'd sold their business, but that didn't mean they didn't plan on moving closer to Tulsa eventually. They'd become close to O'Connor's sister. He might have to start watching that woman more closely.

He still checked Eufaula just in case they were back in town for last-minute packing. Days of nothing, only a few passersby— and then, holy fuck, all three O'Faolain men appeared in front of the door.

Sam sat up straighter, concentrating on flipping through the stills. My, my, Bran must not be over the oldest Byrne after all. Well, this was delightful indeed. A few pics showed Bran seemingly staring directly at the camera. Cheese, motherfucker.

Next still, Bran in the middle of the sidewalk, walking toward the curb. Probably where they parked.

Next still, Hugh and Patrick looking in Bran's direction.

Next still, an eyeball.

Jesus, fuck, Sam startled and spilled his coffee in his lap and over the second half of his bagel. "Damn it all to hell, Sam." He chided himself.

Blotting his lap, he reached over the mess to click to the next photo. This one was taken from a different angle than the camera's previous hiding place would have taken. It showed a hand in the forefront and the top of Triskelion and sky beyond that.

"No. No, no, no, no."

Sam slammed the lid shut on his laptop, left the mess of dishes on the table, and hustled back inside. He may have hours, he may have days, but those bastards had enough money to hire people to find out where the stills were being sent.

Every one of his emergency exit plans was about to be deployed.

26

Bran hung up the phone with Bébhinn Byrne. It was early in the morning, and he was sitting in the kitchen of his Muskogee home. The home that he and Raven were meant to be living in together.

Until he had obliterated that future.

Please, God, let Raven not change her mind about reaching out to him.

With no courteous text— or a single fucking knock on the door— his dad and brother walked into the kitchen where he sat, contemplating the morning sky, the streaks of pink, purple, and orange shooting through the clouds.

"Did you talk to Mrs. Byrne?"

"Was River there?"

Bran was about to say something unkind about their invasion until he saw Pat rummaging through his fridge. Breakfast. He'd hold his tongue.

"Just. And if any of the sisters were there, I wouldn't know, and Bébhinn wasn't of a mind to volunteer information."

"What did you find out?" his dad asked as he sat beside Bran at the table.

"Jo has kept them all abreast of the situation with the stalker — though we knew she would. They've been out of the country, it seems, for the past two months. I hope that means they are safer because of it, but I'm devastated that the woman I love is not even on the same continent as me."

The men stayed quiet. The only noise came from the cracking of eggs and pots and pans. It appeared none of them liked the distance.

"Did you remember to ask if Dad and I could have their new numbers?"

"Their grandma said she would pass along the request. If they agreed, they'd let Jo know. I've been thinking about Bébhinn. I imagine she is with the girls wherever they are."

"Of course, she is."

He would love to flick his know-it-all dad's forehead— just once. He'd get the shit beat out of him, but still, it might be worth it.

"They've probably just been staying with her in Ireland."

"No, Pat. Bébhinn told me they weren't in Ireland. She wouldn't lie. They're somewhere else. I just wish Jo would tell me, damn it! I wouldn't follow her. I just want to know."

His dad only grunted. Fifteen minutes of tense silence later, Pat slid a platter of eggs, toast, bacon, and bottles of water between them before taking his own seat.

"Do you think Raven will talk to you?"

Patrick was piling food on his plate. His voice held little inflection. He was probably afraid to show too much emotion in case the news wasn't good, and Bran might want to avoid answering.

"She needs a couple more months, Bébhinn said. Two more." Bran's fork was digging painfully into his middle finger. He loosened his grip before taking a bite of over easy eggs. "I understand. It's just... damn it, I want to see her."

"Why two months?"

"Bébhinn told me that it's been two months since I accused her of cheating, and Raven believes that had James not come forward and got me to consider that the photos were faked, I would not have wanted to talk to her now. They all knew she was innocent, but I needed the evidence."

Bran grabbed his half-eaten breakfast off the table and took his plate to the sink to start washing Patrick's dishes. "Jesus, the amount of stupidity and arrogance I managed to hold onto over the past months is shocking. I don't blame Raven for not wanting me back right away. If ever."

"Two months is a whole fuckton better than never, brother. You'll win her back."

"And if she says no in two months, we do what I suggested two weeks ago," Dad grumbled. "We hire a private detective, circumvent Josephine, and track them down. If we're standing in front of them, they'll have to talk to us."

"I agree, Dad. I'm hopeful River will let me have her number before then, though."

Dad brought his own plate to Bran, handing it over. He asked what Bran planned on doing with his time while he waited.

"I've got to make a run to the Oklahoma Historical Society in a couple weeks to make the final selection of professors that are going to speak at the fundraising this winter. Then there is Wolves grand opening. It was originally scheduled for this weekend to celebrate the Labor Day crowd. You put it off. O'Connors are pushing for a date." He looked at his dad, raising his eyebrows... well?

Hugh O'Faolain crossed his muscular arms over his broad chest, affecting a casual lean against the refrigerator. "I'll have a date within the week, and I'm paying the O'Connors extra for the delay."

He walked out of the kitchen and the front door without uttering another word.

"Jesus, he's a moody bastard. Beat the shit out of me, Bran, if I ever start acting like our old man."

Patrick was joking, of course. They loved and respected their dad above all others, but he was right about the moody bastard part. Dad exuded a fuckoff vibe more than usual.

Pat went on, "I already texted Jo to put in a good word to River about me. She told me to fuck off, but she didn't say she wouldn't... winning. What else do you plan on doing while you wait for— what is it," looking at his watch, "the beginning of November?"

"I put a countdown in my phone. October 31. I'm trying to be optimistic. If River does give up her number, and you guys talk once in a while, if anything is brought up about Raven, you'd tell me, right?"

"You know I will, Bran. The Byrne sisters aren't the only close siblings."

Bran smiled. True. "As for plans. I'm calling a landscaper today. Gran sent me the name of a woman who's lived in Oklahoma for twenty years but is originally from Ireland. Raven wanted to plant a wild garden of flowers here, and I'm going to make it happen. I'm also going to reach out to the chef that cooked for us the night I... destroyed our relationship."

"Why? He probably heard enough that night to scare him off the O'Faolains for good. You probably don't know this, but the chef opened the door to Dad's study that night to bring in dessert. He quickly backed out, and I'm sure even more quickly left. He may not be interested in hearing from you."

Bran cringed. "I don't care about being embarrassed. I'll apologize to him. Raven loved the bread he baked that night, and she and her sisters talked about some fucking starter or something. I don't really understand what it is, but you make the bread with it. I'm going to learn how to make it and give it to Raven as a gift."

"Wow, okay. You're serious. Noted."

"There isn't anything I wouldn't do to prove myself to her."

Jo CALLED Patrick three days later while he, their father, and Bran were eating dinner and having drinks on the deck.

"Jo, it's good to hear from you."

"Pat. It's your lucky day. River consented to give you her number. I'm texting it to you now."

"Any other news?" Bran asked. Not expecting anything, but hopeful as shit.

"No, that's it. Hey Hugh, do you have an idea when you'll let us open at Wolves?"

"Did you let Rowan know I wasn't happy with the memorial?"

Dad was as close to growling as a human could get.

"River told me that if you were unhappy with Rowan's work, her sister asked that you hire another designer. She wasn't spending anymore unpaid time on the project."

"I would have paid her, goddammit. I would like to pay all three of them for the work they did."

"Well, that's nice, but neither here nor there, I suppose. Rowan did mention that the senior O'Faolain could stick his font up his ass. I'm not sure what left field that flew in from, but maybe it'll make sense to you guys."

"That young lady is impossible."

"I can change none of that, Hugh. I want a date for Wolves' grand opening."

Dad sighed. Clearly knowing when to give in. "Choose what day works best for you. Tell Bran or Pat." He hung up. Conversation over.

27

———

"I can't believe our adventure has come to an end, girls. Well, my part of the adventure anyway. You three are ending one and beginning another when we land."

"And just think, Nan. In six months or so, you'll be a great grandma!"

She laughed, "Oh Lord, I can't wait. I've been trying out names for myself— leaning toward Nana."

They oohed and aahed at the choice. Raven was so lucky to have such loving women in her life. This baby would be spoiled rotten.

"As we're about to land, and I'll have only a few minutes at the airport before my friend takes me home, I wanted to talk to you three about something." They all groaned. "This is not a lecture, but with your attitudes perhaps I should give you one," she hmphed.

Ignoring their chuckles, Nan plowed ahead. "I've been thinking a lot about Bran and Patrick's mother since he called me yesterday." That got everyone's attention. "Now, I've only met Bran in person, but I've been on a video chat with Patrick and Hugh. Despite the nonsense and heartache Bran put Raven through, would you consider the O'Faolain men to be good men — decent and honest men?"

Raven answered first. "Yes, I do."

"Yes."

"They are. Bran is questionable, though." River squeezed her sister's leg and smiled.

"I'm not going to wax on about this, but I do think it's worth saying. That woman, and I won't call her a wife or mother because those titles are earned, and she didn't earn a damn thing, is a horrible excuse of a human being. Raven told me some of the family history that Bran told her.

"So, this Helen married Hugh, and from the sound of it, never planned on a true marriage. I imagine she made Hugh feel unwelcome in his own home, unwanted, and unneeded. Bran related that she never hugged them or told them she loved them, and when she and Hugh divorced, she never looked back.

"Can you imagine, girls, how differently you might view relationships if one of your parents had treated you in such a way? Left you? Made sure you knew how unimportant you were, how... disposable?"

Nan dabbed her eyes with a Kleenex. They all were dabbing their eyes.

"I'm sorry to get so emotional, but I've been a wife and mother and a grandmother. There is nothing in this world so joyous as loving and being loved. You know this because of your parents."

"And you!" They all quickly tacked on.

"Yes, and from me. Hugh stepped up and, from what Bran described, is an amazing father. They all love each other, which is a testament to how he raised them— but in the back of their minds, you know there has to be some residual hurt. They might not even be aware of how much it affects them.

"And I'm not just talking about the boys, but Hugh as well.

That woman left a stain behind. I hope, for their sakes, that they can eventually recognize it and wash it away."

"I hear the truth in your words, Nan. It is something to remember as we go forward. River and Patrick are friends, or they were, and I believe they will be again. Raven is having Bran's child, and I think we all know, including you, sister," she smiled at Raven and winked, "that he will be a part of this family, one way or another."

Raven smiled back and shrugged.

"I've missed Patrick, and I am going to give him my number again. I honestly didn't think he would care about me leaving one way or another. There were times I felt we were getting closer, but it's like, as soon as he would start to open up, he'd get scared. He has a wall, Nan, and I think you are spot on with its origin."

"I want to be clear, though, that knowing they may have reasons for certain behavior and reactions does not give them a free pass. They are grown men. Raven staying her course, allowing them both to see what they're like after a separation is the right course," Nan added.

"I think so too. I, however, am not giving up my number to Pat and Hugh. You do you, River, but Hugh just wants my number so he can be an obnoxious complainer," Rowan shook her head in irritation. "Doesn't like a font. What shite, as you would call it, Nan."

"Don't you dare blame that language on me, young lady!" Now focused on Rowan, Nan asked, "Is Hugh not nice to you?"

Rowan blushed. Suspect. She had begun to suspect her sister had feelings for the O'Faolain patriarch. Hmm...

"I can handle his posturing every day of the week and twice on Sundays, Nan. Don't you worry about me."

Laughing, they all settled down to finalize the first things they would need to do upon landing. Getting the keys to their rental was number one— but Raven planned on wheedling *something* from her sisters about their feelings *eventually.*

MEETING SAOIRSE KENNEDY WAS AN EXPERIENCE. Utterly vivacious. The no-nonsense real estate agent could obviously tell the sisters were feeling overwhelmed and easily put them at ease. Once they'd landed and said their goodbyes to Nan, she met them at the apartment they'd rented to give them the keys and sign a few papers that hadn't gotten sent to them in Switzerland.

"Get unpacked, grab some takeaway, and relax tonight. I'll meet you at nine in the morning at your new building downtown. And," she added with a laugh, "because I'm amazing, my boyfriend is meeting us, who just happens to be a contractor. His job between jobs was delayed, so I begged him to take a look and see if he could get what you needed done in the time you need it done, for the price you *really* need it done at."

"No, Saoirse! No way! You are amazing. Thank you so much," Raven practically squealed.

"You have no idea how much that means to us!" Rowan said, briefly squeezing the real estate agent's hand.

River added, "I hope you do your best work on your back, Saoirse— cause we Byrnes need a bargain."

Rowan and I both yelled River's name. Lord, she was incorrigible.

Miss Kennedy never missed a beat. "I'm a sure bet. No worries, girls. Oh, and before I forget, Jo said you've worked together, and there are no better interior decorators to be found. So, again, no applause necessary, but I've already let several of my clients know that some fancy designers are moving to town. My suggestion is that if you have to pay a little extra to open your doors early, at least the bottom level where you'll do business, do it. You ladies are going to be busy."

After a round of hugs, pats, and air kisses, their real estate agent was clip-clopping away in her designer heels.

"Wow."

"Holy wow."

"Holy shit, wow."

"Okay," Raven sighed, looking at the small space, then sighing again when she realized this was going to feel like a mansion once they moved into their one-room flat over the shop. "Let's get unpacked. I think shit's going to get real really quick in Dublin."

Raven felt a sigh of relief wash through her body. They were going to do this. They *were* doing this.

THERE WAS NO BLOOD, thank God, but sweat and tears— buckets. Raven and her sisters had been working round the clock, seven days a week, for weeks. Business cards, website, finalizing permits and the registration that had been started when they first arrived in Switzerland. Sourcing fabric stores, getting to know local artisans, which Raven thankfully had a leg up on from her previous trip.

Finally, Triskelion Territory Designs' doors were open. Figuratively— it was low 50s outside. Everyone on the streets was bundled in wool sweaters, scarves, gloves, and earmuffs. It was easy enough to see that winter was around the corner. So far, and it was early days, things were going very well.

Triskelion served clients coffee, tea, and a spread of scones and muffins— the cinnamon streusel topping ones were the best — from a local bakery delivered each morning. Just thinking of those sweet treats made her mouth water. Her belly was already so rounded Raven shuddered to imagine four months from now. Treats were not in her near future.

Today, Raven had a checkup with her OB/GYN. They'd taken off the afternoon since her sisters wanted to tag along, and then afterwards they could catch up on some work. Right out of the gate, the doctor mentioned that Raven had lost weight again since her previous visit.

Raven had looked at her sisters, and they'd grimaced. Damn it, they had all been working so hard and such long hours, they had *all* lost weight, and... they certainly hadn't needed to lose any.

To save money, they had only kept the apartment for three weeks before moving into the small flat above their shop. The contractor was amazing, as advertised by his girlfriend, and had gotten the flat livable first. The tiny bathroom plumbing was up to snuff. He'd painted the walls all white and made sure the wiring, smoke detectors, and heat worked, which basically blew in through vents from below.

All their resources had to be concentrated on where they would be doing business. It made sense to stay under budget with the flat in case there were unforeseen expenses below or with the baby.

They made do with a few secondhand pieces of furniture for the living room, as none of their things in storage would fit. They had the contractor hang a large mirror on one wall that they used to do their hair, makeup, and outfit checks. They found a nice plush rug to place in front of the mirror to sit on. They shared a couple of plastic three-drawer stacks on each side of the mirror. All bathroom items and makeup went into those. They used tubs and hanging racks for clothes and shoes. The bathroom was a shoebox with running water— little to recommend there.

They each got a narrow cot and thin mattress lined up opposite the mirror. There wasn't room for more than a queen bed and that would have taken up all the space. This way, they could roll over on their cot and not wake up everyone else. At least they had soft pillows and bedding from storage.

The 'kitchen' was even more depressing. There was room for a tiny card table and folding chairs to sit next to the single countertop, which held a teapot, hot plate, and microwave, with a small fridge under the counter. The single sink had a cabinet above it. They had to keep all their cleaning supplies, dish soap, laundry detergent— don't get her started on lugging everything to the laundromat— and toilet paper in there. The food stayed on the counter. One drawer for utensils, one for spices. Three plates, three glasses, and three coffee mugs sat on a shelf over the toaster.

They'd all gotten into the habit of cooking enough chicken or fish on Sundays to top large salads for lunches and dinners for the week. Protein powder sat on the counter next to Raven's prenatal vitamins. The powder didn't have to be refrigerated and could be mixed with water. They put another mini fridge below to keep cold water for clients.

It was functional and not forever. She and her sisters had repeated that phrase a lot over the past two months. Functional. Not Forever.

So, with their work schedule and not eating as much as they used to, they were thinner, but they all felt amazing and energetic. They'd gotten a feature interview published with *The Irish Times*, a daily newspaper— thanks very much to Saoirse Kennedy! It had been hectic, rewarding, and very exciting.

However, Raven's career was not more important than Baby O's health. So, it was a relief that the doctor confirmed she was healthy, as was the baby.

Raven had gotten so used to referring to her bump as Baby O she could strangle her sisters for it. Rowan had started it as a nod to Bran's last name, but River said it stood for orgasm—what she was probably having at the time of conception. Now, when anyone referred to her tummy as Baby O, she blushed.

Still, Raven wanted clarification that her weight loss was absolutely not a problem for the baby.

"No, no. The baby's growth is where it should be. Healthy heartbeat, weight is perfect. I know you and your sisters have been busy, but you've kept a diet log as I asked, and it is all healthy, good stuff for the little one and you, with plenty of good protein and fats. Just be aware that you will probably need to up your calories in the last trimester, as that's when baby will grow the most. Try eating salmon more often. It's an excellent source of protein and Omega-3 fatty acids. Baby still moving?"

Relieved, she answered quickly. "Oh, yes. All the time."

Rowan and River grinned as the doctor covered her belly back up.

"Baby O is healthy, sis." Rowan and River both patted her bulge, and the baby kicked several times.

Raven laughed. "The baby knows its aunties."

Getting up from the table, she asked Dr. Daley one more thing. "Doctor, I spoke with a woman at the grocery store yesterday that was six weeks further along than me, but... I was the same size! I know you've told me not to judge my belly against others, but I feel really big."

"Raven, relax. Your body is exactly the way it's supposed to be. You're a tiny woman, dear. Someday, if your sisters decide to have children, they will probably experience the exact same thing. My suggestion is to stop trying to cover up the fact that you're pregnant and go out and buy some lovely, fitted maternity clothes. Embrace your belly. Embrace impending motherhood. Enjoy it. I imagine your sisters know just the place to get some clothes."

"Thank you, doctor. Rowan and I were about to have a

Dumpy Outfit Intervention. Raven, get dressed. We are going shopping now!"

"You guys are horrible." She stood from the exam table and decided to spit out her other concern. She didn't mind her sisters' hearing, just the discussion that would follow.

"I plan on inviting the baby's father to Dublin soon." *Silence of the Byrne's* Now Playing at her back. "I've wanted to wait to find out the sex of the baby until he's here in case he might want to... do an ultrasound with me."

"Oh, Raven, of course. If you know when he might arrive, you can make an appointment before you leave today. If you need to cancel, I don't want you to worry. Mama's come first in our office. Sound good?"

Relieved, excited, and very nervous. She thanked the doctor before being whisked to the shops. Obviously, catching up on work wasn't on the schedule.

Jo's PLANE had landed a few hours ago. She'd told them she would drop her things off at The Fitzwilliam before heading to Triskelion to see their new space.

After hours upon hours of shopping, Raven and her sisters were heading back to their shop. She was wearing one of the new outfits. Apparently, they couldn't take the homeless look on her anymore. Bitches. But... okay... she felt glorious. She looked chic and lovely. The doctor was right. She'd been hiding, not embracing. No more!

Everything was happening, it seemed, on one, single, flipping day! Because she was calling Bran tonight. It was time. But first, Josephine O'Connor.

"Oh Lord, you guys. I'm nervous! Do you think I screwed

up keeping Baby O a secret? Jo is going to kill me, then you guys, and finally Saoirse."

"She won't kill anyone," Rowan promised. "She will see that baby bump..." she coughed in her hand, "giant, baby bump that is, and melt."

River laughed hysterically.

"You assholes wait! You heard Dr. Daley. Take a good look at your future." Raven rubbed her belly dramatically as they walked along the sidewalk toward home.

"I'm glad you're calling Bran tonight, Rave. I truly am. He fucked up. Bad. But— dang it, I don't want to cry— I think you guys are better together. I think you both need each other and... I want my niece or nephew to have what we had growing up."

Raven hugged River, matching their strides, scarves flapping between their long hair. "I love you." Pulling her youngest sister in with her other arm, she laughed, "I love you too."

Arm, in arm, in arm. Today was magical.

Jo was waiting outside their building with a giant hulk of scowling man. River was the first to break away and run to embrace their friend.

"Jo, you bitch! Finally! I never thought you would get here. We've missed you."

Laughing, she hugged River back and swung her around. Rowan and I approached. Raven's winter coat hid her 'condition,' but that wouldn't last.

Rowan, sensing her hesitation, moved ahead and held her hand out to Jo's companion. "Honey Bunny, it's so good to meet you. I'm Rowan Byrne. That lunatic hugging part of your, ah, colony, is my sister River, and this," she waved for me to step forward, "is our oldest sister, Raven."

Raven also stuck her hand out... manners and all that. "Honey... Bunny. Raven." She had never witnessed someone having a heart attack, stroke, or any type of life-altering health event, but the look on this man's face had to come damn close. Jaw and eyes clenched shut, he seemed to be doing a breathing exercise before shaking their hands in return.

Rowan turned to Jo for her hug as River got the key out to open the store up. And then, it was time for her hug. Oh God, here it was.

Jo squealed Raven's name and enveloped her in warm spices and golden hair. Tears pricked Raven's eyes. She had really missed seeing her friend. And then, Jo stiffened. Honey Bunny took a step toward them, immediately trying to assess the change in his charge's demeanor.

"Rave?"

She backed up out of her arms and unzipped her fleece coat. Looking at her, Raven smiled. "Meet Baby O." Then she placed a hand on her bump. "Baby O, meet your third auntie, Josephine."

Once inside the warmth of Triskelion, Jo stood, looking poleaxed. HB— seriously, no one could call that Hulk Honey with a straight face— stood behind Jo, a dinner-plate-sized hand wrapped lightly around the back of her friend's neck. A balustrade during a storm of emotions.

"Rave," Jo whispered again. "You're pregnant."

"I only found out at the end of our trip, and I thought it would be fun... to surprise you?"

"Surprised, shocked. Does Bran know? No, no, no," she answered herself. "He would be here if he did." Briefly touching HB's arm, so he would release her, Jo walked to Raven and hugged her again. "Wow. Consider me surprised."

They all laughed then. "We'll catch you up on everything tonight, I promise. But for now, let my sisters and me introduce you to Triskelion Territory Designs 2.0."

"Oh, girls," Jo twirled around, "you've done well. It is stunning."

Jo took in the wide, deep grain of the original wood floors, the cottage feel from the whitewashed walls, floral tapestry-covered chairs, and heavily carved, Gothic revival desks nestled on sumptuous wool rugs. The colors were of a sunlit flower garden, rich golds, greens, yellows, and reds.

Jo sucked in a sharp breath. "You guys... you... oh my." She looked at HB, probably not even realizing what she was revealing. "Honey, isn't it wonderful?" she breathed.

He dipped his head the barest increment. But his eyes burned. Jo was satisfied with his nonverbal cues.

"It's great, isn't it? We love it."

"Beyond great. Saoirse wouldn't give me any hints, that bitch! I see now why you chose this property. My God, I want to spend money just by walking through the doors."

"She has been the best since we moved here, Jo. The best." Rowan admitted.

"Of course, she has. I knew she would be. You guys can tell me everything over dinner, including Baby O details. Let's go upstairs and drink and celebrate finally being together again."

The sisters all looked slightly ill at that suggestion. "Oh, Jo, we planned on wining and dining you in town tonight. Plus," poking her thumb in Raven's direction, "It's Camp Prohibition with Miss Knocked Up as a roommate."

"You guys are hiding something from me."

It's not like they were embarrassed. They cleaned their flat to within an inch of its tiny life, but Jo was definitely not used to such mean accommodations. Perhaps pride was tweaking their tails a bit.

"Our flat is pretty small, Jo. Let's just go out."

Jo moved her hair behind her ears, revealing the earrings they'd given her. Oh God, her eyes looked glassy. HB's jaw was clenched.

"Sisters... you said. Sisters don't hide things."

Raven looked at River and Rowan.

"You're right. Please, sister mine, come upstairs."

Fifteen minutes later, all calm, Jo turned to HB. "Honey. Please call Dom and arrange dinner for five." Then she turned to them. "This isn't going to work. How dare you three live like this and not tell me."

Now Raven was starting to get angry. "Jo, stop being dramatic. You are acting as though we've been sleeping on the streets. We know it isn't ideal, but it isn't forever. Once we are turning a consistent profit, we will reno the space or buy ourselves a house."

"Dramatic? You three are... are... fucking camping at best. We are leaving. Now."

River stepped forward then. "Jo, this isn't permanent, and we are fine. It's cramped but clean. We are going to be successful, and this tiny space will be a distant memory."

Rowan added, "No one ever said success didn't come with sacrifices. Our parents taught us that. We would love to eat dinner with you, but we will return to our home tonight. As you can see, we are no worse for wear."

"You are all too thin," Jo stated, as she defensively crossed her arms over her chest.

Jo looked at HB then, with a 'Help Me' expression. What? Did she want him to forcibly remove them from the premises?

"We have money for food, damn it. It was a choice to not overextend on living quarters. Just for now. As a security of sorts. I just came from a doctor's appointment, and she did mention my weight loss, but she said it was because of our busy schedule. That I was healthy. Baby is healthy. We're good, Jo. Be happy for us, please."

"Yeah, forget the flat, Jo. We sure as fuck try to," River added sarcastically.

Some of Jo's tension eased, but Raven was sure she was only

rallying a better argument. She wouldn't win. Raven and her sisters were going to make it. Their way.

Thirty minutes later, they were at The Fitzwilliam, and Raven was hugging Dom. They were both laughing and crying, and he was touching her stomach in awe.

"Miss Byrne," he looked so happy. "A baby. Mr. O'Faolain must be beside himself."

"Yes." Bran was beside himself, just not the way Dom was thinking.

"Dinner about ready, Dom? I heard Honey Bunny's stomach rumble on the ride here." Jo was trying to save her from any further talk of Bran.

Glancing briefly at the glowering Titan, Dom ushered them toward a private dining room. "Yes, Miss O'Connor. This way."

All sparkling lights and magic. Raven could feel her throat fill with unshed tears as she thought of the last time she'd been in this hotel. She placed her hand over her stomach. Five months.

The food was served, but only after Jo and Honey fought. Silently. HB wouldn't sit down at the table. He stood at the door's entrance. Jo asked him to sit down in a chair that faced the doorway. A compromise. He ignored the suggestion. Jo told the server not to serve anything until the gentleman at the door took a seat at the table.

Five minutes of silence later. Jo asked the same nervous server if a crust of bread might be procured for her pregnant guest. HB sat at the table.

Dinner *was* delicious. Unfortunately, Raven didn't eat much. Her stomach was in knots. She had to call Bran. She'd given her word, but it'd been four months since they last spoke. More time than they were even together.

There was always a chance he hadn't waited for her.

Though, if that were the case, surely Jo would know, and she would certainly say.

Mind made up, Raven placed her napkin beside her mostly full plate and began to move the heavy chair away from the table. Jo's security guard was up and pulling her chair out before she'd even noticed he'd left his own chair.

"Oh, thank you, HB. Those chairs are bigger than I am," she laughed. All eyes on her now, she explained. "Please, everyone, finish your dinner. I'm going to step out on the balcony and... call Bran."

"Oh."

"Oh, fuck."

"Thank God."

"Alright, then." She was still standing in the same spot. "I'm going to do it now." Still not moving.

River and Rowan slipped out of their chairs and stood facing her. Much easier for them without a giant belly.

"No matter what happens on that call, sis, you and Baby O will never be alone," Rowan said.

"Never alone, Rave. You've got me and Honey too. Go on and do it. Bran has literally made me consider changing my number."

Raven walked out on the balcony. There was a table and chairs set up in an alcove where the cold breeze didn't penetrate. There was a standing heater close to the table, making it a cozy corner. Breathing slowly in and out to calm her racing heart, she dialed Bran's number from memory. He answered on the first ring.

"Raven."

28

———

He should thank Bran O'Faolain for finding his Eufaula camera. If he hadn't, Sam would still be performing the same tasks, day in and day out, for who knew how long. He had felt dissatisfaction for a while now. His petty picture stills and occasional voyeuristic endeavors at the women's gym held little appeal.

Even serving those he hated while in disguise had lost that thrilling edge.

Admittedly, he'd known for some time that ruining the Musketeers' relationships wouldn't... couldn't, sustain his needs long term. This was just the end of his first volley. The still picture of Bran's eye, looking straight at him through the camera, he would admit, startled him. Like a horror movie jump scare scene. Over.

So, there was no mad dash to throw everything in a duffel bag and run for the hills. No. He had planned too well for such amateurish behavior. Instead of the plebian totes, tubs, and bins, Sam used a highly efficient packing system for all of his belongings to easily fit into suitcases. His personal belongings, fake IDs, passports, bank account information, ready cash, weapons, drugs, *computer and video equipment, burner phones, and of course, memorabilia of his father— all of it either easily stored in suitcases or already in them.*

He drove to a local U-Haul facility and rented a van, leaving his car in the lot. It wasn't in his name. And he, of course, wore a disguise. A woman this time, in case the police tracked him there and looked at U-Haul's camera surveillance.

Within an hour of returning home, he was packed and on his way to a motorhome dealership. Three hours after that, Tina Burner, a riff on one of his dad's favorite singers and his alias for the day, bought a fully loaded Class A motorhome. His belongings from the U-Haul were on board, and he was pulling out of the lot.

He was untraceable. Untrackable. Unbeatable. Yes, his first game was over. But it had only been a game.

Samuel Delton was invigorated. He had a new purpose. And he had all the time in the world to make those pieces of shit pay.

For now, he might simply enjoy the open road, so to speak. Perhaps try out his new bedroom setup on a few 'willing women.'

He had enough money, even with this last large purchase. Still, he did so enjoy selling some of his homemade videos to his dark web enthusiasts. He was an artist at heart, after all.

Yes, he would definitely take some time for himself. He deserved it. Time enough to deal with the O'Faolains and the O'Connors. He hadn't even begun with James' sister and admitted to a small crush on the youngest Byrne, Rowan. Life was looking up.

Just the open road and new adventures.

29

____

Raven didn't call, text, or email. Every muscle in Bran's body was hot and tight. Miserable. Worse, his eyes were burning. He wasn't losing it. He'd lost it. He considered calling Bébhinn. He'd considered and discarded a hundred things in the past several hours.

He'd hoped yesterday was the day. He still had hope for today. Wherever she was, he was packed. He had their pilot on standby. If she consented to see him, he was there.

He was standing in his father's study, whiskey for lunch in hand, just staring at the fire. He heard footsteps behind him but didn't turn around. It was his dad or brother or both.

"How long will you wait before you take the choice from her?"

Dad then. "I drove her away once, Dad. I don't think showing up, wherever she is, would endear my cause to her." As Bran hadn't turned around, he got a face full of newspaper. Snatching it from his father's clenched fist, he whirled around, ready to fight— anyone for any reason.

"What are you fucking doing?" He looked from his dad to his brother's raised brows. His father's special type of irritating silence answered. Looking at the paper in his hand, he saw a woman smiling at him. The most beautiful woman in the world. Setting his glass on the bar, he began to smooth out the edition of *The Irish Times*.

"Where did you get this paper?"

"Mom gave it to me when I met her for lunch last week."

"Last fucking week! Are you kidding me?"

"Mrs. Byrne gave you a time. That time wasn't up. It is now."

He clenched his teeth together so he wouldn't lash out. His father meant well. He read the article three times. Stopping and staring at the picture of the sisters each time.

"They are opening a new design studio. In Ireland."

"Opened by now."

Bran looked at his brother, who had remained silent. "Did you know anything about this?"

"Nothing." Patrick looked floored. "I thought... assumed, I guess... River never said she was never moving back to Oklahoma."

Bran spread his hands over the pages again. Smoothing the creases where he'd ripped it out of his dad's hands.

"I called Bobby. He told me you've had him on standby for two days. I told him we'd be there in less than two hours."

Bran looked at him, he was sure, with a blank expression. "Dad. She hasn't called me yet."

"Turns out I don't give a fuck. You want to see Raven, and Pat wants to see River. I also know that Josephine flew to Dublin this morning. She must have been waiting for Triskelion to be up and running. O'Connor's pilot and ours are buddies, it turns out. The same pilot also mentioned flying the Byrne sisters to Switzerland about four months ago."

She'd been in Switzerland. It crushed him to know she'd

been so far away while he'd arrogantly believed she'd stayed in Oklahoma.

Dad turned to Patrick. "You going?"

"Already packed. I knew if Bran got a call, I'd needed to be ready too." He shrugged.

Bran wanted to say no. He *wanted* to wait for some sign that she would see him. "My bags are packed. I'll meet you at the truck."

THEY DROVE straight to the airport, where their jet was waiting. One of the airport employees would take the truck to a parking garage. The three men unloaded their bags and headed for the plane. Bobby waved to them as he secured the open door and stairs. Through the windows, Bran could see someone moving around the cabin, prepping for them. Most likely, it was Brenda. He hoped she didn't ask him about Raven.

Bran was tense as they boarded and settled into their seats. He hoped this was the right move. His coat pocket began vibrating. Taking his phone out, he saw that it was an Unknown Number. Oh, God.

Before he answered, he held a hand up to his dad and brother, halting all conversation. His dad immediately got up and walked toward the front. Presumably, to tell the pilot to hold off taxiing for a few minutes if he could.

He answered, knowing in his heart it had to be her.

"Raven."

Silence, and then, "Yes."

Bran fought tears. He fought gulping the deep breaths that his body desperately needed.

"I was afraid you wouldn't call."

"Nan told you I would."

Bran didn't know what to say, where to start. An apology? Tell her how much he loved her? Only her. For fuck's sake, he'd been practicing this very conversation for weeks.

"Thank... I... I'm so glad to hear your voice." Not going according to plan.

"This is harder than... I'd hoped."

"Please don't give up or hang up, Raven. Please don't."

"I would like to..."

Oh God, Raven, finish that thought. He was going out of his mind. His dad was back, sitting by Pat across from Bran.

"I wanted to invite you to visit me in Dublin. At your convenience... and, that is... if you even want to."

She rushed all the words together, but he had never heard anything so wonderful in his life.

"I want to. Immediately. If that's fine." Dad cuffed his head in admonishment for giving her an out.

"Well, we just opened a new Triskelion, so we're pretty swamped just trying to get situated and meeting new clients. A few weeks?"

"I would like..." His dad was getting up to deliver another blow. "Raven, I want to come soon, now... maybe. I won't interrupt your work. I'm so... proud of you for building a new business there."

She didn't say anything.

"Please, let me come."

And then... finally... before she hung up, she sighed but said, "Okay."

Bran leaned his head back. Had someone asked him to move, it would have been impossible. His body had been wound so tight for so many weeks it seemed perfectly happy to be still.

Dad pushed the intercom button on his chair. "Brenda, please tell Bobby we're ready when he is."

"Of course," she replied instantly.

His body was still, but his mind was not. Raven had called. He'd heard Raven's voice. He might be standing in front of her tomorrow. Did she want to tell him in person that she didn't want to see him again? No. He wouldn't entertain that line of thinking.

Reaching over to the box beside him, he briefly touched the lid. A present for Raven. He hoped she would accept it.

"We'll be landing about 5:30 in the morning Dublin time, Bran. We'll sleep as we may on the plane, get a car to the hotel and be able to get checked in, shower, and have some breakfast before we head to Triskelion."

Bran nodded in agreement.

"I looked up their website while we drove to the airport. River must have made it. It's even better than the first one. Business hours are 9 am. to 4 pm."

"I booked us rooms at The Westin. Jo will have booked at The Fitzwilliam. At least, I assume she did. After you and Raven told her about the butler there, I'm sure she'd want the experience."

The plane was taxiing down the runway. Patrick's phone dinged. It had to be River. Did his brother realize he only smiled when he got a text from her? Pat was keeping himself cool and collected, but Bran knew him well enough to see his barely suppressed anticipation at seeing his 'friend' again.

"River text?"

Patrick glanced up and flashed a brief smile before returning to his phone. "She and her sisters are walking home from dinner. She said it's colder than a witch's tit. She must need warmer clothes. I'll see what the hotel shops have and pick some things up before we go see them."

"If she's mentioning the weather, she is letting her guard down. Raven must have told them she called me."

"She would, of course." Dad the Happy Helper.

"You know, Bran, I just assumed we would be going with you to see the girls together, but I will understand if you want to do it alone," Pat said, setting his phone aside to regard his brother.

That was thoughtful. Bran must have been an even more tragic figure these past months than he'd realized.

"No, they'll want to see all of us. I hope they do." He only just considered that he would need to make amends with three women, not one. Four, if he added Bébhinn. "You guys will be a good distraction, at any rate."

"I can't wait to see the new property. What they did in Eufaula was very creative."

"Pat, what exactly are you up to with River?" Before his brother could tell him to fuck off, Bran held up his hands in peace. "I'm not trying to get in your business. I know you would never intentionally hurt River. I only wanted to warn you about Mrs. Byrne. I felt like Bébhinn put me through a meat grinder last time we spoke, and she never raised her voice. Be careful, there, that's all."

Not used to discussing relationships— ever— Patrick's face went blank. "She doesn't think of me as anything other than a friend, which is how I want to keep it."

"Is she not your type?" Bran knew he was poking his nose in more than necessary now. Patrick's type usually started with *social* and ended with *ite*. As long as the women looked good on his arm and in his bed, knew the game and never expected commitment, he was down.

"River would be anyone's type," his brother practically growled.

Patrick immediately returned to a book he'd pulled out during takeoff, effectively ending the Q & A. Bran glanced at his dad, who just shrugged and went back to staring out the window.

"Dad, did you hear anything from the detective before we left town?" The stalker was never far from his mind. Not only was it someone with an unknown vendetta against them and the O'Connors, but he had been following and taking fucking pictures of his girlfriend. It was sick and twisted and made the situation of not knowing where Raven had been living that much harder these past weeks.

"I left a message first thing this morning that we would be leaving town for an undetermined amount of time. He called me before I spoke to you. They found the suspect's house. At least one of them. Data from the multiple cameras were being sent to several addresses. I didn't understand everything he was telling me, but he said, whoever it is, is a pro."

"Holy shit, were they still there?"

"The house was empty but for a few odds and ends. A half-eaten breakfast was still on the outdoor table. They are dusting the place for fingerprints, but it's like the motherfucker wore gloves. They're still hopeful, and they haven't interviewed all the neighbors yet. He said he'd keep us informed."

Bran frowned, "I don't get what ties our two families together. O'Faolain's hired the O'Connors for Wolves. We aren't restaurateurs. The pictures of Jane were taken before we hired them, as well. You're friendly with James' parents, Dad, but you guys don't socialize, really. Maybe at the club or dinner here and there, but always by chance, not design."

Placing his book aside, Patrick joined the conversation. "Neither Jo nor I have been bothered. Maybe it isn't about our families. Could it have to do with only you and James, Bran?"

Bran rubbed his eyes in frustration. "We don't yet know the extent this person has interacted in our lives. Why Jane and not Jo too? They're both connected to James. Were they taking pictures of Raven or Raven and all her sisters? We've been over it a hundred times with the detectives. Why us? Why now?

Could it seriously have something to do with James and I starting a serious relationship? It's ridiculous.

"Our business lives just don't interconnect, so that leaves our personal lives. Who the fuck knows what the psycho is thinking."

"College?" Patrick asked.

"James and I spent hours on a conference call last week picking apart our school years. Nothing so far."

His dad, who'd been fairly quiet up until now, admitted, "That's why I'm glad the girls left the country, Jane left Tulsa, and O'Connor put security on his daughter. Whoever this sick motherfucker is, they're a danger to women. Mom refused security."

"Then I assume the ones you hired must be very good at not being detected."

"Correct. The police believe the camera outside her condo was to see who we were interacting with. If they were important enough to us, we'd take them to my mother's. But— no one spies on my mother. I spoke with Diana Gaines."

Dad's cheeks darkened at the memory.

"Did the lovely Mrs. Gaines make you feel like a dirty, five-year-old chimney-sweep from the Victorian era?"

"She tried, but I have her number. I got up to leave without her asking me to, bad manners again, and told her that I had come to her on a matter of my mother's safety, but if she wasn't inclined to help, I would let myself out."

Patrick whistled through his teeth. "Bold. That bitch scares the shit out of me."

"She told me to sit back down. That my dramatics gave her a headache. Dramatics," he chuckled. "That woman is the very definition."

"Did you tell her what was going on?"

"I did. All of it. She called her secretary in as I was leaving and told her to plan a trip for her and Mrs. O'Faolain. I heard—*think Greece, Italy, Spain. Fabulous. My dear friend needs to relax, and you know I do.*"

"She is something else. I'm impressed you thought to ask." Bran was glad to have another woman he loved away from the stalker.

"No matter her behavior, she loves Mom. I imagine, as both women are widows, they'll be gone for several months. You boys will have to visit your grandmother at some point while she is away."

"And you, too, Dad." Patrick smiled, all innocence and love.

Dad pressed the button to recline his seat and got his earbuds out, dropping down the flat screen above his head. Before he stuck the earbuds in, he answered. "She is my mother. Of course, I'll visit, you little shit." Then he turned on the news.

Patrick started to recline his chair. "Are you ready for tomorrow?"

"No. God, no. I also wish I were walking through Triskelion's door right now."

"I feel the same," Patrick admitted. "It's nothing like you and Raven. River and I are friends, so it feels strange to have this tension."

Pat adjusted his tall frame yet again, giving credence to his words.

"Friends are loved, too, Pat. Friends are missed. It's okay to need River."

He was quick to deny it. "I don't *need* her, Bran. She's just a friend."

Before he put his own earbuds in, he said, "Maybe she needs you, brother."

Raven tossed and turned last night. She kept replaying every word of her and Bran's stilted conversation.

She'd barely spoken when all she'd wanted to do was beg him to come. Right Now! That she loved him still. Missed him desperately. Instead, he'd gotten, 'Okay.'

"Stop mumbling to yourself, Rave. Jesus, you have an appointment this morning. Oh, and unless I'm seeing things, Honey Bunny just got out of that tiny, little car out front."

Sure enough, River was right. HB was leaning back into the compact to pull Jo out of the back. Hold her hand a little longer than necessary, HB? Raven was smiling at their cat and mouse game— fox and rabbit might be more apt.

Rowan was watching the show. "Good thing Honey held on to Jo that extra forty-five seconds. She may have toppled right back into the car."

They all three laughed at their friend's expense. Raven couldn't wait to drill Miss No Time For Men O'Connor.

"Better unlock the door. We open in thirty minutes anyway, and I don't want to make the happy couple stare into each other's eyes longer than necessary." Raven glanced at her chest, which wasn't tiny to begin with for someone her size and blanched. "Wait, I might be able to open the door with my fucking nipples— from my desk."

"You *have* seemed to... bloom." Delicately put, Rowan.

As River opened things up, Raven glanced down once more. "Row. Be honest. This maternity dress is beautiful, and you picked it out, which makes me love it more, but... my body is so different."

The nude-colored, ankle-length, long-sleeved maxi dress fit her body like skin, hugging every curve. Her long, black hair swirled around her shoulders and waist. She wore matte red ballet slippers and a hand-thrown ceramic bracelet in a natural, tan clay with swirls of red glaze. She'd picked it up in town from a local potter.

She was put together and professional. She loved the outfit but obviously had yet to fully embrace her new body.

"There has never been a lovelier pregnant woman. I swear it. Don't you dare change that outfit." They were interrupted by the door being thrown open. Literally, thrown open.

HB must have been the thrower, but thankfully, he was also the catcher, so the door didn't bang against the wall. Jo walked by him without a word, but her elbow 'accidentally' caught him in the ribs. He frowned but didn't say anything. Raven was sure she had never heard him speak.

"You guys are out on the town early today. Any plans, Jo?" River asked as she took her friend's coat and scarf to hang up.

Raven whispered to Jo, "Has he ever said a word to you?"

"Not one, but I know he talks to people. I'll break him eventually," she whispered back. To River, she said, "My BFF and I are going birthday present shopping for Mom. I have to get something and mail it today, or it won't reach her in time. Her latest obsession is *redecorating everything* in the Tulsa house."

"Oh wow, really. When I stayed there, I thought it was stunning."

"Yeah, I think she's midlifing it a bit. It's driving Dad crazy."

Rowan asked what she was planning on looking for. Raven was sure her sisters were thinking something along the same lines— a painting, antique mirror, table scaping décor, bedding...

"Wallpaper."

"What? Seriously?" River. Subtle.

"Not just any wallpaper, but hand-painted silk wallpaper. An antique store here in town has it, and I'm getting it no matter the cost. It has already gone to a conservationist who specializes in art restoration. It's glorious. Soft florals and cupids. It will be stunning for one of my father's study walls."

"Your dad's study? Floral? Cupids? Umm, are you sure, Jo?"

"Oh yes, you girls can help me word Mom's card. Something like, 'In many cultures, floral patterns in a man's private space are supposed to increase his virility.' Something like that."

"I don't think you need any help with the card, Jo. That was Hallmark worthy."

"Has your dad done something to bring this on?"

Jo didn't reply, just crossed her arms over her chest and stared pointedly at HB. Understood.

"Mom will die over the paper. She and Dad will go rounds over the placement. He'll call and beg me to make it stop. I'll make him relent on Honey, he will, and then I'll tell Mom I had an epiphany, and the wallpaper would actually be perfect in her dressing room. Which, of course, is where I always intended it to go."

They all died laughing. "Evil."

"Yeah, I know." Jo smiled and winked. "We really do need to get going, though. I plan on being at the shop the moment they unlock the door."

She was heading toward the coat rack by the door when she whipped back toward Raven. "Oh, oh, oh! Where in the hell have my eyes been?! Holy shit. Sexy Pregnant Mom of the Year Award goes tooooooooo... Raven Byrne!"

Raven laughed as she went to her desk and sat down. She needed to make sure she had all her notes accessible for her first appointment.

"And the views as good going as it was coming," Jo hooted. Thankfully her next comment was cut off.

The antique bell above the door jingled as the heavy wood was pushed open on a gust of wind. Two things happened simultaneously.

The first. HB grabbed Jo and placed her behind his body.

The second. Hugh, Patrick, and... Bran walked into Triskelion. Long wool coats, caps, and scarves flapping in the breeze. Raven blinked. It was like the O'Faolains were filming *Peaky Blinders* in their shop. She noted her hands were gripping the edges of her desk. Whether to push away and run or to keep her in place before she ran across the room into his arms, she couldn't have said.

"Bran." It was a whisper. A prayer.

30

"Raven." Bran's hands tightened around the damn gift box until it was in danger of folding in on itself. My God. She was here. He was standing in front of her. Finally. Four months.

Thank God Rowan broke the tension by recalling everyone's attention to basic manners. Introductions. Her hands fluttered about her neck as if her breaths were too shallow. He could sympathize.

River moved behind Raven's back as the youngest Byrne moved toward his family. She tried to smile. Failed.

"Hugh, Bran, Patrick. How... nice to see you. Please, let me take your coats and introduce Josephine's... umm... security."

Bran thought he heard Rowan swallow an Oh God before she plowed on.

"Honey Bunny, this is Hugh O'Faolain and his sons, Bran and Patrick. Gentlemen, this is Honey... Bunny."

Jo was grinning ear to ear now. Ahh... Honey was blushing red to the roots of his blonde hair. Everyone froze after the introduction.

Bran didn't care about any of that. He wanted introductions over with so he could speak to Raven.

The giant moved one step with his hand raised to shake. "Thomas MacGregor." Scottish. Very, very Scottish. If the accent were any thicker, they'd need a claymore to cut the syllables apart. Jo gasped behind MacGregor's back.

"You are an asshole, Honey. An absolute, fucking douche canoe."

"Such language for a lady, Miss O'Connor."

Or that's what Bran thought he said.

She ignored... Honey. "Girls, I've got to get to that shop, or I may lose the wallpaper. And I want it more than anything in the world right now. Let me know lunch plans. Honey Bunny's about to work up an appetite."

The girls gave their goodbyes. Well, River and Rowan did. Raven was still staring at him. He was still staring at her.

Patrick went over to River and gave her a... side hug... and pushed a $3,000 Burberry wool trench coat into her hands. At her questioning look, he told her she'd been cold last night. Pat was zero help right now.

He looked to his dad to do... anything besides stand there.

He relented. "Good to see you." Stiff. Bran was starting to panic. "Patrick and I would love a tour."

"Yeah, we would. You guys killed it with this place. The property is impressive, and the area couldn't be better. Do you live near here?"

River beamed at Pat's praise. "We live upstairs."

"Oh wow, so you guys kind of set this up like Eufaula."

River's jaw snapped shut. Rowan flinched.

"Yes, we did. We... have plans to..." Raven stopped and fluttered a hand around like she was at a loss as how to keep going. He understood.

As the four moved around the office, Bran walked up to Raven's desk and sat across from her.

"I planned so many things to say, but it really boils down to just a few. I'm sorry. I hope someday you can forgive me. I've missed you horribly. I love you."

Bran watched tears slip down her face. He didn't want her to cry. Damn it.

"I brought you a gift." Like an oaf, he shoved the crumpled box in front of her.

She grabbed a tissue and blotted her eyes. "You didn't have to bring me anything." She touched the ribbon wrapped untidily around the plain brown box and lid combo.

Making things more awkward— at this point he was undoubtedly a contender for the Guinness Book of World Records for Biggest Dumbasses— he added, "I made it. Myself. For you." Jesus. Please, God.

"Oh," Raven exhaled. "Should I open it now?"

"Yes."

The ribbon was green. Raven liked green. He watched as she pulled free the tail of the bow and pulled off the lid. Setting both carefully on her desk. He glanced up for a moment to see that his family and Raven's had stopped what they were doing to watch. He didn't care, but he was starting to rethink his gift.

Oh, God. A homemade gift after he all but threw her out of his life. Shit, shit, shit. He closed his eyes tight, body awash with heat from head to toe. Boiling. Then he heard her gasp, and his eyes popped open.

She had removed the bubble wrap and was pulling out the glass jar. Absently he noticed the other four occupants in the room had circled closer— like Great Whites scenting blood. Raven eyed the tulip jar with its rubber seal and clamps.

"Oh my." River or Rowen whispered behind him.

"Bran, is this starter?" Raven set the jar gently on her desk. The tiny white bubbles looked like Elmer's glue.

He cleared his throat. Feeling the tips of his ears heat. "Yes. I, ah, called the chef from that... last dinner. Damn it," he noticed her flinch, "I'm sorry, Raven, I shouldn't have brought that up. It's only, you and your sisters loved his bread, and... I wanted to use his exact technique. Everyone's method seems to vary, so I thought... it doesn't matter. I should not have called..."

Raven interrupted. "Tell me about it."

Taking a deep breath, Bran went through the process. Bread flour and water to start. Sealed jar. The rubber band around the base to gauge its growth. Feeding it every day by taking half the starter out and feeding in new flour water.

"So, you feed it daily?"

"Oh, yes. You have to if you want a strong starter. It can be very temperamental. Eventually, you can keep the starter in the fridge and only feed it every few days to a week. The more you bake with it, the more you feed it."

Her sisters were next to Raven's sides now, touching the jar gently as if it were a priceless artifact.

"Rave, it's a wonderful gift."

"It looks as good as Nan's. Maybe better." River grudgingly admitted.

Bran was watching Raven. She seemed to be contemplating the world as she touched the lid. Then her eyes met his. "Thank you, Bran. It is the best gift I've ever been given." She dabbed at her eyes and cleared her tear-clogged throat. "I have a gift for you too."

Bran saw the sisters stiffen. "You do? Did you know I was coming in today?" Of course, she hadn't— moron.

Raven swallowed and licked her lips nervously. He glanced at his dad and brother. They seemed perplexed too.

"No, I didn't know you would be here today. I've had this gift for about five months."

Bran stood up. His nervous energy, paired with Raven's anxiousness, wouldn't allow him to be still. "Five months?"

Then she was standing, and he was falling back. Strong arms caught him, preventing him from falling flat on his ass, keeping hold until he had his legs under him.

Oh, God. My God. She was pregnant. "We're having a baby," he finally choked out.

Cupping her hands lightly on either side of... their child, she said, "Yes."

He was walking around the desk before his brain even registered the movement. Her sisters peeled away. When he stood in front of her, tears squeezed from his own eyes. He reached for her, hands close, fingers about to graze her shoulders, "May I hug you?"

"Please."

And then she was in his arms, crying softly into his chest, their child between them. He shuddered. He almost hadn't had this moment.

"Oh God, Raven. I love you so much. Please tell me you'll let me be a part of your life again. Our child's?"

Raven rubbed her face against his chest once more before leaning back so she could look up at him. He slid his hands down her back to support her hips. The sleek, tight-fitting dress allowed him to feel her body as though it were bare.

"I would never have kept you from this child whether we were together or not. When I found out, we were already in Switzerland." She looked away from his face. "I didn't imagine you would believe it was yours."

Bran touched the side of her cheek, bringing her eyes back to his. "I was a fool. Worse than a fool. I will never doubt you again. I can only hope that you can one day forgive me, and..."

He trailed off. Not wanting to go too fast with asking her to love him.

Now she was the one moving his eyes back to meet hers. "I love you, Bran. I never stopped, and though I'm naïve about relationships with men, I'm not inexperienced with how a family loves. You hurt me. Badly. I won't deny it. But love is also about forgiveness, and I do, I *have*, forgiven you."

"I hated to even dream that you might still love me." He took a small step back so he could see the baby bump. "I want to touch our baby." At her nodded assent, Bran placed his large hands about her belly.

RAVEN LAUGHED, "Your hands are so much bigger than mine. My bump doesn't look near as big."

His face was full of wonder and delight. She felt the baby kick, startling Bran. "Holy shit, babe."

"Our baby is a kicker. I hope that stops before it starts school. Oh, I hope you don't mind, but I told my OB/GYN that you were coming to town. I haven't let her tell me if it's a boy or a girl yet. I had hoped... I wanted you there. I made an appointment for next week. I didn't expect you so soon."

"I'll get to see the baby? That is amazing. I can't believe you waited for me. I keep wanting to explain how happy I am, but there are no words sufficient. As to being here so quickly after you called," he smiled sheepishly, "I was already boarded on the jet. I couldn't wait any longer."

"How did you find out where I was?"

"Dad, no Gran, actually. She gave Dad the copy from *The Irish Times* with your article. If I hadn't agreed to leave right then, Dad would have disowned me."

Raven looked around, suddenly aware they were alone.

"Where did everyone go? I thought I heard people arguing a minute ago."

"They went upstairs to your apartment about ten minutes ago. To give us privacy, I imagine. I heard arguing too. As long as there is no bloodshed, I hope they stay up there for a while."

"As long as there's no talk of fonts, it should be okay." Raven felt giddy to be so near Bran. His warm hands cupped her tummy again. The wonder on his face was breath-stealing.

"Please tell me we won't be separated again, Raven. That we'll live together. Be a family. It's all I want."

It was her dream as well. "I do want that, Bran, but after… that night, I had to move on. I made a commitment to my sisters, and nothing, not even you and I getting back together will make me not uphold my end. And it isn't just out of love for them. I want this, as well. I believe we have an opportunity to be extremely successful here. We've already met great people."

"I want that for you. I would never ask you to choose. My work requires travel. Homes in different parts of the world work well for me. I love you. I love Dublin. We'll work out living arrangements."

Hugh's gravelly voice broke through their happy bubble. "Then you'll want to find accommodations immediately. Come up here and see the squalor the girls have been enduring."

Standing at the top of the steps leading to their flat, she saw Rowan standing beside Hugh, clearly pissed. Raven felt her cheeks heat. Jesus, it wasn't like they were living in a cardboard box, for crying out loud.

"What the hell are you talking about, Dad?" Bran's arm slid around her back and waist, his warm hand resting against the side of her belly. Despite knowing Bran would probably react much like his father and Jo about their flat, she couldn't help but feel at peace.

"You are being a prick for interrupting them, Hugh, and for something so inconsequential," Rowan hissed.

"You call that," jabbing a finger behind her, "inconsequential? And perhaps you think I'm too old and senile to see that all three of you girls are rail thin."

Bran tensed against her side. "Raven, what's this about?"

Clearly, Rowan had reached her Hugh-limit. "We've been working hard for months to get this place open. We burned extra calories, you... you... argh! I refuse to explain again."

"Better go upstairs before they kill each other." Raven took his hand and led them up the stairs, around Hugh, stopping at her sister.

"My appointment should be here any moment. Would you mind waiting below? I'll only be a few minutes. Bran can rant and rave and beat his chest with his father once I show him our place," she smiled at her sister.

Rowan's lips lifted in a brief smile. She touched Raven's cheek, silently asking if all was good. Raven touched her fingers briefly to Row's cheek. A way the girls showed strong emotions with each other. "Yes."

Rowan nodded. "Okay then, I'll get below." She walked past Hugh without a single glance. He looked furious and maybe a little... forlorn.

Sighing, she headed through the flat's door— and there sat River looking defiant but hurt. Patrick was leaning against the kitchen counter. Expressionless. Sighing, she was about to show Bran the space, but he hadn't walked in behind her.

She turned back to the door where he was still standing. He looked distraught. Men could be so very dramatic. Looking toward the ceiling, she hoped to find heavenly intervention.

"Okay, guys, listen well, and Bran, I'm warning you, and you as well, Pat, as you've obviously hurt my sister's feelings and your father hurt Rowan's. I would appreciate silence while I go over why we live here."

Patrick straightened from his slouch, looking alarmed. His eyes cut to River, probably only now noticing her stiff posture. Lord save her from O'Faolains. No wonder Jo dragged Honey out of here at warp speed.

"I will preface this by stating what I should think is the obvious. We are not homeless. We have heat and electricity, Wi-Fi and warm water. A bed and a roof over our heads. An alarm system, cell phones, and laptops. Friends. I love you, Bran, and I love your family, but none of you have *any* right to dictate how we choose to live our lives.

"We are intelligent and educated. We chose to do the bare, very bare, minimum to this flat because first, we knew it was temporary and second, and most important, we know that life can change in a moment, in a split second, as our parents' tragedy taught us. We could have used our savings to make this a fucking palace or bought a separate home and commuted, but we plan smart, we plan for every contingency, we plan for tragedies and for miracles like Baby O," she paused to touch her stomach and breathe.

"My sisters have slept on cots and cooked on hot plates because this pregnancy changed our initial projections for Dublin." River started to object. "No, River, it's true. Had it just been us three, we *would* have spent the money. I would have done the same for you guys, so I allowed it."

She looked at Bran's shocked face. Even Raven admitted she wasn't normally this confrontational. Baby O hormones were giving her strength. "Any issues you three have with our flat is a you problem. I have a client coming soon and need to get downstairs." Now that she'd had her say she was trembling and a bit teary. Hormones weren't *always* a blessing.

She tried to walk by Bran, but he grabbed her hand and

drew her close. "Forgive me, Raven. Forgive my family. You and your sisters are three of the bravest women I've ever met. I love you. I respect you. You, River, and Rowan protected yourselves and our child. You chose to play a long game. Safer, smarter."

Raven could only blink. God, her parents would have loved Bran. All the fight drained from her body. "Thank you for understanding. Walk me down?"

"My pleasure." He looked at his brother. "You guys coming down? We need to let the girls get to work."

But Patrick surprised all of them, River most of all. He walked to the card table, gently took her sister's hand, and pulled her out of the chair. "I'm sorry, River. You're my very best friend. Hurting you was not my intent, but... I guess ignorance and arrogance got in the way. Please forgive me."

She could tell River was touched. "Sure, Pat. I'm used to you being a dick." They smiled at each other. "Take me downstairs."

Bran was already leading Raven out the door. He leaned down, his warm breath tickling her ear, giving her full-body shivers. "Is it too soon to admit, I got so fucking hard when you were handing me my ass. Damn, Raven. I won't be able to think of anything but you in this sexy dress for the rest of the day. Jesus, babe."

She grinned up at him but sobered when she considered her body. "I've changed a lot, Bran, from before. You might not think... or like... oh geez, I never was some hot, flashy babe, but now..."

He stared at her before answering. "Rave, if I thought there was any way, *any* way to haul your ass out that door and to my hotel room this very second, I would do it. I'm trying to be mature and make you love me even more for my selfless behavior. You work. I'll plan. You agreed to live with me, no matter what country we're in. Which means I'll be looking at real estate.

"You had your say about why you've been living in that flat, babe, but last night was your last one here. You do realize that? You and I can't fit in a single cot, especially with... Baby O. That is what you call the baby?"

She heard River snort behind her. "Yes," Raven said quickly, "for O'Faolain."

She was still reeling over the living arrangements. Yes, she had agreed they would be together, but she hadn't thought that meant— right now!

As they reached the bottom of the stairs and stepped into the office space, she caught the tail end of what Hugh was saying to Rowan. And holy shit, living arrangements left her brain.

"I'm sorry I overreacted."

"Are you, though?"

"Yes, I just said I was."

"Whatever."

"You *are* too thin."

"Noted. As I get asked out weekly, you'll understand if I'm not concerned about my appearance fading."

"Damn it, that's..."

"Oh, Raven," Rowan interrupted Hugh, "Mrs. Little called and is running late but should be here in thirty. River, you and I can head over to look at Henry's new shipment of carpets and upholstery fabrics. Then all three of us are meeting with Stella, the potter. She has a proposal for us. I imagine she wants us to use her exclusively."

"It won't be a hard sell. She's amazing."

"If money were no object, I would have bought her entire set of daisy dishware," River said dreamily. "A totally impractical design that I would use every day," she laughed.

"And where will you be fitting in lunch?"

Oh, Jesus God have mercy. Her sister was going to stab Hugh. Any. Second.

"The Murphys will drop by some salad or sandwiches, I'm sure. Not to worry."

Raven lifted her eyebrows. Rowan was taunting Hugh, but she might not realize that any second, that taunt would extend to Patrick.

Right on cue. "Do the Murphys deliver food around town?"

"No, the brothers own a pub in town and come 'round on occasion to bring us... food."

Oh Lord, Oh Lord, Oh Lord.

"Why?" Patrick snapped. Hugh didn't speak. I'm not sure he could unclench his jaw enough.

Rowan spoke to Patrick like he was simple. "Raven is the only sister pregnant around here. I imagine they consider River and I single and ready to mingle."

All right. Pat was glaring at River, who was refusing to acknowledge the looks. Rowan was... playing with fire.

Raven looked at Bran. Pleading. He took the hint.

"We need to leave. Now. Let the women work." He even used hand signals to direct them out the door. "When can I see you?"

He pulled her tight to his front, rubbing her back. Distracting. "We close at four."

"Would you let me plan a relaxing evening for just the two of us tonight? We have a lot to talk about, and... I just want to be with you. Know that you are with me."

"I would like that. Are you staying at The Fitzwilliam?"

"No, Westin. I miss Dom."

She laughed. "I saw him last night. I didn't sleep well after I called you. I had a wild idea of him working for Triskelion once we're all big and famous." She laughed. "Do you remember him telling us that his family was all gone? I felt he had something in his past that hurt him, but there is no one more brilliant or organized than that man."

BRAN DIDN'T LAUGH. It was fucking genius.

Raven asked River for Miss Kennedy's card, which she produced with a smile for her sister and a slightly more reserved one for Bran.

"If you're serious about finding a place in Dublin, she's the only real estate agent you need. She and Jo are friends. It's how we met."

Bran pocketed the card, intending to call her as soon as he walked out the door. "You know very well I'm serious." Bran bent down and whispered next to the side of Raven's mouth. "Will you allow me to kiss you before I leave?"

Her hands flexed on his back. "Please."

His mouth covered Ravens before her please had fully passed her lips. He swiped his tongue deep, once, then again, and again, and again. She raised to her toes, he moved deeper in, she moaned, he groaned. And then— fuck, no!

"Mrs. Little is getting out of her car."

"And I think your family would all enjoy a break from the familial soft porn."

He hoped River and Patrick ended up together. Forever. Justice. "Damn," he whispered, pulling back, tucking a strand of hair behind Raven's ear. Bran attempted to have mundane thoughts of food, flower gardens, the stock market— anything but his erection, Raven's swollen lips, and even more swollen belly. God... must stop.

"Rave. Pull it together." River snapped, which made her sister jump and back away from him.

"I'll be here at four."

"Yes. Good," she breathed out. As Bran turned to leave, she stopped him. "Bran, thank you again for the sourdough starter. You can show me how to care for it tonight." Raven looked at him with such raw emotion— hurt, love, passion, and hope.

"We're really going to work?" Raven whispered.

Bran barely heard Raven's question. With no hesitation, he answered, "Forever."

31

———

Bran's relief that he was finally in the same city as Raven was incomprehensible. He wouldn't truly feel settled, though, until they were living under one roof.

He had seen Raven's hesitation when he'd told her she wouldn't be able to stay at her apartment now that they were back together, but he couldn't lie in his bed one more night without her next to him.

Also, knowing she was round with his child was a mixture of euphoria and fucking terror. He needed her close.

Had she truly not been ready to stay the night with him, he would have relented, bought a wider cot, and slept in the cramped flat with her sisters. He didn't think her sisters would have been down with the company, however.

He *had* heard every word Raven said to him and Pat, though. He respected their caution and determination. He was proud that his girlfriend didn't mind roughing it for a greater cause.

And it was rough. Bran grew up wealthy, and with his own investments, he had added to that wealth. He had *never* lived like the Byrnes were currently living. Thank God. There was not one particle of his being not demanding that he remove his woman and child from that situation immediately.

Bran had left Raven's business that morning and looked up and down the block. Next door was a narrow, four-story brick building. The lowest level was modern gray stone blocks. Very different from Triskelion's old-world front of heavy wood and brick, but they complimented each other. He wanted it. When Bran explained his thoughts— a story each for them, with the lowest level walking into a living room and bar for get-togethers. Guest bedrooms in the back— Dad and Patrick wanted it too.

He smiled, remembering Saoirse's initial, "That building isn't for sale, Mr. O'Faolain. Nor have I heard so much of a whisper of anyone wanting to move it privately."

"So, can you find out who owns it and call them this morning?"

She huffed into the phone but asked, "Are you serious about this?"

"My girlfriend, hopefully wife soon, is pregnant and living next door. I want it."

"I see. I'll get my ass back to the office then and make some calls. Keep your phone close. If I can even get the owner to consider selling, I'll need to call you immediately if they give me a price."

Bran, Patrick, and Dad wandered around Dublin for over an hour. They ran into Jo and Thomas. Jo was all smiles and exuberant about her mom's birthday present and how much her dad was going to love it too. Thomas only watched the crowd, and Bran noticed, kept his big body between his charge and the road.

O'Connor obviously decided not to chance his daughter's safety even though she'd left the country. The detective didn't believe that Raven was in any danger, but would the stalker follow Bran to Ireland? He needed to talk to the detective this afternoon.

"Do you guys want to have dinner tonight? Honey and I were thinking of a more quiet, romantic evening." She moved close to Thomas and gave him a side hug. "Isn't that right?"

Thomas didn't so much as blink.

She turned her attention back to them. "He's shy, but I can assure you, it was his idea. He even asked if we could plan dancing. Of course, I told him I didn't bring an appropriate dress. I mean, a woman can't plan for *everything*. Of course, my Honey Bunny is a problem solver, as you'd imagine. And he *insisted* we go dress shopping."

Bran was trying very, *very* hard not to laugh. MacGregor must have really pissed off Jo. "That sounds... fun, but I'd planned on spending the evening alone with Raven tonight."

Jo sobered, all teasing set aside. "Of course, Bran. I'm truly happy things worked out between you two. She's tried to put a brave face on it, but she's been miserable without you. You've been equally miserable but didn't try to hide it."

Patrick laughed. "Truth. He's been unbearable. Dad and I are both thankful Raven took him back."

"Okay, well. No candlelit dancing tonight." She glanced at Thomas over her shoulder. "You even got waxed this morning. Pity." Resuming their conversation, she explained, "BunBun has the cutest tuxedo panties, and hairy... parts... just don't work."

"Josephine." His dad growled from behind him. Bran was surprised to hear him speak. Besides telling him to buy the property, he had spoken maybe five words since the blow-up about the girls' flat.

Jo blushed but ignored the reprimand. "So, we'll let the newly reunited couple have their alone time. Pat, why don't you see if the girls want to meet for drinks, fish and chips, and live music. Honey and I will need to relax after all the shopping today."

Patrick already had his phone out. "If they agree, I'll have River text you for the details. The six of us should be able to find a good table somewhere if we don't go too late."

"Perfect. See you guys. I'm ready, Honey."

As they walked away down the sidewalk, Bran shook his head as they watched Jo lace her fingers through MacGregor's. It was war between those two. His money was on Jo.

"Jesus, Jo is definitely on one. I'll have to tell James to let his old man know to triple whatever price he agreed to pay MacGregor."

Bran's phone started ringing. He answered, "O'Faolain." It was Miss Kennedy.

He put it on speaker and moved into a wide doorway out of the wind. "He wasn't interested. He rents the floors out to different businesses and tenants. For shits and giggles, I asked him to name his price."

"And?"

"Fifteen million. American."

That was only five mil split between them, with another few million in renovations. He looked to his dad and brother. They nodded.

"Tell him we accept. All cash, no contingencies. But I want everyone out immediately."

"Wha... wha... what? That's... you're serious, Mr. O'Faolain?"

"Very. I expect you to call me back immediately." He hung up, deciding to find a warm pub to celebrate.

Bran leaned back in his chair where they'd settled at a small, comfortable pub in the Temple Bar District. His glass of Jameson vibrated beside his drumming fingers.

Finally. Saoirse was calling. "Tell me you closed the deal."

"How the fuck did you ever land a woman as sweet as Raven Byrne— a mystery for Bible study Sunday."

"Miss Kennedy..." Bran was too keyed up to joke.

"He accepted. His man of business is drafting letters to all the tenants today. The grumpy bastard and he *is* a grumpy bastard— you owe me a drink for that— is *actually* paying his renters the equivalent of $3,000 as a Sorry I'm Kicking Your Ass to the Curb with No Notice gift. By the by, it was a hard, fuck off, no, until I mentioned it was a grand gift to the woman you hope will agree to marry you. Turns out, the old geezer is a widower who loved nothing more than his late wife."

"You are extraordinary, Miss Kennedy. A fucking brilliant, mouthy, extraordinary agent. Meet me at The Palace Bar and bring your carpenter boyfriend, Timothy Daniels. I have a proposition for him."

"Oh, feck. Give me forty-five. Have a double of Jameson Cask on ice and waiting. I've got paperwork to do and a boyfriend to track down." She hung up.

"You must be satisfied, Bran," Patrick noted.

"Oh, very pleased. The girls were right. Miss Kennedy knows her shit."

Patrick laughingly agreed. "She might be mouthier than River."

Dad finally decided to join the conversation. "I'm pleased about the building, but I don't need one of the floors. If it works, a guest room on the ground floor is all I need when I visit. I will still pay for part of the building and renovations, of course." He went back to swirling his Guinness.

Both he and Pat regarded their father in silence. What was this all about, he wondered. They always did everything together. They *wanted* to do everything together.

Carefully, because he didn't want to come across as some petulant child, Bran asked, "Is there a... reason you don't want to live there... with us?" Jesus, he inwardly cringed. That wasn't how it was supposed to come out.

His father sighed and moved his glass further from him. "I still hate Guinness. You boys are, for lack of a better phrase, spreading your wings, leaving the nest."

Dad was the one cringing now. Good.

Looking first at the darkened beams above their heads, he looked at his sons again. "Your lives are changing. Bran, you're about to be a father and hopefully a husband before that. Your time will be split, staying where Raven is, which it should be. And Pat, you've been restless, and I hope growing tired of your parties and women. You mentioned buying an old distillery here in Ireland, and perhaps opening a Wolves here."

"What's all this have to do with the property?"

"For fuck's sake, boys! You don't need your old man tagging along on your adventures. And before you ask, no, you have never made me feel like that. Still, a parent has to eventually recognize when they are... or rather, when they need, to step back and allow their children some breathing room."

Talking in complete sentences *and* feelings. Dad was definitely out of sorts. Before Bran could respond, Patrick jumped in.

"I'll clear my end up, Dad. I'm not tired of parties and women. When I mentioned trying our hand at whiskey and a Wolves in Dublin, those thoughts and suggestions were just round tabling our next ventures. 'Our ventures,' Dad. You, me, and Bran. We are smarter and better together. I never once considered it wouldn't always be the three of us."

"Pat's right. We've always been a team. I never want that to change. I know we'll be traveling a lot more with the girls living in Dublin, but they'll also be coming home with us to Muskogee. They grew up in Oklahoma. They're going to want to be there, as well. Plus, I have a plan for a manager for Triskelion, but we can talk about that later.

"We are either all three true partners in this property, or I will revoke the offer. Our lives will always be changing, but not the part where we're together. I mean, you never know Dad, women still fall all over themselves around you, maybe someday you'll decide to remarry. Pat need's a good stepmom to curb his wild ways."

His dad's lips twitched in a smile. "No on the wife, but yes on sticking with you boys. If you promise to tell me if anything changes."

"It never will." He and his brother said at the same time.

"Fine. Then I'll want the top floor, and we'll need an elevator."

Back in business. "One step ahead of you, old man."

"Do you think we'll be able to talk Daniels into the reno? It'll be a hell of a big job, on top of wanting it started ASAP and done fast."

"He'll have a price. We'll pay it."

"We won't know the true scope of the project until we get in the building. It might not be as bad as we think. We just made his girlfriend one very large commission. We'll get him. Another bonus, we'll hire Triskelion for Interior Design."

The very elegant Miss Kennedy and, he presumed, Timothy Daniels were making their way toward them. The three men stood and introduced themselves to Timothy, or Tim as he asked to be called. The waiter took the newcomers' drink orders as everyone sat back down.

Saoirse laid a manilla folder full of documents to sign on the table before relaxing back into her chair. "It's only midday, and I already feel all wobbly in my heels," she laughed. "So, you're the daddy, huh?"

"Jaysus, woman," Tim chided.

Bran barked out a laugh, as did his dad and brother. "No worries, Tim, and good luck to you." Bran smiled, making sure Tim really did know he wasn't at all offended. "In answer to your question, I am."

"I admit, the property is the biggest push gift I've heard a woman receiving, though you're a few months early."

"Push gift?"

"When a woman goes through all that trouble of pushing a child out a part of their body that really, really shouldn't be required to do so, a man gives the new momma a 'push' gift."

"Oh, wow. I didn't know." Bran's mind was racing. "This isn't one of those gifts. I just want to give her an alternative to living in the flat above the store."

"Well, you do love her. Clearly. Good. Now, down to business. While you three sign that bundle of papers, everything is highlighted, explain to the love of *my* life why I had to drag him here." Poor Tim's cheeks were burning.

"Dad, I'll let you outline the plan while I sign this mountain of fucking papers."

"We want to hire you to renovate the new property, four floors. There'll need to be an elevator. Once the current tenants are out, in a few weeks, we'll hire an architect to draw up plans. If there is one you prefer working with, tell us.

"We want you to finish your current job and then devote the next few months to this project. We understand that this size of job would normally take much longer, but my grandchild will have to have a home.

"You'll need to hire extra skilled crews to allow for the schedule. You'll need to hire extra project managers to oversee the site. You can't be expected to work twenty-four hours a day, seven days a week.

"You'll be working with the Byrne sisters for colors and

whatnot. It's their choice, ultimately. My boys and I trust their judgment."

Dad just stopped talking and stared at the wide-eyed contractor across the table.

"I... am very appreciative of the offer, Mr. O'Faolain, but this is a job well above what I have ever done. I... believe you... you would be better served hiring a more experienced contractor with large-scale project experience."

Bran could see Saoirse squirming in her chair, wanting to stop Tim from turning down the offer but not wanting to overstep in his business.

Dad read the situation. "This is your chance to go big, Mr. Daniels. Taking that leap is a scary fucking thing to do. I've been there. Here are my guarantees. We are not frivolous, but we do have deep pockets. You will have the money to buy the equipment and hire the people needed to see this project done right. Consider us as investors in your company. By investing in you, you'll be more invested in us.

"This will change the trajectory of your future. You might be able to get to the point where you run the company, bidding on jobs, not physically working on a project unless you *want* to.

"Oh, and on top of an agreed-upon bid, I'll pay you a half million bonus to get it done before my new daughter has the baby. My push gift to Raven."

Bran could only shake his head and smile. Damn, his dad was good.

Tim grabbed Saoirse's hand, silently asking what she thought. She nodded her head yes. Holding out a slightly shaky hand to Dad, Tim said, "I accept."

Pat added, "As time is not our friend, we need to meet with the architect you choose, Tim, by Monday. You really need to be a part of that process, as well. Saoirse, can you find out what floors have businesses and see if we might do a walk-through next week."

"Oh right, turns out the last renter moved out a year ago, and a tech company rents the space. Better news, it has a service elevator. It would need to be replaced, but, I don't know, I'm not a builder, but it seemed good that the spot for one is already there."

"Very good news," Tim agreed.

Raven called as they continued to hash out a plan. "Hey, babe, What's up?

"The doctor's office called, and they had a cancellation this afternoon. For an ultrasound. Do you want to find out what we're having? Now?"

"On my way."

THE TAXI RIDE to the clinic was quiet. Bran kept rubbing his hands over the top of his pant legs. Raven laid her hand over his mid rub. "Bran, this is a lot for one day. Perhaps... we should cancel or... you could stay in the waiting room."

He looked at her sharply. "What? No way. I want to be right beside you." He gave her a questioning glance.

"You seem tense. Very tense. I thought maybe all of this," she moved her hand in a circle around her middle, "is too much."

Bran turned in the backseat as far as the compact would allow and grabbed both her hands. "I am nervous. I'm normally prepared past the nth degree, but I feel like I'm about to take the biggest test of my life, and I never studied. I don't want to let you down. I was making mental notes on all the things I need to do and find out to be the best partner for you. The best father."

"You've only known about the baby for a few hours. Cut

yourself some slack. You are here. By my side. It's all I need."
She wasn't lying to appease him.

"You'll never regret giving me a second chance. That, at least, is something I am confident in."

"Any luck on finding us a place to live? My due date is February 19th. So, we have a few months, but I would like some time to decorate the baby's room."

"Well, I hope you'll feel up to decorating more than just the one room, babe. My dad, brother, and I have a job we'd like to hire Triskelion for."

"Oh, really, Bran, that's great. We don't want you guys to hire us because you feel you have to, though. We need to be the right fit, and we understand business. You would not hurt our feelings."

Bran grinned at her as they pulled up to the curb outside the doctor's office. "I'd say no one could fit this particular job better. We bought the building next to Triskelion. The four-story one."

"You..." And that's all Raven's brain had left. She'd known Bran's family was next level, but this...

As they walked into the clinic, he explained their informal plans for each floor... the elevator, Saoirse's part in the sale, Timothy's recruitment... the promised bonus for finishing before Baby O was born.

"Pat suggested your sisters stay in the guest rooms until they decide where to live. They'll have en suite bathrooms, and the ground floor will have a small communal kitchen." Bran stopped and got his phone out of his pocket. "Damn it, I forgot to remind Patrick to ask Miss Kennedy to look for a nice apartment for your sisters close to work."

Still having trouble processing so many life-changing events at once, Raven snapped to attention at the mention of an apartment. She placed her hand over his screen. "No, Bran. My sisters won't thank you for the interference."

"But, Rave, you can't think I'd want them to stay there."

"I love that you love them, but what they do and when is their choice. I will talk to them later about it. Come on," she tugged him forward as he reluctantly put his phone away, "let's take a look at our baby."

Bran still looked shell-shocked as they walked back into Triskelion. Her sisters were bent over their large design table, swatches of paint, fabrics, and sketches laid out before a middle-aged woman, who smiled brightly when they entered the shop.

"Oh, my gracious, your sister, I'd guess."

They all laughed. Raven and Bran walked over and introduced themselves. Bran was all charm, but she could tell he was still having some internal meltdown.

"I'm so glad I got to meet you today, Mrs. Baker. Please excuse Mr. O'Faolain and me while we pop upstairs for a... bite to eat." Both River and Rowan looked at her questioningly but waved her away.

"Oh, Raven, when you're ready, we'd love to hear about your earlier appointment."

Raven knew they were dying to hear if they were getting a niece or nephew.

Once the flat's door was closed behind them, she told Bran to sit down. She grabbed two room-temperature bottles of water and sat next to him.

"Tell me what you're thinking, Bran. How can we help each other if we don't confide?"

He took a sip of water and screwed the cap back on before taking her hand and kissing the back. "A son, Raven. My God, we're having a son. I... I'm trying to... picture him." He swallowed, clearly emotional.

"My thoughts are all over the place, babe. I have this irrational need to be clingy like you might change your mind and not want me anymore. I know nothing about pregnancy, so I have to start researching. I'm now frantic to get the fucking building renovated. We need a home before our child arrives. Our son, Rave. You've given me the biggest gift." He finally managed a small smile, "Did I sufficiently confide?"

"You are sufficient in every way. I love you, and you know what? You and I could find a cute little apartment now. Just because it wouldn't be a forever home doesn't mean I couldn't make a lovely space for the baby. It would relieve the stress of you feeling like the monster next door has to be done— which is a gigantically tall order."

"Our son is *not* coming home from the hospital to a... rental. He would think I wasn't capable of providing for him and his mother. Not happening. Between Dad and Pat and I, we'll figure out a way." He smiled, stretching out his long frame and pulling her chair closer to kiss her neck. Tingles shot down her back and around her belly. Mmm.

"You were right. Talking about my fears made me remember something— I don't fail. You know what else?"

Raven arched her neck further in an invitation. "What?"

"It's 4 o'clock and Friday, which means Triskelion is closed, and we have the whole weekend."

"Thank God," she breathed into his ear.

BRAN WAS ABOUT to pull Raven from her chair into his lap when the door opened, and her sisters waltzed in.

"Shit, did we interrupt?" River's smirking face was... annoying.

Before Bran could tell them to get out, Raven squealed and

said, "A boy." It was all tears and hugs for him and Raven, plans and name suggestions, baby room colors, and calling their Nan. Bébhinn cried and suggested names. She loved them all so much, Bran included, and was planning to come see them soon.

That took thirty-three minutes. Forty-five minutes later, Raven finished telling her sisters about the building next door and Triskelion being hired for its interior design, what that could mean for them, and how they would need to adjust their schedules, potential vendors and artisans to be contacted...

"So, what you're basically saying is, we'll make bank off the O'Faolains so we can remodel the flat after Baby O Boy gets here?" River asked excitedly.

"That's one option," Bran interrupted. "Or... you can take option two, which, I have to say, is genius and clearly the best one because I came up with it."

Rowan laughed. "Save me from the O arrogance factor."

"Hear me out. I was going to enact part one of the plan already, but your naysaying sister said I had to ask first, that it was *your* choice." He rolled his eyes.

"You're having a child with this caveman. You realize that, right?" River groaned but smiled at Bran.

He was so going to win them over.

"I'll be blunt here because I want to desperately have your sister naked in my bed as soon as possible." Bran ignored Raven's gasp and the side pinch. "So, here's my idea. I hire Miss Kennedy to find you girls a lovely place to live, close to work. Timothy subcontracts out a company to *completely* gut and remodel this flat.

"Raven and I will make do at The Westin, move to The Fitzwilliam, or lease a condo until the building is ready. Then, once you girls feel you have enough ready cash to build, buy, or remodel, you'll find a place then. I will be renting whatever you choose to live in until then.

"And before you two gasp and reject my high-handed behavior, I want you to understand that this is a thank you to both of you. I hurt your sister, and you picked up the pieces. You loved and supported her when I was too foolish to do it myself. You guys protected the most important person in my life. So, I don't think a few months' rent is too much to ask you to accept."

Bran could tell River and Rowan wanted to hand him his ass on a platter, but he'd made it almost impossible. He could see them attempting to figure out a way to say no, but not look petty. There wasn't.

"Let's say we agree to this, Bran, and I'm not saying we are, but why remodel the flat? Why waste the money?" He couldn't fault River's thought process and questions. Definitely more comfortable than Rowan regarding him silently.

"That is part two of my brilliant plan, which Raven doesn't even know about, even though she's the one that gave me the idea."

"Do tell," Raven grinned, bumping his shoulder, while under the table, she slid her hand over the top of his leg, her fingers coming to rest on the inside of his thigh. He quickly looked at her innocent expression. Her actions were not. He needed to get this meeting wrapped up.

Covering her hand with one of his, he positioned her fingers just that little bit closer to where he wanted to be touched. Her fingers briefly flexed. A warning or anticipation?

"The renowned butler of The Fitzwilliam. Your sister told you about him from our first trip?"

"Yes, Dom." He'd finally managed to pique Rowan's interest.

"He's a wizard at making things happen."

Raven laughed, remembering. "Oh, he is. Remember at Jo's dinner last night? How he handled Honey Bunny's theatrics?

Not a strand of salt and pepper hair out of place. Why are you bringing Dom into your big Plan Reveal?"

Her thumb lightly grazed the side of his increasingly un-flaccid dick. Now he was the one to flex his hand in warning. "Dom is personable but no-nonsense. He is efficient, knows everyone in town, a who's who list mentally stored and cataloged. He knows Dublin and its surroundings like the back of his hand." Bran paused dramatically before the big reveal.

"I want you three to give me permission to approach Dom with a business proposition in Triskelion's name."

Lots of wide-eye blinking. He could see the Negative Nancys formulating creative ways to say the same thing. No. "Hear me out, please. To grow, you guys need the freedom to do what you do best, which is design. Searching the world for just the right piece of art, fabric, artisan..." He swiped his hand through the air to encompass all their passions.

"You need an office manager. One who will make Triskelion Territory Designs the most prestigious, sought-after business it can be. I believe with your talents, Dom's extraordinary organization and second sense of knowing a client's wants before *they* even know, the four of you would be unstoppable.

"He's older and single and could live in the flat once it's remodeled. The shop would not be closed while you're working on a job somewhere, traveling for work, or when you vacation. He could not only make appointments, but once he gets to know you three better, he would know who would serve the new client best.

"I could go on about his skill set and how it would match your needs for hours, but I want to get Raven out this door and into my hotel room within the next ten minutes. So, I'll end with this. I would offer him a moderate salary in the beginning with a small percentage of the business. As Triskelion's profit increases, so will his salary and negotiations for a more significant percent eventually.

"I would like to present him with an offer in the next day or two. Tuesday at the latest."

"I want to hear what River and Raven think, of course. As for me, I'm in. We'd put an office manager as a five-year goal. With Bran's help, we are ahead of River's projections by years. We live for the creative process. Dom, or someone like him, would allow us to immerse ourselves in the side of interior design where we thrive."

"It's one of the very reasons we were willing to put up living in this flat. Sacrifice now to attain future goals. However, I have one stipulation, and we haven't heard from Raven yet. Bran should also get a percentage of Triskelion."

"Absolutely not..."

Raven cut him off. "She's right, Bran. It's only fair. You are basically bankrolling us into a position we didn't see coming to fruition for years. I *know* you know we're good at our job. But given the time to source special pieces for clients and the freedom for endless creativity without the headache of managing the day-to-day— we'd kill it. Consider this just another business investment instead of gifting your new family."

Bran saw the resolve on each face. "I agree, then. I'll have our attorney draft the appropriate papers once we know what Dom agrees to. How about I roll the initial offer out to Dom? If he's interested, we set up a meeting at Triskelion."

32

—————

This had to be the longest but most productively satisfying day of Raven's life. She had Bran back. He was thrilled to be a father. A home was in the works. They might get Dom to work for them. Her sisters had agreed before they left tonight that they would let Saoirse find them an apartment until the building next door was completed, and most importantly, she was alone with her man for the first time in four months.

But as soon as the door shut to their suite, Raven tensed. He was going to see the new her as soon as he got her clothes off, and if the looks he kept throwing her way were anything to go by, he would have them both naked soon.

"I'm going to take a quick shower and get out of this dress if you don't mind." She held up her overnight bag unnecessarily.

"Actually, Raven, I do mind. Don't think I didn't notice you getting partially undressed at the doctor's— under the sheet."

Raven instantly felt her cheeks blush. Damn, she thought that had gone over a lot smoother than it must have. Her first instinct was to deny it, but they'd agreed to communicate their feelings, to be honest.

"I'm sorry. I... did do that. I wanted your first look at my belly to be while I was lying down. It isn't as shocking." She tried to laugh but ended up clearing her throat nervously.

"You need to understand that I will love you and find you attractive no matter what you look like, but babe, you thinking you don't look sexy as fuck is a crime."

Taking her bag from her hand, he dropped it on the floor before pulling her into his arms, running his hands down her back. He cupped her ass, pulling her close, kneading her cheeks as he slowly started working her dress up her legs.

"Tell me you want this, Raven. If you aren't ready for this part of our relationship, I'd understand."

Not ready? His heated words, so close to her mouth, had her aching. She could feel Bran's hard length between their bodies. Her own sex pulsing in anticipation.

"I'm ready. So. Ready."

BRAN HOPED RAVEN didn't notice his hands were shaking as he finished slipping her dress over her head. She was perfection, even lovelier with her swelling belly. She only had on a sheer, nude bra and matching panties. His whole body was shaking now.

"Jesus, Raven. Take off the rest. I want to watch." He had planned on showering together, but that would have to come after— his body felt swollen, hot, and feverish. His skin was a chrysalis. Touching Raven again would tear him in two but also remake him.

Bran had slowly moved them toward the bedroom as he'd stripped off her first layer. He now had the bed in sight. He tore his shirt off, eyes never leaving those hard nipples he was dying to see again, taste.

"Oh God, babe," He whispered as her hands reached

behind her back to work the bra's clasp. His arousal was painfully hard against his zipper. She stripped the bra off, her breasts finally free. His mouth watered. "The rest, Rave. Now. Before I explode."

She must have realized how close he was to losing it and took her time hooking her thumbs into the thin waistband of her nonexistent panties. "Raven," he warned.

There she was. Bare to him, glistening already with her own need. She stood tall, finally proud of her body and showing it all to him. She started to walk closer. He stopped her. He shucked off his short boots and socks. He met her eyes and started unbuttoning his jeans, daring her not to watch what he would reveal.

Popping one fucking button felt impossible, he was so painfully rigid. Raven didn't want to wait another moment—before he could fiddle any further with his fly, she was there, knocking his inept hands aside and freeing his sex from its denim prison.

The moment her tiny hand gripped his solid length, he almost came. Surprising him further, Raven told him to strip now and then backed him the rest of the way to the bed.

"Lay down, Bran, now. Please."

He had some satisfaction knowing she was as out of control as he was. He lay on his back and watched as Raven brushed over her sensitive nipples, rubbing her thighs together to ease the ache. Like a siren from fantasy, she climbed up the bed over Bran's legs and straddled him with her legs.

"Baby, this is going to be fast," he said. "I'm sorry, but I need to be inside you."

She didn't need to be told twice. Raven lifted her hips, stroking the length of his hardness with her slick folds, guiding him into her. Her head was thrown back, crying out as she seated herself fully.

Fierce closeness, deep yearning, soul-stealing— touching her lips with the tips of his fingers before slipping down to grasp her neck. He could feel her heart's heavy beat against his palm, her slightly constricted breath harsh in the stillness of the room.

"Look at me, Raven." When she complied, he let his roughened hand slide further south, using both hands to cup her breasts, pinching her nipples until he could feel her response. Her body clasped his tighter. "There is only you for me."

A single tear made a lazy path down her beautiful cheek. "Only you for me, Bran," she echoed.

Bran squeezed her ass. Raven's movements became furious, forceful, purposeful.

"Baby, yes. Wanted this for so long." Bran was mindless as he watched Raven lift her body high enough that the head of his shaft was close to slipping free before plunging low, taking him again, over and over, until his breath was sawing in and out.

Bran grabbed her hips and, using the leverage, slammed into her body with a hoarse cry of his own. Over and over and over. He slid one hand to where they joined and used his thumb to firmly circle her swollen nub until she was writhing, her rhythm interrupted, her body shuddering with its need to climax.

"That's it, baby, let go. I want to feel you come." Bran continued to work Raven's body. "There, babe! I'm there! Now, oh God, Raven! Fuck yes!"

Bran felt her start to tighten around him. The pulsing, pulling, sucking of her sex around his own set off his own orgasm. He grabbed her hips, pulling her as tight as their bodies could go, filling her full. Bran shuddered, his heart beating so loudly it was the only thing he could hear.

She collapsed on his chest, both of them trying to catch their breath. Their bodies still connected, quivering and hypersensitive. They felt the tiny kicks at the same time.

"Fuck, babe. The baby. Should we have... did we do... let me get you on your back."

RAVEN WAS FLIPPED over so quickly that she and Baby O Boy got a little dizzy. "Bran, I'm fine." She laughed. "The baby is fine."

She melted when he placed his hand on top of her belly. "Should we have done... that... I mean, without asking the doctor?"

"Stop worrying, babe. Sex is fine. For as long as we want." Raven smiled up at him, letting her fingers slowly trace the grooves between his abs. "And I want." She let her fingers drag lower until the pads of her fingers brushed the small patch of white hairs gracing the base of Bran's very impressive sex.

"Raven," he warned.

"I'd like a shower. Join me?"

Raven saw a million emotions race across his face. Lust, love, need, passion. But he hesitated.

He stopped her hand's exploration. "Will you stay here? Right here? I need to get something before we shower."

"Of course."

Bran was off the bed and across the room, pulling out one of the drawers in the dresser that must have held some of his clothes. He unerringly found what he was looking for and turned back to the bed. The city lights from the open bedroom curtains shadowing and highlighting his naked body— the most skilled painter surely couldn't capture the glorious planes of Bran O'Faolain's physique.

Raven sat up on the bed, resting her upper body against the padded headboard. Not worrying about covering herself, confident in Bran's word. He wouldn't lie to her. He truly would love all the versions of Raven Byrne.

Bran knelt on the bed next to her, his serious expression stopping her initial reaction to reach for him. He opened his right hand, one she hadn't noticed had been fisted tight, to reveal a small, black box. Oh... She sat ruler straight now. Eyes wide. Her heart hammered hard enough to bruise her chest.

"Raven, do you believe that I love you with my whole heart?"

"Yes." Her voice sounded off-key, but that was probably the blood roaring in her ears.

"Do you believe that we are meant to be together? Forever?"

"Yes, Bran."

"Then, would you... do me the honor... the privilege, of being my wife?"

He opened the box to reveal the most exquisite emerald ring. Never had she seen anything half so beautiful in her life. Never dreamt of a ring so lovely.

Her hands were shaking.

His hands were shaking.

Raven moved to her knees, looking into Bran's eyes.

"Bran. Oh, Bran. I have never been more sure of an answer in my life." She gently touched her fingers to his cheek.

"Yes."

When he slipped the delicate band on her ring finger, she cried. Holding her hand out to take in the lovely, lovely ring. She reached up and cupped his beloved face between her hands, the emerald catching Dublin's light— green fire.

"You are everything I could ever want, ever need. I will honor this marriage as my parents and my grandparents honored their marriages. But..." She felt him stiffen under her hands and held back a smile, "If you tell anyone that we were both naked in bed when you proposed... I... I will call off the wedding."

She screamed and laughed as he grabbed her hips, careful of the baby, and held her up in the air, grinning.

"Even if our romantic proposal happens to leak to the family

— you said yes, babe. No reneging. Thank you for making me the happiest man in the world."

"Ditto, Mr. O'Faolain. You did damn good on this ring. It definitely weighed in your favor." She grinned at him as she held her hand at a million different angles.

"Would you like that shower now?"

"Yes, I would, but first, show me how to care for my sourdough starter." They slid off the bed, and Raven hugged her fiancé tight, pressing a kiss to his sternum, then over his heart. "I'm excited to be a family with you, Bran Knightley O'Faolain."

DAD WAS WAITING for Bran at the hotel's restaurant for breakfast. He took his seat, telling the waitress that the water already on the table was all he would need to drink.

Bran picked up the menu to look at the omelets.

"I already ordered your food."

"Why? I'm not sure what I want this morning, and I'm hungry."

"You were late, and I was hungry too."

Bran made a show of looking at his phone. "I sat down— at this table— three minutes past when I said I would be here."

"I ordered two minutes ago."

Clenching his teeth and squeezing his eyes shut helped Bran not react to his father's taciturn behavior. Over the years, he'd wondered how he hadn't gotten TMJ.

"I'm sure I'll enjoy it. How was dinner out with everyone last night?" Upon sitting, his dad's expression had been 'a chance of thunderstorms,' but now, it was in the red, all 'tornado warning, take cover.' When would he learn not to ask unnecessary questions?

"I left early."

"Why?" Idiot, Bran.

"I hadn't worked out since we got here."

"So, you missed... one... workout?" Bran dragged the question out, just like his irritating brother— slightly uncomfortable to realize he could act like Pat.

The waitress was back with... the entire menu. Okay, so he wouldn't be whining about not 'feeling' his dad's choice. He took a few minutes to blissfully eat the table buffet before asking, "Did River or Rowan mention what we talked about last night?"

"River didn't."

Do not clench. "Did Rowan?"

"She didn't go."

Ahh. "Oh, I see now." Dad's head whipped up, and he stared at Bran. When he didn't say anything else and continued to eat, some of the tension in his father's shoulders eased. Hmm. Interesting, that.

"Did Raven say yes?"

Thank God Bran had just swallowed his bite, or he would have choked on a sausage. "How did you know I asked?"

"Because I know you better than you know yourself and because you are way too calm and satisfied for sex to be the only reason."

"She said yes, but you're wrong about the sex. I'd be just as satisfied without a ring on her finger— probably more nervous, though," he admitted. He would be satisfied just to be back in Raven's arms, but he freely admitted to himself that having a ring on her finger, especially now that she was pregnant, put him in a much more peaceful state.

Bran's whole body tingled at the best secret his father hadn't taken a guess at yet.

"We're having a boy." Bran felt an immediate rush of heat in his eyes. Damn, it must take a while for the feelings that overwhelmed him to ease when he spoke of his child... thought of his child— his son.

His dad sat his fork down, giving Bran his complete attention. "A little boy. I'm pleased for you both, son. I hope your boy is as sweet as Raven."

"February 19th. That's all the time we have, less really to finish the building renovations when you consider decorating."

"Tim will manage. With the three of us helping."

"I have that OHS charity gala the week before Christmas. I asked Raven to go with me. I was hoping all six of us could go home for it and then have Christmas and New Year's in Muskogee. All three girls want to see Wolves. We could plan dinner there one night."

"I would like that. I'll let Sara know to have the house decorated for the holidays and see if Mom wants to fly back for a couple days. We can't stay long. Having all three of us away from the renovation project too long isn't wise."

"I agree. I wouldn't feel comfortable having Raven out of Ireland so close to the due date. She would be upset if her grandma couldn't be there for the birth.

"Rowan and River agreed to let Saoirse find them a temporary apartment so the flat can be renovated."

"Thank fuck."

Moving quickly on from that grenade, Bran told him about the girls then moving into the guest rooms on the first floor until they felt they could afford to get a place of their own.

"They never have to leave. I don't like guests anyway."

His dad could make things so hard. So exasperatingly difficult.

"Noted. All three are on board to hire Dom, the Fitzwilliam butler, as an office manager if he agrees. He would move into the upstairs flat. But... they wouldn't agree to *any* of it unless I agreed to own a percentage of the business."

"You can't expect them to take handouts with no expectation of paying you back. You know them better than that. *I* know them better."

"I just don't like taking anything that they've worked so hard for."

"What you proposed, and are helping them achieve, has the potential of increasing their earnings tremendously. They know that."

Patrick just walked in and, after a quick good morning, started eating everything on the table that was left. Dad should have named him Hoover after the vacuum cleaners. He didn't chew so much as inhale.

"Why didn't I get an invitation to breakfast?"

"Bran texted me, and last time I checked, I'm not your personal event planner."

Ignoring Pat's tapeworm, Bran finished his conversation with his dad. "Okay, you're right about Triskelion. Raven is meeting her sisters at the flat to pack the rest of her things while I meet Dom at a downtown café before he heads to work."

"Who is hauling Raven's things here?"

"Front desk called a service. Do you guys want to go meet the girls' potential store manager with me?

"Fine."

"Sure. River told me about that last night. Brilliant plan, brother. Oh, and we're meeting everyone for lunch, Honey Bunny's choice, according to Jo. She'll text us *his* plans. You should have stayed last night, Dad. How MacGregor doesn't strangle Jo is like... a Wonder of the World."

"The Tulsa detective called me last night."

His father gave his children so many reasons— daily— to strangle him. "For fuck's sake, Dad, do you think you might have started with that gambit?"

"I didn't want to interrupt your proposal last night, and you were late this morning."

"Three minutes," Bran ground out.

"Wait, you proposed? Jesus, do you fucks share anything with me? Did she say yes?"

"I didn't tell anyone, Dad guessed. She said yes. I would tell you I'm having a son, but I'm guessing your bestie told you that already." Patrick smiled. River obviously *had* told him. He congratulated Bran on the engagement and the little boy.

Back to stalkers. "What did the detective have to say? Anything new?" For the first time this morning, Bran saw a crack in his father's somber façade.

His dad placed both hands flat on the table, either side of his breakfast plate, and sighed. He appeared to be steadying himself, which made Bran extremely cautious, as it must have his brother, because Patrick put his cutlery aside and placed his hands on the table as well, bracing for a blow. Their father didn't let emotion get the best of him often.

"Samuel Delton. He was a high school classmate of you boys and James. The same year as Bran and James. Do you remember him?"

Bran was floored. He'd gone to school with some stalking psycho. "I recall the name. If I looked at our yearbooks and saw his face, I'm sure I would remember more. We weren't friends, but we weren't enemies either, and you know none of us were ignorant bullies. You would have kicked our asses, including James'."

"I know who they are."

That shocked both him and Patrick. Their dad had been very involved in their lives, but not when it came to socializing with parents at school. Half the time, they would hit on him, which embarrassed and pissed him off in turns. The consequence— he wasn't bringing cookies to parent teacher conferences.

"How?" Patrick asked, probably equally as bewildered.

"Samuel's dad, Tom Delton, was an O'Faolain accountant caught stealing. He skimmed funds from several accounts and moved them into offshore accounts. We found some of what was stolen, but not all. He begged us not to press charges to save his wife and son. His son was your age, Bran. I hate thieves, but I had to think of the consequences for Tom's family. My attorneys got what we could, fired him with no reference, took the loss, and moved on.

"I wasn't aware, but I guess Tom killed himself a year later. His wife had already left him and the boy. Samuel's father pulled him from school, and he finished high school online. After Tom died, nothing about the boy was flagged— until they traced where some of the pictures from the hidden cameras were going. It was to a house owned by Samuel Delton."

"I never heard anything about this Samuel or his situation," Pat said. "I was younger, but still, if kids were talking in Bran's class, I would have heard."

"I didn't say anything to either of you boys. It was unfortunate, but it was business, and it was handled."

"We understand that, Dad. I'm as surprised as Pat though that we didn't catch wind of it. Did they bring Delton in for questioning?"

His dad rubbed his eyes, stressed and understandably so. "He was gone. No idea where. The detective wouldn't, or more likely couldn't, give me more information, but he did tell me that Delton is a person of interest to the FBI."

Bran's heart rate shot sky-high at the revelation. The stalker's behavior was worrisome enough, but then to find out he's someone with a personal vendetta against his family, and he'd done something bad enough to involve the FBI...

"Are our loved ones safe?"

"He believes Delton has run for the hills, so to speak, but until he's arrested, we all need to stay vigilant."

"I need to hire security for the girls."

"I knew you'd say that. I didn't already call because you have the right to make those decisions over Raven and her sisters, but I suggest calling MacGregor."

Bran got his phone out to call Jo since he didn't have the guard's number.

Pat asked, "I guess targeting us makes some sort of sick sense, but why James?"

"They believe it has something to do with you three being close friends. It was some sort of trigger."

Jo answered on the first ring, and Bran immediately asked to speak to her guard. MacGregor must have been close because he was on the phone instantly. Bran explained the situation and what he needed. MacGregor said he would handle it. He could have some of his people in Dublin in a day, possibly two. Apparently, he owned the security company and only hired highly trained ex-military.

"I'm indebted. I guess we'll be seeing you at lunch. Jo said you wanted to pick the place." Bran smiled at the growl he heard through the line. "You can let me know what you've found out then. I appreciate it."

33

I t probably appeared to anyone watching Sam sitting alone at the single picnic table at his RV campsite, working away on his laptop, that he was a lonely man. In reality— he was renewed, invigorated— had finally found his passion, his calling.

He traveled when he wanted, stayed where he wanted, and now that he'd bought the small, nondescript SUV, he was even more mobile. His dating life had increased exponentially, which meant more home videos. Though 'home video' gave the impression of a grainy, clumsy attempt when his vids were cinematic wonders.

@SammySoGood— King of Twisted Love Stories was growing in popularity. People couldn't get enough of Sam's special brand of love. It was a shame he always had to engage the old love them and leave them cliché. Because some of his women were worth second dates. It was also regrettable they never knew how gorgeous he made them for his films. They at least got to show their faces. He always had to wear a mask.

Today, in this peaceful park for motorhome adventurers, he was checking in with his less erotic but just as satisfying job of seeing what the People He Most Wanted to Suffer were doing. Revenge against the Musketeers.

He was excited again, even when he had to sort through hundreds of mundane work emails. Gold miners didn't find a nugget of gold in every sieve basket after all.

Most of his cameras had been found, but the not-so-smart detectives hadn't thought to check laptops. Josephine O'Connor deserved an MVP award. Through her, Sam had access to the O'Faolain's emails and all three Byrne sisters.

He was careful to use his remote computer software sparingly. He could enter bank account information, credit cards, reroute prescription medications, anything really, but Sam wasn't about financial gain. He always wanted his revenges to hurt harder and deeper than money.

Such a shame emails weren't used as readily as they used to be. Most people even sent business correspondence through text. There were companies, like a dentist's office, that sent confirmation texts while automatically sending the same message through email.

Case in point, Raven Byrne scheduled a sonogram the following week. That must have been what sent Bran running to Ireland. Hmm. He should consider a trip to The Emerald Isle. Possibly a Christmas present to himself. New Year's?

No need to go before then. Bran would be home for the charity gala he was planning with the Oklahoma Historical Society. And with Raven knocked up, where he went, she would follow. Perhaps even Hugh and Patrick and Raven's sisters.

Mmm, he'd like to make the youngest, Rowan, a star in one of his films. He'd even pictured Rowan and Josephine servicing him together. He used to only dream of the Byrne sister, but what could he say? His imagination was limitless.

He dreamed of it often and knew every angle he would place them in. One dark and one golden. Thinking of them touching *each other intimately made his dick ache for release. He could visualize vividly every still he would shoot as their hands and mouths writhed and moaned— as they traveled over his body.*

Fuck. There was no if Sam would have them, but when. Patience, as in everything, was key.

He continued to scroll through his best source of information, James O'Connor's sister, who so kindly helped Sam plan out a timeline for the next few months. She'd been emailing James' ex, Jane, more than normal. Nothing was said in them that would make him think James had taken her back, but it needed watching...

See... if all of the campers milling around casting him side-eye knew how fucking busy he was, what a genius he had to be to keep all these balls juggling, they would worship the bench he sat on.

34

"Why didn't we hold off until after I had the baby?" Raven wailed. She turned and contorted in ridiculous poses in front of a full-length mirror. They were staying in their original room at Hugh's house in Muskogee.

They'd all flown into Oklahoma a few days ago and had a full schedule ahead of them. They were going to a special dinner at Wolves. A charity gala for the Oklahoma Historical Society at The Dominion House in Guthrie, Oklahoma, a Christmas celebration here, and... a wedding... *her wedding*.

While they were still in Dublin, they'd decided to rent a large house that they could all stay in during the renovation process. It made Thomas MacGregor's security team's job easier if they were all in one place. Everyone agreed. The shocking news that the stalking wasn't random, but a focused revenge, was frightening.

In consequence, they tried to do most things as a group, too, including going to Oklahoma over the holiday. Bran had asked her if she would marry him in a smaller ceremony at the O'Faolain compound. He wanted her to be his wife before the baby came, and he wanted a small ceremony where they could ensure everyone's safety.

She'd agreed to it all. She never wanted a big wedding, and she would love to be married before their son was born. She *didn't*, however, love how she *looked* on her wedding day.

Raven whirled on her sisters and Nan, who were all laissez-faire, reclining in various poses of nonchalance. "You... you... you're all just sitting there like you haven't a care in the world! Meanwhile, I," Raven stopped to reenact a *Wheel of Fortune*, Vanna White wave down her body, "stand before you, looking like this!"

Do not cry. Do not cry. Do not cry.

Nan got up and stood before her, stopping Raven before she could sink deeper into the horrendous Karen & Bridezilla mashup she'd been spiraling in for an hour.

"We've all told you how beautiful you look, Raven, so I won't repeat myself." She grasped both of Raven's hands and held them tightly between them. "This isn't about how you look, and you know it. Bran would marry you if you showed up in a stained shirt and matted hair. You want your mom in this room today. You want your dad to be the one giving you away."

Oh, God. She did. She wanted them here so bad she could barely breathe. She nodded at Nan. "I didn't expect it to hit so hard," she whispered.

River and Rowan walked over to them, handing a bag to Nan, each holding one of their own.

"We wish they were here too, Rave. You have the three of us standing by you, and we'll help you get through it." Sweet Rowan.

"And never forget sis, we all know they watch over us. And I bet they're so happy you're finally marrying your baby daddy."

"You are such a bitch!"

River laughed as Raven tried and failed to kick her sister. Damn, this tight dress.

"That's quite enough language out of you, young lady," Nan sniffed, pretending offense that no one believed she felt.

The mood had shifted, lightened. "Thank you. I'm so glad to have you three with me." Raven was especially grateful to Bran's grandmother. When Tilly's pilot picked her up in Rome, where she was vacationing, she had him stop by Dublin airport to pick up Nan. They were only staying a couple of days.

Tilly was doing Christmas in Paris with Diana. She'd tried to talk Nan into going to Paris with her for the holiday, but Nan said she had plans. Since she was beet red, Raven and her sisters assumed those plans had to do with her widowed neighbor. They didn't tease her... much. They were actually very excited for her and couldn't wait to meet him.

"Okay, ladies. Sorry about the meltdown. Now you guys need to touch up my face." She sighed, looking at herself in the mirror. This time she attempted to appreciate how the dress hugged her belly. Bran had loved the dress she'd been wearing the first day they'd met after their separation.

So, she'd gone for the same, long-sleeved, fitted wedding dress. The neckline was modest and barely off the shoulder. Mikado silk. No embellishments. Nothing shiny or glittery. A Dublin designer had created it for Raven, and it was beyond beautiful. She and her sisters had picked the perfect shade of beige— not too light or dark, not too brown or gold, not champagne or ivory, just perfectly beige.

Her makeup was bare, with a light nude gloss on her lips, and her hair had a slight wave, falling like a dark waterfall down her back. The hairdresser had had her hands full. Thank God she brought assistants for her sisters, or she wouldn't be getting married until tomorrow afternoon.

"Before we touch you up, we all have something for you."

Nan's eyes were sparkling with excitement. They each held up the little bags they'd been holding.

Rowan smiled and, in a singsong voice, repeated the Old English rhyme— something old, something new, something borrowed, something blue.

"You three are determined to ruin my makeup," Raven laughed. "Let's sit at the table so I don't drop anything. If it goes on the floor, I won't be able to find it with Baby O Boy in the way." They all sat gingerly on the edge of their seats so their dresses stayed crease free.

"This one first. It's the 'new.' From Bran." River laughed, scooting the small white sack her way.

Raven removed the tissue and pulled out a small box, the exact same design as the one her wedding ring came in. She couldn't help a small squeal of excitement. She opened the lid. Oh my, oh my, oh my. Emerald earrings to match her wedding ring.

"Lovely," Nan said as she leaned over to see them better.

"Gorgeous."

"Here," River said, picking up the box, "let me help you put them in."

"I wish you could admire the earrings for a while, Rave, but unfortunately, your 'zilla moment took up a lot of time. We have to be downstairs in thirty."

Raven didn't bother correcting Rowan— truth was truth. "Give me the next one. You know I love presents!"

Nan scooched her bag over. "Something borrowed."

Tears forming. Shit. Raven pulled out a linen square, hand embroidered with tiny, yellow flowers, which she thought was the borrowed gift. It was so lovely, but it was only what Nan had used to wrap the actual gift.

She unfolded the square, revealing a polished, silver hair comb with etched buttercups at the top. "Oh, Nan, it's so lovely. I would love to wear it. Would you help me put it in?"

Her grandma blotted her eyes and took a sip of water before she could speak. "I would love to, sweet girl. I would tell you first that your grandfather, my Sean, bought that for me on our first anniversary. Turn it over."

Raven turned the heirloom over and read the inscription.

Bébhinn, mo grá
Always, Sean

She and her sisters were all crying now. "Oh, Nan. I'm honored." No one said anything else as her beloved grandma placed the comb in her hair.

Rowan handed her a mirror. "The comb is perfect in your hair and look how it keeps it back just enough to show off Bran's earrings."

Raven only nodded, unable to speak through her tear-clogged throat. In understanding, her sisters pushed the last gift bag in front of her.

"Something old," Rowan said, and "something blue," finished River.

With shaky hands, Raven pulled out the last gift. It was an antique wooden box. The flat, hinged lid had burned etchings of Native American symbols. A raven, a river, and a rowan tree.

"An artisan from the Muscogee lands, where Mom's mom was from, did the etching."

Raven traced the blackened line work. It was pure art. She looked up at her sisters. "Thank you. I will always, always treasure it."

"Rave, your present is inside the box," River teased.

"There's more? I already need an ice pack for my eyes!" She eased the silver box clasp up and opened the smooth, wooden lid. A bracelet lay pillowed on beige silk... the same beige as the gown... She pulled the piece from the pillowed cocoon and held it to the light.

"Oh. Mom and Dad's wedding rings." Her sisters had their parents' rings added to a bracelet. She was speechless.

Mom's favorite stone was lapis lazuli. Dad had picked out the stone and had it set in a narrow gold band. Mom had gotten Dad a simple gold ring, but she'd had an engraver place **L ♥ D** inside the band.

Raven ran her fingers around the gold bracelet. I can't..."

"A jeweler in Dublin cut the gold bangle apart before slipping the rings on. Then he soldered the band whole again. Rowan and I tried it on several times before he did the final solder. It should fit loose. But you're pregnant right now, so it might fit differently. I'm sure it will fit right eventually. We *had* meant it to be worn for the wedding, so a part of Mom and Dad were with you the whole day... but maybe..."

Rowan placed a hand gently on River's wrist. She was rambling. River never rambled. Raven slipped the bangle over her hand. Her parents' rings caught the light from the fire. Too much, she thought.

Then out loud. "They are not just my rings to cherish. They are ours. Always ours." She took River and Rowan's hands across the table, seeking a moment to compose herself.

"They are ours," she repeated. "I will wear this bracelet today... a happy, momentous day... but you, my sisters, will promise to wear it on your most happy occasions too. Promise."

"Promise."

"Promise."

"Jaysus," Nan cursed, "and just look at our faces, girls! It will take a miracle to put us to rights. Raven, if you cry again, Bran will think you the most miserably, sad bride to ever say 'I do.'"

Raven picked up the hand mirror and peeked at her face. "Good Lord! Please tell me you guys can fix," she made circular motions over her face, "this... and you might want to look at your own faces as well."

Gasps of horror all around. Exactly. "River, text Pat and tell him we need an extra 20 to 30 minutes. No questions answered."

PAT TOLD him the girls were running late, and Bran went into instant panic mode. He *had* railroaded Raven with the whole quick wedding idea, but she'd seemed good with it.

Now, she wouldn't answer his texts.

He paced for all of ten minutes. No, he wasn't waiting. He would *not* wait if something was wrong.

He ran up the stairs and banged on her door. "Raven, it's Bran. Open the door." He heard an 'Oh my,' a 'Seriously,' and a 'Fucking O'Faolains,' but Raven immediately swung the door open. Her face was red, and she still had tears beading her lashes.

"What the hell, babe?" Bran was crushed. "We don't have to get married today. We can do it next month or two years from now. I... shouldn't have pushed."

When Raven gently moved him out of the doorway so she could step into the hallway with him, his body tensed. She was wearing a long, billowy robe that he swore looked like one of Bébhinn's.

When she shut the door behind her, leaving them alone, he freaked the fuck out.

"Pretend you're not seeing your bride before the ceremony," she said while gently touching two fingers to his cheek. His tension eased moderately. It was a sign of affection she and the girls used for each other.

"Raven." Bran closed his eyes and breathed deeply. "*Have* you changed your mind?" He wouldn't be angry or even blame her. He'd put her through hell. He *would* spend however long it took to win her over until she was sure.

"Never, Bran. When I told you that you were it for me, I meant it." She started to tear up again before admitting it was missing her parents that had derailed her. Bran wanted to pound his fists into the wall outside her room. Shout to anyone listening that he was an idiot.

Of course, she was missing her parents on a day such as this. Damn it. Why hadn't he thought of it? He had his father. His mother was gone by choice. She didn't have either, and by no one's choosing.

"Oh, babe. I didn't think. Of course, you want them, miss them. What can I do?" Bran pulled her into his arms and stroked gently down her back. "Would you rather do this at a courthouse? No fuss? Just the two of us?"

She hugged him back tightly before backing out of his embrace and looking up at him. "No. Nan and my sisters got me through it. Truly," she said when he looked at her askance. "Give me time to... do something with my puffy eyes. I promise I'll be meeting you downstairs." She smiled then and touched her ears. "Thank you for these. They're so beautiful."

Bran touched one of the earrings before gently tracing his finger against her jawline. His thumb ran over her lips before he replaced it with his mouth, pressed firmly to her own— a promise. Still sharing her breath, Bran whispered, "Thank you, Raven. Thank you so much for never giving up on me. On us."

"I would never have been whole again without you, Bran," Raven whispered back against his lips.

Moving back a step, Bran put his hands around her biceps.

"You are all I see. Your love is all I'll ever need. I'll go downstairs and wait because you've promised to meet me, because you said you would, and I trust you... with me... with my heart." Placing one more gentle kiss on her mouth, he left Raven to finish getting ready.

Forty-five minutes later, Bran watched Raven, arm in arm in arm with her sisters, walk toward him. His dad and Patrick touched his back as they neared, perhaps as moved by the site of the Byrne sisters as he was.

Dad and Patrick stood to his left, River and Rowan to his right, with Raven facing Bran. He took her delicate hands into his much larger ones. As the priest had them recite vows— promises— he was honored... humbled that this woman would be his... that he would be hers. Always.

Bran was married. He had a wife, and Raven had to be the most beautiful bride in the history of brides. They'd cut the cake, made toasts, kissed, hugged, and gotten advice from Gran and Raven's Nan. Now he held a low ball of Tullamore Dew and watched his wife, River, and Rowan sit with the matriarchs of the family, laughing and probably saying all sorts of unflattering things about Bran. He couldn't care less. He was the happiest of men, even with the threat of Delton and the security guards looming in the background— the luckiest of men.

Jo was handing a gift box to Raven. They were smiling and laughing as she undid the tan-colored bow, probably beige. He'd heard the name of that color about five hundred times in the past several weeks.

His wife slipped the lid off and set it aside. Pulling the tissue off, Raven glanced at Bran, smiling mischievously as she pulled out a nude-colored, silk... transparent... something... nightgown? He released his wall lean, pulled slowly toward his bride. The thought of his wife wearing see-through anything— magnetic.

Almost where he needed to be, by her side, she stood, still

clutching the slip of silk, and turned to... MacGregor? To Bran's shock, and most assuredly the guard's, Raven hugged the man whose arms were frozen like pillars at his sides.

"Thank you for the lovely present, Honey Bunny. It's one of my favorite colors." MacGregor's eyes found Jo's— retribution would be swift. Bran didn't think the determined Ms. O'Connor cared.

Raven stepped away and turned to Bran with a wide smile. "Husband mine, are you ready to get this party started? Baby O Boy and I are feeling this song." *Set You Free* by Sam Ryder.

"I'm feeling *you*, babe." Bran pulled Raven close, cupping her back tenderly but with enough firmness to create an unbreakable bond around their son. "I'll remember every single moment of this night, Rave."

Raven tilted her head up and smiled brightly. She placed her hand on his chest as they moved around the small dance floor and told Bran, "We've had a few beginnings. Today marks our forever."

Bran and Raven spun slowly around taking in their family and friends. Dad, Patrick, River, and Rowan. He hoped each of them found— *this*.

35

S am had his new-to-him Chevrolet Equinox fueled, neatly packed, and ready for a road trip. He'd paid cash for the nondescript, wine-red, mid-size SUV. He had snacks, a cooler full of water bottles, clothes and toiletries, his makeup cases, and, most importantly, multiple camera bags.

It was such an honor that the Oklahoma Historical Society hired him as one of the photographers responsible for documenting their fancy charity gala. Driving to Guthrie, Oklahoma, from his Arkansas RV park would take three hours and forty minutes. The event would be held in the historic Dominion House— so lovely for the Okie elites. Sam had rented a cheap motel room on the outskirts of town. He would need at least two hours to transform.

If he were less attractive, the level of effort could have been reduced. As it was, well, it was no use playing coy; his face and body required considerable time to become unexceptional.

This holiday season marked the last of his small, irritating retribution jabs. A few last little pricks to irritate the prick O'Faolains.

Phase two of his revenge tour wouldn't be as sweet and innocent as his past plays.

Sam always wanted to visit Ireland.

ABOUT THE AUTHOR

Anne Gregor is a Contemporary Romance writer and the author of *Raven*, the first book in The Irish Wolves trilogy. Anne loves using her master's degree in history to sprinkle a little of the past into a modern package. When she is not writing, reading, or book reviewing, she is obsessed with true crime documentaries and cooking challenge shows— a combination like fish and cheese— sometimes it works. An empty nester after her three children started adulting, she still loves getting together for family game nights. Quiet evenings are reserved for reading and peanut butter.

She lives in northeast Oklahoma on the Grand Lake O' the Cherokees and is passionate about all things Okie.

ALSO BY ANNE GREGOR

The Irish Wolves Trilogy

Raven

River